"DO YOU REALLY WISH
FOR ME TO LEAVE?"

She touched him then, a soft, tentative stroke of one fine-boned hand upon the broad expanse of his back.

He flinched.

She placed her cheek next to where her hand rested, feeling the warmth of his skin through the fine silk of his shirt. Slowly, inch by torturous inch, her hands reached around his waist, their warmth conveying gentleness, caring, and tender innocence.

It was the tenderness that caused him to look at the ceiling, then close his eyes tight against her naive gesture. His teeth, ground together tightly, muffled the moan expelled from his throat.

She moved closer, her breasts pressing against his back.

Must he be tormented by her? He was a man, damn it! Trapped in the body of a monster. Was she so ignorant that she did not realize that her touch vibrated through his body? Did she not recognize that his pride and his restraint were within inches of being thrust aside, of being supplanted by another, fiercer emotion?

"Get out," he repeated for the third time. He cursed the mask that shielded his look of rage from her.

He felt her move away and his shoulders sagged as if she had released him from some terrible burden. He stood unmoving, anticipating the sound of her departure from the room, but instead heard only the rustle of movement behind him.

He whirled and almost reeled with the shock.

She stood without a stitch of clothing on her white, velvety flesh, meeting his incredulous gaze with her own direct look, as if daring him to banish her now.

Tapestry

Karen Ranney

ZEBRA BOOKS
KENSINGTON PUBLISHING CORP.

ZEBRA BOOKS are published by

Kensington Publishing Corp.
850 Third Avenue
New York, NY 10022

First Printing: May, 1995

Printed in the United States of America

To my son, John

and

to

Yolanda Grau

who taught me, by example,
that laughter can follow tears.

Book One

One

"Please, Miss Laura, do not do this thing. Nothing good will come of it; I feel it in my bones."

The warning seemed to hang in the air, a wisp of words tinted by pleading tones. Laura shook her head, as if dismissing the memory of her nurse's parting entreaty. Jane could not possibly understand.

There was no other choice.

Laura slapped old Gretchen on the rump, knowing that the pony would soon amble home in search of oats and a rest. She savored the respite herself for a moment before crossing the bridge that spanned the Wye. Although the house was splendid seen from all sides, the most beautiful view of Heddon Hall was from the river. She had deliberately taken the pony cart the long way around, perhaps for the view, perhaps for additional time to consider the ramifications of her plan.

It *must* work.

An ancient square dove house sat near the road, its narrow ledges filled with cooing birds—the first sign of welcome from Heddon Hall. Waving gaily to them, she topped the rise of the bridge, glancing down into the clear, sparkling waters of the Wye.

On the other side of the humped bridge the massive towers of the Hall were visible above the treetops, harmonizing so well with the countryside that it was possible to believe the imposing house was as old as the knurled oaks and rolling hills that encircled it. There had always been a Heddon Hall. The bricks, mellowed over the centuries to a silvery gray, merged with the seasons—warm and welcoming in summer, taking on a greenish tint in winter, as though covered with moss, thereby adding a touch of color to the bare white landscape. In spring, as now, the stonework seemed imbued with gentle shadows, a muted backdrop for the verdant fields and glorious flowers surrounding Heddon Hall.

A steep grass-carpeted incline rose to a great oaken doorway that opened to the first court. The door was never locked, and she pushed it open with no feelings of trespass. She had spent almost as many hours here as in her own home, Blakemore.

She strolled through the garden, savoring the fact that although she had not visited Heddon Hall in four long years, there were few changes. The garden was as immutable as time itself. Topiary animals—boars and peacocks and a unicorn—acted as sentinels in the corners; the yew hedges were the same height, their perfume filling the air. The roses massed along the inner wall dropped their petals in pink profusion. There were only pink roses at Heddon, never red or white.

As she reached the wicketed gate that marked the second courtyard, or Winter Garden, she looked above her head for the statues. They were still there: three grotesquely carved gargoyles perched on a ledge circling the tallest tower.

She smiled as she opened the last barrier to the inner courtyard. By force of habit she strode through the archway, but stopped herself from entering the house by way of the steep granite steps. Turning left, instead, she crossed the grass path to the kitchen gardens. A hastily muttered prayer was the only prelude to her quick knock on the kitchen door.

He watched her stroll through the Winter Garden with the insouciance of a lady of the manor and not a peasant girl seeking work. He stood at the arched windows of the Eagle Tower and continued to observe her as she looked left and right, studying his world as if she had a perfect right to stroll upon the carefully manicured grass and through the famous gardens of Heddon Hall.

In amazement, he watched as she discarded the ugly straw bonnet and loosened that silly-looking cap. Her hair gleamed in the sun, a beacon of red tinged with gold. Her dress was too short, showing her ankles when she walked, but she seemed oblivious to her swirling skirts with the same unconscious grace that she swung the cloth bag in one hand.

When she stopped and smiled up at the wall of gargoyles he abruptly stepped back so that she would not catch a glimpse of him. He rarely wore his mask when he was alone, knew full well a fleeting glance at his face would be enough to make her abandon her carefree air and run screaming from the courtyard.

He was, strangely enough, loath to frighten her.

Finally, when she entered the second courtyard and disappeared from sight, he reluctantly returned to his desk.

He massaged his left hand absently, the constant cramp from injured muscles and torn tendons almost second nature now, like the shadow pain felt from an amputated limb. It was only one of many reminders of his mortality. The other lay inches from his good hand.

It was a Birchett breech-loading flintlock pistol, one of a pair. The barrel of this constant friend was eight inches long, and etched into the butt of the grip was a silver medallion embossed with the Cardiff heraldic emblem.

One day, perhaps, the loneliness would become too much of a burden to bear. One day, perhaps, the horror of his solitary existence would be too much to endure.

He had learned, in this past year, that he was capable of many things. Capable, for one, of the staunchest courage when viewing himself in the mirror. His left eye was gone, a shattered bit of white scar tissue that left him gasping in breathless horror when he had first viewed himself. That was not the worst of it, however. If it had been, he could have donned an eye patch and pretended piracy. But a genial free-booter would never be his masquerade. No, Fate had grimly rewarded his survival with a mocking foretaste of his future—generously presented to him every day in the sight of his burned flesh—knitted and knotted into a lumpy and twisted caricature of his face and chest.

The hideous face, nearly blinded eyes, and the claw that had become his left hand doomed him to remain just outside of humanity, a tortured, twisted hunk of flesh that frightened the man he had been.

And terrified anyone else.

His mask was a charity to them all.

His servants, however fearful, were careful to hide their aversion to him. As long as he paid their inflated salaries, he was entitled to their lowered eyes and carefully deflected faces.

His stepmother was the only one who did not mask her antipathy to him; not once did she deign to conceal her re-pugnance whenever she looked upon his leather-clad face or mask her thinly disguised shudders when their paths could not help but cross.

Despite Elaine's contention that he was trying to beggar her, he had sent her on her way with enough money to main-tain a luxurious lifestyle in London. She had not bothered to act the hypocrite, departing his home enraged at his insistence that she not only manage to live on the amount he'd advanced but that she remain in London rather than intrude upon his privacy at Heddon Hall.

It was a cloistered existence, this, a monastic life that pulled at him with razor-sharp talons, as if his flesh were half-healed.

He was proficient in coping with his half-blindness, grop-ing infirmity, and daily pain, stifling his anguish beneath a thin-lipped silence. Yet, he did not know how much longer he would be capable of living alone, of listening to the echo of solitude, the awful emptiness of his own existence.

It had only been a year since the cannon's explosion, yet he was near to screaming with it.

Dying might be preferable to this.

It would not be self-pity that thrust him toward self-destruction. He had long since challenged that god of ego and won. He did not anguish over his circumstances, nor bemoan his fate. He was cursed with too much self-knowledge; a brightly polished internal mirror by which he resolutely examined himself. He was sometimes autocratic, but command had come easily to him, both at sea and in his new guise as earl. He was self-sufficient, a trait distilled from leadership and a solitary childhood; his older brother separated by more than years, his father disinterested in the fate of a younger son, his mother dead two years after his birth. He was stubborn, but his pride and his occasional dogmatism were the only things to hold on to in a world suddenly skewed and unfamiliar.

It was his stubbornness that demanded that he alter, in small, decisive steps, his helplessness. He refused to believe that he could not make his undamaged eye focus on the words swimming on the document before him. He had gradually, over the last year, begun to see with that eye, despite the warnings from the Navy surgeons and the caution of his own physician. It had begun as a sense of color and light. Then the blurry outlines had become clear, and he had regained his vision of far objects.

As his sight slowly cleared, he set himself another task: that of reading again. He detested having to depend upon his secretary for assistance in the most basic of chores. It chafed at him, this sense of reliance. He hated wondering if the letter was written exactly as his secretary read it, or if the expense was as high as had been represented to him, or the report of crop damage as onerous as Hartley reported. He loathed being forced into a child's role. Ironically, his self-imposed mission of trying to read once again began with a child's hornbook, the engraved drawings becoming discernible only with patience and the presence of bright light.

Now, sunlight streamed through the arched windows and a branched candlestick stood beside him with other candles resting near his arm. Yet, despite the sunlight and the artificial light, he was no closer to being able to differentiate the written word than he had been yesterday or the day before.

He threw down the quill with an oath and glanced at the gun on the table before him. No, it would not be self-pity that coaxed him to destruction; it would be an act of sheer, puling desperation that finally impelled him to squeeze the trigger.

He could bequeath his title to a distant cousin and seek anonymity someplace where the demands of his rank would not be so onerous. Yet, the same reason he was reluctant to do so was the same reason the gun lay unused on the table.

Hope: somewhere it still existed. Battered, as bruised as his ego, but sewn together with pieces of his past and distant, fleeting glimpses of a brighter future.

It was unique, this feeling of being part of mankind, yet so supremely set apart. Dear God, all that he wanted was to be treated as a man. Not as a monster. A man who dreamed, who still lusted, who even now ached for those things he had taken for granted before—friendship, the ability to laugh, the tenderness of gifted love, the hope of tomorrow, the softness of female flesh pressed against his in ravenous need, the sounds of pleasure, music shared, bawdy jokes, wine sipped and savored in company before a fire, a future bright and promising.

He was as unlikely to be granted those favors as he was the ability to read again.

His sigh was heavy and leaden in the silent room. He bent to his task, determined, stubborn, grim. He spent the next hour ignoring the faint sounds from the courtyard, the bustle of maids, the gurgling of the reservoir mounted on the roof behind the Eagle Tower.

He could not, however, ignore the female screams that tore through the kitchen garden.

The first part of her plan had gone quite well, Laura thought, until an unexpected complication. She'd had no trouble obtaining a position, quite frankly lying about her references, giving Blakemore as her last employer. When asked her name she calmly stated that it was Jane Palling, with mental apologies to her nurse.

Yes, the first part of her plan had gone well, until she had learned that the new earl had strange notions about cleanliness. She was escorted, none too gently, to the kitchen garden by the heavyset butler, Simons, and divested of her meager cloth sack, her cloak, and her straw hat.

She had stood calmly, if not a little confused, until Simons had motioned to two of the footmen. If she had known the fate in store for her, she most certainly would not have remained meekly in place. Nor would she have screamed each and every oath she had surreptitiously learned from the stableboys at Blakemore if they had just warned her that she was to be doused from head to toe with gallons of vinegar!

She sputtered, coughed, and could hardly breathe for the stench.

"M'lord will not tolerate fleas or lice," Simons starchily intoned as he motioned to the footmen again.

"No more!" She slicked back her wet hair from her forehead with one trembling hand, glared at Simons and his willing henchmen, and wondered if they weren't deriving too much pleasure from their task.

She was drenched. Her gray dress was almost black and clung to every curve. Her muslin tucker lay on the muddy ground beneath her feet, and her hair had come loose from the careful bun at her neck. Even the cheap hose and leather shoes she had purchased from one of her maids were sodden. Her eyes stung, and she tasted the briny vinegar on her lips.

She also smelled. No self-respecting louse or flea would dare invade her person.

"Enough!" she yelled after the second dose, but her command did not seem to dissuade them. She clenched her teeth and squinched her eyes shut in preparation for the next drenching.

It did not come.

Instead, an eerie silence drifted over the three. She slitted open one eye, glancing at the suddenly subdued Simons. Neither of the footmen raised their eyes from the muddy ground.

She blinked furiously and looked up.

Behind Simons was a tall, broad-shouldered figure.

He stood, legs braced apart, one hand behind his back, surveying the scene like an iron statue. His leather mask hid his expression and his face from her view. Only a slit appeared where his nose would be and another for his mouth. One eye was completely shielded by the black leather; the other seemed disembodied, as though it were floating apart from his face, watching her with an expression she could not read.

Alex.

Two

The rumors were true then.

He was dressed in black, as if to complement his mask. His trousers were severely tailored down to thigh-high boots, their jet surface gleaming in the bright morning sun. His waistcoat was embroidered ornately, black upon black, as was the shirt whose stock ended in flowing ebony lace and whose sleeves were fastened neatly at the cuff by large onyx stones. Everything about him spoke of dispassionate elegance, effortlessly and apathetically obtained. Such refinement did not, however, detract from the sight of the black leather that shielded his face from prying eyes.

The awful rumors were true. Even Jane could not refrain from repeating what she'd heard—that the new earl had been maimed during the war. That the reason he'd shuttered and closed himself off from everyone was not due solely to grief at the loss of his father and older brother.

She didn't care what the reason was. Laura only knew that for almost a year her letters had been returned, those notes inscribed in such a careful hand that her fingers had trembled as she addressed each envelope and then dotted it with her own scent. For almost a year he had returned each one with no explanation, no message, no hope. Nor, according to neighbors, would he accept visits from old friends.

Which is why she had decided to don a maid's garments, scandalize her nurse, and do something so absurd as apply for work at Heddon Hall. He might bar her from his door, but the great house still required servants.

She had succeeded in the second part of her plan—to see him, to coax him from his refuge, and yet she had not envisioned their reunion taking place under such bizarre circumstances. Her imagination had conjured up a more fitting scene, perhaps against the backdrop of the Winter Garden. Certainly she had never seen herself standing before him drenched in vinegar and smelling as pungent as a vat of pickles.

Nor had she considered that he would not recognize her.

For despite his scrutiny of her, there was no glimmer of recognition in that obsidian eye. She was no longer the tempestuous child, the fourteen-year-old girl who had clutched at his sleeve and wept over his new uniform. That fixed gaze swept down her figure as if she was a stranger.

It had been four years since she had last seen him, but the memory of their parting was as clear to her as if it had occurred only yesterday. How like a young god he had always appeared, her Alex, but never more so than on that day so long ago. His mouth could turn up with wit or thin with anger or, as then, show the slightest trace of impatience to be about his future. His raven hair had shone blue-black in the morning sun. His mysterious black eyes that could flash with humor or soften with contentment had been filled with barely veiled irritation.

Even then she had loved him. Nor had the intervening years altered that emotion. She took a step toward him, suddenly uncaring of her sodden appearance or his altered one. That small step seemed to shock him. His head jerked and he stepped back.

Simons turned to face his lord, but his eyes never quite reached the leather mask or that single peering eye that had not swerved from Laura.

She watched him, wide-eyed. It was not fear that prompted her soft gasp or the sweet smile that curved her lips. Her eyes scanned the leather mask, the ties that were knotted be-

hind his head. His hair was still raven-colored, but there were
streaks of soft white at his temples. He stood as tall as he
had on that day when he had bid her farewell four years ago,
his shoulders erect, his stance enhanced by a newfound military bearing.

Her Alex. Changed, true, but still hers.

When her parents had died it had been Alex who had come
to console her. Alex, whose words of kindness had been her
only comfort. It had been Alex's arms that held her in a tight
embrace, rocking her back and forth as if he had assumed
the role of parent, brother, friend.

It had always been Alex.

She stared at him, entranced, and remembered when he
had ridden to Blakemore when she was eleven to present her
with the best of Sally's litter of puppies. The little springer
spaniel had been her best friend, partly because the puppy
was a gift from Alex, partly because she had just lost her
parents and desperately needed something upon which to
shower affection, something to love her back.

When she had wanted to play Queen Anne he had joined
in her game, a kind companion to a lonely little girl, singing
the verse along with her own high-pitched voice:

> *Come smell my lily, come smell my rose,*
> *Which of my maidens do you choose?*
> *I choose you one, and I choose you all,*
> *And I pray Miss Blake yield up the ball.*

She had laughed and giggled, and although Alex was ten
years older, he had forgotten his stature and his consequence,
ignored the fact that he was at Cambridge, and had played
like her equal.

It was Alex who sat at her bedside when she was ill, re-
galing her with stories of school and teasing her spotted face.

Her Alex.

Four years ago he had held her tight when she had cried

over his new uniform, and blotted her tears with impatient tenderness.

She met his gaze and did not lower her own, remembering that day a year before when she had learned of his being wounded, when she had desperately wanted to go to him, to comfort him, to put her arms around him and hold him close. Only her uncles, and distance itself, had stopped her then.

There was nothing to stop her now.

She had no inkling that he was stunned by her eager perusal of him. He fixed his eye upon her, but she only met his look and smiled brightly. She did not turn her gaze from him, embarrassed, nor did she flush and look away.

She did not realize that her single hesitant step was the first time a human being had willingly come toward him since that horrible day more than a year before.

Even the young maids assigned to fetch him his meals or tea were filled with fear as they approached the State Bedroom and the great oaken double doors that led to his kingdom. He suspected they were greatly relieved to be spared the trip to the Eagle Tower, which he had claimed as his own refuge. He could not blame them; he would have escaped himself if he could. Which is why he could not refrain from staring at the young girl in front of him, at her wide and sparkling eyes and the look that shocked him to the core. It was open and trusting and totally devoid of fear or revulsion.

"What is the meaning of this, Simons?" he asked, his voice emerging as a raspy whisper from behind the black leather mask.

Simons looked from one to the other, confused and uncertain as to whether or not he should explain. Was he not, after all, acceding to the earl's own wishes? "Fleas and lice, m'lord," he said hastily in the silence, thinking that it was a blessing that the earl had fixed his evil eye upon the new girl and not him.

"Have you finished?" the earl asked calmly, still watching the girl. He doubted, frankly, that this new servant needed to be doused for vermin. She was dressed poorly, true, but she looked clean enough.

He noted the fact that the contours of both pert breasts and their hardened tips were readily apparent beneath the clinging cloth of her sodden dress. He also noted, with not as much detachment as he would have wished, that she was lovely, even though she was drenched with vinegar, her hair plastered around her flushed face and her thick lashes blinking furiously over glade-green eyes. Her lips were parted, and, as he watched, an eager tongue darted out and licked them clean. He felt himself tighten at the simple gesture and then almost smile at the look of distaste that flickered over her face at the tang of vinegar.

"Yes, m'lord," Simons said, motioning to the footmen to replace the bucket. They obeyed with relief and almost ran from the courtyard.

"I believe she is de-loused," he said brusquely.

His voice had changed; it no longer bore the melodious tones she remembered. Yet this voice seemed to fit the man who stood before her now, as though everything about him had been altered to conform to his tailored mask. His shoulders were broader than she remembered, and although the Alex of four years ago had had a lean, whipcord grace, this one radiated a more substantial presence. His chest seemed broader, his arms more muscular beneath the silken shirt, his legs empowered by ropes of muscle that could not be hidden by the taut material of his trousers.

She inspected him for other changes with a connoisseur's eye as he stared at her in bafflement and something like dismay. Despite himself he felt a flush emanate from his toes, tracing upwards on his rigid body, accompanied by her sweeping and somewhat less than maidenly scrutiny.

Something stretched between them then, in the long space of moments in which they stared at each other. Something that shimmered in the air with a heaviness of its own. She, bemused by the sight of him after so long, was not surprised at it. He, with stunned incredulity at her wide-eyed wonder, was more than shocked.

Laura took another step toward the masked figure, but he moved back again, his gloved hand coming forward and resting on his hip, as if to push her away if she came too close. His legs were braced apart, one knee slightly bent, as though standing on the deck of a ship.

"Go about your duties, Simons," he said finally, pulling his gaze from the lovely young servant and fixing his stare upon the butler.

Simons gulped and bobbed his head as the earl turned. In one movement he had vanished from the doorway.

She stared after him.

Simons thought she was truly daft: first, to stare at the earl as though unafraid of his demonic appearance and now to stand in the kitchen garden with a faraway look in her eyes and a small smile tilting her lips.

Laura ignored the sharp, assessing gaze of the butler.

What had she expected? To see him and have him fall into her willing and waiting arms? To announce to her that he loved her as she had loved him all her life? He had not even recognized her. She suspected that this new, reclusive Alex would be as little receptive to her womanly emotions as the stalwart and handsome one had been to her childish feelings.

Which put her at a distinct disadvantage that was softened by only one thing: She was no longer a child, and she certainly would not be dismissed as one. He might shun the others, but he was not immune to her appearance. She had not missed his quick glance at her drenched bosom. Nor had she missed his sudden stiffness as he had watched her tongue lick her lips.

Her own response to his sharp gaze had been instantaneous and without thought. Her body felt flushed, as if internally heated; her blood acquired a feverish beat, a rhythmic pulse that grew louder and faster the longer he'd stared at her. Even

her breasts seemed to swell as he watched, her nipples lengthening beneath his look.

Jane was right; her plan was absurd, but only because she
had not thought it through. He was the Alex she remembered
and yet he was not. There was an almost palpable feeling of
isolation that emanated from him, as if he had created a moat
around himself. She doubted, frankly, if any entreaty would
sway this man. She also had the distinct impression that if
he was annoyed, even the tiniest bit, by her presence, he
would not hesitate to dismiss her on the spot.

She would need to be more brazen. Something more would
have to be done. She grinned broadly.

Simons looked at her, rolled his eyes to the heavens, and
wondered how long the loon would last.

Three

"Mrs. Wolcraft's Academy has a lot to answer for," Laura muttered to herself as she scraped ashes from the kitchen fireplace.

She had frankly detested school, but not because of a mind dull and incapable of learning. If she loathed Mrs. Wolcraft's Academy for Young Ladies, it was for another reason. Since the age of ten she had been tutored by the uncles in classical Greek and Latin. Uncle Percival had schooled her in botany and horticulture, and she had learned animal husbandry and farm management from Uncle Bevil. Instead of bedtime stories she had spent her evenings sitting beside both of them in the withdrawing room and listening to their rousing arguments on the fate of the Empire. She had discussed the rights of man before she was twelve and learned geography from an old globe taken laboriously from the attic. She studied mathematics beside a candle-strewn table in the dining room.

Uncle Bevil, who was the more practical of her two uncles, had stenoriously announced that she had a great deal to learn, since she was an heiress.

She could quote per capita consumption of the beer that was manufactured in her father's brewery just outside London, could calculate the annual profits from the forestry industry, the iron forges, and each square mile of land that was ably managed for her under the uncles' stewardship.

She had thought that her education had prepared her for

the world. It had not prepared her for Mrs. Wolcraft's Academy for Young Ladies.

Books were used not for study but to balance upon the head, thereby guaranteeing the victim a graceful, willowy walk. She practiced sitting, backing up like a recalcitrant carriage horse until she felt the chair seat nudging against the backs of her knees and then collapsing gracefully upon the chair, a delicate flurry of hoops and lace. Endless hours were devoted to managing her limbs, to walking with a pigeon-toed saunter so that her skirts swayed gracefully and to tucking her elbows tightly to her chest so that she would have the marionette look of her peers. She learned how to converse agreeably on a variety of acceptable topics, only to be taught that it was gauche and ill-mannered to speak of anything more tantalizing than the weather.

Sewing samplers with silly expressions on them was not her idea of learning. The sentiments carefully embroidered upon the limp and slightly soiled linen squares did not seem worth the effort. *Patience is a virtue, Virtue is a grace, Both put together, Make a very pretty face.*

Nor did the sentiments copied in her handwriting book, such as "Knowledge procures general esteem," or "Misfortunes are a kind of discipline," seem adequate for the world outside Mrs. Wolcraft's Academy.

She did not sing well, but she sang loudly. After a few sessions even Mrs. Wolcraft decided that her forte was not the musical arts. She was also excused from spinet lessons when several of the girls complained that the instrument always needed tuning after Laura finished practicing.

Mrs. Wolcraft's students were expected to cultivate taste in decoration and furnishing, to the extent that Laura could now identify a Chippendale chair from one with more history. The arts seemed interesting until she discovered that Mrs. Wolcraft's perception of them included sewing, lace-making, and an occasional pallid watercolor of bowls filled with fruit.

Yes, Mrs. Wolcraft's Academy for Young Ladies had a great deal to answer for!

It was one thing to learn how to supervise a domestic staff and quite another to know what they actually did. None of her training had given her an insight into the workings of a great kitchen the likes of Heddon Hall's.

She was, in fact, beyond irritation.

For the first time in her life she felt inept, and she did not enjoy the sensation. None of her uncles' long nightly speeches on philosophy or religion had prepared her to scrub heavy iron pots. None of Mrs. Wolcraft's lectures on decorum or proper elocution had prepared her for the simplest of practical duties.

During the first two days she was desperately afraid she was going to lose her job.

As a child Laura had scurried to Blakemore's warm kitchen in winter and sat at Cook's knee, savoring her treat of cooling gingerbread topped with clotted cream. It was doubtful, however, that anyone had ever sought comfort in the kitchens of Heddon Hall. The dimensions of the room were as commodious as the rest of the hall. The ceiling itself was over thirty feet high, with an open cupola on top. Near it was the larder, the brewhouse, the laundry, and a storeroom for fruit, with rooms over them for servants, including the tiny one she had been assigned. She had been informed in a supercilious snort by the housekeeper, Mrs. Seddon, that the upper sort of servants were lodged in the older wing. On top of the servants' quarters sat a leaden cistern holding a thousand gallons of water, to supply all of the water needs of the great house plus the fountains in the courts and gardens.

Mrs. Seddon did not resemble the motherly housekeeper at Blakemore, nor did the cook's stare seem filled with warmth.

On her first day Laura allowed the great fire in the kitchen hearth to grow cold, and when she went to light it again she realized this elemental chore was beyond her. She could quote Plato and Aristotle; she could recite Shakespeare with the greatest of ease; she could tally a long column of numbers, but it took one of the maids to show her how to light a fire!

It looked simple enough.

Finally, after three attempts, the cook grabbed the tinder box from her and lit the fire in one movement. Then the same maid who had taken pity on her stupidity was sent to tell Simons that the earl's breakfast would be late due to the clumsiness of the new girl.

Both the cook and the kitchen apprentices waited for her to be summarily dismissed.

"His lordship does not require breakfast this morning," a confused Simons reported. He did not add that the earl had listened patiently to his complaints and then stated that the new girl was to be given a chance to prove herself. Which, to Simons, was as much as declaring that m'lord had an interest in the foolish female.

For some reason the earl's charity seemed to annoy the cook even more; Laura was set the daunting task of stirring some noxious concoction over the fire.

The fireplace was wide enough and of sufficient depth to make room for seats on either side. An iron fireback rose behind the fire, decorated with the Cardiff heraldic emblem. Across the opening ran a sturdy oak beam, and from that ran a system of pulleys and cranes that allowed the heavier pots to be moved easily. Of course the cook did not tell her that, and it was not until there was outright laughter from some of the apprentices that someone finally took pity on her blistered hands and aching back.

She was not let out of the kitchen for a whole day. Nor was the next day any better. She was not to be trusted, she was told, to dust the valuables residing at Heddon Hall. Not with her obvious clumsiness and lack of skill at the simplest chore.

She could not, honestly, blame them.

It would set back her plan a few days, but the experience she was garnering in the kitchen of Heddon Hall was enough to make her bless her own situation in life. With luck she would never again be asked to boil a kettle of water for tea. Even that small task seemed beyond her capabilities.

Kettles had small iron trivets, or stands, so that they could be pushed into the smoldering ashes and thus heated faster. Of course she did not know that, and hung the teapot above the fire. Consequently, it took twice as long for the water to boil.

She burned the bacon drying in the smoke chamber in the flue over the fire. How was she to know that she should have opened the stupid thing before setting the meat upon the spit?

She even charred the wooden toast dogs, the whimsical bread holders carved and painted in the shape of hunting dogs. They should have been held by the tail and gently placed into the flames so that the bread would brown evenly on both sides. No one told her that she should not have set them in the flames and walked away.

The kitchen was always dim with a mist of roasted meats and spiced breads. That is, when it wasn't covered in smoke from one of her fiascoes.

It was an absolutely horrible two days.

She had not known that she was so clumsy, or so lacking in the basic necessities of life. That knowledge depressed her almost as much as did the realization that reaching Alex was going to be more difficult than she had thought.

Even if she could have marched past the retinue of maids and footmen who seemed eternally to patrol the corridors of Heddon Hall armed with dustbins or polishing rags, she doubted that he was going to be overcome with the sight of her attired in a spotted gray dress, smelling of smoke and the lingering scent of vinegar.

From the gossip in the kitchen it was evident that he held himself aloof from everyone—and that Heddon Hall's servants were grateful for his reticence. Their comments about his appearance and his evil eye only made her more irritable.

Could they not see that he was still Alex?

Despite her fatigue, and the tiny little room to which she had been assigned, she found it difficult to sleep at night. Her hours of staring out at the moonlit garden finally reaped an unexpected reward on her second night at Heddon Hall. As if in reward for her patience, Alex moved into view, walking unerringly around the sloped garden, his limp barely noticeable, his figure as perfectly beautiful to her as if the moonlight had bequeathed him an unearthly grace. She propped her chin on her crossed arms, watching Alex as he strode in the serenity and stillness that was midnight.

She did not realize that the lone candle illuminated her figure, creating a halo behind her so that she appeared a ghostly white shadow, her hair streaming wildly down her back. She did not realize that he could see her quite clearly.

He did not, surprisingly, resent her intrusion into his solitary vigil. Midnight had been his ally for months. Rather than let others see his uncertainty and his clumsiness as he tripped or stumbled around unfamiliar rooms, he had relearned his home in secret. As his servants slept, he roamed Heddon Hall until each room was drawn into a fixed and unchangeable pattern in his mind. He had issued orders that nothing was to be changed; if a belowstairs maid dusted in the dining room, she was to replace each object exactly on the same spot from which she had removed it. If the carpets were beaten during spring cleaning, each massive piece of oak furniture was to be set down exactly on its previously designated spot. The failure to do so meant instantaneous dismissal.

He knew that there were forty-eight steps up the grand staircase of his home and that the treads were ten feet wide. He knew the feel of the etched panels and the handles upon each door, the brass rubbed bright and smooth beneath his fingertips. He had prowled through the chapel in the dawn light and touched the ancient frescoes on the wall with his right hand, stumbled against the gigantic carved chest that once contained the vestments of officiating clerics and now bore only the dusty tracks of curious mice. He had traced

the family motto etched into the plaster above the fireplace
in the dining hall—*Drede God and Honor the Kyng*—and felt
the carved faces of Henry the Seventh and his queen, found
in a dainty frieze..

He had learned his gardens again, identifying the plants
there by their smell, recognizing the topiary figures by their
leafy shapes or his memory of them.

Darkness held no fear for him, but he welcomed the light
he had begun to see as his vision had gradually returned.
Now if he prowled through his home long past the time others
lay abed it was in an endless quest for peace.

He was well aware that he frightened the servants just as
he knew that the young woman smiling down at him from
her perch upon the sill was not afraid of him.

The poor girl was simple.

Which was a damn shame. A body like a siren's and a
mind like a sieve. At least that was the description he had
received from an irate Simons, who had braved his lord's
displeasure and knocked upon the door to the Eagle Tower
countless times in the past two days. The man had been covered in soot and redolent of the noxious odor of singed wool.
It was only after numerous complaints from cook and even
little Mary, who was the bravest of the maids, that he had
discerned that the new girl was as devoid of intelligence as
she was amply provided with nature's abundance.

Which was a perfect waste of a glorious figure.

He wondered if God, who had stripped her of reason, had
felt, at last, only pity. Had such a merciful God gifted her
with beauty in a supreme gesture of appeasement for her lack
of wits?

What we have never had, though, we cannot miss.

He could not simply dismiss her. It was evident from her
lack of skills that she would soon starve. No, Heddon Hall
had its share of misfits; what would one more matter?

They were quite a pair, the two of them, lit by the strong,
radiant light from the full moon. He laughed, a mocking, self-

deprecating sound that carried past the yews and up to the window where Laura sat, bemused by the sight of him staring up at her. She withdrew finally and sought her bed, but sleep was as elusive as the fourth Earl of Cardiff.

Four

Laura was chopping onions on the great center table, her eyes streaming with the chore, when Cook abruptly thrust a heavy silver tray in her hands.

"Take this to the earl, girl, and mind, don't drop it."

"What about Mary?" she asked. The very last thing she wanted to do was meet Alex again clad in her spotted gray dress, with the odor of onions clinging to her skin.

"Mary's sick," Cook said shortly, "now go."

She followed Simons's instructions implicitly, entering the large hall by a doorway she had never seen before, its outline cunningly concealed in the pattern of the frescoes. She turned left and found herself before the grand staircase. Soaring above her head was the domed roof, filled with carved statues of gods and goddesses.

She had raced up these steps as a child, seeking a hiding place during an impromptu childhood game. She smiled as she remembered colliding with Alex, and the strong arms that had prevented her fall.

He had scolded her then, telling her that the steps were dangerous and no place to play, and that a fall could result in her being badly hurt. She remembered looking up into his flashing black eyes and nodding whenever he said, "Do you understand?" Truth to tell, she could not remember much of his lecture later, only the sight of his mobile lips and the long, long lashes that seemed to swoop down over his eyes like black silken wings.

She mounted the stairs slowly, not savoring the return of memory as much as she was conscious of the weight of the tray. It was not easy climbing the steep steps and balancing the tray with its silver teapot and Spode china. There were three types of jam, white bread toasted just the correct shade of brown, delicate slices of fruit, and starched linen bearing the Cardiff crest.

The walls beside the stairs were covered with a set of pictures done in the school of Raphael. She recognized the style from her instruction at the academy, which was the only part of her education she had been able to utilize thus far.

From a wide landing at the stair's head a massive set of double doors opened into the lord's apartment, the state bedroom.

She placed the tray on the ornately carved mahogany table in the hall and gently knocked on one of the doors. She waited for a moment and knocked again. When she received no answer she turned the brass handle and pushed the door ajar. It swung heavily inward on well-oiled hinges.

She peered into the room. The first thing she saw was the magnificent draped bedstead to her left. Over fourteen feet high, the four-poster was hung with rich green embroidered velvet. It held no occupant.

He stood with his back to her, standing at the entrance to the small conservatory built adjacent to the master suite. The light from the windows illuminated him, as if he stood in a shower of sunlight. He was dressed in black trousers again, but his shirt was white silk, exposing a broad back and stiffly erect shoulders. He stood with his hands on his hips, looking out at the panorama of Heddon Hall before him. Next to the Eagle Tower, it was reputed to have the best view of the massive house and its environs.

"Put it on the table, Mary," he said softly, without turning.

She did not bother to correct him, but gratefully disposed of the heavy tray. She glanced around the room curiously;

she had never been in this room and had only heard of its beauty and its treasures.

A massive fireplace lay opposite the four-poster, surmounted by an alto-relief of plaster representing Orpheus in the act of charming the beasts. The furniture was heavy and ornately carved, its massive size balancing the dimensions of the room. Beneath it all lay a brightly patterned octagonal carpet. In the center of the room sat a huge circular table, a massive crystal bowl set upon its polished surface filled with hundreds of pink roses from the Winter Garden. Their fragrance perfumed the air and vied with the scent of bay rum for dominance.

She thought how different Heddon Hall was from her own home. There was nothing at Blakemore that was traditional—stately, somber, built to last, and marked by a patina of age. It was all new. Blakemore's floors were laid with Dutch oak boards instead of shining mahogany, the rooms wainscotted and painted instead of plastered and decorated with intricate carvings. Marble slabs surrounded their fireplaces of brass, not friezes that were the work of masters. The doors were thick and substantial, with brass locks, not paneled and etched with gilt. The furniture was light and delicate, painted beech or walnut, upholstered with leather or cane, not the handsome mahogany and oak that marked generations of use, or accented with tapestry covers that represented countless hours of work by generations of willing hands.

Blakemore was barely thirty years old, while Heddon Hall dated from the twelfth century. Yet it was not only age that differentiated the two. One represented the seat of generations of power, the other, only money.

Upon the vanity in the corner was a dim oval mirror with an elaborately lacquered frame. She walked toward it slowly, oblivious to his watchful stare.

When he had heard no shuffling, hurried footsteps he had glanced around. Instead of Mary the new girl was there, curiosity evidently overcoming her fear.

He had not been able to forget her eyes. They were the green of thick pine forests, of the yews at dusk. He turned and watched her. Her auburn hair, the tresses that were not hidden beneath that silly-looking cap, seemed to shimmer in the faint light from the windows, as if each skein sought out a mote of sunlight. Her skin was milky white and her lips were full and peach-colored, as if she had just nibbled on a fruit. He wondered if they would taste the same.

The gray dress did little to hide the sweet swell of her bodice or the curve of her hips, which moved with unconscious grace. He looked down; her ankles still peeped out from the too-short skirts.

For a few moments, when he had first seen her, she had lifted something within him, something hard and heavy that lodged in his chest like a giant beast whose talons gripped his flesh. She had moved toward him and he had felt hope stir. She had looked at him directly and he felt the blood course through his veins, so thick and hot that he could not speak except in short, clipped sentences. He had felt no fear within her, and his heart had stirred.

Of course she was simple. Only a fool would look upon him without shuddering.

Now he laughed, and the sound caused a shiver to lance up her spine.

She stopped in the act of admiring the mirror, as if remaining motionless for his intimate perusal. He did not know it, but the sound had brought back memories to her. Memories of when she had deliberately tried to charm the laughter from Alex and had succeeded, despite his claim that she could not. The sound had changed through the years, and she suspected, wisely, that the reason for it had, as well.

"It is very pretty, is it not?" he asked, speaking of the mirror in front of her. His voice was deliberately soft, unwilling as he was to frighten her. Laura looked away, tracing the pattern of the mirror's frame with one tremulous finger. She nodded.

He stepped closer to her, each footfall cautious and measured, as if testing her tolerance for his nearness. He wondered if Mary's duties had proved too much for her, and Mrs. Seddon and Simons had seized upon this likely replacement because she was simpleminded.

What a pair they made: a luscious little loon and a frightening monster. One with too little sense to be afraid, the other with too much awareness of his own ability to invoke fear.

He still did not recognize her.

She frankly did not know whether to take it as a compliment to the way she had changed, or to be insulted that he had not remembered her. How could he forget? She would have recognized him no matter how many years and miles they had spent apart. As it was, there were four blank years and a gulf of more than miles between them.

There was the distance that Alex had put between himself and others, even his servants.

There was the distance that her masquerade was causing, as even now she pretended to be someone she was not.

He did not move closer, but continued to watch her with an impassive stare. She wished that she did not feel the almost physical sense of withdrawal from him. The mask was not his only barrier from the world, she realized with a flash of insight. It only represented the line of demarcation as surely as if he had drawn a circle around himself and proclaimed, *do not trespass here*.

She was more certain than ever that her initial impression was correct: He would see her love as only pity. She did not pity Alex; there was too much about him to love. His wit, which had charmed her since she was a little child. His gentleness, which had been gifted to the lonely little girl who was his neighbor. His fairness above all, his sense of pride and decency, his way of looking at the world.

She did, however, come very close to understanding the enormous magnitude of the gulf between them in that moment, as he remained out of range of the mirror and she stared full face into it.

She wanted, desperately, to be part of his present and his future. Not in the way she had been as a child, but as a woman. She wanted him to recognize her and her love; then she wanted to pull aside the shield of the black mask and tell him that it didn't matter that he was scarred, or that he limped or could not use one hand.

"The mirror was a gift from Queen Elizabeth," he said in that harsh, grating voice. "She once stayed in this room."

She did not speak or comment. He had not expected her to.

"Rumor has it that she rewarded my ancestor with far more than a mirror," he said. Tension and the strangest urge to keep her there, webbed in a net of his words, made him wish that he were less unused to the company of others. He was rusty in conversation, and unused to the company of women, even one as sweetly fragile and childlike as she.

She looked at him calmly, still tracing the outline of the mirror.

He stepped back.

"Please," she said quietly, turning, "do not go." She extended one hand to him, and he looked at it dispassionately, the sudden widening of his eye the only sign of his surprise.

He grasped her hand between his gloved one and his warm flesh. He peered down at it, at the faint burns and the blisters. She had been given too many tasks, this sweet little idiot.

"Would you like to bring my meals from now on?" he asked, thinking to spare her the heavy kitchen chores she had been given. It was a kindly gesture he made, one of pitifully few in many months, and he recognized it as such with a tinge of self-mockery.

She only viewed it as a way of seeing him again. She nodded.

"Then you shall," he said softly, still stroking her palm.

His touch was different, somehow, from what she had

thought it would be. She had not imagined his eager perusal of her in the courtyard, but now he acted almost paternally toward her. That was fine for when she was a child; she wanted more from Alex now. She looked down at her spotted dress and, in the mirror, at the ruin of her hair. She was a poor Salome, she thought in disgust. A rueful smile wreathed her lips, which caused him to cease his visual exploration of her hand and glance at her in surprise.

He noticed her white, even teeth, the porcelain beauty of her skin, the soft flush that tinged her cheeks, and wondered if he had made a mistake.

She might be simple, but she was still a woman.

Nor had he forgotten, although the world had, that he was a man.

Five

"You stupid, clumsy creature! Now see what you've done!" The slap was sudden and vicious, the strength of the blow forming a stark red imprint upon the pale and frightened face of the young maid.

Maggie Bowes stepped back in a frantic bobble of motion, two things uppermost in her mind: to remove herself from the reach of the dowager countess and to maintain a respectful attitude while doing so, so as not to anger the countess further.

She had been far away from the vanity when the perfume bottle had overturned, spilling the countess's favorite scent. She had been on the other side of the room, in fact, carefully finishing the packing that had been her chore for most of the afternoon.

But then, it was not the first time she'd been the brunt of undeserved rage. It took little to beckon blistering words from the countess, or sharp blows from that deceptively small hand.

Maggie's only sin in life, if such could be called that, was that she had been born plain. Worse than plain, if you were not Christian and saw the port-wine stain that swept over her cheek and her neck as the Devil's mark itself.

Marriage was beyond her, but not honest work. So, in hopes of a future and in fear of strangers who did nothing but stare and ridicule the birthmark that had caused her such grief from the time she was a tiny child, Maggie had come to Heddon Hall. The rumors said that even the most infirm

could gain employment where the only requirement to draw
a fair wage was a willingness to do the work.

Somehow she'd caught the eye of the countess, and instead
of remaining as a belowstairs maid, where she would have
been only one more of the score of servants employed at
Heddon Hall, Maggie now had the terrible task of serving
the countess herself. It had been a dark day indeed when the
dowager countess had spied her.

Maggie herself winced at the sight of the two of them,
framed in the expanse of the gilt-edged mirror. It was such
a shocking contrast that the first time she'd seen their reflection she had known instantly why the countess had chosen
her. It was not any skill she might have possessed that had
recommended her; it was her ugliness, against which the
dowager countess appeared even more ethereal, fragile, and
delicately formed.

Her ugliness, and only that. Her fingers were clumsy; she
knew nothing of the latest fashions; her hands trembled when
she arranged the countess's blond curls.

If she had known that she was to be chosen by the countess, she would have stayed in her parents' cottage, never mind
that the little ones always wore pinched looks of hunger and
the strain on her mother's face was there for all to see.

If she had known that she was to be whisked from Heddon
Hall and spirited away to London, she would have fled back
to the country. Being in the countess's employ had meant
endless nights of remaining awake until the countess returned
and endless days of servitude to a woman who invoked more
fear than loyalty. Nor had she had one day off in the month
they had been there.

And where would you go, Maggie girl? London scared her.
It was dirty, filled with nothing but people and noise. No,
she was a country lass and long these many days she had
wished she was back in the country.

Now it looked as though she was going to get her wish.
She wondered if the earl knew.

There was bad blood between those two, if belowstairs gossip could be relied on. The grapevine had spoken of shouting in the Orange Parlor, hissed words from the countess, and her fury upon leaving Heddon Hall.

How well Maggie remembered that day. The countess had been in a rage, for sure, her anger translated to her hapless servants, all of whom went out of their way to avoid her pinching fingers.

The dowager countess made Maggie nervous. There was something in the look of those lustrous blue eyes that were, more often than not, slitted and lit by a brilliant gleam, as if the woman knew a dreadful and delicious secret. Something in the lilt of her voice, carefully modulated, carefully controlled even in the midst of her rages. Maggie had learned, to her discomfort, that the countess was at her most dangerous when that silky voice descended in tone and her words were almost whispered.

There was something about the dowager countess that made her want to cross herself, for all that she was not a Catholic.

It was a sentiment unexpressed, but unanimously felt, throughout the Weston town house.

Which would have shocked all of Elaine Weston's admirers, of whom there were many. She was feted and praised for her fragile, doll-like beauty, her charm, her sparkling and easy wit, the smile that etched her bowlike lips and her creamy complexion, with its shell-pink hue. She was the subject of many a parlor whisper, a whiskey-induced ode to her fair beauty, a challenge among the younger hotheads of the day.

No one noticed, unless it was the more perceptive of the female sex, that her lips were oddly red, a shade rarely found in nature. Few realized that her fair complexion was enhanced by rouge and the lead-based treatments she employed every morning and night. No one knew, except for Maggie, that the sparkle in her eyes was due to drops she used regularly.

Nor did any of her companions ever discern that her fair hand, delicate and topped with pink nails, could strike such a hardy blow. Or that she used her deceptive strength often and without regard to the subject of her rage.

She was small of stature, which made even the most puny of men feel protective and masculine. They did not realize that her small frame contained a will and a strength of purpose that would have rivaled the strongest man's. Her blond hair fell in pale, golden ringlets, surrounding her heart-shaped face, which publicly bore either a look of simpering sweetness or a riveted interest in a speaker's words. The smile she practiced often in the mirror never quite reached her eyes, however, had anyone looked closely enough to notice. Nor did any of her many admirers know that this same delicate face was often twisted by rage or marred by a look of cunning.

As it was now, in the privacy of her luxurious bedchamber, with only her maid in sight.

She was out of money and it was the monster's fault.

Money she had earned, in five long and endless years of marriage to the doddering earl. Five years!

Years in which she had played the dutiful, precious wife to the old earl. Years in which she had been discreet and demure. Years in which she had suffered the earl's touch, his possessiveness, and the contempt of the Weston sons.

Five years of her life.

They owed her something.

More than an allowance doled out by a misshapen lump of a man. More than a paltry sum that would not allow her any of the comforts of life and none of the joys. They owed her.

She had been barely seventeen when she had left her home, a stately manor house suffering from years of neglect. The paint had weathered, the gardens overgrown, and there never seemed to be enough money to adequately feed and clothe the large family, despite the titles her father bore too proudly. A baronetcy could win entrance to an exclusive gentlemen's club but could not be bartered for the latest fashions. An Honorable before his name could guarantee that his chits would be valued, but her father's word had no value with the shopkeepers in their small village. From her earliest years she was the only one who seemed to notice. She had wanted something better even then, even when her elder brothers and sisters laughed at her ambitions. She could have told them, at the age of five, that her life was charted. She knew exactly what she wanted.

Money, power, and freedom.

Power and freedom were attainable only with money. It was a lesson she had learned as a child. It was one she never forgot.

She settled for the money first, trading her fresh young body for a title accompanied by wealth.

She did not come to her marriage bed a virgin but had tested her talents before settling on the Earl of Cardiff as a worthy goal. He was fantastically wealthy, old, and so filled with passion for her that he dismissed the warning words of his two grown sons and the coaxing ones of his solicitors. He thought himself in love, enough to be overcome by her cries of pain on their wedding night, which were real enough. The knife she had hidden beneath her pillow had cut her thigh too sharply.

It had been almost too easy.

The old earl had clung to life with a tenacity that she could have admired if it had not been in the way of her own ambitions. He had outlived his usefulness, the old fool. He had nearly outlived her charade. Her boredom had been so great that she had taken chances, stupid chances. She had cuckolded the great and mighty Earl of Cardiff with every male within thirty miles of his precious Heddon Hall.

If he had only known . . . but then, perhaps, toward the end, he had realized that she was not who or what he believed her to be. Yet his newfound knowledge had not spared her his attentions.

He had crawled into her bed often enough. She had been the greatest of actresses on those nights, when his wrinkled body brushed against hers and he touched her with lips that were chapped with age and hands that were gnarled by life. He had touched her and moaned over her and thrust inside of her with his old man's body that smelled of camphor and the sweet-sour stench of decay. How she had loathed him at those moments, when his excitement fueled hot words and she moaned and encouraged him with sounds that barely, just barely, concealed her hatred of him.

Yet her time had come, finally. The roads had been icy; the earl and his precious son and heir had been traveling to London; the groom had been enthralled with her body and her promises. That was all that was needed, at the end. A quick knife cut to the harness, a wheel that was loosened, a few smiles to the groom, an afternoon tumble in the hay.

It had been so simple, really. So absurdly simple.

Except for the will.

She had waited too long. Perhaps the old earl had known, had somehow discovered that the only thing she ever lusted after was his money.

She had no trouble feigning shock on that date, when she learned that instead of inheriting Heddon Hall and the vast fortune that accompanied it, she would, instead, be placed on an allowance. An allowance! Administered now by the crippled and hideously disfigured new earl, who sat at Heddon Hall and issued dictates from his position of power.

He had left the hall soon after his father's marriage, after having argued vehemently against it. When he returned, a prodigal son—a caricature of the handsome young man he had been—it was to a title and a future filled with the wealth that should have been hers.

Now that parody of a man sat on a fortune and doled out a pittance barely enough to sustain a beggar.

She stared into the mirror, ignoring the blotches of color on her cheeks, remembering his words upon her departure from Heddon Hall, a brick prison in which she had suffered for too long.

"Do not feign affection for me, madam," he had rasped behind that hideous black mask. "I am well aware that your motives are more couched in the love of money than the love of kin."

"You were my husband's favorite son, Alex. Would you allow rancor to come between us?" She had smiled her sweetest smile, but the monster had turned away.

"I was my father's second son, madam. A spare, if you will, who is ill equipped for the post he now occupies."

She had gone to him then, placed her hand upon his sleeve, even though the effort cost her much. Surprisingly, the feel of the steely muscles beneath her palm had thrilled her, and a tantalizing thought entered her mind. What would it be like with the son?

However, he abruptly shook off her touch, as if soiled, and then had the effrontery to laugh at her expression.

"Let us not mince words, dear Stepmama," he had said sardonically. "I want my privacy and you want your money. Go to London. Live well. But stay away from Heddon Hall."

"And the money to live in London, Alex? Will you provide that?"

"Your allowance is available, madam. Make it last."

But it didn't last, not if she wanted a decent wardrobe, or played a few friendly games of whist, or paid for the privilege of having James Watkins in her life. He was a treat she had no intention of relinquishing. Not as long as her golden lover remained in her bed, beguiled by her talents and veiled hints of Cardiff wealth.

At the moment, however, her credit was extended to the limit and the collectors had started showing up on her doorstep with the duns in hand. She was out of money, and the freak was living in state at Heddon Hall.

He could have that moldering pile of bricks, with its overtones of ancient history, its drafty rooms and hints of ghosts.

He could have the forever green, rolling fields, the unearthly silence, and the lack of amusement. He could have the serenity and the stultifying boredom.

She just wanted the money.

Did the new earl prize his privacy so much that he would pay for it? She would simply have to find out.

She smiled into the mirror, noting the presence of the maid, who remained in the room, her hand still pressed against her burning cheek. Her smile changed a little, shifted as she stared at the girl.

Maggie thought it was the most evil look she'd ever seen.

Six

Mary was grateful to be relieved of the task of taking the earl's tray to him. More than grateful, she confided to Laura, smiling in the first gesture of honest friendship she had been given since walking into Heddon Hall's formidable kitchen.

" 'Tis the mask," Mary whispered, as if the earl was listening. "Mind you, he's never done nothin' mean or cruel, an' Heddon's a place to call home for many a poor travelin' servant, but it's the way of his lookin' through that one eye that puts the fear of the Almighty in you."

Laura had no words to counteract the young maid's sincere aversion. She, herself, had felt the jolt of that drastic change in Alex's appearance. Yet his appearance did not mean that the man himself had changed. Had they forgotten the young Alex who had laughed through the halls of his home and played ball upon the lawn near the Winter Garden? Didn't they remember the young man who had made his father smile, or caused even the stern-faced Simons to grin reluctantly? A bit of black leather might conceal his face, but it could not mask his true nature.

It would become a crusade of hers, to reveal the man beneath the mask.

It was not going to be as easy as she had innocently supposed. From that day on it was Laura's duty to help prepare Alex's meals. Sometimes he would speak to her as she delivered the heavy tray. Their conversations were simple, consisting mainly of the state of the weather. More often than not he would say nothing, simply glancing up from his desk in the Eagle Tower, his work interrupted until she once again shut the door quietly behind her.

She was no closer to him than before. Even her slight attempts at broadening the conversation were met with silence, as if he weighed her words with more import than necessary. As if she had thrown out a conversational trap and he was wary of it. She longed to linger, but his look indicated that he preferred that she depart as quickly as possible.

She never noticed that he gripped the quill more tightly in his undamaged hand when she was in the room. Nor did she hear the swift, expelled sigh or the muttered imprecation after she left it.

She did, however, have time to reacquaint herself with Heddon Hall. She would delay her return to the kitchen, skirting the presence of the many servants occupied with cleaning, and investigate yet another room.

She experienced Heddon Hall slowly, like a rare flower that opened its petals only for the very patient.

Her first self-imposed chore was to find the tapestry. It was her most prized memory, the one thing she instantly recalled when thinking of Heddon Hall. She slipped into a small room beside one of the bedchambers.

The memory of childhood had not imbued it with false magic. It was as wonderful as she had recalled.

A fully armored knight stood helm in hand beside his destrier, staring directly and unflinchingly forward, as if his eyes met those of the watcher. Once, she'd thought the tapestry had been of Alex. She had been corrected quickly, informed that it was at least three hundred years old, designed by a master. A master whose subject had borne the same Weston dark looks, the identical black, flashing eyes, the same curl of hair near his brow, the same slight upturn of his lips on the left side, as if he had not decided which type of smile to bestow—a mocking smirk or a tender grin.

It was, she thought, a smile to haunt one's dreams.

Quickly looking to her left and then her right, she pressed two fingertips to her mouth and then to the lips of the proud knight. She smiled brightly at the unchanging figure and continued on her mission of exploration.

The Music Room was adjacent to the Withdrawing Room, where she noticed several recent additions to the supply of instruments. In addition to the spinet in the corner, at which she only winced, there was a lute, a virginal, and a viola de gamba.

She entered the Withdrawing Room, directly above the Dining Room, and went immediately to the dainty recessed window from where she could view the gardens and the river.

She traced the letters etched in the glass. She had been banished to Blakemore House for a week after that incident. She found the tiny heart and the initials DAW linked with her own—Dixon Alexander Weston and Laura Ashcott Blake.

Alex had come to Blakemore finally and explained what she had done. The glass in the windows had been blown, he told her patiently, by craftsmen in Venice. A blow pipe was put into a crucible of molten glass and blown while being twisted rapidly, with the result that a large, thin disc was formed at the end. From the outer parts were cut the panes of glass for the upper windows. The center, where it had been attached to the pipe, was thicker and had a knot when broken off. This formed the bull's eye seen in the lower windows of the Withdrawing Room. The light was caught and reflected from the different surfaces until it was a rainbow of colors.

She had been tearfully apologetic, but he had ruffled her head and sighed and said that Chatsworth, the great mansion across the river, had similar evidence of youthful exuberance in the Latin doodles of Mary, the doomed queen of Scots.

She had cried because she had made Alex angry, not because she was sorry for what she had done. She could not honestly say that she was sorry now. She touched her lips with one finger and then the finger to the spot on the glass where their initials met within a hastily etched heart.

She passed finally through the Long Gallery, said to be the chief glory of Heddon Hall. She only found it strangely disconcerting, as though she should whisper and tiptoe through it lest she disturb the ghostly dancers that she could imagine treading lightly on the boards. To reach the doorway she had to ascend a semicircular staircase of solid oak, cut from the trunk of a single tree, whose branches had furnished the planks for the floor of the great chamber.

Without much effort she could hear the strings of the lute and see the swirling skirts and severely executed movements of the lavolta, pavan, or saraband. The coloring here was rich and warm, the paneling, with its carved boars' heads, peacocks, mermaids, and frolicking nymphs, had mellowed over the years until it resembled walnut. Originally the parqueting was etched in gilt. Although traces of the gilt still remained, winking gold in a stream of sunlight, the bright paint had faded until it was only pastel.

The ceiling above was frescoed with gamboling satyrs, Pan with his flute and other imps frolicking around ladies dressed in costumes that were as scanty as they were delicately carved. In alcoves cut into the wall other statues rested, dimly lit by the afternoon sun. The central bay window was as large as an ordinary-sized room and let in the light, which seemed to float down on dusty sunbeams to dance upon the floor. It was a room strangely silent now, waiting for motion and laughter and music.

She loved Heddon Hall and she cherished the memories of her visits as a child. Strangely, though, Alex's brother never entered into her thoughts. Charles had been an adult even then, separated in age from Alex by twelve years. He had always been away at school or involved in some adult pursuit by the time she had first visited Heddon.

She had been here for days and she was no closer to Alex than a stranger would have been. She did have, however, a clear and detailed idea of how kitchens operated. She also had a great appreciation for those silent workers in her own home and the seemingly effortless appearance of food upon her table. She did not think she would ever view her own staff in the same light.

"He's done it again," Simons said sourly the next day. "Gone and sacked Hartley." He sighed heavily as the housekeeper, Mrs. Seddon, looked over at him in complete accord. "And now he wants a replacement! Where, I ask you, am I to find a likely candidate for such a post?"

"The earl's not an easy man to work for," Mrs. Seddon agreed. "You'll have to advertise in London again, Simons."

The butler scowled at her. "I know that, woman. It's the time I'm worried about. He says he must have a new secretary in a week's time. Or before! Now, he's shouting that he needs someone to read to him!"

"I can read," Laura said softly from her post at the oak table. She had been set to cleaning the old boards with vinegar, and she hated the odor.

Both Simons and Mrs. Seddon ignored her. She put down the cloth and advanced on them. "I can read, I said," she repeated, coming to stand between them. It was not, after all, a great feat of which she boasted—most females were schooled in basic skills. Although it was true, of course, that not many were privy to the varied and eclectic education meted out by her uncles. She had no idea that it was not her education that was held in doubt by both upper servants but her mental acuity.

Simons looked at her appraisingly and then smiled. He exchanged a long glance with Mrs. Seddon, who nodded once.

It was a perfect way to rid themselves of the idiot.

The earl had been too kind to this simpleton. With her protestations of learning she would incur his wrath for good this time.

A few moments later she was mounting the steps to the Eagle Tower, armed with a dog-eared copy of Marcus Aurelius's *Meditations*.

From the Long Gallery she entered the Orange Parlor, so called because of the draped Chinese silk of its walls. From there she reached a corkscrew staircase that climbed to the Peveril Tower and across the open walk to the Eagle Tower. She hesitated at the door and turned to look down at the roofs, courtyards, and green Heddon meadows.

She took a deep breath, summoned her courage, and firmly knocked on the door.

"Who is it?" came a clear, impatient voice.

"Jane," she said simply. There was a long pause, as if he was trying to recollect who she was. Why should she think that he would remember her from the vast numbers of servants at Heddon?

He should have, anyway, she thought irately. He had seen her every morning and every evening.

There was the sound of a bar being drawn across the door, and then he thrust it open. The black mask was tied tightly into place.

"What do you want?" Once again his voice was muffled, made harsh and raspy by the effort of speaking through the leather. That was the cause for the delay, then. He had once again put on his mask.

She held up the book for him to see.

He stared at her for so long that she thought he was going to deny her admission. He finally pushed the door open far enough for her to enter.

She had been strictly forbidden to walk the narrow path from the Peveril Tower as a child, but the enchantment of the Eagle Tower had been too much of a lure to resist. She had come here once, just once, before she was discovered by Alex and sent home in disgrace once again. She remembered the Persian carpet and the odd shape of the room: rounded, with long narrow windows. Upon one curve sat an open grate, serving as a fireplace. Opposite were built-in cupboards lining the curved walls.

She eased past Alex, scanning the room quickly. Other than

the addition of one long table and two solid oak chairs, the room was as sparsely furnished as she remembered it. She walked to the other side of the curving wall and peered from the arched window. From here she could see the footbridge crossing the Wye and the little dove house beside the road.

He would have reached for the book, but she swung away from him.

He sat on the chair beside the wrought-iron candelabra and watched her. She finally sat, too, opening the book slowly. She raised it up for him to see, hoping he approved of Simons's selection.

He wondered what game she was about then, his little loon.

At first her voice was tremulous; then, as she continued to read, it lost that reedy tone and reverted to her natural voice, vibrant and low.

He sat straight up in the chair and studied her intently. She did not notice when his posture became rigid, or when his right hand gripped the arm of the chair.

He said nothing about the fact that she was reading Greek.

Finally, after she had turned the pages twice, she began to be aware of his rigid stillness. She looked up at his words.

"I do not understand that last passage," he said quietly.

"Oh, it's quite simple, really," she said in the patient tones of one who would explain something to a child. "They are rules that Aurelius has decided for himself, you see. He does not have a cheery attitude as much as he has one of forbearance. He says that one must have the will to continue to do the best even in the worst of all possible worlds."

"Translate that last part," he said, in the most quiet of whispers.

She thought nothing of his demand, but calmly re-read that section, translating as she went. " 'I can neither be harmed by any of them, for no one can fix on me what is ugly, nor can I be angry with my brother, nor hate him. For we are made for cooperation, like feet, like hands, like eyelids, like the rows of the upper and lower teeth. To act against one another then is contrary to nature, and it is acting against one another to be vexed and turn away.' "

"Who are you?" he said, still not raising his voice. The poor simpleminded girl had just translated Greek better than his Cambridge don.

She placed the book on the table and traced its gold-leaf spine with her finger. He did not glance away when she looked directly at him.

"Who are you?" he repeated, but she only examined her hands as if to find the answer there.

"Who are you, damn it!" he finally shouted, goaded beyond reason by her silence.

It was not, she thought later, that she wanted so much to deceive Alex as she wanted to prevent him from throwing her out upon her ear, which was exactly what he looked like he wanted to do at that moment. Despite the fact that only one eye peered through that damnable mask, she knew the expression it concealed.

Sheer rage.

Alex was never to be argued with when he was in such a mood.

So she did what any prudent soul would do in such a circumstance.

She lied, straight-faced.

"I do not know what you mean," she said helplessly.

"You know full well what I mean," he continued adamantly. "Why did you let me think you were simple?"

She looked shocked, he thought, and not a little indignant.

"It's true, I have no experience with domestic pursuits," she said huffily, "but that is no reason to think I lack sense." The rumble of thunder caused her to look through the arched window at the sky. She hoped that God would not cause a bolt of lightning to strike her dead for that confession. It was, at least, the truth. "But my father was a poor country parson, richer in learning than in his purse, I fear." The thunder rumbled again, and she looked down at her hands once more.

"And is Greek your only virtue?"

She shook her head, mumbling toward her clenched hands. "No, I fear not. Latin, too."

"Did you have no brothers he could teach, or was he limited to a poor female?"

Poor female, indeed!

She lowered her eyes before her look of indignation gave her away. Not quick enough, however, for him to miss the spark of fury in their green depths.

"I have three strapping brothers," she invented, deciding that if she was forced to lie, she might as well embellish it a little. "Brian, Neville, and Bruce."

"What? No sisters?" He leaned back in the chair, crossed his arms over his chest, and watched her as she frowned. She still had not returned her gaze to him.

"Three sisters, too. Agnes, Marsha, and Petunia."

"Petunia?" He could not help a snort of laughter, which surprised him and irritated her. She was not used to dissembling on the spur of the moment. Normally she was given some time to think about it.

"No wonder your father was poor, with such a brood to support."

The thunder rumbled closer, and she decided God had been put to enough of a test.

"Can you cipher?"

She nodded, grateful not to be forced to lie about that.

"And do you write a decent hand?"

"I have been told so," she said stiffly.

"Can you sit and not prattle for hours at a time?"

Since she had been barely allowed to speak in the kitchen for the past few days, she nodded again. Heddon Hall had taught her too much about her own unknown capabilities.

"Then you shall act as my secretary until Simons procures another." He stood and extended his hand and she grasped it, thinking that he meant to shake hands in the way of men.

His skin was warm, and although his palm was hardened, his flesh was still soft.

If she had been rational, she would have confessed all, right then.

If she had not loved him so much, she would have counted her experience as one of pure stupidity and departed Heddon Hall posthaste.

If she had not been so foolish and so young, she would have recognized the danger for what it was.

She looked at him, then, standing in the Eagle Tower, and felt the barest shiver of anticipation. Only later did she recognize it for what it was.

A warning.

He could not stop staring at her, the silly chit, clutching his hand like a lifeline and refusing to let go, even though he had only wished the book from her. He looked at her wide eyes, the faint smile on her face, and absently shook his head.

If he had not been so lonely, he would have barred her from his door.

If he had not been so filled with horror at his own life and his dismal future, he would have dismissed her beauty and her talent and sent her reeling away from Heddon Hall.

Only later did he realize what the small shiver of anticipation he felt at that moment really meant.

A promise.

Seven

"Jethro Tull's *Horse Hoeing Husbandry* is a good source to verify my information, m'lord," she said with irritating aplomb.

Her pretense at subservience didn't fool him. He had never met a less meek female in his life. Nor did her smiling acceptance of his irritation dampen it in any measure.

"Of course," she continued, "if you would prefer that I not speak on the subject at all, I can understand that, too." She continued to smile at him, which only added to his mounting exasperation.

He frowned at her, which seemed not to discompose the girl one whit.

"What about it, Matthews?" he said, with all the patience of which he was capable, which wasn't much, considering the fact that he had been the object of her gentle chastisement all morning.

The steward of the home farms crushed his hat between his hands and stared at his boots which had left clumps of mud upon the floor of the Eagle Tower. He hesitated before answering, not sure if his response would be accepted with another glare, or if the young lady's smile would be the prelude to yet another lecture. Not from the earl, because the man had been suspiciously silent, but from the young lady herself. And how would she be knowin' such things? he thought to himself. Women had no business messin' with man's work. Women, well, women were to keep a proper meal

on the table and order about the house, and leave the work
of providin' the meal to the men.

"Aye, sir," he said finally, avoiding the earl's black-leather
face and the girl's smiling one. "It would work."

"Then do it," he said shortly, turning back to the source
of all his problems for the past few days. Matthews left the
room with relief.

Laura noted his departure with a frown and then turned to
Alex. It was not the first time she had noticed that none of
the servants at Heddon Hall dared to look at their master.
Alex could not help but be aware of that omission.

"Are they all afraid of you?" she asked gravely, and he
turned at her question, surprised. Not at the seriousness with
which she asked it, but the very nature of the question itself.

No one else would have dared.

Yet she had done many things during the last two days
that no one else in his limited circle would have been brave
enough to do.

He had never envisioned a secretary who *argued* with him.

He had thought that she would simply transcribe his instructions to his steward. He had never imagined that she
would toss the quill down upon the desktop, shake her head
as if he were a recalcitrant tot, and then proceed to challenge
his orders.

This morning she had recommended that he look over Mrs.
Seddon's accounts.

"Your cook is selling off drippings and cinders, receiving
too many commissions from the shops that supply Heddon
Hall. Also, there are too many mistakes in the entries for the
servant's livery and wigs, an error of £300." She had grinned
at him when she delivered that news, as impishly as she had
earlier smiled at him and proceeded to educate him in seed
selection and planting in furrows!

"If you will but alternate turnips, grasses, and corn, m'lord,
you will provide winter food for the cattle and avoid having
to let the land lie fallow once every three years," she had

patiently explained, as if he were not the earl and in charge of his own estate.

He paced in a circle around the table where she sat. It was, she suspected, an exercise of his leg as much as it was a show of frustration.

" 'It shows a will most incorrect to heaven, a heart unfortified, a mind impatient,' " she muttered and bent her head to her task again, when it was quite evident that he was not going to answer her.

He stopped his pacing and stared at her intently.

"You have a bad habit of doing that," he accused. She only smiled, remembering that Uncle Bevil had said much the same thing. She could not truly help that she remembered things so well. After all, was that not what an education was for? But, if he did not wish to be quoted to, like Uncle Bevil, well, she would try her best.

He wished, fervently, that she was not so damn lovely. Her beauty only reinforced his own ugliness. It was torture, but he welcomed it. It was anguish to sit and watch her as she read, her lips forming the words as if they were framed for kisses. It was hell to see her brush back her hair with one fine-boned hand and wonder if it felt as silky and smooth as it looked. It was agony to smell her scent, a blend of roses and something else, and wonder where she placed it. Was it on the crook of her arm, at the nape of her neck, or between those full and lovely breasts?

She was immune to his ranting, as if she was indeed simpleminded. Hartley had cowered when he had roared at him. She merely smiled.

She stared unflinchingly at him when he spoke to her, meeting the sight of his one eye as if it were the most natural thing in the world to be addressed by a cyclops in a leather mask.

It made him strangely irritated.

She did not flinch when he handed her something with his

gloved claw. More than once he had felt her gentle touch on the back of his leather hand and had withdrawn it quickly.

That did not please him either.

He could not help but see that soft smile that lit her face as her eyes glazed over and she stared at the wall, as if seeing a picture placed there. Undoubtedly her daydreams were of a lover somewhere, which made him unaccountably angry.

Angry enough to berate himself for enjoying conversing with her, anticipating the mornings when she would arrive in the Eagle Tower all freshly scrubbed and smelling of roses.

Angry enough to make him dream of another time, when he was young and handsome and had all the women he wanted. Now, he was older and worse than ugly, with a countenance that would send her screaming into the forests that surrounded his home.

It did not mean that he was less than human, however, or did not remember the feel of warm, soft, silken skin next to his, or the plump fullness of rounded breasts cradled in the palms of his hands. His injuries had not, unfortunately, stemmed the tide of rising manhood that seemed to expand in her presence.

What the hell was he doing?

"Are they not wise to be frightened?" he asked finally.

She grinned at him then, an irrepressible smile that held the warmth of the sun in it, the promise of a new day, the hope of tomorrow, and a gaminelike challenge that held him immobile for a moment.

"I think you use your mask as another man would use a whip, m'lord," she said softly.

"Explain," he said curtly, moving to her side. He noted that she did not edge away, or move the chair aside; she propped her chin in her hands and watched his movements.

"Another man might carry a whip and never use it, merely to frighten others into thinking that one day he might. Your mask serves the same purpose, I think. Each of your servants fears your presence, and yet you do nothing to reassure them. It's as if you wish them afraid."

"Why should I do that?" He stretched out one hand and almost touched the fiery glint of her hair before he caught himself and restrained that recalcitrant limb.

"I wonder," she said seriously. "Is it because, perhaps, you have grown used to your apartness? That other people, instead of offering comfort, now only offer a threat?"

He stared at the young woman who had become such a trial to peaceful sleep. Who had replaced his nightmares with sweet welcome and frightening warmth, and caused him to awaken sweating and needing and hurting with the surge of hot manhood, left unappeased and unassuaged.

He nearly laughed. "Is it such a sin, then, to crave my privacy?"

"Your privacy, or your solitude? They are different things, you know."

What would she know of solitude? What, damn it, did she know of what he wanted? Did she imagine, in that sweet, innocent, naive brain of hers, that he longed for nights without end, of sun-basked days seen from the slit of black leather, of the scent of roses masked by the tang of tanning oil, of the touch of paper, quill, brick, soft woman, forever to be translated through a glove? Did she think, did she presume to infer, that he was what he wanted to be?

He was suddenly furious, his rage emanating from him in the guise of his stiff gait across the room. He threw open the door, bowing mockingly to her.

"What I want, right now," he said harshly, his anger swallowed by the slit of leather, "is to be left alone. It matters not if you call it privacy or solitude."

She stood and walked, unconcerned, to the door. He might frighten the servants, but he did not frighten her. She smiled as she passed him.

He thrust one arm out across the doorway, leaning down

to her face, so close that he could breathe in the air she exhaled.

"Do I not frighten you?" The question lanced through the silence, carrying its own burden with it. Did he want an answer? If she said yes, would this growing affinity for her presence be magically severed and disconnected? Would her truth act as a wedge between them, stemming his own feelings, sealing him into a crucible of despair and loneliness that seemed, somehow, less palatable now that he had breached his self-imposed solitude?

And if she said no? Would that single word act as a bridge between them? Would it be a swinging rope above the gorge of reality, binding her to him with inexorable ties?

She glanced at him, a soft smile curving her lips. Her eyes sparkled with merriment. How could he ever have thought them dull or witless?

"Do you wish to, m'lord?"

He ignored her question and asked another of his own. "Does this," he said, touching his mask with fleeting fingers that betrayed him by their tremulousness, "not cause you alarm?"

"Should it?" she asked, with unreasonable woman's reason. She did not deflect her gaze, but stared at him straight-faced, her lack of artifice infinitely painful in that moment. Did she trust him so, not to reveal himself? Or was it simply another measure of her innocence that she would look at him full-faced, a small, gentle smile playing upon her coral lips, and know no danger?

"Or what may lie beneath it?" he asked harshly.

He wondered later why he had not tested her then. It came to him suddenly that he did not want to know her reaction. It would either be a replica of his own horror as he daily witnessed the ruin of his flesh or a placid acceptance of it, as if he was no more important to her than a freak at a London sideshow.

She did not tell him that she could not change what Fate

had done to him, but she could ache for the loss of laughter in his life, or hate the almost palpable isolation that surrounded him. She could not change the fact that his own servants were in awe and fear of him simply because an accident had altered his appearance, but she could give him her own gift of acceptance.

All of his scars were not on his flesh; he betrayed by a hundred small gestures his wariness of the world, a bleak acceptance of his isolation. If he had been a different man, he would not have minded it so, but the Alex she had known had compassion for a lonely little girl, awareness of another's pain. Those feelings that had made him so beloved to her—empathy, sensitivity, tenderness—were now his own two-edged sword. Rather than suffer the derision of others, he separated himself from them. Rather than be condemned he simply removed himself from the source of condemnation.

The only thing she could do, the only talent she had in this moment and another thousand timeless moments was her unalterable love for him. Beneath the scars, the bitterness, the mocking derision of his world lay the man he had been. Her knowledge of him was simple and elementary. He was Alex; a thousand times injured, he would still be Alex.

She stared steadily at that one unblinking eye.

"No," she said simply and finally.

Eight

"What is it now?" he asked, peering dourly at the book she had left on the bench. "Greek, Latin, mathematics, farming, or Shakespeare? Tell me, how do you manage to be so diverse?"

Barely an hour had passed since she had sought out the sanctuary of the rose garden. She took the book from him, matching his scowl with a frown of her own. Yet she could not help but think, as she glanced up at him, that this was where he should always be, lit by the sun, not hidden in the Eagle Tower like a badger gone blind. It was the first time she had ever seen him outdoors.

"Are you reading some weighty matter to lecture me upon next?"

His tone was slightly mocking, and she took immediate umbrage to it. She had, after all, been the most tolerant of souls. The least he could do was be civil. Especially since everyone else thought there was only the warmest civility going on between them.

The fact that the earl utilized her as his secretary, albeit temporarily, caused murmurs and sidelong glances from the female staff and outright leers from the males.

She wanted to reassure them that she was as safe now as she had been in the bosom of the kitchen.

Too safe.

In fact, her life barely changed at all.

Mrs. Wolcraft would howl with laughter to learn that her

unwilling pupil had willingly accepted a taskmaster a hundred times stricter.

When she blotted her paper Alex made her transcribe the letter over again. He fussed at her for wasting paper, of all things. She almost slammed her wages down on the table and demanded that he subtract the cost from them. Yet the few pennies she had earned, she realized with a sigh, would not have purchased his ink. She was reminded of his grumbling when, as a child, she had come away from Blakemore with no coins of her own and he had been forced to pay a penny for her passage to the Russet Well.

He disputed her sums of the monthly costs of upkeep for Heddon Hall, until she had called out each number twice!

She took her lunch in the kitchen and he questioned her tardiness. When she searched the library for a book he wanted he grumbled at her for taking too long.

Now, he had banished her from the Eagle Tower and then searched her out as if she was not supposed to obey his first instruction! Would she never understand him?

"Most of the world's knowledge, m'lord, can be found in books. Do you begrudge me my ability to read, or merely my capacity to remember it?" She stared up at him, her gaze less angelic than an hour earlier. Now it was tinged with a spark of pure aggravation.

"It is too bad that your premise is not altogether correct, or cooking would not be such an obstacle for you."

She disliked being forcibly reminded that the cook had sighed with relief when she had been freed from her kitchen duties.

"Is not experience the best teacher?" he said, his tone still slightly derisive. "Are the lessons one learns personally not imprinted upon the mind and the soul with more fixed purpose than the lessons one reads in a book?"

"Are you saying that all of the experiences of others should be discounted simply because you have not firsthand knowledge?"

He moved to the bench and pushed her skirts aside before seating himself. He looked around absently at the Winter Garden, the profuse roses, the scent of growing things, and thought that this was where she belonged, with life and promise and the hint of spring. His land. His home. He spoke absently, as if the thoughts were not important, but the words were uttered in such a somber tone that Laura turned toward him.

"I worked for my command through countless hours of tedium and long hours of study. I conferred with battle-hardened men and studied the exploits of others, in book after book. I never learned war until that last year, when all I read was translated into reality. You may read of battle, my earnest secretary, but you will never experience it fully until you smell the oily smoke of cannons and hear the screams of dying men."

There was an echoing silence between them. She ached to end it by stretching out her hand, as if a human touch would bring him back from that uncertain boundary of memories. He looked so alone then, seated so close to her, as if he was the most solitary of men.

"What happened, m'lord?" she asked in a gentle voice that was as soft as the spring breeze that lifted a tendril of auburn hair and brushed it past her cheek.

He touched his mask with a fleeting finger. "This?"

She neither nodded nor spoke, but her soft green-eyed entreaty was plain enough.

What could he tell her? How could he possibly explain? He amazed himself when his lips moved, spewing the words in a carefully controlled torrent.

"But for my own luck in being born an earl's son, I would not be sitting beside you now." He did not tell her that there had been long months in which he had prayed earnestly for death. But for his birthright he would have been trapped belowdecks in the tiny, windowless compartments that held their massive cannons. But for his own fortune in having the funds he would have been one of the fresh-faced lieutenants, none of whom had survived the suicidal battle of Quiberon Bay in 1759.

"We should have made for Torbay, for a haven, but we were riding out the gale, with our spritsail tucked under the bowsprit and the triangular head sails still unfurled."

The serene gardens of Heddon Hall dimmed, the profusion of pink roses changed shape and became gale-lifted waves. "If we didn't crack a mast, or become breached by the weight of the heavy sails, then we had a chance to stay afloat." The stay sails, mounted between the masts, held the ship in the wind for a longer period in coming round. That same method of maneuvering, easier than on previous warships, caused them to list severely leeward. Great art and cunning was required to handle a warship of the *Sceptre*'s class. He needed no skill then. They had no real maneuverability in the face of the gale's fury. They were simply trying to stay afloat.

He had been astounded at Admiral Hawke's orders, had exchanged surreptitious glances with the other captains of the fleet. None of them had looked too happy about their task. He had wondered, that night, standing in the wardroom of the admiral's flagship, how many of them would still be alive at morning light.

Morning light had brought the fury of the storm, but it had not brought new orders.

Their mission was to destroy Conflan's fleet, to prevent his eighteen-thousand men from embarking on their plan to invade Scotland. It was too much to wish that Conflan had the sense to turn tail and run; the Frenchman was as intractable as his own admiral.

One cannon blast followed another as the fire and smoke from the guns seemed to merge into the roar of the storm. Their volley became automatic, monotonous, deadly.

They had all but gutted the enemy, blowing massive chunks out of her side, slaughtering the gun crews on her lower decks.

They were not, however, immune to the carnage. Two of his lieutenants were down on the open deck, and lethal splinters had killed a third. A goodly number of his crew were badly wounded or dead. The *Sceptre's* decks would have been thick with blood had not the rain and the wind washed them clean.

He gave the order to maneuver closer still, and they continued to hammer the reeling ship, whose men were forced to continue their futile fight with a mere handful of guns.

Starboard, another French ship maneuvered closer, and he again gave the order to fire. They were so close that the blow back of splinters from the French ship ravaged some of his own gun crews. Screams now sounded above the booming guns and the whistling winds of the gale.

The French ship was dismasted and out of control and ran its bowsprit into the *Sceptre's* rigging. Clasped together like warring lovers, the two ships continued to pound away at each other from a scant yard's distance.

The upper guns were largely out of action. He raced to the lower gun deck, flooded almost to his knees. Half of his gunners were dead. With the help of those remaining he lowered one of the larger cannon's barrels toward the French ship, loaded it with a charge of five hundred musket balls atop a sixty-eight-pound ball, impelled by twenty pounds of powder. He stepped back, lowered his arm as a signal for the fuse to be lit, and the gun exploded.

In his mind he heard the sound of screaming; harsh, despairing wails of horror from his own throat. He buried his face in his hands.

Her touch, her incredibly delicate touch upon his arm, brought him back. Brought him back from the memory of the black, red hell of his burning skin.

She knew why no one had breached his privacy before. Why no one could intrude past that barrier he had erected. It was as defined and as palpable as if it existed in truth, a wall of remoteness he had created to shut out the world. She loved him, yet there were times even she despaired of breaching that fortress. He kept a distance between them, not only measured in feet but in his thoughts.

He had allowed her to intrude this time, to pass beyond some demarcation line set in his mind, but he would retreat now, quickly. She was so attuned to him that she could feel it, sense his withdrawal as if he had posted a sign.

"They told me I was a hero, and that a grateful country had rewarded me with an annual stipend of two thousand pounds," he said mockingly, the derision so much more apparent by his soft tones. "At the same time those idiots bragged about Admiral Hawke, proclaiming him a military genius, the Battle of Quiberon Bay a splendid British victory." He laughed, bitterly. On that day he had only turned away, his silence unaltered. His detachment toward the outside world had not troubled him much. He had also been strangely unaffected by any agony of the soul. He had felt numb, as though his injuries and his disfigurement had taken all of the energies he had left. When they told him hesitantly, as he was being transferred from the makeshift hospital ship en route back to England and then to home, that his father had died, he had accepted the news stoically and without comment. When they told him of his elder brother's death in the same carriage accident he had not blinked one lashless eye. When they addressed him as m'lord and said he was the fourth Earl of Cardiff he had simply turned his scarred and ravaged face into the cover of his pillow and shut his eyes. When they asked what he was to do with his good fortune he began to laugh. A laugh utterly devoid of humor, but filled with bitter mockery, so caustic and so cruel that the few who heard it shivered as the sound touched them, and felt the chill.

"I, for one, am glad you were an earl's son," she said, her voice as tranquil as if they had been discussing farming and not his injuries. "And I am glad that you survived to sit beside me on this lovely day." She could say nothing more; her throat was clogged with tears, her eyes awash with them. She turned away so that he could not see. He would, with his inflexible pride and his stiff-necked arrogance, construe them as pity.

She did not pity him. She loved him. But he would not see it that way. He would erect more barriers between them, more obstacles for her to overcome. She blinked into the breeze, wishing her tears away by a supreme act of self-control. Tears would not help Alex now. Tonight, when she was alone, she would weep for his injuries, for his pain. And in the darkness, perhaps, she would weep a little for herself, and the ache she felt even now to be held within the safety and warmth of his arms.

"Because I have never actually plowed a field then, my knowledge is as nothing?" she said lightly, changing the atmosphere when he did not speak. She knew that if she did not, he would leave her, striding away with his mood descending into bleak melancholy. "Because I have never planted a crop, I am to take nothing from others who have done so?"

He laughed, then, a great barking laugh that swirled around the garden, and seemed to lodge in the region near her heart.

"Advise all you wish, little secretary. It is true that I have learned more from you in two days than I have learned in months on my own." He had been ill-equipped for his duties, being trained for the sea. The mantle of responsibility had fallen heavy upon his shoulders, and he had been painfully aware of his own lack of information. Nights of Hartley reading to him had not prepared him as well as a few days in her presence. He should have been grateful that he was assisted so ably in the running of his estates. Instead he was curiously irritated.

"My caution to you is just this," he said shortly, "because you read about something is not to say that your knowledge is as full as if you have experienced it."

"Then why bother to read, m'lord, if experience is the only teacher?"

"Perhaps as a warning," he said pensively, still not looking at her. "Perhaps the author writes to purge his soul—the reader reads to refresh his. I do not know. Those thoughts are for more philosophical minds than mine."

"I will be old and gray long before I have experienced life, m'lord," she said, smiling because he was no longer staring at the hedges as if seeing visions of war.

"Somehow I don't think that altogether true," he said softly, and then carefully directed his attention to something else. Anything but her lovely face, framed so artfully by tendrils of auburn hair. She was so young and so eager for life. She had visions of what life should be, so carefully crafted from books and youthful dreams. Despite the fact that she was forced into servitude, it was quite evident that she had been reared for better circumstances. She should be kept locked away to preserve her innocence and her purity, shielded from what would inevitably be her disillusionment.

"Surely you did not seek me out to discourse on books, m'lord?"

"No," he said slowly, turning again to her. "I did not. I have come to apologize," he said, with a mocking laugh, "and find myself mouthing philosophy."

"I accept your apology and your philosophy, m'lord," she said, smiling. "With gratitude for the former and a slight disagreement with the latter." This conversation was the longest they'd had, yet the only conclusion he had drawn was that she was innocent of the world, with no real knowledge of it.

Nor was she likely to have any, if it was left up to him.

She had gone too far and yet not far enough, she realized. She had perpetrated this masquerade too long to suddenly face him and divulge her identity. Nor was she so idiotic as to imagine that her revelation would result in his sudden acceptance of her love. Alex was not a archetypical hero like the ones in her carefully hidden novels. It was doubtful that he would ever kneel to her with outstretched hands in supplication. Alex would never beg for her affections.

It was entirely possible that he would banish her from Heddon Hall.

He was indisputably arrogant—he had done nothing but shout orders at her from morning until dusk. He was auto-

cratic and demanding, imbued with a pride that she sometimes despaired of breaching.

Yet he had insisted that she take a break from her chores
and walk in the gardens. He noticed when she had not slept
well and commented upon the evidence of her puffy and reddened eyes. She had bristled at his words but had felt a leap
of pleasure to know that he, at least, had noticed. He bade
Simons fetch their afternoon tea, so that she would be spared
the heavy tray. No, the signs were there. The arrogant earl
was not the despot he wished to appear.

He had still not yet gleaned her identity, but the proof was
there each moment in his presence. She had changed, true,
but she had not changed so drastically that her eyes were
now different, or her skin a lighter hue, or her smile altered
from that as a young girl.

Her voice bore the accent of others in her speaking, but
she did not speak as they did anymore than Alex's speech
mirrored that of Simons or the footmen.

She had given him every clue and he had ignored it.

Yet she had not missed the ones he had unwittingly divulged. She had suspected, from the first day, that he could
not see well enough to read. She had tested that theory by
scribbling nonsense on a paper, and all he had been able to
see was the blot upon it.

He could see her well enough, though, and it seemed to
make no difference in his treatment of her.

She had been patient and kind when he was in the most
surly of tempers, and he had simply continued with his grumbling. She had smiled when he was intemperate and forced
herself to recall sweeter memories of him. Yet, the man acted
as if she was not there; or, worse, as if she was no more
than a child. A sweet, innocent, slightly stupid child.

She wanted him to recognize her of his own accord, true,
but most of all she wanted him to notice her as a fully grown
woman.

She had not worried and wondered and dreamed all those

years for him to ignore her now. She had not suffered through Jane's home remedies for her freckles and buttermilk compresses for her skin for him to blatantly dismiss her. She had not balanced books upon her head in order to learn to walk with grace for him to dismiss that small skill.

She would have tolerated it much better if he once looked upon her as a female and not simply as a piece of furniture.

She had arched her back, reaching for a paper she had artfully dropped to the floor, and he had turned his eyes away from that swell of bosom she displayed.

She had tucked her skirts up beneath her belt and allowed her stocking-clad ankles to show, and he had averted his head.

She had swung her head and allowed her hair to fall from its severe bun and pushed its coils off her neck with one hand, and he had not moved from his stance by the window.

She wished that she had not left home without one pretty dress in that sad and lumpy-looking carryall. She wished, too, that she had brought the special salve Jane had made for her face.

As it was she was forced to run errands for him without the straw hat, which he had confiscated, and her skin was becoming red and blotchy. Not only that, but the gray dress had never quite recovered from its dousing with vinegar, despite her efforts at sponging it clean. It was a sad, wrinkled ruin and, from his treatment of her, she evidently looked just as sad and wrinkled and ruined wearing it.

She sighed heavily but did not demur when he stood and extended his hand to her. She took it, rose, and followed him back to the Eagle Tower to another endless afternoon of work.

Something more would have to be done, she thought, fixing her eyes upon his stiff back.

Something more.

Nine

It was less an uncertain virgin who climbed the stairs of Heddon Hall the next night, laden with Alex's dinner tray, than a young woman determined to act upon her plan. A plan that, heretofore, had accomplished nothing.

Time was running out.

She had only a few days to return home, or a hue and cry would be raised about her whereabouts. Jane's promise of silence was no match against her nurse's diligent conscience. She had agreed to the plan only under duress, had finally been coaxed to give Laura a week in order to broach Alex's self-imposed solitude. The uncles, quite free and generous with their permission to visit a school friend, would hardly think that this was what she'd meant in her hastily scrawled note to them.

She could well imagine their reaction, or society's, if they learned of her plan for this night. Jane's unwilling cooperation would not extend to seduction, for whatever good intentions it masked. Uncle Percival might smile before locking her in her room, but Uncle Bevil would not have a glimmer of expression on his face as he reached for the tawse.

She was, after all, not an idiot. Only in love. Had not Sir Walter Raleigh felt the same, when he penned those words— "But true love is a durable fire, in the mind ever burning"? That was what her love for Alex was: a fire that had been carefully nurtured and nourished all these years, despite the uncles' determined dousing of it, Jane's words, Alex's ab-

sence, or time itself. It had flickered and smoldered, this patient, loyal flame, until it was once more a roaring blaze.

She had lain in her bed last night, musing on her failure,
so far, to entice Alex into reprehensible behavior. She had
done everything possible, short of stripping in front of him
and begging him to ravage her.

She had the most horrible thought. What if he had been
terribly injured? More than what appeared? Dear God, what
if he had been, well, emasculated?

That would explain his withdrawal from the world, his
avoidance of her touch, and his anger.

Uncle Percival had educated her, at length, about the male
animal. Of course Jane had been horrified when it was discovered, but not before she had been shown detailed drawings
and Uncle Percival had kindly and enthusiastically answered
all her questions.

It was, after all, the age of enlightenment.

Had she not read Aristotle's *Masterpiece* herself at school?
Granted, it was kept hidden beneath the mattress, but still, it
had provided almost as much information as Uncle Percival's
copy of *Fanny Hill,* but not as much as *The Innocent Adul-
teress* and *Venus in the Cloister.*

She pummeled her pillow with one fist, glared at the ceiling, and remembered his words—*because you read about
something is not to say that your knowledge is as full as if
you have experienced it.* She ached to experience it, but Alex
seemed curiously lacking in receptivity.

It could not be his new nobility.

The Duke of Devonshire had three children by the duchess
and two by Lady Elizabeth Foster, who lived under the same
roof!

Was it not, as she had heard whispered, taken for granted
that maidservants were fair game for philanderers? That the
gentlemanly thing to do was to take advantage and then provide for any resulting offspring?

Then, what was wrong with Alex?

How could she possibly compromise him into marriage when he was being more noble than a duke?

Something more would have to be done.

Perhaps it would have been better for her modesty to admit that she was overwhelmed with horror at her own daring. Although she was nervous, it was not due to thoughts of implementing her plan. No, if she was just a little anxious it was because Alex might, even now, reject her.

Which, while not exactly a maidenly point of view, was certainly an honest one.

She'd had no trouble procuring Alex's dinner tray, explaining to Mrs. Seddon that the earl wanted to work during the meal. It was one thing to contemplate the act of seduction with the backdrop of candles and soft night, quite another to think of it occurring during the day, with the sun beating brightly through the windows of the Eagle Tower. Even she did not have the courage for that.

No, she definitely needed to beard the lion in his den, and this, frankly, was the only thing she could think of.

This afternoon had been her half-day off, and she had taken the precaution of bathing earlier and dusting herself with rose-scented powder, a birthday gift from Jane. She had not, as much as she wished it, replaced the old gray dress. According to her plan, she would not have it on long, anyway.

She brushed her hair until it shone and clamped her lips together all the way up the stairs so that they would look red and ripe when she saw him.

She placed the tray on the table, knocked softly, and awaited his curt response. When it came she smiled softly, entered the room, and nudged the door shut with one foot.

The room was almost dark, the shadows in the corners barely illuminated by one feeble candle placed on the bedside table. Beside it stood a bottle of sherry, its rich amber color mirroring the flame. The air was sweet with the scent of the flowers massed in the glass conservatory and warm with the lingering heat of the day.

The tap of rain upon the glass panels was the only sound, its patter mocking the beat of her heart.

She placed the tray on the table and clenched her hands together in front of her.

He did not turn after one quick glance, which had surveyed her quickly.

"I have brought your dinner tray," she said tremulously.

"Just get out," he said, refusing to turn and see her again, standing in the glow of the candle. He closed his eyes, but she was still imprinted on his lids, a clean, sweet vision of wholesomeness. A country girl with an innocence he could only soil. A simple girl with learning, true, but unknowing of the ways of the world. Unaware of forces she had churned into life, powers that swirled at her artless beckoning even now.

"Do you really wish for me to leave?" she asked softly, walking slowly to him upon the plush expanse of carpet that separated them. She touched him then, a soft, tentative stroke of one fine-boned hand upon the broad, silk-covered expanse of his back.

He flinched.

He had wondered all afternoon about her absence, after being told by Mrs. Seddon that it was her half-day off. Was she walking out with someone—one of the footmen, perhaps? Or a village lad ready to make an offer? Was she exchanging kisses with him, or hugs, or did their pleasures extend to other, forbidden fruits?

"Get out," he said again, and wished she would obey him. Perhaps she was a simpleton in truth not to recognize the warning for what it was.

He held up his gloved hand and then brought it sharply down, as if dismissing her with one stroke.

Despite the fact that the atmosphere in the room was that of a soft cocoon, an oasis of serenity and privacy, his loneliness, his apartness, screamed loudly to her. This was the unapproachable earl, a man who stood apart, rigid, imbued not simply with autocracy but with bitter resignation and an aura of hopelessness.

This was Alex.

She ignored his dismissive gesture and placed her cheek next to where her hand rested, feeling the warmth of his skin through the fine silk of his shirt. Only the taut muscles, stiff and tense, betrayed his knowledge of her action. Only his clenched hands conveyed his response.

She desperately wanted to stroke back his hair, or hold him in her arms as he had comforted her so many times in the past. Slowly, inch by torturous inch, her hands reached around his waist, their warmth conveying gentleness, an acute caring, and tender innocence.

He had always been there for her, a gentle man with time enough to spare for a child's tears.

She was here for him now.

It was the innocence of her touch that froze him in place. It was the tenderness that caused him to look at the ceiling, then close his eyes tight against her naive gesture. His teeth, ground tightly together, muffled the moan expelled from his throat. His hand, clamped in a rictus of tension, remained by his side, its only motion a fist, knuckles white and bony, tendons flexed and taut. His breath, hot and heavy like a stallion run too hard, was too much for his mask suddenly, and he wanted to be rid of it with the frustration and longing of a man doomed to darkness when others live in a world of bright white day.

But he did not move.

With the tips of suddenly sensitized fingers she smoothed the silk of his shirt in small, uncertain strokes, unknowing that he waged a battle in which her innocence fought valiantly against his lust. She moved closer, her breasts pressing against his back, unaware that she was tempting the scales toward rapacious behavior. That her scent was enough to make his loins full and heavy. That her breath, exhaled against his skin and cloaked from his flesh only by a thin layer of silk, was moist and warm and summoned memories of wet flesh and helpless murmurs.

"Get out," he repeated for the third time, like a swimmer caught in an undertow. The current of her scent pulled him toward her and he swayed. Each muscle, each sinew, each flushed and hard and ready part of him, from his rapidly pulsing blood to his swollen organ, wanted to press back against her, this silly chit with the brazenness of a harlot and the sweet smile of a babe.

Still she did not move.

Must he be tormented by her? He was a man, damn it! Trapped in the body of a monster. Was she so ignorant that she did not realize that her touch vibrated through his body? Was she so innocent that she was unaware that her scent blossomed in the air around him, carrying with it a hint of sweetness mixed with the scent of woman. Pure woman. Was she so foolish that she did not know the danger? Did she not recognize that his pride and his restraint were within inches of being thrust aside, of being supplanted by another, fiercer emotion?

His only coupling would be done with heirs in mind, not for the sheer pleasure of it. There would be no delight in it for his wife, either. Only a swift midnight entry, both into her room and into her body.

Gone were the days of trysts beside the river, of the tickle of leaves against his back, or grass upon his lover's. Gone was sunshine and brightness and laughter and perfect moments of rapture that made him close his eyes and exult in the power of his youthful, trim body. Gone was a room lit softly by candlelight, surprises of the flesh, supple movements of grace.

Gone.

He was condemned to darkness now, like a demon of the shadows. Murky shadows that would shield him and protect him from revulsion and gasps of horror.

He felt her move away, and his shoulders sagged as if she

had released him from some terrible burden. He stood unmoving, anticipating the sound of her departure from the
room, but instead heard only the rustle of movement behind
him. He clenched his teeth.

"Leave me!" he shouted. If he must, he would summon
Simons. He cursed the mask that shielded his look of rage
from her.

He whirled and almost reeled with shock.

She stood without a stitch of clothing on her white, velvety
flesh. She faced him with no thought to modesty, meeting
his incredulous gaze with her own direct look, as if daring
him to banish her now.

He took in the sight of her hungrily, from her full breasts
tipped proudly with their coral nipples to the delicate arch of
her feet, and back again. Her mound was fleeced with tight
auburn curls that mimicked those swept into the bun at her
neck.

She did not look away from his mask but kept her eyes
upon him, as if to read his thoughts. Inside she was quivering,
trembling beneath his avid gaze. The buoyant bravery that
had carried her up the stairs and into this room settled into
her stomach and raced through her heart as she watched him
take one uncertain step toward her.

He must not reject her.

She would not let him.

She did not smile but continued her level stare as she
slowly extracted one pin from her hair and threw it down on
the carpeted floor like a fragile gauntlet.

As he watched, dry mouthed, another fell at his feet, still
another in the cold fireplace. He stared as she tossed her hair
until it swirled like a molten flame down to her hips.

Her green eyes lowered suddenly, quickly veiling a fleeting
look of panic. If he had not studied her so raptly in the past
days, he would have missed it. His attention was riveted for
a second to her bottom lip, gently caught by her teeth in a

parody of pleasure. Was she nervous, this gorgeous, seductive creature?

She was more than nervous; she was terrified. Other than that one halting step, he had not moved. Would he reject her, then? The action of stripping herself of her clothing had been done with quick, numb fingers. Standing before him, naked, was an act of sheer bravado.

Her courage was waning with each breath.

He had dared only to dream of kissing her, nothing else. To fantasize of burying his hands in the autumn flame that was her hair, while coaxing her lips open beneath his. He had wanted to touch his tongue to that full lower lip, bathe those white, even teeth with his breath, lick the corners of her mouth, the middle of her upper lip, which curved so tantalizingly.

He had yet to kiss her, but now she stood before him with all the wiles of a harlot, the seductiveness of the truly initiated and the winsome gravity of a virgin, ready to be sacrificed for the greater good.

She extended her hands to him slowly, palms up. They trembled. He thought his heart would burst from his chest.

"Why?" was all he could say in the aching silence. Why? It seemed a stupid word, but no less idiotic than the situation itself. "I do not need your pity," he said harshly, clenching his good hand.

She lowered her arms to her sides and raised her head. The look she leveled on him was devoid of innocence now, and if she felt panic, she hid it well. Her chuckle was a low, throaty sound in the quiet of the room. Her smile was pure daring.

"You do not have my pity," she said, walking with seductive grace to the bedside table. She turned and smiled impishly at him before bending to blow out the flame. The arching sweep of her back and her rounded buttocks was the last sight he saw as the room was blanketed in darkness. It was, he thought, a sight to last him for a lifetime.

She was all coral and white, autumn and winter. The russet of mellow leaves of oak and the purity of snow.

She approached him softly in the darkness, reaching out both hands to him. He did not know that her knees shook so forcibly that she despaired of ever completing that short journey.

When he allowed her to grip his hands, matter-of-factly holding his gloved claw as if it were not a thing of horror, he felt the faint tremors flowing from the tips of her fingers.

"Come," she coaxed, leading him the short distance to the massive bed. He stood with his back to it, so close that his shirt brushed against her breasts. Still he did not touch her. She pushed him gently back upon the bed, and he found himself yielding to her dominance, unable to speak and unwilling to demur.

He was shocked a little, true, but mostly bemused by her actions.

She mounted the three steps to the bed and stretched out beside him, placing her left arm around him. She buried her face against his chest and could not help but notice that her rapid heartbeat was echoed by his.

He did not speak, nor did he touch her.

For long moments she lay there, feeling the warmth of him, the solidity of him. It did not seem incongruous to her that she was praying frantically at that moment. Praying that he would not banish her from the room and Heddon Hall. Praying that he was not injured. Praying that, later, he would forgive her for this act of harlotry. Praying, finally, that her instincts would guide her and that love alone would be all the experience she would need.

He smelled as he always had, of bay rum and the soap he used and the undefinable scent of his own body. She smoothed her cheek against the broad expanse of his chest, as a kitten would nuzzle against a soft coverlet. She was trembling, but not from the chill dampness of the room. Her shivers were caused by her own daring, a tinge of fear and the feel of him, so close and yet still entombed in his own apartness.

Even now he did not make it easy, her Alex, but lay unmoving, a solid wall of arrogant disbelief.

"What are you about?" The sound emerged from him in an incredulous whisper.

"A bit of comfort in the night, m'lord," she intoned softly. "Surely you do not begrudge me that."

"I have said that I do not want your pity," he countered, his words not as forceful as before. His hand began to stroke her arm and then the soft curve of her swelling breast, as if it had an independent mind and was not ruled by his nobler impulses. Those fingers registered the softness, the promise of her flesh, and it was by will alone that he ceased his explorations before touching those hard little nipples that even now pressed against his shirted chest.

"Can we not pretend for one night, m'lord, that you do not wear a mask, and I am not your servant? Just for one night?" Her voice sounded thin and reedy to her own ears.

He did not answer her.

She took advantage of the moment by slipping her arms around his neck. His shoulders were as muscular as they looked, and despite the fact that she was only a few inches shorter than he, she felt petite next to his strength.

She traced the leather mask with shaking fingers. It felt cool against the warmth of her hand, slick and shiny. He grasped her hand and held it against his chest, a solid wall clothed in cool silk. She wanted to trace her fingers down his bare skin and explore him, learn him, until she satisfied that enduring curiosity about him and his man's body.

"I cannot kiss you with your mask on. Can you not remove it, m'lord?"

He shook his head, not trusting himself to speak. One part of him shouted for him to continue. Good God, he had been offered a chance to bid farewell to this damn celibacy. He had been without physical release for too long.

Another part of him argued that she was just a young girl. *With the seductive wiles of a harlot.*

She was gently bred.

She lay upon your bed naked.

She was a servant in his own home.

For one night, she wished to pretend otherwise.

"Please, m' lord?" she said sweetly, and it took a moment for her request to register.

"Alex," he said shortly and harshly. "If we would pretend, then my name is Alex."

He slipped his hands behind his mask and untied one tie. This was utter stupidity, he told himself. Yet it was dark enough in the room.

He untied the other tie, and the mask dropped to the coverlet. He placed it beneath his pillow.

She put both hands on his shoulders and raised herself to where his lips should be. He drew back.

He traced her face with his hands, feeling the fine bones of her jaw, her sweeping throat, her hairline, and the fine arched line of her nose. His fingers traced the outline of her full, warm lips. He slowly lowered his head. He found her lips unerringly and nearly sighed aloud at the feel of them. They were moist, as though she had licked them, and swollen, as if his teeth had already grazed them playfully.

They tasted better than peaches.

They tasted of woman, sweet and acquiescent, warm and lovely, soft and welcoming.

His tongue barely skimmed her lips and then dipped inside them, where he could feel the echo of her heartbeat beside one tiny spot. His thumb edged her chin, offered gentle pressure so that her lips would open more fully.

It was a sweet abrasion, tracing, teasing, as he licked the outline of her lips. Sweet, God, she was so sweet.

Her lips parted beneath his tender assault, as he explored the warm, wet cavern of her mouth, until her lips grew more full and seemed to swell beyond their borders and reached to suck the next kiss from his own ready mouth.

His tongue touched hers, and at first she seemed surprised by the tender contact, until she lost her reticence and they dueled in mock battle. Where he led she followed, their timing preordained by nature itself.

She moaned slightly, a raw and sensuous sound against his mouth. He flinched, so highly attuned was he to her every move, every gesture.

She raised her hands to place them on his face, but he grabbed her wrists, imprisoning them in a tender grip.

"Please," he said softly, his voice soft and low without the mask. "No."

She understood.

He lay her gently back upon the bed. The darkness gave him freedom but denied him a vision of her. His hands would be his eyes.

With knowing fingers he traced long, sweeping lines upon the tapering contours of her hips. Her concave belly was the canvas for small invisible circles, drawn as targets for his gently sucking lips. The backs of her knees were soft hollows for his thumbs; her legs, long columns for his warm palms.

She placed her hands upon his shoulders again. He was still fully dressed. "Alex," she said, her voice quivering with the feelings he had effortlessly evoked, "will you not disrobe?" She skimmed her hands down his arms, feeling the strength in the corded muscles.

He hesitated for the longest time.

He finally slipped the shirt from his shoulders, and her eager fingers slid up his chest and halted. She did not need the light to see the scars she felt. She shocked him then by tenderly placing her lips against the greatest of these, a trail where iron fragments had torn through and burned his skin. He slid from her touch and stripped off the rest of his clothes before returning to her side.

He held her for a moment against the length of his naked

body, breathing in the scent of her hair. It was of roses and spice, as though she had sprung full grown from a garden. He sighed.

The feel of her, her ripe, smooth flesh against his was almost more than he could bear.

And her breasts. He resisted that temptation for too long, until anticipation was coring at his vitals, leaving a column of fiery hunger there.

He gently palmed them, hearing her soft murmur with complete accord. She echoed his own unspoken feelings with that sweet, lost sound. Instead of assuaging the need, each touch upon her ivory body seemed to embed the memory of her in his mind.

He would never forget her.

He would never forget this night.

Slowly, so slowly that he screamed at himself in impatience, he lowered his lips to her hot and heavy breasts, feeling her thunderous heartbeat just below the skin with lips that were suddenly capable of detecting the most finite sensation. He licked the underside of her breasts slowly, tasting the salt of her skin, teasingly avoiding the straining nipples. She gasped and gripped fistfuls of the sheet with clenched fingers and he wanted to absorb all of her. He wanted to lave her with his tongue and suck her into his mouth and feel her quivering flesh, and stroke her with timeless patience until she writhed some more and gasped out his name, and he wanted to impale her now and end this insufferable anticipation that was nearly his undoing.

He settled for plucking one lengthened nipple between two tremulous fingers while his mouth suckled at the other. Her flesh was puckered and hot, elongated and eager, and he nearly died of it. Her breasts and their straining nipples were havens of erotic nourishment, and he drew upon her until his cheeks hollowed, until she thrashed and gasped beneath his ministrations. He felt, more than heard, her whimper, and then the arch of her back as if she was offering, then pleading for more. He rolled the other, lonely nipple between his fingertips, gently pulling until the sounds from her lips were sweet gasps.

When his teeth grazed that aroused nipple it was echoed in the soft core of her womanhood, as if he touched her there, too, creating a volley of beats, a timeless rhythm that resounded like the most primitive drum.

She whimpered and the sound was achingly loud in the silence of the room, quiet except for the soft lapping of his lips, or the brush of his soothing hands upon the fire that had become her body. She felt as though she were drowning in a pool of hot, wet feeling. What fear she had felt in those breathless moments had been replaced by heat. Her skin was burning beneath every soft movement of his fingers, her breasts swelled, her nipples were fiery points of aching flesh. She licked her swollen, heated lips as if to cool them, only to have her tongue replaced by his.

She, who had begun this seduction, was now the seduced.

He stopped his exquisite torture and returned every few minutes to her lips, as if in apology for leaving them lonely. Her lips opened for him before he touched them, seeking something that was answered by the flickering touch of his tongue, delving, deep, so deep. His mouth was hot and wild and wet and as voracious as hers.

She moaned slightly, until he took the sound within his mouth and transformed it into an answering growl, so low and resonant that she felt the sound down to her toes.

She was nothing more than sensation. Nothing more than feeling, as if her identity had been compressed into the molding of his hands, as if his will were now her own. She shivered at the soft, darting strokes of his teasing fingers, pulling him to her in wordless need. She could not seem to get close enough to him.

She felt the tumescence of him throbbing, lengthening, engorged against her thigh, and instead of maidenly reticence she felt only wonder.

Dear God, thank you.

It was a prayer echoed by both of them.

She, because it was Alex and she loved him so.

He, because she was granting him a gift he had thought long denied—a lovely woman's cooperation and eagerness.

His tongue traced a path between her breasts, tasted the pungent oil of perfume. He smiled in the darkness. He had his answer, then. He continued his path of exploration while her hands gripped his back and swept from his nape to his firm buttocks. Her head rolled from side to side, but she would not have been denied this sweet torture for anything.

His tongue dipped into her navel, swirled and descended still lower, laving her belly in small circles. Her hand reached through his hair and he tensed, but relaxed when she lowered it to his back again.

He straightened and kissed her again, his tongue delving deep inside her mouth.

"You are so lovely," he whispered, but she only moaned. He knew just how she felt. Hot, and thick, with a need that seemed to encompass every other thought or feeling.

His hand explored her while he kissed her, invading her secrets, feeling her wetness and the sudden voluntary widening of her legs. He smiled at her eagerness. He felt the same.

She arched against his hand, higher, harder; her movements more than an entreaty, they had become a demand. His fingers slid between the swollen and slick folds of her flesh, in a gentle glide, a teasing stroke. Her heart lurched with the feel of it, the almost pain of his touch. That sensation was so sharp, so narrowed, as if her world had compressed until all she felt was the touch of his fingers. All she heard were his coaxing murmurs and the exhalation of his breath. All she saw was the flash of his fingers dappled on her skin and the shadow darkness of him near her, over her.

He raised himself above her and hovered there for a moment until the pain of needing to be within her was too much to endure any longer. He entered her with one swift movement, feeling the barrier of her virginity break with not only his sudden thrust but the surprised arch of her body.

"Why?" he spoke next to her ear, preventing his release by sheer effort of will.

"I love you," she said simply, and it was almost enough to drain him of his lust.

The fact that he had been celibate for too long and the feel of her tight sheath around him soon overcame his lingering conscience.

It was, after all, what they both wanted.

He parried his movements, stabbing her with short, gentle thrusts that were all the more potent for the restraint he showed. He bit his lip as he ached to plunge and thrust within her, but moderated his own movements until her own gasping motions nearly unmanned him.

She felt the hot heat of him between her thighs and inside of her and moaned aloud at the solidity of him, the feeling of being joined so completely to him. Where he was hard, she was soft. Where he was large, she was small. Where he invaded, she welcomed. The momentary pain and discomfort was being replaced by the driving rhythm he had begun, and that was being answered in the involuntary movements of her own body, as she arched to meet him and then fell beneath his powerful thrusts.

He reached between them, palmed her mound, unerringly found that sweet soaring place of sensation and gently smoothed his fingertips across it, around it, circling, until she froze, all her senses attuned to the movements of his hand.

He raised himself up on his elbows as he eased slowly from her. She moaned slightly in objection and raised up to pull him down again, but he lowered his head and kissed her again, a blinding kiss that seemed to suck her down into a vortex of pleasure.

His fingers found her again, and her soft imploring moans almost made him drive into her again, hard. But he never forgot that she was virginal and that her only joy this night would not be from his invasion, but from his skill. He reached down once more, plucked her softly and then with less restraint, his fingers probing, teasing, driving her beyond need into flushed arousal. Her head rolled from side to side, her nails bit into his arms. Her breath had narrowed to a pant, the little sounds she made a counterpart to his own driving desire.

"Soon, sweet," he murmured, his restraint evident in his raw and hungry tone. It was a delicious torture to hold her like this, feel her hands upon him, the arch of her body upwards as she demanded that he finish, quell that ache within her.

"Now," she demanded softly, grabbing his hips with two urgent hands and forcing him fully into her as something magical and wild swirled around and through her.

All feelings of restraint vanished with her innocent movement. He plunged within her until her moans echoed his.

This was Alex and he was in her body and she was part of him and he was a part of her and it was glorious. The feeling grew until it shattered, leaving her gasping and helpless beneath his thrusts.

He would have screamed at the sheer pleasure of it, but his voice forgot how to make a sound. All of his senses were concentrated on the feel of her sheath constricting around him, until he exploded in a shower of white sparks that seemed to encompass every one of his senses until he felt it down to the tips of his toes. He lay replete over her, his arms shaking, his breathing still erratic. Her arms extended around him, holding him tight when he would have moved to spare her his weight.

" 'So eagerly in Venus' toils they cling, while melt their very limbs, o'ercome by violence of delight,' " she whispered weakly a few moments later.

He laughed, the first unrestrained laughter he had felt in months.

"You would quote Lucretius to me now, Jane?" he asked,

nuzzling her neck with his lips. "I'll bet you did not learn that from your parson father."

"No," she admitted slowly. Somehow it did not seem appropriate to tell him that her name wasn't Jane. At least not now.

Besides, to be thoroughly compromised, would she not need a witness?

Mary would do, when she came to bring his breakfast tray.

She wriggled a little, loving the feel of him still within her. She sighed, thinking that she would rest for just a few moments.

A few moments became a few hours, until he gently awakened her with a kiss.

"Do you not remember the rest of the poem, Jane?" he asked. " 'But when at length the gathered passion from their limbs hath burst, there followeth for a space a little pause in their impassioned ardor. Then once more, the madness doth return.' "

It certainly did.

Ten

"Have my trunks brought in, Simons," the Dowager Countess of Cardiff said imperiously, fixing a small, gratuitous smile upon the shocked butler. He bowed, as punctiliously as ever, despite the fact that dawn had just appeared on the horizon and despite the fact that his attire consisted of a frowsy-looking robe that made up in comfort what it lacked in style. He signaled to one of the sleepy-looking young footmen and stood impassively watching as the trio mounted the staircase.

Samuel, a new addition to the retinue who served Heddon Hall, carried the heavy valise ostensibly bearing the countess's jewelry. What no one knew but Maggie and the resourceful dowager countess, was that the more valuable pieces had long since been substituted by paste. The weight of the case was due mainly to the sheer quantity of jars of creams, unguents, rouges, and powder pots deemed necessary by the dowager countess to maintain her youthful beauty.

The trip from London had seemed endless to Maggie. Three horrible days of being subjected to the dowager countess's rages. Three miserable days of genteel imprisonment in the swaying coach. At least here, at Heddon Hall, there were no amusements to keep the countess up until dawn and herself hunched over her own knees, praying for wakefulness but nodding off regardless.

Maggie nearly stumbled up the massive staircase in her

fatigue, smiling shyly at the tall young footman, who extended an arm to steady her.

Simons hadn't batted an eye at the dowager's unannounced arrival, but he frowned as he caught a look between the footman and the countess's maid. There was no dalliance allowed between servants. It was hard enough to employ enough staff for the huge house as it was—he did not want the added complication of romance gone sour. His organizational problems took his mind, fleetingly, from the problem at hand.

It returned all too quickly.

What was the earl going to say about this new development?

He should be informed, posthaste, despite the early hour.

She lay sleeping in the morning light, unaware that he stood beside her, as consumed by his feelings of guilt as he had been consumed by passion hours earlier.

He realized that his loneliness had given birth to actions he should not have committed. He should never have taken her to his bed. He should never have taken her innocence. He should not be remembering every nuance of movement, every gasp she had uttered, the silken feel of her next to him, the soft sheath of her body tightening around him.

He wished, more than anything else he had wished for since he was a boy, that he could bend and waken Jane and that they could once more share their passion in the dawn light. That he could forget such nebulous beliefs as honor and dignity. That he could forget, for a day, a week, a month, the trappings of his peerage, his obligations, and the contract he had signed with a flourish and kept carefully hidden in the secret drawer of his desk.

Marriage. Once postponed because he simply had no time for a wife. His Navy career was a jealous mistress who had demanded more and more of him and finally too much. He had agonized for long hours before he had signed the documents proffered to him as if he were the prize and not the young innocent who would be his bride.

He gently bent down and brushed Jane's slightly parted lips with a gentle finger. Her lips were soft and warm and too beckoning. His throat ached as some deep, hidden part of him wished desperately that he could find another solution than the one honor dictated.

Dear God, what had he done? If he had not actually seduced her, he had certainly fallen into her plans with little struggle. He had been shocked by her actions, but his incredulity had lasted only as long as it had taken to touch her silken flesh. Nor was his restraint in evidence when he had first felt that thin barrier that denoted her innocence. He should have stopped then.

He had gone to war willingly, had suffered through it, had nearly given his life. Had certainly devoted months of anguish and pain to the greedy demands of his country. He had remained stoic and unyielding through months of torturous healing. He had been silent when other men had screamed. He had assumed the mantle of his earldom with reluctance, but he had done so. He had provided for his family, the servants who had fallen under his stewardship. During all the challenges that fate had provided for him he had performed with as much dignity and honor as he was capable. Yet, he knew in that instant, as he stared at her and remembered the feel of her body around him, that he finally made a disastrous mistake.

It was the least honorable thing he could have done.

It was the most glorious act of passion he had ever shared.

She had been innocent, unknowing, unaware that what they had experienced was different somehow. As different as a child's scrawl was from a Botticelli masterpiece. It was not just an act of lust; it carried other overtones, deep, mysterious longing melded to a unique feeling of belonging that was as rare as it was unplanned and unwelcome now.

He had compromised her, but there was little he could do, honorably, to mitigate his actions.

She had given him laughter and reason and sun-drenched days of smiles, but more importantly, hope. A hope that had been dormant, barely living, but that had flourished in her presence.

In the past few hours he had begun to believe that it might be possible for him to live again, as a man would live. He had forgotten, for those few hours, that his face was so scarred that it caused others to shudder in revulsion at the sight of him. He had disregarded the awkward limp that was worse during wet and humid weather. He had dismissed the talon that had once been his hand.

She had surrendered her purity and in so doing had fed his own lost innocence. She had brought back to him, for a brief span of time, memories of those lost days of his youth, when he had simply been a second son off to war and to his future with grandiose hopes and not a little recklessness.

Jane had done it all, with her scholar's talent, her unflinching way of looking upon him as if he were no different from other men. Jane, who refused to step aside when he ranted and paced, who explained and taught him and spoke of such things as Cicero and cow dung as other women would discuss coiffures and frocks.

He did not doubt that her motive had been pity, however much she might deny it. Or that her softly spoken words of love were only her conscience's way of rationalizing her recklessness. She did not know him, had only spent a few days in his presence. She, therefore, could not love him. Yet her passionate response had been a surprise, as pleasing as her words had been unwelcome.

He studied her as she slept, this lovely girl with her hair streaming across the pillow and the trusting nature of her soft movements toward the spot where he should have lain. One hand lay curved against her cheek, its surface smooth and pink-tinged. She smelled of roses and rainwater and the essence of their loving. The only disturbance to the deep and heavy silence in the chamber was her occasional murmur and his own harsh breathing.

He could almost believe in miracles, watching her as she moved in soft slumber, stroking her warm, full arms with the most delicate of touches so that she would not awaken, gently grazing the tips of her breasts, which puckered instantly beneath his tender, questing finger.

In a few short days she had imbued his life with something more than simple horror. She would not, however, reap the rewards of her efforts.

He shifted restlessly. How could he do this? How could he turn away from her now? He had no other choice. A bell of honor resounded in his mind, a peal of stern conscience.

He was horribly scarred, but perhaps his future wife would see beyond the scars.

Like Jane.

Yet what had begun as a simple selfish longing for physical and emotional release had been transformed into a need that surprised him and shocked him not a little.

He did not want to let her go. He wanted a few stolen days before he took on the mantle of responsibility again.

She was giving and loving, open and trusting. Yet she deserved a man who could open his arms to her and welcome her into his life.

He could not do that. He would not offer her a place here, as his mistress. That would not be fair, either to her or to his new bride. Neither woman had been raised for such a role. Jane's upbringing as a parson's daughter had not prepared her to accept a life of sin with equanimity.

He could not keep her in his household. It was bad enough that a section of his heart was already reluctantly apportioned to her. He owed his wife fealty and dignity. She deserved his honor, if not his heart.

He smiled mockingly. Honor demanded too high a price. The kindest thing to do was to cut Jane out of his life now.

To provide for her future, but to send her away as quickly as possible.

He had lost his career, his command, his identity, his personhood, the ability to merge into a crowd without being stared at by horror-struck passersby. He had given up everything. And now he must give her up, too.

He did not think he could do it. And yet what other choice did he have? None.

He had duties to perform. Duties that he would like to refuse, but that, as well as being onerous, were also mandatory. He had not wanted to become earl, but he was. That was an indisputable fact. His own wishes were mutable compared to the duties he owed his station and, in a lesser sense, his country.

He could not give it up because of a lovely woman. Yet how much more would his life demand of him?

In a few short days she had changed his world, expanded his boundaries. He was still plagued by moments of melancholy spiced with rage, yet because of Jane he had returned the pistol to its place in the gun room and did not think he would ever again remove it from the locked cabinet.

She had brought him acceptance, which was a greater gift than her wondrous passion. She did not flinch when he looked at her; she did not cringe when he moved toward her. She met him, head on, with a smile on her lips and a look of wonderment in her beautiful green eyes. She had shivered when his claw touched her, but in passion, not in revulsion. She had extended her arms around him in delight and not in dissembling. She was both his most precious gift and his most dreaded liability.

He could not help but hurt her.

He watched as the dawn touched the sky with pink and purple fingers of light and wished to God it could be easier than this.

He finally roused her an hour past dawn. Her only sound was a faint moan into her pillow, her face shielded by the waterfall of her loosened hair. She wondered, fleetingly, if she was up to the challenge. He only laughed gently.

"You ascribe to me powers beyond mortal men, Jane," he said softly. She brushed back the tangled mass of her hair, opened one eye, and peered up at him.

The mask was back in place. She could see it well in the faint light from the conservatory window. He was also fully dressed. Again he wore black, but this time his somber attire was offset by a snowy white stock and the waterfall of lace at his throat. His black coat was piped with silver braiding. The shine of his boots was mirrored by their silver buckles.

He looked the very picture of nobility, satiated from a night of debauchery with a poor peasant girl. The poor peasant girl felt just as satisfied.

She eased up in the bed and drew the sheet around her, realizing that she was a little tender in spots that had never before known another's touch. She flushed and looked away.

"Have you no valet?" she asked in the silence between them, realizing that she had seen no manservant about.

"I pensioned him off when I returned home," he said, still standing beside the bed. "I crave my privacy more than I do my comforts."

"Do you not find it difficult to dress?" she asked, thinking of his injured hand.

He laughed as he sat upon the bed and ruffled her already mussed hair. Hair that he had entwined around them both last night and that had been used to pull her face gently to him so that he could reach her lips again.

"Are you always this excessively curious at dawn?" he teased gently.

"I am interested in everything about you," she responded seriously. It was the truth. She wanted to flesh in those blank years between them.

He could not, however much he tried to prevent it, refrain from staring at the curve of her hip, neatly outlined by the sheer material of the sheet.

Nor could he stop himself from recalling her abandon, the soft murmurs she made when he was inside her, her clutching fingertips that had left faint trails of their passage upon his skin. He had reveled in her passion when he should have regretted it. But that knowledge did not stop him from smiling softly behind the barrier of his mask.

Even now he wanted very much to kiss her.

Even now he wanted very much to enter the wrinkled sheets with their warm scent of love and touch her everywhere. He laughed at his own ardor.

"If I am excessively curious, m'lord," she said with pursed lips, "you seem in an extraordinarily good mood." Her widened eyes were filled with sudden defensiveness. He placed his hand upon her arm, feeling the soft silkiness of her skin. He looked down at her white flesh, the contrast in the textures of their skin startling against the backdrop of the sheet.

"I was thinking that perhaps I do have powers greater than mortal men, sweet," he said ruefully.

She looked at him quizzically, and he gently drew her hand down to show her. She felt the evidence of his interest and smiled impishly.

His steady glance encompassed her exposed breasts, full and lovely in the early light, before he gently covered her with the sheet.

"Not now, my eager little maiden," he said, but she could swear there was a smile in his voice.

He stood abruptly, walking to the windows of the conservatory. She watched him as he surveyed his newly acquired empire, Heddon Hall touched with the pink glow of a new day. Even now faint noises were sounding in the hallway, the sounds of activity, the bustle of servants about their chores.

His back was broad and straight, his shoulders erect, his bearing as proud as if he stood on the deck of his own ship, command evident in every angle of his body. From this angle she could imagine that he had never been injured.

"Thank you," he said abruptly in the silence.

She raised herself up more fully until she was seated upright in the ancestral bed.

"I do not know if last night was due to charity," he said softly, "or pity, but I thank you, regardless."

"It certainly was not because of charity," she said brusquely, not seeing his small smile at another sign of her defensiveness. "Nor do I pity you."

"For whatever reason," he said, turning, "I am grateful."

"I do not think," she said, irritated beyond measure, "that I want your gratitude."

"Then what do you want?" He reached the side of the bed in a few long strides.

This was the perfect time to confess all. It was the ideal time to make a clean breast of it and divulge her secret. Then why didn't she? She opened her mouth a few times, but the words would not come out. They simply froze there, on the end of her tongue. *Alex,* she should have said, *I am not who you think I am. I have lied to you.* She could not say it. She would regret that she did not speak then, for a long, long time. Yet how could she, when the magic was still between them. His gaze was still reminiscent of the night before, and she still ached so wonderfully in a hundred spots where he had kissed her and bathed her with full and tender lips.

She could not, dear God, allow him to hate her.

He watched her blush and then her small, open-mouthed movements and grinned. He sat on the edge of the bed, gathering her hands between his own.

"If it were within my power to grant you my kingdom, I would do so," he said softly. "You have given me back what I thought I had lost."

She looked up at him, at the dear face she had loved so much clad now in black leather to hide it from the world, and felt the tears mist in her eyes.

"I have given you nothing," she said, her voice husky with emotion, "that you did not always have."

"Ah, but you have, little one, and you do not know it. You

have given me faith, when my faith was broken. You have given me hope, and I have lived without it for so long. You have given me peace, and I have not known peace for a very long time."

She extracted her hands from his tender grip and threw her arms around him suddenly, holding him tight within her grasp. She had wanted to do this for so long, to simply hold him.

"What is this?" he said, pulling back. "I have made you cry?"

"No," she said softly, burying her face into his neck.

"Your tears call you a liar, little one." She continued to sniffle into his neck, and he could not help but smile gently. He cursed the damnable mask that prevented him from kissing her.

"I am not little," she said, brushing her hand across her cheeks. No, she was not, yet there was a space in his arms that she fit into, as if it was carved there in anticipation of her presence.

He was content to hold her and rock with her and knew that for a small space in time he was blessed. He had cheated the fates and found a haven, one that was lovely and warm and giving. A woman with intelligence and honesty and charm, who would be hurt by his actions and his sense of honor. Who would probably hate him when she knew.

She held him as tightly as he held her. And prayed that he would not hate her when he knew.

"No," he agreed, finally, "you are not. You are beautifully formed."

"Thank you," she said, and did not see the humor of the situation, with her kneeling naked upon the bed, politely accepting a compliment in a drawing room tone of voice.

He did, however, as he laid her gently back upon the bed, and covered her up with the sheet.

"Rest, little one," he said, his lips quirked in genuine humor. "You have slept little this night. I would not have my secretary nodding over my papers, or blotting my transcriptions."

"You would undoubtedly make me pay for them," she said crossly, her words softened by a smile.

He sat watching her for a moment, unmoving, his head tilted at an angle, his fingers rubbing idly upon her arm, from her wrist to her underarm and then, gently, upon the swell of her breast.

She shivered and wished he would return to the bed.

He wished he could join her, but the dawn light was his enemy. He stood, bent over her, feeling their breaths exchanged, watching the pulse of one eyelid, stroking her hair gently with one tremulous finger, feeling something precious and beautiful and rare crushed beneath the weight of responsibility.

The tentative knock upon the door ended his reverie.

"She is what?" Alex demanded, at Simons's announcement. His rage was muted by the leather of his mask, moderated only by prodigious restraint.

He closed the door swiftly behind him, but not before Simons had a glimpse of the young girl attired in nothing but a sheet, seated in the center of the ancestral bed. Not by a word or deed did he betray his shock.

Simons sighed, following the earl, knowing that the furor was not over yet. He only wished that things could go back to the way they had been over the past year. Quiet and peaceful, without the interference of women who did not know their place and greedy widows who assumed too much of one. However, the ways of the gentry were strange, indeed, as well he knew from his father before him and his father before that.

"Of course I'm staying," Elaine Weston said, calmly stripping off her gloves, one finger at a time. She smiled coolly at her stepson's leathered face and then flipped her hand at her maid. It was enough of a dismissal for Maggie to quit the room with relief.

"Like hell you are!" The rage was evident in his voice, but his stepmother seemed immune to it, or to the sudden clenching of one fist.

"Alex, allow me to refresh your memory: I have every right to reside here, in my husband's ancestral home. I do beg you to recall the terms of your dear father's will."

"It is the reason for your visit to the country, madam, that intrigues me more. What brings you here, our pastoral peace? The fear of London pestilence, or is it perhaps that you tire of the social life?"

She slowly unfastened her cape, draped it across the nearest piece of furniture, and looked around the Orange Parlor. She hated the Chinese silk arrayed on the walls—the color did nothing for her complexion, causing her to look almost sallow in the mirror above the fireplace.

"Alex, don't be tiresome. Perhaps I missed your charming smile."

The mask hid the sudden gritting of his teeth.

"Go away, Elaine."

"Where?" she asked, smiling at her reflection. She touched the corner of her mouth with one finger, as if testing for wrinkles.

If the man had any culture at all, he would have offered her the use of the State Bedroom. The furnishings there were a perfect backdrop for her coloring. It had been her husband's domain, of course, and the fact that she had not crossed that threshold willingly while he was alive was beside the point. Her own solitary tenure there had been brief. Too soon, the prodigal son had returned. Too soon.

"Go back to London," he said, his voice clipped.

"Regretfully, dear boy," she said, despite the fact that he was a few years older than she, "I have no funds with which to do so." She reluctantly turned from the mirror.

"You have squandered your allowance?" He stood in the middle of the room, his stance as rigid as if he commanded a ship.

His military bearing was wasted, she thought. As was his aura of command. Did the misshapen earl think to rule her? She smiled at the notion.

"That magnificent sum you speak of was barely adequate to support a scullery maid," she said mockingly, her voice as brittle as the finely etched crystal in the ornate cabinet beside her. "I defy a member of the *ton* to exist on such a paltry amount, dear Stepson."

"Those funds were enough to support a family of four for over a year, madam!"

"Perhaps, Alex," she agreed with equanimity, bestowing upon him a smile that had never failed in its charm, "but not if they reside in London."

"Very well, madam," he said, ignoring the smile and the careful, watchful look in her eyes. "Enjoy your stay at Heddon Hall." It was not bitterness or anger that made him throw the next words in her face. "Do not become too enamored of the role of mistress here," he said softly, rewarded by the sight of the Dowager Countess of Cardiff's pale face being colored by twin spots of rouge—nature's flush this time, and not from a jar.

"Do I detect the sound of wedding bells, dear Alex?" she said, a soft mocking smile wreathing her lips, her shining eyes narrowed. "Has the lure of Cardiff wealth procured a willing bride for the reclusive heir?"

"Money can buy many things, Elaine," he said shortly. "Did it not purchase you?"

She smiled fixedly at the Earl of Cardiff and wished him dead.

Eleven

Laura stared at the door long after Alex left the room. She was blind to the raised panels, the gilt upon each carefully carved scroll. The stern voice of her newly awakened conscience, even now stentoriously denouncing her actions, held all her attention.

What would he think of her when he knew? Alex prized his privacy so, what would he think if she brought scandal to Heddon Hall?

Uncle Bevil had told her once that she was impulsive to a fault. He had announced, in a gruff tone that belied his warm and loving heart, that there would come a time in which she would pay for her inability to think before she acted. He had been referring to her childish acts of hiding, naked from her bath, while Jane called frantically, or attempting to help one of the gardeners by harvesting an entire bed of poison oak, or assisting with Uncle Percival's experiments, causing them both to be surrounded by billowing smoke. He had not been speaking of her singleminded passion for Alex. Yet his words came back to her now. She had been reckless and impulsive and had not thought her plan through.

She had thought she loved Alex before. Yet the memory of her feelings was a dim and shadowed version of what she felt for him now. The change had, at its root, the four years of separation. Four years in which to grow up. She had not known that his entrance into a room could charge the air or cause her pulse to race, or that she longed to banish that

damnable mask, kiss his scars, and tell him that it did not
matter—he would always be whole and strong and virile to
her. She had not realized that she would feel such a sense of
protectiveness for him, a wish to shield him from pain, or to
grant him a sense of belonging. She had no idea that she
would ache to enfold him in her arms and give back all of
the love and comfort and warm caring he had once so lavishly
bequeathed to her as a child.

She had not, above all, been prepared for her love to
change overnight into something so vital, so tangible, so
strong that it was almost a living thing. She had experienced
such joy with him. One touch from his gentle, warm fingers
could turn her into a mindless creature, whimpering and begging for release.

When the passion had been spent, however, her amazement
and wonder were tempered with guilt. She would do anything
rather than hurt him. It was a paradox she had not considered,
a duality of emotions she had not thought possible. Even now
part of her wished to escape Heddon Hall silently, while another, stronger and fiercer emotion decreed that she never be
banished from his side.

At first she had only wanted to see him, and then had
planned, calculatingly, to compromise him. Her actions of the
past few days seemed childish and thoughtless in retrospect.

She had wanted to reach him, to convince him of her love,
and all she had succeeded in doing was perpetrate the most
horrible of deceits. He had praised her and blessed her presence in his life and it had been nothing but a masquerade.

Dear God, what had she done?

She would, for better or worse, tell him her identity. Then,
from the foundation they had formed already, they could build
a relationship, one of trust and honesty, not fraud and deceit.
She loved him, but she had lied to him. She loved him, but
she had cheated him.

She was quite frankly ashamed of her actions. Not the act
of seducing Alex; their coupling had been a natural extension

of the love she had always felt for him. No, she was shamed by the untruths she had told him. She wanted an end to the fear that came from a misstep or a word uttered without thinking.

He would be angry, but she would deal with it somehow. She would find a way to repair his torn trust and make him love her.

"Optimism is a mania for maintaining that all is well when things are going badly." She shook that thought from her retentive mind and scrambled from the bed, winding the sheet around her, toga fashion. In frantic desperation and with a trace of clumsiness, because the sheet kept becoming entwined around her feet, she pulled on Alex's dressing gown. She tugged it up against her ears, breathing deeply of the scent of him within it.

She quickly dressed in the other room, returning and searching for the rest of her hairpins, but they were gone. Her fingers were clumsy, and the task of subduing her unruly hair seemed destined for failure. When she was finished she opened the door, sparing not one glance to the rumpled bed.

She must find him. Now, before any more time had passed. Before this charade grew beyond the already monumental proportions it had assumed.

He was not in the Eagle Tower; his quills were neatly arrayed and there was no trace of previous occupation in the pristine stacks of papers arrayed on the corner of the desk.

She nearly skidded to a stop at the top of the stairs. She turned and heard the muffled bellow of a voice. His voice. With a sense of dread growing in direct proportion to the feeling of unknown urgency, she stopped at the entrance to the Orange Parlor.

He was there, his stance unmoving and nearly frozen with rage. Any other man might be difficult to read without the clue of facial expression. Not so Alex. There was no doubt when he was angry—it showed in the line of his back, as stiff and solid as one of the stone walls of Heddon Hall. It was betrayed by the military precision of his bearing, his chin at a right angle to that broad chest, his neck straight, his shoulders squared. It was discernible in the clenched hands at his sides.

He was not alone.

Laura gripped the fabric of her skirt with one nervous hand and slowly stepped back from the doorway. Too late. Alex whirled, his movement clearing the path to his visitor, enthroned in a tufted chair as regally as if she was the owner of Heddon Hall and all other lesser mortals simply visitors there.

Laura closed her eyes for a moment, willing the vision away. But when she opened them seconds later the dowager countess was still there, still examining Laura with venomous eyes. Not an inch of her person was spared from that intense perusal, from the top of her unruly mass of hair to the tips of her leather shoes, scuffed and dusty. She cringed inwardly at the inspection.

It was the one confrontation she had dreaded.

Even when she was a child Elaine Weston had had the ability to make her feel unwanted and barely tolerated, as those cold blue eyes had scanned her with a disinterested look and then dismissed her as unimportant and unworthy of her attention. Laura had the notion that no female was important to the dowager countess, except as a source of potential rivalry.

"Are you not going to introduce us, Alex?" Elaine said, her lips curving into a smile that did not quite meet her calculating eyes. "Or shall I draw my own conclusions?" she said to Laura's shocked look. She had not missed the sudden pleading look the girl had directed at Alex, nor her stepson's almost imperceptible protective move toward the chit.

Beneath the other woman's intense scrutiny Laura felt more naked than she imagined possible. It did not matter that the gray wool of her much-abused dress covered her chemise and stockings; she felt exposed and vulnerable. If Alex had not recognized her, there was no reason the dowager countess should, a small, nearly hysterical voice deep inside whispered. It was not a very reassuring voice.

"I am surprised, though, I must admit," Elaine said, glancing at the girl's tousled mane of auburn hair, at the lips that were swollen from kisses and the sudden flush of color on that peach complexion.

Alex still had not spoken.

"Is this the little bride? How unlike you to flaunt convention so, dear Alex," she said, her blue eyes slitted.

"Shut up, Elaine," he said curtly.

"Bride?" Laura asked helplessly, looking from one to the other. Alex had turned away again, staring at the wall above Elaine's head as though it was the most fascinating sight in the room. Elaine's eyes moved first to her stepson and then to the frozen countenance of the young girl who stood so still and immobile in the doorway. Her smile was filled with delighted malice.

Laura was paying no attention to the Dowager Countess of Cardiff. She only noticed that Alex still had not turned.

"Did you not know that the Earl of Cardiff is to gain a bride soon?" Elaine asked with a small smile, watching as the girl's face turned a leaden white. "Wedding bells will soon peal over Heddon Hall." The softly spoken words had the desired effect. Laura's eyes swiftly veered from Alex's back and she stared at Elaine in shock.

"I don't understand," Laura said, gripping her two hands together in front of her. It was the only way to still their trembling.

"Which words did you not comprehend?" Elaine asked bitingly. "Bride? Wedding?" The gleam in her eyes was bright, wicked, and thoroughly entertained by this impromptu tableau. "I had always imagined that if Alex took a whore, she would have to be as maimed as he. But you, girl, you definitely have possibilities. You are wasting yourself in this godforsaken place, however. Or," she said speculatively, "does Alex pay you too well to stray?"

Alex lowered his head and stared at his stepmother. In that instant all of the revulsion and loathing he had ever felt for her choked in his throat. Granted, the words should have been said, but not this way. Not with Jane looking at him with those lost, stricken eyes, as if she were a child and he had promised her something and then taken it away as quickly. She was no child, and there was no promise he could have ever made to her.

Which only made his self-loathing greater, if that was possible.

"You've spewed your venom, madam," he said abruptly. "It is time for your treacherous tongue to be still."

"But Alex," the dowager countess said, her tinkling laugh brittle in the frozen silence, "what did I say? Is not every word I've spoken true?"

"Alex?" Laura said, looking at him. He turned, slowly, and watched her, noting that her flush had paled and only stark whiteness was in its place.

There must be some mistake. Some horrible, hideous mistake. If he was to be married, then a contract was already in force. A binding contract that could not be broken by whims or wishes, which meant that she had been a fool. And it had all been a lie.

His tender gratitude this morning was only that. He did not love her, could not love her if he was promised to another. The Alex she had known and loved for so long was to be married to someone else and she had been a night's diversion—nothing more. She had spared him any effort at seduction, had fallen into his arms like a ripe plum. She had played a stupid, idiotic, childish game and she had lost.

Lost.

She had felt such guilt, and even that was misplaced. She had sought him out to confess her duplicity, yet he had been guilty of his own deception.

He had not even the decency to inform her himself, but had let this hateful woman speak the damning truth. There was no honesty between them. Neither hers, nor his.

She looked stonily at Elaine, refusing to let her see the reaction to her news, not realizing that her stricken eyes betrayed her emotions.

Laura ignored the pleased lilt of laughter as she whirled and left the room. She did not see Alex's sudden helpless gesture as he extended his hand to her and then let it fall impotently to his side.

What she wanted first was to be away from this place. Her feelings of humiliation would not be witnessed by others. Her pride, which had been so lacking in her actions of the past night, was now firmly in place.

There would be plenty of time, later, to experience her pain and her disillusionment. For now she wanted to be quit of Heddon Hall and its master.

She descended the sweeping staircase with a regal demeanor that Mrs. Wolcraft would have applauded.

"What shall I tell his lordship, miss?" Simons asked carefully as he opened the door for her. True, she was not gentry, but she had occupied the earl's bed. That very circumstance, while not elevating her in rank, certainly set her apart from the other village girls, causing Simons to tread very carefully around the girl he'd once thought as crazy as a loon.

Crazy as a fox, more like it, he thought, as he stared at her pale face and downcast eyes.

No, one could not overstep here. The earl would not be happy with this day's work. Not happy at all. He did not want the earl's wrath to be visited upon him.

There was, after all, his pension to consider.

"Tell him whatever you wish, Simons," Laura said serenely, the only sign of her distress the death grip of her fingers upon her gray and wrinkled skirt.

She left Heddon Hall without a word spoken in farewell and without a backward glance.

* * *

"Damn you!"

He turned from the doorway and glared at his stepmother. She remained seated in front of him, unconcerned, preferring to study her nails rather than watch his reaction. She shrugged, her mouth a thin-lipped smile of derision.

"My dear stepson, why attribute me as the cause for your domestic problems? I simply informed your whore of your pending nuptials. It was bound to be common knowledge soon enough."

That, at least, was true. The servants' invisible link with the outside world had informed him of her exploits while his father still lived, her long line of illicit liaisons, her excesses in London. It would have only been a matter of time until talk of his marriage was fodder for the servants' gossip.

Yet he would have had a day, a few hours at least, in which to soften the blow.

"How did my father manage to stomach you for five years of marriage, Elaine?"

She leveled her eyes upon his mask and laughed. "You would talk of tolerance now, Alex? When your servants slither away from your presence and you must hide from the world rather than have it retch at the sight of you? I am only surprised that you managed to lure any woman to your bed." She laughed, and the sound ate at his composure and his restraint.

He left the room, returning moments later, hefting a small drawstring bag filled with gold coins in one hand. He had thought that he would give it to Jane; a dowry, a gift, a way by which she could start again, be prepared for an uncertain future.

It had been a paltry gift compared to what she had given him, but he had wanted to protect her somehow.

He tossed the bag to his stepmother and was not unduly surprised when she caught it with ease.

The gold coins clanked together in a golden shower onto her palm. She watched each one of them fall, a smile flitting across her face, a look of triumph sparkling in her eyes.

"There is a fortune there, Elaine. Enough to carry you to London and beyond. All that I ask is that you quit Heddon Hall with all possible speed. If not, I cannot guarantee either my tolerance or your safety."

He turned, sparing himself a glimpse of her gloating face, the mocking smile that wreathed her mouth and sent frissons of revulsion through his soul.

He answered Elaine's taunt in silence, in the echoing emptiness of his own bedchamber later that day after he had sent Simons out to search for Jane and bring her back.

She could have sought an explanation from him. He remembered her stricken expression as the words seemed to form a barrier around her as he watched. That sweet smile, frozen in the act of curling up her lips, that lambent look, so filled with promise, so replete with satisfaction, replaced by emerald shards glittering in her eyes. Even her hands had stilled in the act of supplication. What would she have done, then, if he had turned and walked out of the room and pulled her with him? Would she have followed? Or, would she have proceeded down the stairs and through the great doors of his home with the regal bearing of a young Elizabeth?

What if she had asked him? What if she had turned to him and asked for an answer to the question lurking in the depths of those frozen eyes? What would he have said? What could he have said?

That he had been forced by circumstance to do the honorable thing? Yet honor was a commodity, he understood in those bleak and lonely hours when no word came of her whereabouts, that demanded too high a price.

She had softly stroked his arms and kissed his chest, oblivious to the scars that marred his body. She had given her innocence to him and the gift of laughter and love.

How short a time she'd spent with him, and how blessed

he felt by her presence. He would not, now, be able to walk in the Winter Garden without smelling her scent, or rest upon the bench without remembering her compassion, or work in the Eagle Tower without remembering her spirit.

She was not reared to be a whore, nor was she prepared, he thought with implacable honesty, to be paid for her favors. It had been a stupid idea, that bag of gold. But what could he give her, that sweet and generous young woman who had graciously gifted him with her time, compassion, empathy, knowledge, and the most precious gift of all—a young girl's passionate dreaming? Even though it would never have lasted, this romantic attachment, she'd allowed him to play Lancelot to her Guinevere. He owed no one a greater debt than that.

He had no other choice.

Yet he was as responsible for her future as she was. True, she had been the one to broach his self-imposed exile, but he had wanted her as much. Would it not have only been a matter of time until he had taken advantage of her gentleness, her sweetness, her innocence?

She was too gentle to earn her living as a scullery maid, too intelligent to be forced into servitude.

Yet what did he want for her? A courtesan's existence?

He had hated his circumstances before, with a deep and vile hatred of war and of men who would make it. He had hated what he had become, a creature of the night, of solitude. He had not hated himself.

Until now.

Twelve

"Did you know, my boy, that they think me overly awed by the crown?"

The remark was not answerable, and the young secretary wisely remained silent. He gathered the sheaf of dictation he had been given that morning, watching as the great minister's valet smoothed a blue frock coat over shrunken shoulders. It had been a bad two weeks for the minister; lines of pain were etched upon the man's sallow face. The mind that had carried England safely through the perils of the last three years was encased in a body too frail, too gout-ridden.

"I've heard one wag say," William Pitt said, smiling at his secretary's silence, "that if I bend any lower, my pointed nose is in danger of being caught between my knees." The laugh belonged to a stronger, more boisterous man. "What they do not know, my boy," he continued, waving off the unctuous valet and staring full-faced into the mirror, "is that George II is a stupid man, a dull monarch, a true Hanoverian. He can barely utter a few words of English, does not comprehend the good and loyal citizens of this great country, and loves sweets more than reason. The fact he is old is a sin that cannot be laid upon his doorstep, as age is one master none of us can rule."

There was most assuredly nothing one could say to that remark, Robert Liltian thought. Silence, as usual, was always the best policy around Mr. Pitt.

"The year 1759 was a good one, my boy, but I fear we'll

not see its like again soon. Too much divisiveness," he continued, as if Robert had had the courage to broach the question. "Too many damn fools out to make a name for themselves. They have no idea what England wants or needs. They see only their name in the history books. What do you say, Robert? How will history reward these years and ourselves? What will great minds say to my exploits?"

It was the time in every conversation he dreaded; the time when Mr. Pitt asked for his opinion. He crafted his words carefully, thought about possible ramifications, weak points that Mr. Pitt would pull upon like the unraveling of a sock by a ravenous terrier. Conversation with William Pitt was never a comfortable thing, he thought, but it challenged the brain, the heart, even his bowels. Today he felt less like pontificating than seeking his quarters with a wet rag upon bloodshot eyes. That's what he got for the sin of pride. He could almost hear his Cornish mother's stern words. He had been feted last night at Gooseley's, had eaten for free and drunk too much ale passed to him by friends in awe of his standing with Minister Pitt—"the minister given by the people to the King." Little did they know that most of his days were spent wavering between abject terror, dreading just such moments as these, or overwhelming gratitude that he was a witness to the sleights of hand that created history itself. He wet suddenly parched lips and decided that an impatient William Pitt was to be avoided at all costs. Better a fool than a dawdler.

The voice was shy and timorous, and for just a second, too short a time to be actually observed, a genuine smile appeared on William Pitt's face. His secretary could roar with the best of the young sprouts at a London tavern and hadn't he heard him himself, bounding down the corridors when he'd thought himself unobserved, whistling loudly and vulgarly?

"I do not know what history will say as to the events of our day, sir," he began, wisely looking directly into the minister's twinkling eyes, "but I know that England is behind you, sir, and the people believe you have their best interests at heart."

"Damn it, boy," he said in a reasonable voice, for all that his curse shimmered in the air, "I am up to my not insubstantial ears in bowing and scraping. My countenance will tolerate the truth, or each man's version of it. Speak your piece, and this time let the words flow through a well of thought, not vanity."

Robert gulped. "Yes, sir."

"And do you not think I'm crown proud, Robert?"

"I think you do what you should, sir, in order to do what you must."

Robert's look of confusion as to his own words was punctuated by Pitt's fond laugh. He placed his hand upon his young secretary's shoulder and used him as a support to reach his desk. "I think that, despite your ale-addled wits, Robert, you have expressed it well after all."

Once he was seated behind the imposing desk he stared at the pile of dispatches that arrived every morning. "We all must do what we must now, Robert," he said, dismissing everything from his mind but the chore at hand. Time was the one commodity he could not press down and bid to wait. Time oozed from between his fingers and spilled upon the wooden floor, and still he could not have enough of it. He wanted the time to do the job right, to interpret what was happening through the missives of his generals, his soldiers, his sailors, all those brave and gallant young men ready to fight and, if need be, die for England.

For three years England had been at war on various fronts. From India to America, the world had divided itself along allied lines. Those not with Britain, Prussia, and Holland were with France, Austria, and, if rumor were correct, Spain. He had scandalized military minds by replacing the older, more seasoned men with younger men of his own choosing. Men like Clive in India, who were brilliant in battle and not afraid to do something different. Young men who, under normal conditions, would spend most of their lives in subservient posts were now commanding the battalions, the infantry and the great, glorious warships that made up the might of England's Navy. Their battles had never been more bravely won—like the fiasco at Quiberon Bay, where Admiral Hawke's actions had been insane, but insanity had quickly turned to victory.

A small frown added itself to the lines of Pitt's face. Quiberon Bay sparked another memory, another face, and he closed his eyes as a broad, relieved smile wreathed his thin lips.

Thirteen

Blakemore House

"Are you certain you are well, Miss Laura?"

"Perfectly well, Jane, but thank you for your concern."

"Your head doesn't ache?"

"No, Jane, I feel perfectly fine."

"No stomach grippe? No chills? No tightness in the throat?"

"I am very well, Jane, I assure you."

"You are not sleeping enough, Miss Laura, that I know."

"I am more than rested, dear Jane."

That was how it had been for weeks now. Her charge had sat there with perfect decorum, not moving or fidgeting as she was wont to do. Although her responses had been short, they were perfectly modulated with a young lady's refined speech. Above all, there had not been that sense that she was laughing behind her hand at the dictates of her elders.

If only she could dismiss that feeling that something wasn't quite right. She stared at the door that Laura had closed firmly and quietly, with all of the aplomb of a genteel lady of breeding. Not the usual slam as she bounced from a room.

Jane Palling adjusted her muslin tucker in the mirror above the bureau and stared into her own brown eyes for a moment, not seeing their muddy color, but instead the direct green gaze of the young girl she had mothered for years. The child had changed since that silly escapade she had insisted upon, an episode that now brought a flush of embarrassment to Jane's weathered cheeks. What had she been thinking of, to let Miss Laura do something so rash? It was bad enough that she had been coerced into uttering falsehoods to the uncles. By all rights Miss Laura should have been away at school, but the pleading note from her charge had frightened her so much that she had sent Peterson in the carriage to bring her home—only to find that Miss Laura was as right as rain and fit as a fiddle, never mind that she had then embarked upon a plan that was just this side of lunacy. There was a soft spot in her heart, if not her head, for the young girl. She shouldn't have dallied in that nonsense, anyway. If she had had any sense at all, she would have sent the child to her room and informed the uncles of her plans. And what would they have done? Chucked her under the chin and applauded her self-reliance, no doubt.

They might insist upon tutoring her in the most outlandish notions and treating her as if she were a man by filling her head with nonsense, but if it hadn't been for her, the child would have run wild. Well, perhaps not quite a child, either, she thought, considering all the changes a few short years had brought.

No, despite Miss Laura's words, there was something definitely wrong. Why else would she be so pale? Jane hoped with a fervent prayer that the young woman she loved as much as she would have her own child, should the Good Lord have provided first a husband and then offspring, was not ill. Sickness, however, was not enough to explain the dead look in Laura Blake's green eyes. The mischievous glint had not been there. Nothing had been there. Just a flatness that gave away none of her thoughts or feelings. She had always been able to tell when Miss Laura was up to something because those glorious eyes gave her away.

Now they were almost lifeless.

Something was definitely wrong.

The greatest clue was the absence of one name from Miss

Laura's conversation, a name that had bedeviled Jane for years until she thought she would scream with the sound of it. If nothing else should have alerted her, the absence of Dixon Alexander Weston as a topic of conversation should have.

Even as a child Laura had trailed after him as if he was not ten years older and wise in the ways of the world. No, the young man who was now the Earl of Cardiff had too much patience for the little orphan. Not for the first time Jane wished that he had been brusque with Laura instead of tolerating her childish adoration. If he had only condemned her youthful antics instead of gently laughing when she did something outlandish, or forbid her the freedom of Heddon Hall instead of welcoming her into the great house as if it was, in truth, her own, Miss Laura's childish passion would have died a natural death.

Had time done that instead? Or—and this misgiving was so ominous that Jane clutched at her bosom and stared at her reflection in dismay—could something have happened in the week Miss Laura was gone? Of course not, she assured herself quickly. She would have known.

Yet something was different. Miss Laura had pinned her hair back into a bun; she sat with hands neatly folded on her lap; her posture was studiously correct. She had all of the grace and finesse of a woman of breeding.

Was that it, then? Jane nodded to herself in the mirror. She had succeeded in the impossible task of turning a hoyden into a lady. Of course; that was what it was.

Over the next few weeks she prayed her initial judgment was correct. Instead, Jane had the oddest feeling that something else was terribly wrong. Something substantial, and not easily repaired.

Laura no longer laughed, and even her smiles were wan, pale imitations of her usual bright expression. She seemed perfectly content to sit in a room, quietly reading or conversing with the uncles. Her tone was low, well-modulated, never the breathless, excited one Jane had tried to quell for years.

Blakemore House could be a dismal place when it rained, which it seemed to do often that spring. Laura never seemed to mind the weather, but walked through the gardens in the mist and did not seem to notice that her shoes grew wet and the hem of her hooded cloak trailed along the damp cobblestones of the circular drive.

When the day was bright and cheery her mood remained somber. She sat in the garden when the sun shone, practicing her watercolors. Even the tangled embroidery threads, once dismissed as a useless occupation, were unearthed and delicately and unerringly transformed into a very credible rendering of multicolored flowers, worthy of the most ardent needlepoint student.

Something was definitely wrong.

Laura had no idea of the worry she was causing either Jane or her uncles, both of whom had met in whispered debate with her nurse. She was focused inward, her once indefatigable energy transformed into thoughts instead of actions. She did not *do* as much as she *contemplated,* did not *perform* as much as *pondered.*

Uncle Percival had once said, in answer to her irritation about having to attend Mrs. Wolcraft's Academy, that the purpose of her education was not to teach by rote but rather to help her learn about learning. "If you do not question," he had said, in one of the few times his eyes had lost that vacant and faraway expression, "then you will never understand the why of things. *Why,"* he continued, "is the greatest word in all the world."

Why kept reverberating in her mind.

Why had she done something so stupid?

Alex was to be married. It was a thought that was echoed not in her brain but in the region of her heart.

She could tell the uncles what she had done, and her outraged relatives would undoubtedly compel him to marry her, but that action would only bring scandal to Alex. He prized his privacy so, it would not be a fitting beginning to a relationship between them. It would, in fact, bring her little but his contempt. Besides, she did not honestly see how she could tell her fond and doting uncles what she had done. They had been more than generous with her, protecting her, allowing her to bend the boundaries of propriety more than just a little. Above all, they had loved her. But their benevolence had its limits.

Why had she not told Alex who she was before she had gone about the business of shedding her virginity? She could have spared herself this misery if she had just confessed her masquerade before he laid a hand upon her. If not before, then *why* had she not told him that next morning, when the opportunity presented itself? Why, why, why, kept bouncing around in her head like a tennis ball gone awry.

She had no one to blame for what had happened but herself. She was truly a reckless, impulsive, miserable fool. Dear God, what had she done?

God did grant one whispered prayer, and that occurred three days after she'd returned home. She went to the armoire where the cloths were stored for her monthly flux and returned to the bed, thankful that she would not bear a child out of wedlock. Yet even that comfort was a dubious one at best.

Now she would never bear a child for Alex. There would be no children between them, no little black-haired boys with winsome grins or curly-haired girls with green eyes. There would be no bond between the great houses of Heddon Hall and Blakemore, only the product of an alliance between the one man she would always love and a stranger whose face and name were as much a mystery as before.

Alex was to be married.

Despite that knowledge, which weighed upon her soul like a dark-winged creature, she could not banish him from her thoughts. He was as much a part of her life as he had always been.

Yet this time her thoughts carried no illusion of hope.

Someone else would live with him and laugh with him and love him. Someone else would share his days and his nights and his dreams and his hopes. Someone else would know when he was in pain or when he was sad. Someone, not she, would tell him when the last of the Winter Garden roses were blooming, or that the turnips should be unearthed, or that the winter crop of rye should be sown. Someone, but not Laura Ashcott Blake, would stand hand-in-hand with him before the three muses, or walk with him beneath the crenelated towers of Heddon Hall and plan for the future.

Someone else's future was etched in silver and banded by gold. Her own future seemed gray, untouched by color and as drab as a winter day. She could not conceive of a life without Alex. He had been her icon, her god for so long, that the thought of another man taking his place in her heart made her almost physically ill.

If her own life stretched out before her without excitement, only dread, she had no one but herself to blame. With implacable honesty she faced what she had done, the fact that she had lied to him about her family, her life, her identity. She had bent the truth in so many directions that it looked like a badly used hairpin. He had not been honest with her, yet his sin of omission seemed strangely innocent compared to her actions, like a tarnished angel standing knee-to-knee with the devil.

The only truth she had given him was her virginity and the response of her body.

Alex was to be married.

Alex would share that wonderful rapture with someone else, and she would hate the end of day, knowing that sunset would bring a sharing of that glorious passion. Someone else would stroke those broad shoulders, ache to share the burden of his unvoiced pain, or stroke his ravaged face, or hold him within the gentle comfort of her arms.

His bride, not her, would hear that harsh whisper muffled by leather, be teased by those knowing hands that had learned each contour of her body so intimately and so quickly that it was as if the pads of his fingers had been granted sight in the darkness.

She hoped, with a fervent prayer, that this mysterious bride would see past the mask into the soul of the man himself and give Alex the love he needed so desperately. She wished that he was happy and content and that occasionally a smile would wreath the face she had not seen in so many long years. She prayed that one day he would feel secure enough to reveal himself to his bride and not be mocked or scorned.

If she did not love him, this unknown bride, then Laura's thoughts were not so charitable.

Her own future stretched out in a long line of interminable days of longing for Alex. Her life seemed endless, a symptom of the young; but she knew, with a wisdom as old as the earth itself, that she would never love anyone the way she loved Dixon Alexander Weston.

Fourteen

His niece was having hysterics, Bevil Blake surmised, since it was the only reasonable explanation for her reaction to their news. She had been transfixed by gales of laughter for the past few minutes. He was hard pressed to discover a reason for it. It was not like her at all. In fact, her actions of the past weeks had not been like the young girl he had known so well.

Probably that damn school. She had been fine before she attended the last semester of that silly Wolcraft woman's school. Never should have listened to Jane. Ever since, she had been a pale and withdrawn replica of herself. Probably thought she was more ladylike that way. Put him off, it did. Liked her the way she'd always been.

Today she was eighteen years old, and until a few weeks ago she had been filled with life, so enthusiastic and thrilled about each day that her joy was contagious. No one in her small circle of family, and those servants treated as such, had ever bothered to tell her that she should not experience life with such radiance and joy. Her smiles often softened his own habitual scowl and summoned enchanted memories of her mother for Percival. Her escapades made Jane laugh, for all that he was sure she told herself chastisement would be the best course.

According to Mrs. Wolcraft, she had scandalized the girls at school with her earthy conversations about the sights in London, although she had only been there once, when she was twelve. Her knowledge of the reproductive habits of insects had almost put the old biddy in a faint—although he supposed he should have told Percy that discussing such a strange and novel topic with their niece was not the proper thing to do. She told outrageous stories and quoted Shakespeare at the oddest occasions. She laughed too loud, smiled too much, and enjoyed life with such robust anticipation that it endeared her even more to those who loved her already.

At least until a few weeks ago.

Now her gleeful laughter, excessive enough to bring tears to her eyes, was not at all Lauralike. In fact, the entire conversation had definitely been un-Lauralike.

"You did what?" she whispered, her eyes growing wider with the implication of their news. She sat abruptly, and without regard to years of delicate, ladylike manners, upon the yellow wing chair opposite her uncles. The parlor furnishings had not changed since her mother had redecorated Blakemore House upon her marriage. In fact, the yellow draperies and striped sofas made the room the sunniest in the house, especially during this spring, which seemed the gloomiest in Laura's memory. Right now, however, the yellow seemed particularly bilious, especially since both Uncle Bevil and Uncle Percival were grinning like hungry cats who had just discovered a family of lazy mice in the gardener's shed. When it finally occurred to her what they had done or, more appropriately, what *she* had done, hysteria seemed the best recourse.

Bevil Blake, whose sideburns covered most of his well-fleshed face and whose glowering exterior hid a wonderfully warm heart, wondered if he had simply misjudged the entire situation. He stared at his niece, attired in the ivory lace gown he had given her for her eighteenth birthday, and realized that she was more than surprised and perhaps less than happy with her second present.

No, that was not it either, he thought, as he watched her attempts to compose herself. Her radiant smile finally eased his worry just a little, enough for him to tell himself that she was simply shocked, that was all. She was undoubtedly ecstatic.

Which is why, of course, she had gone into peals of hysterical laughter at the news of her betrothal to her childhood idol.

Percival, who was thin and tall and sometimes seemed perplexed by the most ordinary of events, never noticed his brother's frown. He was more concerned about the sudden look of worry in his niece's eyes and the paleness of her skin, now mottled by a flush that swept from her neck to her cheeks. He vowed to speak privately with his niece at the earliest opportunity. Eighteen or not, their camaraderie had not altered over time, and he suspected she would not only benefit from a private chat but would actually encourage it. For now, however, both uncles eyed her with curiosity and not a little concern, Jane's many warnings finally taking root in their busy brains.

Both men had been unprepared for the guardianship of their niece but had relished the girl's lively enthusiasm and fine mind. Now they each stared at this lovely vision of womanhood as if she had grown two heads. They looked at each other and then at her. Their broad smiles had vanished moments before.

"I can only hope that you are transfixed with joy at the news, my dear," Bevil said a little crossly.

She managed, finally, to compose herself. She did not bother to explain that it would have been just as easy to cry at their news as it had been to laugh.

Dear God, they were so proud that they had been so secretive, had divulged with pride their plans and their hidden manipulations in her life. If she had only known, had only suspected, then she would not have been transfixed with hysteria at their gift. Dear God, if she had known, there were many things she would not have done.

"Oh, uncles," she said a little breathlessly, "you cannot simply wrap Alex up and present him to me on a platter."

Her smile was fond as she looked at the two who were as
dear to her as parents. They had, in fact, taken the place of
the father and mother she had lost when she was so young,
and because of their love and affection for her she had never
found herself lacking a feeling of family.

"Your dower has already been paid; we have already signed
the contract," Uncle Bevil stated firmly, being the more practical of the two. What was left unspoken was the fact that
he was quite willing to nullify the contract if the union did
not please his niece. He would not have her unhappy. The
words did not have to be said. She smiled at him fondly, not
disturbed one whit by the fierceness of his look.

"I thought that we had agreed that no marriage was to be
contracted for me without my consent," she said softly. If
they had only consulted her first, she would never have embarked on her harebrained scheme. She grimaced, thinking of
Jane's thin-lipped questions ever since she had returned to
Blakemore. She could well imagine her nurse's words if she
knew the truth about that week.

"But, Laura, dear," Uncle Percival exclaimed, "we simply
did what we knew you would have wanted. You've fancied
the man since he was a boy."

"Has that changed, child?" Bevil demanded.

Her quiet response reassured him somewhat.

"No, Uncle, it has not changed." How could she tell them
that everything else had? Now was not the time to divulge
the truth of her actions; she must bear that burden alone. She
was, after all, getting exactly what she wanted, wasn't she?

She sighed and stood, looking down at her guardians. If
she had only known. If she had only left well enough alone.
If she had never perpetrated that stupid masquerade, she
would not now have to recant almost everything she had done
and said. If she had only gone to the uncles first. If she had
only told Alex.

If, if, if . . .

Her heart leaped with joy; her head warned her of the

consequences of her own actions. She was not so foolish as to lie to herself. Most marriages began in benevolent ignorance; hers would begin with a less stable foundation. Yet did not Cicero say that where there is life, there is hope? She ignored the fact that he also said, "There is nothing so ridiculous but some philosopher has said it."

"I am pleased, Uncles," she said softly, "and I love you both. Very much."

They both looked mollified by that remark and the swift, hard hug she gave each of them.

They separately ignored the niggling feeling that something wasn't quite right.

Fifteen

Heddon Hall

"Damme," William Pitt said, leaning heavily upon his crutches, "these legs of mine are but two stumps upon which I heavily rest. It would do me better to be tied to a child's wagon than to amble like a crab with its legs tied behind him!"

"Yes, sir," Robert said, careful to agree with the minister. One did not argue with William Pitt. Even the king had learned that.

"Is the earl at home? I have not come all this damn-fool way for nothing, Robert."

"I believe he is, sir. I made the point of sending a dispatch when we rested last night at the inn."

"Do not call that flea- and pox-infested hovel an inn, boy. What earthly good it does me to have a warming pan spread over sheets that have seen the likes of hundreds of sweaty bodies, I do not know."

"We could have carried our own linen with us, sir," the young man suggested, careful to keep his voice servile enough for the irascible Pitt.

"Bah!" Pitt snorted. "If we took the time to travel like kings, we would be as mad as the old king. There are wars to be fought, Robert, not dainty comforts in mind!"

The young man forbore to mention that it was Pitt, himself, who had complained about the filth.

He was assisted up the steps to the broad oak door of
Heddon Hall, grumbling under his breath as his secretary announced him to the starchily imposing butler. Simons's face
broke into a broad grin, and he ushered Pitt into the front
drawing room with the treatment he would have given the
king. William Pitt's success as minister was due to two
things—the astute ability of his brain to sift through and retain minutiae that would overwhelm a less intelligent man
and his immense popularity with the people of England.

He nodded to Simons, stepped inside the parlor, and gratefully accepted the chair placed near a footrest of adequate
height. He raised both feet upon it and nodded when Simons
offered tea. Spirits were out, according to his doctor. The only
reason he acquiesced to that idiotic dictate was the acute pain
in his lower limbs. He would, quite frankly, sup with the devil
himself if it meant that he would be given a few hours' respite
from the incessant, pounding anguish.

Alex paused at the entrance to the parlor, then quickly
stepped to the old man's side. He pushed him down gently
when he would have risen.

"Do not get up, sir, I beg you," he said, shaking the man's
hand. "Is it your gout again?"

"Again and still, Lord Weston," Pitt muttered.

Alex chuckled, a strange sound muffled by the mask.
"Please sir, let us stand on no ceremony between us. I was
lowly Lieutenant Weston when you first met me; Alex will
do for now and the future."

Pitt peered up at the tall man who dwarfed him even when
he stood.

"Damme idea, that mask, Alex. Seen you without it, you
know."

"I know, sir. Let us say it keeps my domestic staff happier
this way." He pulled up an adjoining chair and sat near his
visitor. His mouth was wreathed in a genuine smile. It was
Pitt who had been responsible for his rapid rise in the hierarchy of the Navy; Pitt who had expedited his captaincy. In-

deed, he had suspected Pitt's fine hand behind the speed with which he was returned to England after he was injured.

"I'm on my way out, boy," William Pitt said, seeing no reason to belabor the point.

Alex inclined his head and did not speak. Pitt motioned to his secretary, who retrieved the leather valise kept always by his side, handed it to the minister, and tactfully left the room.

"Spain has no choice but to enter the war, Alex. No choice at all. Newcastle is nipping at my heels. That damn Frenchman, Choiseul, will not give up his plotting, and no one will agree to a declaration of war against Spain."

"I have no knowledge of politics, sir, nor frankly do I wish any."

"If you had, this would be the last place I would be, my boy. I have had enough of trailing sycophants to last me a lifetime. You do, however, have a keen mind with regard to analyzing naval strategies. I would have you do a little of the same now."

"In what regard?"

The voice was so cautious, so careful to remain detached, that Pitt forgot the pain in his feet for a moment and laughed.

"Do you dread I would send you to Court, my boy? Even I would not do that. No, you are made for grander schemes. You wear your proof of courage each day," he said, sobering. "Alex, I need one man I can trust who knows how I think, someone who knows the intricacies of battle, who has been there in the flesh—unlike most of my advisers, who consider fighting London traffic their greatest crusade. Use your brain for something more than to set a wig atop it. What do you say?"

"I think, perhaps, that I should listen further and speak less," Alex said, his mobile lips in a hidden smile. He well knew Pitt's machinations; how he could stir the populace with his fervent speeches. The man was a brilliant leader who could rouse a bloodthirsty mob to prayer, if prayer would be good for England.

Pitt laughed and then moaned, as the movement jarred his aching left foot. "Very well, my boy," he said fondly, eyeing the mask with some dislike. "Every week I receive dispatches from Amherst, Boscawen, Wolfe, and Lord Howe in North America. Abercromby—and I will not have you call him Mrs. Nabbycromby, as some of you younger men do—is better than Loudoun, thank the good God. His dispatches are not book-length. Clive, when he is not fighting, informs me of India. I haven't the time to interpret every squiggle, to delve into the intricacies of what they say, my boy. I need someone who can put the pieces of this world puzzle into order, whose mind is trained, in whom I can trust."

"There are more experienced men, sir, who may serve you better." And who may be able to read with more ability than his halting discernment of the written page. After all these weeks he had regained some ability to read, but the results were not as well-advanced as he would have wished. If he took on Pitt's chore, it would be for love of England, and this man. Some would say they were one and the same.

"Perhaps," Pitt said, "but they are either aligned with Newcastle or they are known to the new king and his tutor." These last words were spit more than said, and Alex almost laughed at the expression on Pitt's face. There was no more disgusted visage than Pitt's when he was irritated. He had served one abortive term under George II and had now been returned to power by that same popularity. "I know I can save this country," the minister said now. "I know that I am the only one who can save it."

"The king does not agree with your concerns about Spain?"

"George III still hates his grandfather and anyone associated with him, which includes, unfortunately, myself. He would choose any method to rid himself of me. Do you know what he said when Montreal fell? A battle, I might add, that was a splendid victory. He said, 'I can't help feeling that every such thing raises those I have no need to love.' And, in the very next breath, he referred to me as a popular man 'who is a true snake in the grass'! No, Alex, these Hanoverians are strange rulers. The best thing I can say about George III at this particular moment is that at least England finally has a king who can speak our language."

"I will help you if I can, sir," Alex said. The words were anticlimactic; they both had known he would assist Pitt in whatever scheme he had in mind. There was too much at stake for him to refuse.

"Good; then perhaps we can clear some of the smoke from this hideous mess. If I am forced to resign, at least I can protect England before I go. Will you come to London, Alex?"

"I regret that I cannot, sir," he said, then paused and spoke again. "I am to be wed this evening."

Pitt laughed, a genuinely humorous laugh, at the news. "So, you've found yourself caught at last, eh, Alex? Who is the woman who would tie the noose?"

"An apt description, sir. But for her, not myself. She is a neighbor I've known all my life."

He smiled inwardly, thinking of the imp of mischief, the little mistress of Blakemore, who had been such a trial to his young manhood. He could not help but remember when she had fallen once, scampering after him. He had turned and picked her up, examining her torn stockings and wounded knee. She had flung her arms around him and declared her twelve-year-old love for him then and there.

"It does not matter, Alex," she said, squinting her eyes up tight against the pain of her scraped knee. "As long as you are here," she said, sighing against his chest.

Strange, he could barely remember her face, only that brilliant cloud of bright orange hair and her way of twisting it between perpetually grubby fingers. That, and the sound of her voice, high-pitched and a little squeaky.

He knew that his relationship with his future wife would be one of patience and understanding. He would need to nourish her childhood affection, coax her into forgetting his appearance, lead her to believe that their union was not as lamentable as she might believe once she saw him at the altar and realized just what, exactly, her bridegroom had become.

It was the reason he had not seen her.

He could not bear to see her look of trusting adoration transmuted to one of horror.

She would need all of her childish affection for him to overcome his failings. With any luck at all Laura's enthusiasm would find a toehold in his armor and her laughter would still be as bright and lilting as it had been as a child, and would sparkle through the halls of his home and lift his own fog of recurring despair.

With any luck at all she would also be capable of banishing other, more insidious memories. Memories of red-gold hair and deep green eyes and sparkling laughter from coral-kissed lips.

"The best kind, Alex," Pitt said, interrupting those unwelcome and unbidden thoughts. "Never marry a woman you do not know well. They keep surprises, like handkerchiefs, up their sleeves."

"I would be honored if you would stay, sir, and be my guest."

"Ah, I would not miss this ceremony for the world, my boy. At last Domino is caught like the rest of us mortal men."

"Domino?"

"It seems an apt code name, do you not think?" Pitt said, waving to the mask.

Alex only grimaced.

Sixteen

By day's end she would be wed.

George II had delayed her wedding by choosing an inopportune time to expire in the privy, but even that excuse could not delay her nuptials forever.

She escaped quietly down the hall and through the heavy iron door to the courtyard, entering the secluded garden with a sense of profound relief. Here, at least, it was serene, without the bustle and the noise she had come to expect and dread during the last few days. The staff had not increased in number because of her wedding, but it seemed that their capacity for speech had doubled, as had the requests for her time, her opinion, her presence.

The garden was dormant now, swept clean by the keen winds anticipating winter. The rose bushes were mulched carefully by Harold, the oldest gardener, whose love for Blakemore's many varieties had caused him, in past winters, to burn small pots near the bushes, protecting the tender plants from frigid blasts.

Winter, however, was still some weeks away, and the hedges surrounding the circular path braced this area from the worst of the winds. In the center the fountain was drained and silent, its cupid archer balanced upon one plump foot, bow extended. His arrow, primed to be released toward some unwary victim, was frozen in time. Around the base of the statue were some artfully reclining maidens, undoubtedly recuperating from having been wounded previously, Laura thought with a smile.

Only the sound of denuded branches clicking together and the remnants of brittle leaves skittering along the icy blades of grass disturbed the peace of the courtyard. That, and the tenor of her own thoughts.

The death of the king and Alex's wish for privacy had decreed it to be a small wedding, thank heavens—she had no idea how she could have managed a larger ceremony. For the same reasons her wedding would take place in the evening, with candles illuminating the great Cardiff chapel. It had been one of her favorite places as a child; it was only fitting that her marriage take place there, too.

Her dress was finally finished, the delicate stitches having taken the seamstress and her apprentices more than a week to complete. The final stitch, according to tradition, would be sewn after she slipped on the gown. She had chosen a beautiful shade of emerald green for her dress and nearly laughed aloud when Jane had cautioned against it.

"No, Miss Laura," she had said earnestly, " 'Marry in green, ashamed to be seen.' "

There didn't seem to be many choices left open for her. Marry in yellow, ashamed of your fellow. Marry in red, wish yourself dead, or the one that seemed most appropriate— marry in black, wish yourself back.

Dear God, if she had only known, she would have wished herself back. No, she thought, shaking her head within the warm woolen cloak as if to negate the thought, she would not think that way anymore. She must think only of the future, not the stupid mistakes she had made in the past. There was little, after all, that she could do about the situation. Her conscience, deciding to make its presence known as if making up for lost opportunity, reminded her that it was one thing to become the bride of the Earl of Cardiff as simply Laura Ashcott Blake. Another entirely, when he knew her as Jane, the young maidservant.

She wondered what Alex would think when he saw his bride. Would he be happy to discover her true identity, or would he be as angry as she feared?

She would simply have to explain, that was all. Explain and hope that her explanations made sense to him, even though they sounded woefully inadequate to her own ears.

She had not seen him since the uncles' announcement. He had wanted it that way, they said, perhaps hoping to shield her from the reality of his injuries. His wish for privacy had shielded her, too, because he had no chance to cry off.

There were to be no raucous festivities because of the king's death, although the villagers of Heddon would find a way to celebrate regardless of George II's death. It was difficult to truly mourn a monarch who made no secret of the fact that he detested all things English. There would, undoubtedly, be good English ale secreted somewhere and enough food to give out portions to take back to dimly lit cottages. There would be subdued dancing and fiddles playing, she had no doubt, but there would be no cheers for the Earl of Cardiff, no chants of a lascivious nature toward the bride and groom. There would be no jeering, no bawdy remarks, no showering of the happy couple with grain to signify fertility.

There would be few guests invited to the chapel, the smallness of the gathering serving Alex's interests also. It would be difficult for him to expose himself to a large crowd. It would be a calm and simple ceremony, more a solemn finale to negotiations that had taken place for over two months. He had been informed of her holdings, of the land she owned and the capital she possessed. If he had been surprised by the extent of her wealth, it had not been mentioned by either Uncle Percival or Uncle Bevil, who watched her with curiosity as the day advanced.

Clutching the warm woolen cloak around her, she sent a beseeching glance to the sky. It was not the approaching storm she noted, nor the orange and red streaks of a waning sunset. She sought some sign of God residing among the gray wind-tossed clouds. If God was in the heavens, perhaps He could look down and see a truly penitent girl, someone who was abjectly apologetic for her actions of a few months before. And, if this same God was in a mood to be benevolent, then she prayed in that moment that Alex would forgive her. And if he could not forgive, then let him at least understand.

"Have you decided to escape from all the blather, then?" Percival Blake asked softly, his thin lips turned up in a wide smile.

She whirled and greeted her uncle with a swift hug, trying, but not quite succeeding, to smile the way a bride on her wedding day should smile. The effort did not diminish the worry on her face.

"Would it work, do you think? My effort to escape, I mean. Do you think Alex the type to fly over hedgerows trying to find me?"

"And do you wish to escape him, now?" The fact that she nervously clasped her hands in front of her did not elude Percival. Neither did the gesture of wringing them—it was not from the cold; her gloves adequately protected her from the elements.

"Uncle Percival," Laura said, deliberately facing him and resolutely forcing her chin up so that he would see straight into her eyes. There would be no more dissembling, no more white lies. Those had gotten her into this mess. Nothing but the most honest truth was going to get her out of it. "Have you ever done something so idiotic, so stupid that you could barely face yourself in the morning?"

Percival smiled. He was, despite his niece's beliefs to the contrary, abjectly human. As such, he had run the gamut of idiotic behavior, from becoming sotted on wine and spirits in a London tavern when barely graduated into long pants to falling irrevocably in love with Laura's mother. He suspected that most men could claim a few deeds that could easily be construed as stupid, foolhardy, or naive. Yet stupidity was not merely a province of the young.

He managed, however, to stifle his smile. Had the two of them managed to meet somehow, and Laura had done something she considered irreversible? Had his impulsive and reckless niece offended Alex? If anything, life had taught him that there were few things, death being the only exception, that could not be mended.

"I am afraid that I can only answer your question in the affirmative, my dear," he said, in response to her earlier question, "as much as I would like to appear saintly. I have too many witnesses, your Uncle Bevil included, who would be more than happy to recite a litany of my youthful indiscretions. Is it worry about something you've done that disturbs you so, or concern about what is to come?" He devoutly hoped that Jane had introduced his niece to those subjects she needed to know. There were a few subjects in which he had no intention of educating his niece. He prayed fervently that one of her concerns was not the wedding night and that she would *not* ask him for clarification.

"Sometimes," she said, sitting on the rim of the now empty fountain. "I wonder how people manage to get along at all. Life can be very difficult."

Was there any hope that they could make a true marriage from their abortive beginning? That he would not be horribly disappointed when he discovered the identity of his new bride? That he would not be enraged?

For once she wished she did not know him as well as she did. There seemed little likelihood that Alex would excuse her masquerade as a reckless adventure. It was doubtful that he would simply smile upon her unveiling and then proceed to walk down the aisle with her proudly on his arm.

She'd be lucky if he didn't drag her out by her hair.

"Speech," Uncle Percival said, sitting beside her, "is what differentiates us from the animals. That, and the ability to plan for the future. Whatever you are feeling, whatever problem you have, you cannot rid yourself of it, you can't overcome it, unless you verbalize it first. Sometimes you must talk a problem through, my dear."

Her facile tongue had gotten her into the predicament; talking was not going to get her out of it. But rather than hurt her uncle's feelings, Laura smiled brightly and reached up to plant a kiss upon his forehead. "Of course, Uncle Percival, you are quite right. Thank you." Still smiling, she waved at him, leaving the garden and her confused uncle behind.

Soon she was sewn into her wedding gown, a confection of green and ivory lace that fell to a train four feet long. Because it was simpler than the gown she would have worn to a state wedding she would not be assisted with the train. Her veil was attached last, draped and pinned into place over her long flowing hair, which indicated her maiden status. She hoped God would forgive her that one lie. Surely she was not the first woman to be bed before she was wed.

They passed over the bridge to Heddon, the house brightly lit with the flames of a thousand candles. She shivered as the wheels of the carriage rumbled over the wooden planks.

The carriage halted before the steps of the chapel. Both Uncle Percival and Uncle Bevil dismounted, extending their arms to help her down. They had drawn lots to see who would escort her down the broad aisle of the Cardiff Chapel, but in the end she would not short either of them. She would be given away by both uncles, who were as dear and as precious to her as her own parents.

The chapel stood in the southwest corner of the courtyard. It was topped by the third of the Heddon towers, from which a bell of indeterminate age would peal the news of the culmination of her wedding. The rich heraldic glass of the west window was dim in the darkness, but the chapel was still a place of warm color, illuminated as it was by great branched candlesticks. Near the entrance doors of carved oak was a short flight of stairs that led to a dark balcony, used as a choir loft. No choir sang there this evening. On the walls and ceiling were ancient frescoes, but the brass monuments celebrating past earls of Cardiff and their countesses were gently covered by stiff embroidered cloths. It was unlucky for a bride to see such signs of death or mortality on her wedding day. The floors were laid in black and white marble in the shape of lozenges. The broad aisle passed high back stalls carved from stately oak and circled around a baptismal font decorated with smiling white cherubs before reaching the raised altar. There, before the severely patterned wrought-iron gates, is where she would kneel beside Alex.

Due to his rank, the earl was entitled to be married by a bishop, but Alex had not slighted the village parson. He stood, his robes gleaming with rich embroidery, at the dais before the altar, as proud as a bishop himself.

Only Jane, a few of the retainers from Heddon Hall, and one strange and wizened old man sat as witnesses to her marriage.

Laura placed one hand upon each uncle's arm and was led down the altar to where Alex had slipped from the nave and now waited. She blinked through her veil. He had cut away the lower portion of his mask, disclosing a firm, chiseled chin and mobile lips. Those lips formed into a reassuring smile, but she only gulped and forced her feet to move.

She was taller than he remembered, but then he chided himself. She had only been fourteen when he'd seen her last. She was fine-boned and not plump, although the expanse of bosom of her green and lace dress hinted at a voluptuous figure. His smile did not seem to make her fingers any warmer, or quell the sudden faint trembling of her hand.

Why should she not tremble? He was a daunting bridegroom, with his mask gleaming in the candlelight and his gloved hand. She had a right to tremble, his little Laura.

She only wished it over.

She heard her own responses with a dulled hearing and listened to Alex's with the same hideous detachment. She felt her fingers being touched as the words of the bond were mouthed and then the heavy Cardiff wedding ring slipped upon her finger. She gazed down at it dully, seeing it through the film of her heavy lace veil.

Soon, too soon, she received her wish.

She stood beside the man she had loved since she was a child and aided him in sweeping back the veil that had hidden her face from his view.

She flinched as he took one step back and stared at her with that one unblinking eye.

He noted her pale face, the large, wide green eyes. She looked frightened, he thought dispassionately.

As well she might.

"Hello, Jane," he whispered harshly, and proceeded to shock the few witnesses to their marriage by striding down the aisle and through the church.

He slammed the double doors hard behind him.

Seventeen

He had searched for her for two months.

There was no impecunious parson's daughter with six siblings. There was no Jane in the neighborhood, unless you counted the aged nurse employed at Blakemore. There was no lovely auburn-haired girl turned woman with the education of a scholar and the power to enchant.

She did not exist, his Jane.

At the end of his search it was painfully obvious even to his hopeful mind that she had simply vanished, as if she were a figment of his lonely imagination. In fact, he had found himself asking about her to Mary and to Simons and even to the pursed-lipped Mrs. Seddon in order to convince himself that he had not conjured her up, that she was not the stuff of another wishful dream.

She had simply vanished. She had refused to speak, Simons said, but had simply glided through the hall, through the double doors and down the stone steps of Heddon Hall, disappearing from sight.

Now she had miraculously reappeared, as ghostly white as a wraith, her lovely green eyes wide with fear.

As his bride.

He had been played for a fool, a comedic figure in her little drama.

He strode up the stairs of his home and slammed past the startled maids and footmen, who swallowed the words of congratulations on their lips, through the Long Gallery and across the balustrade to the Eagle Tower.

He could not face her yet.

He had sat at this very desk for endless weeks, trying without success to force his eye to focus upon pages of documents, unwilling to have her replaced, but in the end being forced to. His secretary never came to this room, however; it was too replete with memories of her.

He pulled open the hidden drawer of his desk and extracted the six hairpins he had jealously guarded. How many times had he held them in his palm, as if seeking to conjure her up from a bit of metal? An auburn hair, tinged with gold, clung to one still. In the past lonely months he had had no trouble in summoning the glorious waterfall of her hair to his mind's eye.

He turned and stared out at the courtyard, brightly lit by hundreds of lanterns in celebration of the marriage of the earl. The wind had picked up, and there was a storm brewing; as he watched, several of the lanterns bobbed and were extinguished. Just as memories were being doused in his mind as he stood there.

It had ceased to be a haven, his home. It was a safe place no longer. She would be there.

How she must have laughed, his little actress. She had tried out her husband-to-be, to see if he qualified for such an exalted post. The little heiress with the pots full of gold and a heart as cold. He had been secretly appalled at the staggering fortune that had been amassed in her name. Appalled and a little chagrined to discover that her wealth topped even his.

She was a consummate actress, he would have to give her that; first playing the fool and then the innocent lover. He wondered if that had been a great joke, too.

He had hated himself that day and in the days since. Had hated himself with all the fury and the passion of which he was capable; had felt remorse too sharply to live with himself easily. He had called himself three kinds of a fool, had lamented the unconscious cruelty of Elaine's words, had ached with some hitherto unknown emotion that even now defied description.

What would the chit have done, he wondered, his sense of irony pricked, if he had repudiated honor and begged her to remain at his side as his mistress? That would have put her in a difficult position!

The door swung open with a bang and he confronted his new bride. Her veil was askew and she grasped her skirts in her hand like a child running for a treat. She had chased him down again as she had as a child, ever demanding attention.

"Get out," he warned her, and this time his voice did not hold a pained resignation, only a fierce and growing anger.

"Alex," she began, but he cut her off.

"Do not address me, wife," he sneered. "Do not speak to me. Just simply remove your unwelcome presence from my room and find yourself a burrow in which to hide. I do not wish to see you, or speak to you, or hear your name spoken."

"Please, Alex," she said, her hands outstretched.

" 'Please, Alex'?" He mocked her. "Please what? Please believe me? Why? Please be kind? Why, again? Please what, my lovely little liar?"

She stared down at the floor. The room was dark, but the full moon illuminated it enough for her to see his clenched fist. She took one step backward and nearly tripped on her train. Her clumsiness caused him to laugh, bitterly.

"If you do not want to suffer the consequences of your actions, get out, Laura, or Jane, or whatever name you are currently using!" he shouted.

She felt despair steal over her like a fog. How could she possibly explain to him? How could she tell him that it had begun as a way of reaching him, to convince him of her love, and that circumstances had escalated to where she was trapped in her own masquerade?

"What consequences could I possibly suffer now, Alex," she asked him, her voice low, "that I have not already suffered? Will you banish me from your life? You did that once. Will you refuse to speak to me? Years have passed with no word from you. Will I feel guilt that I deceived you? Anger? Loss? I have felt them all. Please, Alex," she said, extending one hand to him. "I love you. That is why I did what I did."

He laughed again, and the sound almost caused her heart to break. She entered the room slowly, reaching the table, uncaring that the door still stood open and the wind from the approaching storm blew her hair about her face and tore the veil from her head. It swirled and dropped to the floor.

He stared at her with no expression at all. He calmly extended one hand and, with an economy of movement, lit the branched candles on the table. The flames flickered wildly in the wind.

"You said you loved me. The exalted Lady Blake, oh, pardon me, Lady Weston, loves me? I think not, my dear. I think, perhaps, it was because you wanted to know what you were getting. You wanted to rehearse the role of wife, audition your husband-to-be, to see if he was good enough for the little heiress. Laura always gets what she wants, doesn't she? Always the spoiled little miss, now the spoiled darling of the uncles, feted and pampered and given everything she ever wanted. When it was me you could not rest until you had obtained that little prize for your collection, could you?"

"Is that how you see me, then?"

"No, lady wife, that is the charitable angle of how I see you. The truth lies somewhere to the right of it. You are a capricious woman with no thoughts or feelings but your own. You craved a sweet and you schemed to obtain it. You twist the truth around to fit your purposes. That is how I see you, madam wife, as a liar, a cheat, and a consummate whore."

She only stared at him, the paleness of her face deadening to a leaden white hue. He was as angry as she'd feared he'd be. It was a relief of sorts, she thought in a strange, detached way, to have it finally out in the open. Now she no longer would have to live in dread of this moment.

She leaned down over the table, planted both palms upon it, and bent down until her face was only inches from his. She smiled softly, and he almost flinched at the tender look in her eyes.

"How else could I have reached you, Alex, when you were ensconced in your ivory tower, playing the world's greatest martyr?"

"You would accuse me of that, madam?"

"Yes, I pretended to be someone I was not," she said, her smile sweet and damnably irritating, he thought. Her ability to lecture to him had survived her masquerade. He grit his teeth and pretended not to notice that her posture caused her rounded breasts to be within inches of his face. "You had sheltered yourself from those who loved you, so well and so ably that there was no other way. I did not see you refusing what was offered, Alex. It takes two to play at love's games, m'lord."

She stood then, folded her arms in front of her, and glared at him. The gesture irritated him even further, for which he was infinitely grateful. It took his mind from her proximity.

"And as for twisting the truth, I seem to recall that there was something you had neglected to mention."

"Are you berating me for not divulging my marriage to you?" he finally said, biting out the words. "It is hardly the topic of conversation when one is being seduced, or do you now deny that, too? Do you know, I was going to pension you off with a sack of gold the day you disappeared. Isn't that the supreme irony?" He noted, with too much interest, the mounting flush in her cheeks. Was she angry, embarrassed? Whatever emotion she was feeling, it only enhanced her beauty, a fact that added to his irritation. Damn it, he should not be sitting here appreciating the curve of her waist, or the fact that her skin looked as pure and white as Devonshire cream, or that those damn eyes were as hauntingly lovely as he remembered.

"Did I not play the whore well enough for you, Alex?"

She pulled back, standing tall and proud before him, asking the question with a slow and daring smile.

He laughed.

"Do you know why I was going to send you away, my little cheat? My conscience was troubling me. I did not wish sweet Laura to suffer any pain because of my actions. I did not wish to cuckold my future wife!"

She stared at him for a long time. Long enough for him to be bemused by the strange and winsome smile that blossomed on her lips.

He stood finally and circled the table.

"You think me a martyr, Lady Weston?"

"You have been, Alex," she said, turning her eyes to meet his mask.

His hands reached up to untie one knot of the leather tie that held the mask in place. He released the second tie, moved the candelabra so close that she could feel the heat of the flames. He bent down until their faces were only inches apart.

"Is this not enough, then, to want to hide from the world?" he whispered, as his mask fell to the floor.

The smile neither altered nor slipped from her full lips. If he had not been watching her so carefully, he would have sworn that she was an expert at masking the revulsion she must have felt at that moment. But, no emotion, other than tenderness, crossed her features. No horror, no quickly veiled disgust. Only that tenderness, which had the power of a thousand knives to slash at the suddenly vulnerable part of his soul.

He stepped away abruptly, but her eyes followed him, unflinching in their examination of the ruin of his face, the man she once thought as beautiful as Apollo. Her fingers clenched against her skirt and her heart nearly stopped beating in her chest, then lunged and began booming loudly again.

One eye was white and sunken, a deep, crimson gouge lanced through it, as if struck by a long, heated object. His forehead, now knotted into a scowl, was marred by deep black scars, as if he had been neatly scored there with a thousand red-hot needles.

"Well, do you not think this sufficient reason, then, lady wife?"

His words focused her attention on his full and mobile lips, upon that aristocratic chin, that, even now, pointed imperiously at her.

The rest of his face was a ruin.

The skin upon his right temple, extending down one cheek, was thin and scarlet, as if scraped clean. On his other cheek his flesh looked as though it had been melted like wax from a candle, red and angry, thick and bubbled. His nose looked to have been pinked delicately with shears, leaving gouges where flesh had once been.

She did not speak, but continued to look at him, her heart expanding with each long second that she stared.

Dear God.

He had been hurt and she did not think she could bear it. He was still Alex, and she did not care that he was scarred.

"No, Alex," she said softly. "It is not enough." She continued to look at him with that idiotic smile on her face. He stepped back, warned by that smile and the continued tenderness shining through those emerald eyes.

He stared at her, thinking that his original assessment had been correct.

She *was* simple.

Or he was.

He shook his head as if to clear it.

She reached him in a few steps, and despite the soft smile tears pooled in her eyes. She placed her hands on either side of his face. She shocked him then, his little Laura, effectively robbing him of the power of speech.

She kissed his face.

She did not just brush her lips across his slack mouth, but she kissed him on the forehead where the shrapnel scars lanced into his skin like the claw marks of some ancient mythological beast. Her lips darted across his useless eye, as shriveled and grotesque a picture as a fevered imagination could conjure. Her lips swept past the bridge of his nose to the side of his face, where most of his skin had burned away. He felt the tenderest touch of her tears and he bowed his head.

"Spare me your pity, Laura," he said, his words meant as a warning but emerging from his tight lips with too much softness, too much hidden emotion.

"I have loved you all my life, Alex," she said, the tears in her voice adding a thickness to it. "As a child, and then as a woman. Did you think me so without merit that I would pity you now? Or so lacking that I would run from you if you were seen as less than whole?"

"Pity, compassion, regret. They are all cut from the same cloth," he said finally, pulling away from her. He turned, retrieved his mask, and replaced it with his back to her.

She did not stop watching him and he grew distinctly uncomfortable beneath her gaze. This was not going the way he had envisioned it. She was not faint from fear and she did not eye him with horror. There were tears in those deep green eyes. God, he had missed those eyes.

"I do not think the less of you with your scars, Alex," she said softly, placing her hand upon his back. He pulled away at her touch, but she continued to look at him tenderly. There was, however, a slight glint to her eyes that he did not see.

"They are the least of your flaws," she said in a teasing voice, a small smile tipping her lips. "You are stubborn, inflexible, and sorely lacking in humor, even though you have a surfeit of honor and pride. Your hackles rise at the least little occasion and you wear your mask like a shield against the world. You must learn, dearest Alex, to be less rigid."

"You would assess my character now, madam?" He whirled and stared at her.

"Good heavens, yes, Alex. Who, after all, is better to judge? Everyone else is afraid of you, and those who aren't are too stupid to count."

She advanced on him, and if his back had not been against the wall, he thought he would have retreated farther. She stood with her hands pressed up against his chest, her lovely face upturned and smiling into his.

"You would accuse me of too much pride, lady wife? Am I then to thank you for your lies?"

She sighed. She would not now allow him to hold his pride up before her, as if it was a sacred relic, something to be hoarded and sheltered and treated with reverence. Pride be damned, she thought with a small smile. She loved him. That was all that mattered.

"Alex," she said, smiling at him, "you are surely a lesson in patience."

"I hope you've learned your lesson well," he said curtly. "Be careful what you wish for; you may get it."

"Yes," she said, that simpleminded grin still playing about her lips. "I did, didn't I?"

She should have reeled from his anger. She should, at the very least, have been intimidated by it. Instead she was lecturing him as though he were still in short pants. She had the daunting ability to diffuse his rage with that silly smile. A smile that seemed to coax an answering grin from his own mouth. He compressed his lips firmly and turned away.

"You may as well admit it, Alex. You may be surly or curt, cutting or haughty, but you may as well know this now. I love you and I will not cease loving you."

"Your damn flaws in judgment are not my concern," he said sardonically.

Her laughter disconcerted him. He had the distinct feeling that he had lost control of the situation. He scowled at her.

"Alex," she said, brushing her lips across his shirted chest, "surrender. My terms will not be harsh."

"I will surrender nothing when it comes to you, wife."

" 'He that is proud eats up himself, pride is his own glass, his own trumpet, his own chronicle.' "

"Shakespeare?" He stared at her incredulously. "Now?"

"Troilus and Cressida," she said amicably, her hand upon the open door.

"Where do you think you are going?"

"To our guests," she said, that small smile still playing about her lips. "Am I not the Countess of Cardiff?"

Neither the French nor the stench of war and smoke had given him pause, but she did. He stared after her, wondering why he felt as though a major battle has just been fought. He also wondered why he didn't feel worse about being vanquished.

Good God, he thought, shaking his head, he should have raced from the Eagle Tower when he had first noticed her, strolling casually across the expanse of the Winter Garden. He should have locked the wicket gate and posted a sign. He should have dismissed her the moment he had first seen her, dripping with vinegar and smiling crookedly at him.

The storm broke, relentlessly pounding the roofs and walls of Heddon Hall, and filling the reservoir; the flash of lightning visible through leaded glass windows. Gusts of fierce wind whistled through open casements. The force of the storm blew open the door of the Eagle Tower and drenched him, but still he stood, watching the darkness as if his new wife would emerge once again from the shadows.

He shook his head.

He finally stepped back from the door and slammed it, hard. It blew open again, empowered by a playful gust of wind, and he was again inundated by the storm. He raised one gloved fist toward the sky and then realized that his gesture against nature's fury was as futile as his rage against his bride.

Dear God, what a wedding night!

Dear God, what a wife!

"I do not see why you are shocked," Elaine Weston said, surreptitiously surveying her appearance in the mirror over the fireplace. She was not displeased with what she saw. "They both acted sorely lacking in breeding or refinement. But I suppose that's to be expected."

She had arrived too late to attend the wedding, but not too late to be regaled with the tale of what had occurred. How like the monster to create a scandal. Yet there were her interests to guard. She would take pains to ensure that the little bride was suitably cowed by her own presence. There was still all of the delightful Weston money to consider, for all that the chit was rumored to be an heiress.

The wedding guests milled about in the Orange Parlor, being warmed by the fire lit against the storm and the small amount of sherry Elaine had confiscated from the sideboard. She sighed and turned to face the others once again.

"Why do we not simply take our cue from our hosts and ignore the niceties," she suggested in exasperation. "Why must we wait here, when there is a perfectly good meal set aside in the dining room?"

"It is Laura's duty to lead us to table, Elaine," Bevil Blakemore said curtly, in defense of his niece. He eyed the dowager countess with distaste. He had never liked the woman, for all that she had been married to his old friend. There was something not quite right about her, and her recent remarks did nothing to alter his attitude. The uncomfortable scene in the chapel was on all of their minds, but Elaine was the only one who saw nothing wrong with voicing her displeasure. She would have been better served, he thought, to have kept her thoughts to herself.

"Well, she is probably crying somewhere," she responded, adjusting the waistband of her new dress and turning to the side to see her profile. "I know I would, if married to Alex." She shivered.

Her dramatic gesture was met with stony silence and not a few quelling looks.

"I do hate to rusticate in the country. As much," she said,

with badly concealed impatience, "as I hate waiting for that chit."

Laura walked regally through the Long Gallery and serenely faced the group that had gathered in the Orange Parlor. One hand clutched her torn veil; the other held her short train aloft. Her hair flowed around her in disarray; her face was flushed and there were traces of tears still in her eyes and upon her cheeks. She had never looked more magnificent.

The uncles were conversing quietly with a wizened old man leaning heavily upon crutches. Jane glanced at her anxiously. The Dowager Countess of Cardiff smiled her cat's smile and hid her shock.

Conversation halted as they stared at her.

Uncle Percival stepped forward, restrained only by the simple movement of his brother's arm. Bevil stared open-mouthed at his niece who, despite her appearance, looked radiant. He shook his head at Percival, when he would have pulled free of his restraint. No one said a word, not her uncles, not Jane, not the old man with the crutches. Even Elaine Weston was silent. Laura smiled and entered the room.

The uncles rushed to her side as she halted beside Simons, who was standing imposingly beside the sideboard, guarding the sherry. He would not meet her eyes.

"Please forgive our delay," she said, addressing them all with a small smile. "I know the evening grows late and I'm sure you are all more tired than hungry. Shall we dispense with the wedding feast?"

She kissed each of her uncles in turn, nodded in greeting to the stranger, and approached the dowager countess with the air of a young queen, fixing her smile upon the older woman's rigid stare.

"La, dear, so sorry to have missed your wedding," the dowager said sweetly, "but this rain has made the roads so terrible. Isn't it odd, this storm? An omen, perhaps?" She smiled her thin-lipped smile, which was calmly answered by the new Countess of Cardiff.

"Even though the roads are bad," Laura said, just as sweetly, "there is an inn not far from here where you may rest the night. It will be more than adequate to house your retinue. I'm sure that you and your servants will enjoy your stay there until you depart once again for London."

The dowager looked at her from between slitted eyes.

"Have the dowager's trunks placed in her coach, Simons," she said, "and then attend to our other guests." Her voice was mild, utterly serene, and as rigid as Mrs. Wolcraft would have demanded in addressing recalcitrant servants.

Simons nodded and smothered a smile.

"Marriage has given you courage. You will need it, to be married to that monster."

She met Elaine's look of mounting rage with her own warning glance.

"You will not speak of my husband in that fashion," Laura responded quietly. "I will neither tolerate your vicious words nor your disloyalty."

"Who do you think you are?"

Laura had absolutely no doubts about her new position.

"I am his wife," she said sweetly.

Now if she could only convince Alex.

Eighteen

Alex left the Eagle Tower, finally, forcing himself to attend their wedding supper. He walked into the dining room prepared to be apologetic. He steeled himself to accept the congratulations of his guests with grace, their sidelong looks with aplomb. Although he had been, he allowed, sorely provoked, there was the matter of his rudeness in the chapel. He was even prepared, he conceded, to grant Laura some measure of politeness as his countess.

Except that the dining room had been cleared, their guests were missing, and only Simons's stuttering explanation filled in the gaps.

He strode up the steps two at a time, threw open the door with a bang, and found her in the bathing chamber beyond the dressing room.

She splashed, like a child, but she also sang, a bawdy melody that only made him wonder about some aspects of her education.

She did not sing well. She sang horribly off-key, in a tuneless voice that made up in enthusiasm for what it lacked in tone. He should have been surprised at her nonchalant pose, but somehow he wasn't.

"What have you done with our guests, madam?" he shouted at her.

She glanced at her irate husband and smiled, thinking that the changes to his mask made him appear very handsome, indeed.

"Alex, why is it that you treated your servant with more respect than your wife?"

"What are you talking about?"

"Very simply, Alex," she said, in the most beguiling of tones. "I do not remember being yelled at once while I was Jane. Why is it that the only tone you adopt with me now is one of rage?"

"Do you not think me provoked?" he shouted. "Do you not realize that one of the most powerful, if not the most powerful, man in England was at our wedding? What have you done with William Pitt?"

"I truly do not know, Alex. Perhaps he's at Blakemore, with the uncles. The only person whose whereabouts I am reasonably certain of is Elaine. I have no wish for her to be let loose within my childhood home. Elaine, I believe, is resting at an inn."

She stood, oblivious to his presence, drying herself calmly before the fire. He wished he was as unaware of her nudity as she. He shifted impatiently, knowing full well that the minx was challenging him. He was no rutting ram; had he not denied his own bodily urges for over a year?

Somehow that year seemed infinitely shorter than the time it took for her to finally don her robe.

Her hair was still pinned at the top of her head, but she let it swirl down past her waist with one swift movement.

He remembered well that night when she had let the auburn mass of her hair swing free.

He glared at her. He did not want to recall other scenes, not at this particular moment.

"I am tired, Alex," she said sweetly. "Tired of sparring with you. Are there no other diversions you can think of to occupy our time? It is, after all, our wedding night."

"Is it?" he said, curtly. "I think not."

She followed him to the bedroom, pretending that she did not notice how the robe gaped open at the top or allowed glimpses of her legs as she walked. Grabbing one of the chicken legs arrayed upon a silver tray, she scrambled up the steps to the bed. She had requested that Simons provide them a simple meal, not the remains of their wedding supper. Heddon Hall's servants would dine well this night.

Sitting in the middle of the bed, she munched contentedly, watching him glare at her. Alex could glower quite well, even with his mask.

"Alex, concede," she said, still nibbling at the chicken with unruffled composure. Her calm was only surface deep, however. Inside she was trembling.

Surely he would not continue being angry.

He advanced on her, his good hand clenched into a fist.

"I should have throttled you when you were a child."

"Ah, then think of all the fun we'd have missed." She sat cross-legged on the bed, uncaring that the robe gaped around her. "There was a time, Alex, not so very long ago, when you would have thought this situation very appealing."

"That was before I realized exactly who my bride was, and before I realized the extent of her deceit."

She kneeled in the bed, placed the chicken bone upon the bedside table, and licked each finger. She placed her hands on her thighs, looking at him in exasperation.

" 'Thou art the Mars of malcontents.' "

"No more!" He threw his hands up in the air and advanced on her. "I will not be quoted at, madam!"

"Very well," she said agreeably, moving aside to give him room on the bed. "What would you like to do?"

He remained standing beside it, staring at her. His lips were pursed in a thin line, and she thought that he looked very angry indeed.

She smiled again, and he thought that it was a daunting task he had been given.

"After throttling you?"

"Do you truly wish to?" She smiled at him. Her teeth were white and perfectly formed. He thought they should be sharpened into fangs.

"At this moment? Yes." He thought she had never looked more like a hoyden. Nor more appealing.

"Why?" She thought he had never looked more imposing, even with his silk shirt dotted with rain and his black hair swept low across his brow by the wind and his rage.

"You dare ask it?"

" 'Of all the causes which conspire to blind Man's erring judgment, and misguide the mind; what the weak head with strongest bias rules; is pride, the never-failing vice of fools.' "

He had had enough.

"Oh, Alex, do sit down; that vein on the side of your neck looks ready to burst. What have I done that merits such anger?"

She had not believed that he could hold on to his rage. Nor had she considered the fact that he would have sought any chamber this night but the one meant to be shared by the two of them. She had not believed that he would glare at her, then calmly turn to leave the room.

She knelt in the bed, the object of his small, triumphant smile.

"Quote to the shadows, madam," he snarled. "I do not wish to hear it!"

Dixon Alexander Cardiff, fourth Earl of Cardiff, Captain in His Majesty's Navy, decorated veteran of Quiberon Bay, respected for his mind and his ability to assess a situation, gathered the tattered remnants of his pride about him and studiously ignored the sudden bereft look of his new wife.

He retreated to one of the guest rooms.

None of the heroines in any of the novels she had read had had remotely the same experience. They had all been applauded for their courage, placed on a pedestal for their charms, abjectly apologized to by the hero who had been shown the error of his ways. In *The Virgin Wore Lace,* the hero had cried. In *The Vicar's Downcast Daughter,* the duke had nearly killed himself for love.

They hadn't remained virtuous either, these damsels in distress. Perhaps they had not embraced their downfall with such eager enthusiasm as she, but they certainly had not remained chaste.

None of them, however, had acted so stupidly as she.

Yet, had he not told her, *You have given me faith, when my faith was broken. You have given me hope, and I have lived without it for so long. You have given me peace, and I have not known peace for a very long time.*

He had thought her capable of that—could he not think her capable of being a wife? Of course, she had acted rashly, she would concede that—but she had done so in order to lure him from his seclusion. She had donned her masquerade in order to reach him when he had isolated himself.

She had loved him as a child. She had loved him a few months ago. She loved him now and would continue to love him as long as she lived. He was Alex and he was hers.

She had, after all, nothing to lose. He had screamed at her and she had only given him smiles. He had been the most irate of husbands and she, the gentlest of wives. He had threatened her and she had merely pointed out the error of his ways.

How else could she reach him?

She sat on the edge of the bed in the state bedroom and realized that she hadn't the slightest idea how.

The only thing left was conversation. "Speech," Uncle Percival said, "is what differentiates us from the animals."

Right now she wanted fervently to plan for the future, but her wedded life looked rocky, indeed, unless she could talk to Alex.

Perhaps that was the answer then: simple speech.

She felt like the strangest of all the rumored ghosts of Heddon Hall, softly opening the doors of the unused bedchambers until she found him.

He was only a blur of a dark shape, huddled upon his side.

She left the branched candelabra upon the table in the hall and crept into the room.

"Alex," she said softly, thinking that she could not allow one night to pass between them like this. It was not a fitting foretaste of marriage.

"Alex," she said again, as she sat gently upon the edge of his bed. "I am sorry." She cleared her throat and waited for him to speak. He remained silent.

Very well; it was to be this way, then.

"Alex, when I came to Heddon, it was with the intention of trying to get you to see me. I had tried writing, but you would not answer my letters."

Only silence. She was not daunted.

"You see, I have always loved you. Perhaps I should have told you immediately, but I was afraid that you would send me away. Then, when I found out you were going to be married, I wanted to die. How was I to know that I was the bride in question? Besides," she added, with a touch of irritation, "you never recognized me. Not once."

This was not going well.

Still, only silence. She decided to make a clean breast of it.

"Very well," she said, a little crossly. "I admit it: I came here, first, only with the intent to see you, but I changed my mind. I crept my way into your affections with the intent to compromise you. There, are you satisfied? I was going to seduce you and then, once you knew it was me, I was going to force you to marry me."

She bowed her head and wondered why he did not speak.

"You were quite trapped in your little drama, were you not?" he said calmly from behind her.

She whirled and stood.

"Perhaps we should leave our guest now, wife," he said, exasperation heavy in his voice. "Now that you have made him privy to our most intimate secrets."

She stared down at the lump in the bed.

He could see her look of shock by the faint light of the

candles as he went to her and led her from William Pitt's chamber.

She was beyond humiliation.

The great minister of England simply smiled and began to laugh, blessing the fact that she had not thought to sit near his aching feet.

Alex did not speak all the way back to their room.

She would have slumped into a graceful faint except that she doubted such a ruse would have worked at this moment. She cursed her hearty constitution.

He left her at the door then, trying not to notice how the robe exposed her white, full breasts. From her downcast profile he could see that her face was flaming. What an impulsive little creature she was, he thought. He leaned down and tipped up her chin with one long, steady finger.

"Sleep well, Laura," he said in a low and reasonable voice. So reasonable and so calm that she could only look at his departing figure with incredulity.

What a wedding night!

Nor did it improve much from that moment onward.

She scowled up at the velvet hangings of the bed, restlessly turning again. This bed was too wide and too empty and bore too many memories for her to rest easy.

Besides, who ever thought a bride should sleep alone on her wedding night?

He was the most intractable man. He was the most wonderful man.

She punched her pillow, frowned, and wished that she could think of something. She must find some way of reaching her husband. She stabbed her pillow again with one fist and moaned in the darkness.

She awakened from a troubled doze when Mary brought her chocolate and toast.

"I'm sorry, m'lady," Mary said, bobbing. "I didn't mean to wake you."

"It is all right, Mary," she said, easing up in the bed. She did not demur when the little maid brought the tray to her. This morning she had wished to awaken in Alex's arms, not alone in the cavernous Weston bed.

How was she ever going to manage a reconciliation? How was she ever going to defuse his anger? She might as well still be a maid for all the attention he gave her. He had paid more notice to her when he had thought she was a penniless parson's daughter.

Mary bobbed a little, opened the armoire, and peered within. A few of her trunks had been unpacked, and her day dresses looked odd arrayed next to Alex's clothes. At least their garments had a chance of being close.

"Pardon me, m'lady," Mary said, peeking from behind the door, "which dress would you like me to put out?"

Her cup stopped halfway to her lips and she looked at Mary with wide, sparkling eyes.

A few moments later Mary skirted the second floor, descended the servants' staircase, ran through the kitchen garden and up the back stairs to her tiny room tucked beneath the eaves. She returned by the same circuitous route, a brown wool dress tucked tightly under her arm.

Nineteen

If she had only known the tenor of her husband's thoughts, Laura's mind would have been greatly eased.

It had been a long and trying night.

Not only was he finding it difficult to retain his anger—in the hours since he had left her he was acutely conscious of her presence as his wife—but he was finding it almost impossible not to simply walk into the bedroom and greet his wife the way a wife should be awakened in the morning.

After all, he reasoned, he had spent many restless, damning days searching for her, missing her with such an acute longing that he had almost begged off from his own marriage.

After all, he reasoned, she had said from the first that she loved him. Her actions, although extraordinary, had not been those of a grasping, spoiled woman; they had been the impulsive gestures of the young girl he'd known for so long.

In that regard she had not changed much.

She was right, though; he had not recognized her. He had not put those sparkling green eyes into an alluring face, but had set them in the pixie profile that had been Laura's at fourteen. He had not thought of that orange cloud of unruly curls transformed into long, silky auburn hair that wound around his wrists and smelled of roses. He had not thought of her skinny and childish frame as being made womanly, willowy with supple curves and softer than silk skin.

Yet she still bedeviled him, much as she had when she was a child.

He had walked out of the chapel and she had followed him. He'd shouted at her and she had shouted back. He had shared the ruin of his face with her and she'd kissed it.

Nor had she stopped there, but had gone in search of him, had attempted to reason with him even then. This morning he studiously avoided the chuckles from his guest and bade William Pitt farewell with the remnants of his composure and dignity.

"Believe me, boy," Pitt said, leaning heavily upon his cane and tapping his host upon the shoulder with an imperious, withered hand, "I would not have missed that wedding for the world."

"I am gratified that you enjoyed it, sir," he said stiffly, which caused his guest to chortle louder.

"Your maid insisted upon explaining the situation to me, Alex," he said, his laughter restrained only by the sight of the other man's tight, compressed lips.

"The maid, sir?" He stared unflinchingly at William Pitt's florid face, but the minister of England had faced down the king; he was not unduly daunted by Alex Weston's glower, covered as it was by black leather.

"Quite an unusual staff you have here, my boy," he said, allowing his secretary to assist him up the steps of his coach. It was not the only sign of his infirmity. The constant pain in his feet caused him yet another grimace of discomfort as he laboriously sat back against the tufted seat.

"The maid, sir?" Alex only repeated, his suspicion growing with each second, his benevolent thoughts shifting to rage and his well-reasoned logic to ideas of strangling her.

"What the bloody hell do you think you're doing?" he demanded when he found her, not in the bedroom where a rational man might expect to find his wife in the morning, but hunched over the fireplace in the Orange Parlor, scraping out the cold ashes and attired in the ugliest dress he'd ever seen.

He stared at her and she meekly lowered her eyes and

brushed her soot-covered hands over the front of her dress and bobbed at him as if she was the lowliest servant.

His wife!

The Countess of Cardiff playing maid!

"Cleanin', m'lord," she said, and bobbed again.

Simons answered his roar, followed by a subdued Mrs. Seddon. His mask no longer muted his words; on this occasion sheer rage and a simmering temper pushed past the boiling point were the impetus behind his near unintelligible shouts. Somehow, he made his demands known, but both his well-paid employees remained silent. They were unwilling to state that the new countess had simply and nonchalantly strode into the kitchen this morning, shocking the entire staff assembled there by being attired in Mary's old dress. Calmly retrieving the brush and ash pan, where it was stored in the small cupboard near the larder, she had left again without a word spoken. No one had thought to stop her. Of course, to do so would have meant spoiling one of the more pleasant moments of the day, with hot tea, buttered biscuits, and convivial atmosphere.

"Are we not substantially served by maids, Mrs. Seddon," he asked the thin housekeeper sharply, "that my wife need not perform such tasks?"

She could only stutter, look down at the floor, and curse the day she'd ever taken the post at Heddon Hall.

Laura eased around Alex's stiff back, ignored his drilling of the redoubtable Simons, and retrieved the ash pan. The noise of her scraping halted Alex's tirade in midsentence. He turned and looked down at his wife incredulously.

Her chore was immediately interrupted by the grip upon her arm and the fact that Alex was hauling her, none too gently, up the stairs. They entered the double doors side by side and went into the cavernous room where she had spent her wedding night.

Alone.

He was so enraged that she surmised words were neither

necessary nor prudent. Nor was she feeling excessively charitable at this particular moment, considering that her wrist still
stung where he'd gripped her ferociously and pulled her up
a flight of stairs.

"Why?" he shouted at her, and Mrs. Seddon and Simons
heard his shout from the foot of the stairs. They exchanged
a wordless glance, each relieved that they had escaped, although by a hair's breadth, the use of such a tone on them.

Laura noticed that the vein on the side of his neck seemed
to beat in time with the fastest metronome, and that his neck
was cherry red.

But he was not ignoring her.

He planted both substantial hands upon her shoulders and
shook her. He frankly wanted to do more. He wanted to haul
that god-awful dress off his wife's pert little rump and beat
the daylights out of her.

She didn't have the sense to look the least bit afraid.

"Why?" he shouted again, and she realized he was asking
for more than an answer to her masquerade as a maid. She
met his anger with composure, serenity the only expression
on her face as she stared at the black expanse of his mask.

"You do not wish me as a wife, m'lord," she said demurely,
deciding that she would handle one problem at a time. "I
seem to recollect a kinder time when I was but a servant."

"You would recall those days, madam?" he raged, and
wished that she did not look so alluring, even attired in a
dress too short and snug for her lovely figure. If he didn't
know better, he would think she'd planned the fit of the ugly
garment, which cinched in her slender waist and pushed out
the thrust of her breasts until the laces almost popped with
the exertion of holding her modestly within. Come to think
of it, he didn't know better, and he slanted a glance at his
recalcitrant wife.

She squirmed free of his grip and stepped away, placing
the great circular table between them.

"If you wish to act, Lady Weston," he said, his soft tones

as seductive as another man's leer, "I have another scenario in mind."

He circled the table and reached her side, thinking her witless indeed to continue to smile so amicably at him. As he pulled her close, one hand reached out to separate the lacings of the servant's dress. Instead of pulling away she reached up and touched his white shirt with the tips of her soot-covered fingers. And she smiled, damn her.

"Don't ever wear brown again," he muttered. She should be dressed in white or ivory or green, not something so mundane as brown.

"Certainly, m'lord," she said, glancing down and surveying her decolletage, a gesture that mirrored her husband's ardent look. She could look regal in rags, he thought, and voluptuous in a blanket.

She gently pulled away from his grip, determined not to make this too easy for him.

"One moment, m'lord," she said, bobbing again. He raised his eyes to the heavens and prayed for patience. He watched her cautiously as she washed her hands in the basin, dried them calmly, and then divested herself of the huge and ugly mobcap.

She walked back to him then, her hips swaying saucily, the smile curving her lips as wicked as the mischievous sparkle in her eyes. She calmly finished unlacing the bodice of her dress and pulled it down until a coral nipple peeped through the sheer expanse of her beribboned chemise. He extended his gloved hand and rotated one finger lightly around its surface. He watched as it lengthened under his touch.

His smile was wolfish as his right arm reached out and encircled her so that she was crushed to him.

"Does it not give you a thrill, my dear," he whispered, "to know that even now my loins react to your presence while my brain cautions me to be wary of you?"

The alterations to his mask allowed her to see his smile and the wry upturn of his mouth as he could not help but glance at her full breasts. They were all but bare to his gaze beneath the sheer gauze.

She felt no embarrassment, no shame. This was Alex. She had no modest inhibitions since he had first touched her. No, she corrected herself, she'd never had thoughts of modesty around him. While other girls dreamed of a white-horsed knight, his shining silver armor hiding his identity from their wishful eyes, she had always known who he'd be.

His full lips parted slightly in a rakish grin as he pulled her to the edge of the table, bending her back upon it.

"If you wish to playact, lady wife, pretend you are a whore on the streets of London. You are so good at pretending, aren't you? Pretend, if you will, for a few moments, that we have bargained. Your favors for my money. It is an apt trade, is it not?"

"Only if you allow my participation in your play, m'lord," she said, forcing her hand between them and shocking him by grasping his manhood firmly. It was not a near virgin's touch; it was experienced, talented, and hungry, stroking against the length of his manhood until he was longer and harder than he'd ever been, straining against the fabric of his trousers.

He was definitely not ignoring her now.

She smiled, then, a wicked, crooked smile, and he almost grinned in response.

He had a feeling he had created a demon.

His hands reached down and gathered her skirts up around her waist. His fingers trailed above her stocking tops, found the spot he sought, and ran through her curly fleece.

" 'The joints of thy thighs are like jewels.' " He touched her higher, his fingers gently probing, intrusive. " 'Thy navel is like a round goblet.' " Still higher stroked his fingers, until his hand was splayed flat against her stomach. Her skin was warm and growing hotter even as her eyes widened and her breath seemed to grow more agitated. " 'Thy belly is like a heap of wheat set about with lilies.' " He stepped back only inches and smiled into her startled eyes. He palmed both breasts, one with a gloved hand, the other with the warmth of his palm. " 'Thy two breasts are like two young roes that are twins. Thy neck is a tower of ivory.' " His gloved hand felt cool against the warmth of her breasts, and his fingers, clad in the leather, plucked at her nipples until they were swollen and aching.

He reached forward and traced his tongue around her gaping lips and murmured against them, " 'And the roof of thy mouth like the best wine for my beloved.' "

"The Bible?" she asked incredulously. She had been out-quoted, she thought.

He laughed at her look.

There was such a contradiction about her, he thought, as he stood watching the play of emotions across her face. One part of her was a temptress, the other a puzzled child. He never knew which part would emerge.

Each stroke upon her soft, full breasts was matched with a stroke upon his manhood. He lowered his head until his mouth was close to her coral-tipped breasts. He hesitated, feeling the arch of her back, as if she would present them to him. A feast of fantasy, he thought, before he blew upon one as if to cool its heated tip, and her skin puckered further. He licked it quickly with a raspy tongue and blew upon the wet tip again.

She shivered, and he smiled.

When she thought she could stand it no longer he finally engulfed a straining nipple with his mouth, sucking gently. She moaned and pressed harder against him. His leather finger softly caressed her other breast, and he watched her coloring change gradually from pale to a rosy hue that seemed to flush her throat and breasts.

"Does that feel good, Laura?" His throaty murmur was taunting but tender.

She would not turn her eyes from his. "As good as this, Alex?" she asked just as teasingly, freeing his staff to slide engorged into her hand. "You feel like the softest velvet, Alex, upon a rod of iron," she murmured as she grasped him firmly between both hands to slide down his turgid length.

He closed his eyes against the feeling of it, and she chuckled.

He inserted his finger inside her, mimicking the action of his manhood, inserting, withdrawing, then pushed her legs easily apart with his own, not realizing that his victory was hers also. As he laid her gently back upon the table, the antique bowl rolled and crashed to the floor, crystal shattering, water and pink Winter Garden roses splayed upon the carpet.

Neither noticed.

He watched her through his mask, filling her with one gloved finger and then two, stretching her as his other hand descended to her bodice, plucking at her nipples as if they were ripe fruit.

"Your breasts are lovely, wife," he said, pulling at one nipple with two fingers. His mouth followed, and it was her turn to close her eyes with the feel of him.

"You are as lovely, Alex," she said in response.

She gripped him with one hand, cradling the underside of his shaft and the pouches that dangled beneath it. He stilled for a moment. One false move and he would be emasculated or in great pain.

They both knew it.

She grinned again, and he could not resist kissing her until the grin disintegrated beneath a moan. His mouth loomed over hers as hers widened to receive him. Pulling back, he breathed softly against her lips, his words low and soft and unbelievably seductive.

"Do you want me, Lady Weston?"

"Yes," she said, turning her eyes to meet his mask. "Always," she added with a soft smile.

He kissed her then, his tongue exploring her warmth and heat, touching the tip of hers, then sliding to trace her bottom lip and the corners of her mouth. She moaned as his lips left her mouth and descended once more to her breasts.

He impaled her with one thrust, feeling the wetness of her passage. She was ready, and incredibly hot. He filled her with his own heat and engorged flesh, and she closed her eyes again, her breathing erratic.

"You have many sins to make amends for," he said roughly, trying not to notice how hot and satiny and tight she was.

"Mea culpa," she moaned and ground against him.

He laughed, and wished that he could remember his anger. He felt nothing but acute pleasure at this moment.

"You are incorrigible." He had the feeling that she would continue to be. What would his life be like, with a countess who was such a hoyden, for all that she looked like a lady? She reasoned with a Jesuit's logic and she loved like a temptress. She said things that no one ever dared say to him, and did things that young girls were cautioned against. She bent the bonds of propriety over and over, yet her only quest had been him.

"Possibly," she agreed, encircling his neck with eager arms.

"You are still a brat," he said as he thrust within her, closing his eyes and willing himself to hold on. She had other ideas as she gripped him tightly at the hips and urged him still further inside her.

It came to him then, as he kissed her full and glistening lips, that his fate had been sealed since she was ten years old.

She'd wanted him then and she wanted him now.

She had refused to allow him the sanctity of his home, his privacy, and his loneliness, but had burrowed into his life and his mind until he suspected she would never be shaken free. Even now she refused to stay in that safe little niche he had crafted for her, but was excavating past it, into his heart.

What chance did a mere mortal have against such an obsession?

He kissed her, his little intransigent bride, spiraled into the deep darkness of her answering passion and tried to remember a time when a woman had wanted him enough to go to such lengths to attain him.

What possible avenue was open for him in the face of such resolve?

He nearly screamed his release. Her only response was the sobbing of his name over and over and her tight grip about his neck.

"I love you, Alex," she said softly and, with soft and gentle fingers, untied his mask. He sighed as it fell, and she traced the lines of his scars with knowing, delicate, acutely tender fingers.

"What am I to do with you?" he said when he could breathe again. He had not only weakened, he had capitulated. Despite his blustering, he had surrendered now, as fully and as completely as if she had fired a broadside across his bow.

In truth, he had surrendered long ago.

If she did not sing, he thought, or continue quoting at him, possibly he could deal with her.

"Love me?" Her words were mumbled as her lips traced the path of his scars.

"Do I have any choice?" he asked, placing his hands on either side of her face and looking deeply into her eyes. They were wide and glade green and brimming with love.

"None." Her lips quirked in a smile, just before he found them and softened them, and his arms went around her and held her tight.

Twenty

"I think," she said much later, while munching on one of Cook's biscuits, "that we both need a little time alone. Without," she said fiercely, "the duties of rank, privilege, obligation, or station."

"You do, do you?" He grinned at her earnest look.

"Yes," she replied emphatically, nodding. "I have burned and blistered myself for you; I know the kitchens at Heddon better than you do, I believe. I have fetched and toted and been at your beck and call. I have also," she said, her words softened by her tender smile, "spent many weeks in abject misery because of you. Now I simply want to relax with my husband and my friend."

He looked at her quizzically.

She laughed merrily and dropped crumbs upon his chest.

"I mean you, Alex. Do you not know that you're my dearest friend?"

It was a unique thought. He had seen her as a childhood torment, a tempestuous love, an intelligent companion, a smiling witch, an obdurate wife, but he had never envisioned her as a friend.

"Besides, I think that it is time we really learned about each other."

"What have you left to learn?" he leered, his fingers straying up the back of her bare thigh.

"No," she said, gently pushing his hand away and propping herself up on her elbows, using his chest as a base. And such a nice chest it was, too. "I am serious. I know the old Alex very well, but I want to know about the new one. What do you want in life, to become? Do you still like rice pudding and dislike lamb? Is blue still your favorite color? Do you still play chess, or do you have another game that you like as well? Who are your favorite authors?"

"One at a time, little one," he protested, angling himself so that one arm extended around her, his hand softly stroking her silk-covered back.

"Well?" she prodded impatiently, as he stared up at the velvet draping above the Weston ancestral bed and pondered her first question.

He smiled and softly pinched the curve of buttock beneath his hand. "Quiet," he said autocratically, "I am thinking."

She sighed heavily and squirmed beneath his wandering hand.

"Once I wanted to be a captain," he said, staring up at the emerald green draperies above the bed, "and all I wanted was to command a warship. When I attained that rank my wishes compressed into surviving from one battle to the next." He did not tell her that there had been times when he had despaired of doing so. Nor did he mention that there had been too many occasions since the cannon had exploded when life's definition had been hopelessness and little else. When each morning he awakened from a hideous, sweating nightmare only to realize that it was no nightmare at all, that what he was living was real and as immutable as the sun rising above the towers of Heddon Hall. He suspected that Laura would not understand that sense of despair. She was gentle and compassionate and warm and loving, but she had never been so sorely tested that she wished to give in to the deep, black melancholy of hopeful dreams of death rather than the struggle to live.

"When my father died, and then Charles," he continued, "it seemed that fate had taken an active part in planning my life."

"If you were not earl, what would you be?" She looked clearly at him, the gaze of her green eyes so direct that he wished he did not have to dissemble or deal in half-truths. He wanted nothing but honesty between them, but he was also conscious of his mission from Pitt.

One side of his mouth quirked in a humorous grin. There was little between them but one thin layer of Laura's silk gown. Silk and truth, a disarming combination.

He did not realize his thoughts had gone so far astray until she tapped him playfully on the arm. "I am very organized," he said, and ignored her snort of disbelief. She had seen the inside of his desk. "Not perhaps in the way you mean," he said, ruffling her hair, "but in making sense of plans and strategies. I enjoy plotting things, with an aim to their end. Battles fascinate me," he said cautiously, turning his head to meet her look. "Does that make me sound strange to you?"

"No," she said hesitantly, "but I'm not sure I understand."

"It is like chess in a sense, but with real men and real ships." He looked away, seeing in his mind the carnage of Quiberon Bay. "I enjoy the planning of it but cannot forget that men die, and women will grieve."

"Then perhaps you are better suited to be a minister of war," she said seriously, "than a man who forgets that."

"No, my planning will be relegated to our crops and enclosures, not to the machinations of men who forget that their doodles upon a map represent thousands of souls."

"I would think," she said, looking at her husband with interest, "that such a man as yourself would be a gift to England. Not like the ones who forget that lesson."

"Perhaps I could have attained that post once," he admitted, a soft smile playing around his mouth as he looked at her. The next five minutes suddenly held more interest for him than the next five years. "Those days are gone. I cannot traffic with politicians."

"Then why was Mr. Pitt at our wedding?" Her lips were still orchard perfect, he thought, still as tempting despite the fact that he had tasted them repeatedly. They still curved winsomely over straight and even teeth. Little white teeth that could nibble like a carnivore, he thought, grinning, remembering the marks upon his shoulder.

"He is an old friend, sweet," he said, distracted, moving his hand up her back beneath the silk, feeling the satin of her skin and the perfection of taut, youthful flesh. With a sudden taste of foresight, a blinding moment of clarity, he could see himself doing this in twenty or forty years, his wizened hand traveling up a spine not so youthful, feeling just as randy as he caressed skin not as supple, nor as limber. What a pair they would make then, he thought, grinning, and wondered if they would manage to shock all their progeny.

She looked up from her perch upon his chest, wiggling at his caress but making no more than a halfhearted attempt to escape. "Alex, a minister the stature of Mr. Pitt does not absent himself from London at a time like this merely for the wedding of an old friend."

"I worked in the ministry for a year before I left for sea duty, Laura. He was instrumental in gaining me my captaincy. Would you begrudge the man a friendship?" His fingers stroked down her back and around her slender waist, where they began a slow and calculated ascent toward one breast. It was a campaign designed to seduce, but who was becoming the seduced, he wondered, as each touch brought on another wish to stroke, the skin of her body beckoning, taunting. He felt his breathing quicken, and had he not suddenly been empowered by a terrible, lancing need, he would have laughed at himself. Where was his legendary control? He was not a battering ram and Laura was not an intransigent wall. Not all the loving in the world had to be done between now and sunrise. He sighed heavily, and not at all inaudibly, and stayed his hand in its progress. The movement, however indiscernible, was enough to make her open her eyes from her languid response to his caress and glance at him curiously.

"I have studied the past, Alex," she said softly, turning

into his embrace like a small, contented kitten, "yet I am no closer to understanding war than I am the most delicate of embroidery stitches."

"Or singing? What you lack in tune you make up for in enthusiasm," he said, forgetting his intentions and nuzzling her neck. He had an excuse; he was tempted beyond belief.

She nodded, chuckling.

"It is economics, pure and simple, little one. Oh, the great statesmen will orate that it is because of pride in one's country, or enslavement, or tyranny, or even religion, but it comes down to pounds and shillings."

"Have you ever noted," she said absently, staring intently at his wonderful chest—true, it was marred by scars, but still it was a lovely sight, with its muscles and supple skin—"that when we love England it is called patriotism, and it is to be applauded. Yet when the French love their country it is called nationalism, and is something to be feared? How is this war based on economics, though, Alex? From the speeches in Parliament, it would seem that we are in imminent danger of being invaded by the French."

He looked at her, surprised, and then wondered why he should be. Her uncles were astute men who delved into many fields. They had discussed agriculture and dung with her. What made him think she would not be as well-versed in politics?

"The French, and to a greater extent the Spanish, have a vested interest in the new world, as much as we do. There are places in the Colonies, for example, where two forts nearly adjoin, one English, the other French. The same is true in India. Whoever controls India, and the new world, controls their vast wealth. The Dutch empire, for example, is a declining power, yet it is mainly due to their colonial settlements that they have been able to amass such commercial and financial might."

"Yet it seems as though this war is being fought on all

sides, Alex. Is there no one immune from it? The colonies, Prussia, India, West Africa, France—where will it end?"

"It is, sweet, possibly the first war in which the entire world is occupied. Perhaps it will be over soon, if Pitt can stay in power with the new king."

"You have such faith in him, then?"

"The Great Commoner is irascible and prideful, and yet he is extraordinarily eloquent. He owes no allegiance to any group, although he systematically attempts by his gruffness to offend them. He has two abiding and strong beliefs: England and a strong Navy."

She chuckled.

"Therein lies the reason you like him so much, Alex," she said, placing tender kisses upon the much admired chest.

"The Navy?"

"No," she said softly, "because he is irascible, prideful, and extraordinarily eloquent. You have a great deal in common, I think."

His chuckle was all the response she was going to get. "My favorite color is still blue," he said teasingly as he began to nibble one particularly appetizing-looking earlobe. She heard his words as if they came from very far away.

She wondered if it was wrong to thank God for the deaths of his father and brother, if their deaths meant that he must, now, consider his obligations. She wondered, also, if she pressed him, if he would promise to never again go to sea or to war if his country summoned him.

She shivered, as if some premonition snaked across her soul, and leaned against him, wanting him to hold her close. He spoke so easily of command, of war. Pray God, nothing would keep him from her side. "Alex," she said, her voice soft, "promise me something."

"What is it, little one?" he asked as his chin nuzzled her hair. He hoped the pledge she would extract from him would not imperil the oath of secrecy he had already given. He could not tell her what Pitt had requested. It was a daunting task the man had set aside for him. Not only must he force his eye to focus upon pages of documents, but he must keep these papers from Laura. He wondered exactly how he was supposed to accomplish that.

"Promise me that you will remember Heddon Hall, and me, and your obligations here."

He pulled her up so that he could see her face. She would not meet his gaze, and he put his hand beneath her chin and raised it so that he could see her eyes. They were pooled with tears.

"Why would you ask such a thing of me, Laura?"

"Because I know you, and I can't help but think of something Thucydides said."

"Another quote?" He smiled wryly.

"It could be said of England, although he spoke of Athens," she continued stubbornly. " 'Remember that this greatness was won by men with courage, with knowledge of their duty, and with a sense of honor in action.' You are like that, Alex; a man of courage, duty, and honor."

He was troubled by her words, but more so because of the commitment given to Pitt. He did not answer her, but pulled her once more into his arms. They lay like that for several moments, each contained within private musings.

"Alex," she said, forcing a smile, anxious to dismiss the pall of her thoughts, "I have a present for you." She rose from the bed and went to the armoire, as oblivious to her near nakedness as he was acutely conscious of it, fetched her small jewel case, and carefully extracted a wrapped article from it. She carried it back to the bed.

Now he stood and walked to his dresser. From the second drawer he retrieved a velvet box about four inches square, engraved in gold upon the top. She, in turn, sat on the bed and watched him with open, curious eyes. His scars did not detract from his appearance; they somehow enhanced it, as if he wore his badges of honor proudly, without reservation. His shoulders were broad, his back sinewed with muscle, his legs thick and powerful. His chest was broad and tapered down to a firm stomach and further down to a nest of hair that cradled his manhood. As she stared, it seemed to grow, and he sent her a look that was half-lust, half-resignation, and laughed at her open wonder.

"For me?" she asked, her kiss of welcome gratefully accepted and returned, despite the fact that their parting had been of only a few seconds' duration. He wondered if she spoke of the gift he held in his hand or another, more obvious, token of his esteem.

He laughed when she held the package within her hands and looked up at him with the eagerness of a child. His little heiress was not so spoiled that she could not anticipate a gift.

"You first," she said emphatically. He shook his head.

"If I'd known your inability to carry a tune, little one," he said with a grin, "I would have arranged singing lessons as a gift."

She stuck out her tongue at him, and he laughed.

Inside, nestled upon ivory silk, was a small box, its etched gold top encrusted with four magnificent rubies outlining the Weston coat of arms.

She looked at him curiously, but he only said, "Lift the lid."

She did, cautiously, and a rich, melodic sound emerged from the interior. She glanced at him with an amazed smile, and then studied the bejeweled crest. Finally she discovered the mechanism by which it was wound.

"It's beautiful, Alex," she said, suddenly moved.

"I remembered how you loved music as a child," he said, a little embarrassed.

She put the box between them and leaned over to kiss him. He wiped the tears from her cheeks with one finger and sighed with mock exasperation.

"Tears of happiness," she explained, sniffing.

He smiled and hugged her close.

"What have you for me?" he said, with the same happy

expectation. It was her turn to chuckle as she handed the oblong package to him.

He unwrapped the muslin padding carefully, looked at her, confused, and then untied the string. He stared down at the contents and then back up at her, doubly perplexed.

She laughed then, and extracted the glasses from the muslin, and told him to remain still as she wound the earpiece around and then balanced the spectacles upon his nose. One side contained thick glass; the other was of an opaque amber color.

He said nothing for a moment, but both hands went up to adjust the earpieces. She handed him her book on the bedside table and opened it.

"See?" she said. "Now you can read."

He calmly removed them and blinked a couple of times. He would not look at her.

"Alex?" she said, placing her hand on his chin and trying to tilt his head in her direction. "Have I done something wrong?"

"You knew?" he said finally, and his voice was harsh.

"Yes," she said softly. "I knew. Are you angry?"

"And you still wanted to marry me? Half a man? Scarred and without ability?"

He still would not look in her direction.

"You have served your country in war, my dearest love. How could I ever fault you for that? You are a greater man with your scars than others who are perfect and without blemish. I love you, Alex," she said softly, "everything about you."

He put both arms around her and she sighed into his neck. He would not suffer so, she thought, if he was not a man of great conviction and unswerving pride. Perhaps he would not be the Alex she knew and loved without those attributes. But it certainly meant that he would need convincing. Often.

She smiled and thought herself worthy of the task.

Stroking the leather of his glove, she massaged his hand absently, mimicking the gesture he often made. She slipped one finger from the glove, but he did not demur. Another, then a third finger was uncovered, and he still did not move. She glanced up at him, and he was watching her.

"Do you truly wish to see?" he asked her quietly, and she nodded.

"It is but a claw," he said. He was, surprisingly, not offended by her curiosity. It was honest. She saw nothing wrong in speaking the truth. Her open candor was a delightful change from sidelong glances or whispers that seemed to float about him when he was in the presence of others.

He slipped off the rest of the glove slowly, watching her face as he did so. She gasped at the sight of his twisted hand, and yet he did not misjudge her gesture. Had she not viewed his face with that same aching regret?

The hand was arched back upon itself, with fingers clenched into a perpetual curl. The flesh on the back and the palm was red and thin. She extended her own unblemished hand and held his softly, not meeting his eyes. She bent down and kissed his hand, and he closed his eyes at the tenderness of her gesture. He had thought that he was spared any feeling but pain in that claw, but he felt the tears dripping slowly upon his palm as she rained sweet kisses upon it.

"Do not grieve so, my sweet. It is over," he whispered.

"I can't help it," she said, her voice thick.

He pulled her close in his embrace, holding her tightly, as tightly as she held his maimed flesh. She unmanned him with a touch. Months of white-lipped courage were dispelled by a single tear. What power she had, his little Laura, what great love capable in that beautiful frame.

He smiled at her then, his Jane/Laura/witch-wife, and knew that she would lead him a merry chase for the rest of his days. She would annoy him and irritate him. There would be times when he'd want to paddle that luscious backside, almost as many times as he would want to gently stroke that smooth skin. There would be occasions when she would hurt him, and in which he would hurt her. Yet there would be days he would not venture from this bed, and nights he would love her until they both could barely walk the next day. He would hold her clasped to him in friendship and need and she would respond with love and companionship. Even now he was overwhelmed by her; the sight and the scent, the spirit and the essence of her.

The look on his face was so solemn, so filled with all of the emotions he was feeling that for once she said nothing, only went gently and sweetly into his embrace. It was, she thought later, a moment more meaningful than their wedding vows.

Later, in that great cavernous bed, he held her, both of his arms around her as she lay on her side, her back pressed up against his chest. His left hand curved around her waist, his fingers laced through hers. The mat of hair upon his chest tickled her back, and she pressed harder against him to stop the feeling. She was almost asleep, her gestures those of complete and satiated weariness. Their linked fingers lay upon her breast, his hard palm brushing against her nipple in a lazy circular motion. She sighed, thinking that it was a wonderful way to fall asleep, with his flesh pressed next to hers.

She arched her head back and his lips found hers easily, quickly, both mouths open and tasting, the sleepy invasion of his tongue a final good night. She yawned and sighed again, and wiggled comfortably against him. Life with Alex would be everything she had wanted, and more than she had expected, she thought.

He held her close and thought that the fates were not laughing now.

They were smiling softly, and winking at him.

Book Two

Twenty-one

"Absolutely not!" He scowled fiercely at her, but she only giggled.

"Alex, you are inflexible."

"It is not inflexibility, my dearest love; it is simply a wish to preserve my hearing."

She leaned over the upholstered bench and pinched his nose gently between her fingers.

"Boor," she said crossly.

"No," he said, once she'd released him, "just an epicure of audible delights." He grinned, and she stuck out her tongue at him. His fingers trailed along the keys of the spinet, and she recognized a country ballad.

"I truly do not see why you will not let me sing," she said, planting her fists on her hips and glaring at him. The fabric of her skirt brushed up against his legs, and he smiled at his sudden, wicked thought.

"You may not even hum," he said, directing his attention to the keyboard. He was, however, very conscious of his wife, of the scent of roses that seemed to float around her. She smelled of springtime.

"You are a cad," she accused, her rancor in contradiction to the broad smile on her face. Her attention was on his hands, moving across the keys, one supple and moving quickly, the other halting and webbed by burns.

"True, but I still have my hearing."

He ducked as she threw a pillow at him.

"Come here and we'll play a duet," he said, standing suddenly and pulling her close. He held her tight for just a moment, then released her.

"Why? You say that I do not play well, either." She looked at him suspiciously as she allowed herself to be coaxed to the spinet. He had, over the last few months, permitted himself the luxury of being without the mask for long periods of time. He still donned it whenever there was a chance he might be seen by the servants or the rare visitor, but with her he had dispensed with what she called his "vanity."

"You don't," he said, ignoring her mutinous look. "But my playing is good practice for my claw. Without it, I doubt I should be able to move any of my fingers." He pulled her so that her back rested against him. He sat again, with her imprisoned within his arms upon his lap.

"What sort of duet is this?" She turned and glared at him, but he only leered at her.

"The best kind," he said, and showed her the melody he wished her to play.

"No, no," he said impatiently a few moments later, "your fingering is all wrong. Do it this way."

Again she fumbled at the keys, a slight smile curving her lips.

"If I did not know better, I would think that you are doing this on purpose," he said, glancing sternly at her.

"Are you criticizing my fingering, Alex?" she asked sweetly.

"That, and your technique. Did they teach you nothing at that ridiculous school?" Not as much as she had learned from him, she thought with a grin.

She wiggled a bit, then reached down and traced her hand up his leg until she found the spot she sought.

He looked at her with a frown. It was, she thought, a daunting look, until she noticed the twinkle in his eye.

"What are you doing now?"

"Practicing my technique, Alex," she said softly, turning slightly so that she could meet his lips. "And my fingering."

He chuckled and caressed one rounded breast with his hand.

"You have the most damnable way of turning me from my duties, wench," he said softly, her fingering already producing the expected results.

"Ah, but I'm your greatest and most onerous one, m'lord," she said, and stood. She pulled his arm until he knelt on the floor beside her.

"Here?" he said, looking beyond to the half-opened door.

"Our staff is well aware of our proclivity for training them in the art of love, Alex. What is another lesson, more or less?"

"You are incorrigible," he said firmly as he carefully closed and locked the door and then lowered himself to her side. She was already skimming out of her clothes. She turned, and he unerringly helped her unlace her dress. A great deal of practice, he thought, grinning, made him a virtuoso at this task.

"True," she agreed, "but you would have it no other way."

"I would prefer my knees not be rubbed raw by every carpet at Heddon," he said with a smile.

She raised herself up and grinned. "There is a way to prevent that, m'lord."

"Oh?"

She scampered naked to the bench and draped her upper body upon the keys of the spinet. Her legs wiggled in widespread invitation.

He shook his head in wonder.

"Shall we see how musical I am in this position, my love?" She laughed as he lunged toward her.

He thought later that she was no more tuneful in her screams of passion than she was in her singing.

* * *

Alex scanned the dispatches with a frown, adjusted the spectacles upon his nose so that he could focus with his good eye, and frowned again.

Either Pitt had made a mistake, or he had deliberately slipped some translated papers detailing the French plans for Portugal into his case. He scowled again, and looked for the date scrawled on the front of the packet.

Pitt never made a mistake.

The man had an affinity for detail. He did not make errors that other men might. His was a brilliant tactician's mind. No, he had included these for a reason, but Alex was damned if he knew why.

He read the translation again, and went to the cupboard. He sorted through the sheaf of maps until he came to the one he wanted and unrolled it upon the expanse of the table.

If Pitt was right, then Spain was indeed involved. He read the missive again.

He wearily ran his face over the faint itch of his scars and closed his eyes. With luck he was wrong. Yet the very fact that Pitt had pointed him in that direction was proof that he was not. His mentor had the unwelcome habit of quizzing those around him, as if challenging their minds would enhance their thought processes, ensure they were better thinkers. Perhaps the tactic worked, but right now Alex did not want to be tested by Pitt.

Besides, the conclusion was obvious: Spain was going to invade Portugal. And unless England did something, Spain was going to win.

Pitt's naval strategy, although rash, had been brilliant up to this time. The raids against the French coast were unpopular, but they not only destroyed war materials stored in French harbors but also struck a blow against French privateers who made their homes in those harbors. It was a war of nerves, and the British Navy was winning it. Pitt's general plan also sent expeditions to Cherbourg, took the town, and demolished the harbor. His naval strategy was a unique combination of moral victories coupled with large battles undertaken by brilliant military minds, most of whom were handpicked by the minister.

Pitt was not afraid to attack a vast army with a handful of men, believing that determination, a feeling of right, and the belief of British supremacy would overcome all.

From what Alex read from the commanders in Pitt's naval hierarchy—Coville in America, Holmes in the West Indies, Palmer in Indian waters, Saunders in the Mediterranean, and Rodney in the Channel—it was working.

But if Spain entered the war, another factor was added to the more than complicated mix. Spain had a might of its own to reckon with. Could England's Navy, as overburdened as it was, bear the added toll of having to fight on yet another front? Or would Spain's entry into this war cause the balance of power to shift, and England to lose its edge as the world's greatest naval force?

He wished to God it was over.

As early as two years ago Pitt's men had intercepted dispatches that indicated that the French minister expected Spain to enter the war at any moment. There was activity in the Spanish port of Havana, in Cuba, and in Manila, in the Philippines.

He sat and wrote to the minister, his feeling of dread a strange, unwelcome thing. He loved his country and he honored his king and William Pitt. Those feelings, however, were not enough to make him forget what war was truly like, nor discount other, newer emotions.

Such as love for Laura, and a newfound peace.

He sent the dispatch to Pitt by the next messenger.

He was a peer of the realm, but he did not wish to walk in the presence of kings. He was a nobleman, but he wished to consider himself more a noble man. He was titled, and yet the only title he wished for was the soft sound of Laura's lips murmuring "husband." He had, grudgingly, accepted

Pitt's assignment and had performed his task with the most care he was capable of.

Most nights he worked late, leaving his replete wife in slumber in the state bedroom, duty the only impetus that would compel him from her side. But for Laura, he would not have been able to perform this onerous chore. He smiled at her foresight and compassion each time he adjusted the small magnifying glass in front of his eye.

He was, if he honestly admitted it, a loyal English subject who frankly did not wish to be reminded of it every day. His world had narrowed. He no longer missed the sea, the blue-green mirror of the Mediterranean or the gray slate of the Atlantic. Now his world consisted of a few acres of cultivated garden, large sweeping expanses of farmland, grazing cattle, and the arms of one sweet and gentle woman.

He sat, idly twirling his quill between his fingers, smiling softly. He wondered what she would come up with tomorrow. Life had become a magical tapestry around Laura. Just like the one she had insisted upon bringing into their bedroom.

She pressed her finger against her lips each night and then placed it upon the knight's lips. Although he had told her, many times, that the tapestry of the knight dated from the thirteenth century, she still insisted upon calling it Apollo.

"Life is like a tapestry, don't you think, Alex?" she had asked him one day, cuddling up next to him on the settee in the Orange Parlor.

"How so, love?"

"Well, the threads in it all represent something. Like my tapestry, for instance. There are threads for hopes and dreams and thoughts and aspirations. There is a thread for Uncle Bevil and Uncle Percival and Jane, and one for all the servants at Blakemore, because they've touched my life and I've touched theirs. Then there's Mrs. Wolcraft and the girls at school. And Elaine." She grimaced. "And there's you, of course," she said, her frown changing to a tender smile. "You are the brightest and most enduring thread. You weave

throughout my entire picture. But I wonder if it isn't until
your life is almost over, and you look back upon what all of
these threads have formed, that you know what sort of picture
you've made."

"That sounds very profound, little one," he said, scooping
her into his arms and holding her tight. "What do you think
your tapestry will look like?"

She thought for a moment and smiled softly. "Just like
Apollo, I think: rich with color, bearing your resemblance, of
course, with lots of wonderful little Westons forming the
background."

He smiled. Apollo, indeed.

She insisted that he remove his mask around her, and he,
Dixon Alexander Weston, fourth Earl of Cardiff, tried, above
all, to do what his wife wanted. He chuckled and leaned back
in the chair. She always brushed her lips against his ruined
face and chided him for his reticence, and like as not would
do something outrageous. Like this morning in the Music
Room.

He stood and went to the arched window, looking for a
sign of her. She was either cowing Simons again, or repotting
new roses that simply refused to grow in the old beds, or
harassing his third secretary in as many months.

He might as well admit it; she was jealous of his seclusion
with another person and would find a reason to bedevil the
poor soul so much that he quit. He should go ahead and
utilize her as his secretary. It would be cheaper and easier in
the long run.

Yet if he did, it would be impossible to keep the almost
weekly dispatches from her. As it was, she was intensely curious about the messenger who appeared like clockwork.

He sighed and returned to the table. His life had never
been so complicated. Nor wonderful, nor filled with joy. He
threw down the quill on the table, stored the papers in the
cupboard, and laughed at himself.

He was in love with his wife. Gloriously, ecstatically, fully.

He missed being around her. He delighted in her mind, her wit, her radiant beauty; he cherished holding her in his arms or watching her read another play or some horribly obscene novel. "But I get such wonderful ideas from these," she would always protest when he said that her choice of reading matter was trash.

He grinned. Another shipment of novels had recently arrived from London.

He wondered if she was reading now.

Twenty-two

She sighed as the crate of books was carried past her into the library. What a pity she had not time for a good book today. This morning she had planned to arrange for Alex's birthday present to be installed in their bedroom. At least she was, until Jane thought it her duty to smother her with more attention. Of course she knew better than to move the circular mahogany table by herself; that was why she had summoned one of the footmen to assist her. And of course she would not usurp the maids' place and straighten up the room before the new desk was carried in and arranged in the entrance to the conservatory. But couldn't she at least move the small rug lying upon the polished wooden floor so that she would get some idea how the desk would look there?

She would have stayed to watch them carry the heavy desk up from the wagon, but Jane was badgering her to rest, for heaven's sake. As if she wouldn't have months and months to rest. She sighed heavily, not at all pleased with her old nurse's instructions. She was no longer five years old, for heaven's sake! She ascended the stairs to the state bedroom, her mouth wreathed in a grin. If she was still five years old, she thought, chuckling, she wouldn't be in this condition in the first place!

But Jane could still be as stubborn as she had been when Laura wanted to explore the woods, or play in the mud with her best doll, or touch that wonderful plant that ate flies. Jane simply did not understand.

Despite the fact that Jane was obstinately refusing to comprehend that she felt wonderful, and not at all sick, Laura was glad of her presence. Although she was ashamed to secretly admit that she had not missed her nurse—in fact, she would not miss anyone as long as Alex was there—she impulsively hugged the old woman now. She was shocked to feel the fragility of her bones and, seeing the wrinkles around her pursed lips and the long lines near her eyes, resolved to speak to Alex soon about Jane's pension. She did not want her old nurse to want for anything, nor feel that she had to continue to stay in service only to keep body and soul together.

"And what's all this about, then?" Jane asked, but Laura could see that she was pleased by the hug, despite her grumbling. Truth to tell, she suspected that Jane was still a little irate for being kept waiting these long months until her honeymoon was over. But Laura had wanted nothing and no one, even so beloved a person as Jane, to interrupt the two of them, or mar those beautiful months alone.

The last year had been the most wonderful of her life. Alex was not only the most wonderful lover any young girl could have dreamed of, but he was an amusing companion, a cherished friend, a challenging chess partner, and a witty and thoughtful conversationalist. Their talks, and their arguments, ranged from the Hanoverian rulers to the role of women in modern-day England. Anything, any subject, was fodder for their discussions.

She watched as the new desk was moved carefully into the corner of the room. This way, Alex could work at night without having to be ensconced in the Eagle Tower. It had not eluded her that he left her most nights, as if the duties at Heddon Hall weighed upon him heavily and he must perform them before sleeping properly. He was a good overseer to his inheritance, the broad acreage that surrounded the Hall itself, the farms stretching off in the distance. He studied great tomes of agricultural books, asking for her advice as to the most valuable. When he had exhausted her knowledge he had turned to both the uncles, grateful for their tutelage. She never commented when he left her, but the bed seemed colder and too large without his presence. This way, he could be as able a steward for their existence as before but would not have to brave the cold and lonely battlements to reach the Eagle Tower.

"It's a strange gift, I'm thinkin'," Jane grumbled, staring at the massive desk with its carved legs and broad, imposing chair.

Laura simply glanced at her and did not bother to comment. She did not want to enter into an argument about Alex's birthday present. Besides, it was only a little present. She had a much more important one for him.

She was radiantly, gloriously in love, and everything about Heddon Hall charmed and delighted her. Even Simons.

He had become almost doglike in his devotion, assisting her with packages, being there when she needed a door opened or something fetched. A tray of tea would be at her elbow before she barely voiced the request. She smiled often at him, until he had lost that bulldog expression, and even coaxed a rusty smile from him in response.

She wanted everyone to smile. She wanted, most of all, for everyone to be as happy as she was. She noticed the bloom of color on her own face with pride. Her breasts swelled, and tingled just the tiniest bit, and although she was tired most of the time, she did not suffer from that awful sickness Jane had warned about.

She was going to have Alex's child.

She cupped her hands across her stomach and wished she could feel the movement of her child, but Jane had said that it was much too soon. By her counting, and by the absence of her flux, she could be no more than two months along. In seven short months the heir to Heddon Hall and the earldom would be born. Although Jane had scoffed, and said there was no way she could tell, she knew she carried Alex's son. Her little boy, with bright eyes and raven hair.

She was as happy as she had ever been in her life, and tonight she would tell Alex.

She had planned several ways. At first she thought that she would be knitting something delicate, and when he asked she would calmly say that it was a booty, and hold it up for him to see. He would scoop her up into his arms and tell her that she was the most talented of women, and show her how much he loved her.

But, she realized with some chagrin, she could not knit, and she knew that the minute she voluntarily picked up needlework of any kind, Alex would become suspicious.

Then she had planned to leave delicate hints all over their bedroom. Sprigs of baby's breath, the christening cap of the Weston babies.

She had decided the idea was very clever. Too clever.

She decided finally to ply him with wine and candlelight and a glorious evening of marital debauchery, and then, when he was satiated and replete, she would gently whisper the news.

Wasn't it wonderful?

Weren't they wonderful, to have done something so brilliant?

He read Pitt's note with shock, and then disbelief.

Only an hour after he sent his message to Pitt another harried courier had arrived and thrust this letter into his hands.

He almost reeled, and then straightened, beginning again.

Lord Weston, Pitt began,

As we spoke of late, I stand alone without support. A lone stand is an impossibility, and retreat becomes a matter of principle. I was called by my Sovereign and by the Voice of the People to assist the State when others had abdicated their service of it. That being so, no one can be surprised that I will go on no longer since my advice is now neither solicited nor heeded.

Therefore, my boy, I have resigned my post as minister, and have informed the King of such.

Yet, I can only pray that when Spain enters this war, my plans are so well prepared that the final victory is winged by my foresight.

I do not take this tack lightly, but I bid you venture to Saunders, in the Mediterranean, and discuss the plans that you and I have recently mentioned.

Upon you, Lord Weston, the future of England rests.

Fare you well, and God speed,

William Pitt

It was the worst possible news.

Pitt had led England through five years of war, through campaigns on most of the continents of the world. It had been his brilliant mind that planned the Canada strategy, who gave Clive all he needed to succeed so admirably in India. Pitt had been the rudder for England's ship, the sail that unfurled and blew her to a safe harbor. It was not Newcastle, or King George, either grandfather or grandson. Pitt, and only Pitt, had rallied the common man, had argued so loudly and so vociferously in the House of Commons.

He knew the plans Pitt was referring to, the detailed plans that would protect Portugal against a Franco-Spanish offensive. The battle would rage, and once again English ships would be at the forefront. Spain must be defeated, and quickly, or England's overstretched resources would be no match for yet another player in this war.

Saunders, the commander in the Mediterranean, must be informed. And, somehow, the packet of papers and maps and confidential assessments of Spain's might and assembled war weaponry must reach Saunders without delay.

What would England do without Pitt?

What would Laura do, without him?

Twenty-three

Blakemore House

"Damme thing about Pitt," Bevil Blake said emphatically. He had admired the man's fight against Newcastle, had enjoyed meeting him at his niece's wedding. Even though Pitt was gruff, with few social skills, he was possessed of a brilliant mind; that was easy to see. He had led England through this war. Now, with the end in sight, he had been forced out of favor by the king's boyhood tutor! Bute would be unpopular—not only was he a fawning fool, but he was a Scot, on top of everything else.

"Doesn't seem fair," Percival said, slanting a glance at his brother, and hoping that Bevil would not choose this moment to launch a rousing debate on the deficiencies of the present royal family. Anyone, even Bevil, could see that this was not a social occasion and that it was quite evident, even if you could not see his face, that this visit was a trying one for Alex. In fact, the whole situation must be a difficult one for him, but not by word or deed did he reveal it. No, he was being too damn stoic, and that in itself was the greatest indication of all.

"No, it does not," Alex agreed solemnly.

"Well, there's duty to be done, my boy, and we will look out for Laura in your absence," Bevil said heartily. Percival wanted to kick him.

"I would appreciate that, Lord Bevil."

"Nonsense, boy, it's about time you and I were on a more familiar footing. Call me Uncle. Feels strange not to be addressed that way, anymore. Yet I can remember a time when the thought horrified me."

"You were little prepared for the honor," Alex said, with a humorous twist to his lips.

Bevil laughed. "Honor? The chit was a wayward little lass. Don't suppose marriage has changed her any?" He winked at his niece's husband, whose mask prevented him from seeing his expression. He was not so obtuse, however, that he could not detect the slight trace of color upon the man's neck.

"You will remember what I told you," Alex said, his tone somber.

Bevil looked at him with a directness that echoed Laura's. "Hope not to use it, boy," he said slowly. "I don't know what the chit would do without you."

"Yet if anything happens, use the name, and see Pitt. He will know or be able to find out."

"Very well," Bevil said, disliking even the vague thought of that errand. He prayed that he would never need to use the information. "I will look out for her as I have all these years. You can count on both of us."

"Thank you," Alex said, simply, and walked through the foyer to the door.

"You have not told her yet, have you?" Percival asked, following his imposing figure. Alex stilled, his stance as unmoving as if he had been hewn from granite. He stared beyond the open door to the courtyard that fronted Blakemore, at the great circular drive filled with white granite stone. His gaze was ostensibly on the steps below him, but Percival suspected he was recalling another day, another time when he had said good-bye to Laura.

She had mourned for a long time then. How well he could remember her standing there, looking down the road, her glade green eyes focused not on what she could see but on what her heart could envision. If anyone had been willed back to Blakemore by sheer determination and love, Dixon Alexander Weston had been. And now? Would love and determination be enough? What would this parting be like for her now that she was married to the man? He would have driven through the gates of Hell rather than be in Alex's shoes.

"No, I have not told her," Alex finally said, and turned and bid farewell to his wife's uncle. His very stillness precluded another question, because in that moment Percival knew that the parting would be as difficult for both of them.

He watched as Alex mounted his horse and trotted down the paved walk that led to the road between the two homes. How often he had seen little Laura and her pony cart travel that same path, or an older Laura striding relentlessly down the path and up again. Or, and this was the memory that hurt him the most and gave him the most bitter foretaste of things to come: The sight of Laura standing upon that path, her hands clenched into fists beside her, her eyes staring down the road as if to will Alex home again.

Dear God, he thought, as his mind veered from envisioning it, what would she do if Alex never returned?

He sat at the table in the Eagle Tower and realized that he could not tell her. She would say nothing, but her green eyes would pool with tears, and that chin would quiver, and she would be brave. Too damn brave.

He stood and paced, his restless energy keeping time with his thoughts. How could he leave her? How could he face danger again with the knowledge of her painful vigil always at the back of his mind? How could he bear the idea of her patiently and anxiously waiting for him?

Much better if she did not wait for him at all.

Much better if she grew angry and her temper boiled over and she ranted and raved about the stupidity of man's duty when his wife and child needed him.

He wondered when she was going to tell him, as though

he could not feel the fullness of her breasts or the tiny swelling softness of her waist. He was going to be a large baby, his son. A soft smile banished his frown.

Pitt's strategies would be the only way to defeat Spain, and Spain was most definitely in this war, whether or not the king and Parliament wished to acknowledge it.

He remembered her words. *"Promise me that you will remember Heddon Hall, and me, and your obligations here."*

How could he not? He no longer had the freedom he had once, leaving as a young man. He was no longer the second son; he now had estates, the duties to his title.

Most importantly, he had Laura, with her zest for life and her healing passion for him. Who had decided that he was worthy to love, and so he felt worthy. Who had deemed pride too fragile a barrier between her love and him. Who touched him every day with her laughter and her thoughts and her gentle fingers and made him whole again.

Who had said that he was a man of courage, duty, and honor.

Courage. It was not that he was afraid, although any prudent man would think twice about his mission. He must somehow run the blockade of French ships and reach Saunders with the dispatches and the word from Pitt before the king and Bute countermanded his orders. He was acting only slightly shy of treason, and he knew it.

Duty. If he was not the only one to take Pitt's orders, he was one of few. He had no idea of the other shadowy figures in Pitt's plotting, and truth to tell, he did not wish to know. It would make him a target, and suddenly his own safety was far more vital to him than it had ever been.

Honor. He was a Navy officer first, despite the fact of being forced to resign his commission. He had the obligation to carry out his orders. He could not live with himself if he did not. He thought of all those other men who probably ached as he did now for home and hearth and family. Unless he acted, they would be slaughtered.

Dear God, he had never felt so torn.

Laura. She believed in him, contradicted all of the horror of his existence. She had brought light and love and happiness into his world, and now that secluded, isolated world was being invaded from the outside by forces beyond his control. His peace was being destroyed by his conscience and by the war that had finally, and inevitably, reached his doorstep.

He hoped to God she would be strong. That he could return from his mission before their child was born. That she would not hate him for doing his duty, but that her prayers and her love for him would follow him wherever duty would lead him.

He sat finally and forced himself to pen the note. He finally accepted his fourth attempt, and sat back in the chair and read it through the glasses she had given him.

He sighed then, and buried his head into his folded arms.

When she asked Simons to arrange dinner in their room, amidst candles and the best linen, Simons only sighed. "M'lord has already requested it, m'lady," he said, careful that his words always bore the proper respect.

"He has?" An anticipatory smile played upon her mouth. What was Alex up to, then?

She went to the Winter Gardens and snipped the blooms from the first of the spring roses. She looked around her, thinking that it had been only a year since she had first come back to Heddon Hall.

Only a year, and so many changes. She was wed to Alex, and now she was going to bear his child. Could anyone else be so blessed?

She had been extraordinarily privileged in her life. Although she had lost her parents at an early age, she had never felt the lack of loving relatives, since Uncle Bevil and Uncle Percival had stepped into the void so quickly and ably. She had never had to worry about money, nor would she for the rest of her life. She was titled and young, but more important than all of those things, she was in love with the most wonderful man in the world, and shortly she would bear him the first of the heirs to the Weston-Blake dynasty.

They would name this first child Dixon after his father and they would call him Dix until he was breeched. She smiled, and inhaled the aroma of the stately pink roses. Perhaps later they would have a daughter, and then another son. She would fill the house with Weston children, all with their father's black hair, save perhaps one with her own reddish locks. They would have black eyes, or green, and they would all shout and run through the gardens and be shown the most fascinating places to play and be taught the legend of the three muses.

She looked up to the wall where the statues sat poised to guard the entrance to her home. Once, when she was a child, Alex had told her that the first was to wish upon, the second was to curse one's enemies, and the third was the judge, set apart from the other two to decide which of the wishes or the curses would be granted.

She sent her wish to the first and could imagine him nodding in the dusk. She had no curses to utter, for right at this moment she wished only the best of things to happen to each person who populated the world.

She only hoped that the third of the gargoyles, the judge, would not find her wish lacking, and would grant it.

Before he returned to the room he had bathed and dressed in his finest silk shirt, with the stock tied so that the lace at his neck was full and broad. He fixed the onyx links to his cuff and dusted his boots once more with a linen rag. He supervised the placement of the table in the conservatory and bid Simons to fetch more candles, which he would place among the plants there.

He was surveying the whole of it when she entered the

room, flushed with a glow that came from being out in the spring sun and her anticipation of the evening.

He kissed her on the forehead and stepped from the room, giving her privacy. He descended the stairs slowly, looking about his house, lit with the flames of a hundred candles. The light and shadows played upon the domed roof at the entrance and cavorted among the gods and goddesses carved there. He stood in the middle of the broad steps and noted the fluted columns by the doorway, the marble flooring that led to the great door.

He loved his home, had done so since he was a boy, but now he felt the enormous burden of it, as if it called to him from a distance that already existed in his mind.

He had left word with his secretary to give the household books to Laura—she would know how best to manage Heddon Hall in his absence. The steward of the home farms and the foraging enclosures had been met with and he, too, had been instructed to go to the countess if anything was amiss in his year-long plans of cultivation. He had taken Laura's advice, and already the rents on their enhanced land were larger than ever before.

He'd met with his solicitor and updated the will he had made as a captain. He had not been forced by any terms of primogeniture to relinquish Heddon Hall. If he should not return and Laura not bear a male child, only the title would go to a distant relative. Heddon Hall would not be passed along with the title, as it had to him through his father's death and his brother's. It would now belong to her and their child. He had seen the uncles last, unwilling to share his concerns with them, but prompted by some faint dread to make arrangements for her. He could not bear the idea of her endlessly waiting for news of his fate, if the worst thing that could happen did in fact come to pass. The uncles were to go to Pitt, who with his connections would be able to obtain information more quickly than anyone else.

He entered the library, little used since he had returned

until Laura had, with her usual foresighted tenderness, gifted him with the glasses. Now he had no trouble discerning the printed word. It no longer swam in rivulets, like wiggling tadpoles upon a page. Now the words were stabilized and held fast to their moorings.

He picked a book at random from the shelves, and chuckled when it turned out to be one of her dreadful novels. He laid it on the desk and went to the window, looking out among the hills that swept down to the river Wye. The grass was black-green, the shadows of night almost upon them. He felt an acute tenderness that bordered on pain.

At dawn he would ride away from this place, his home. He would leave behind the one person he held most dear in the world.

Oh, Laura, he thought, resting his forehead against the cool pane of glass, how I will miss you.

He had thought once, long ago, that he needed no one. He had since realized that he needed her. He needed her to tell him when he was being terribly autocratic or inflexible or when the melancholy was descending in a slow, vaporous fog that was invisible to him but so obvious to her. He needed her to believe in him and trust him and, in doing so, give him back part of himself.

He needed her, but England needed him, and he had not been granted a choice.

He prayed that she could see that he did this in spite of the love he bore her. That he must perform his duty, however unwilling.

He stood at the windows and watched until dusk became dark. He saw a ghostly shape glide by, and jerked. Then it waved and he laughed.

He reached the door before Simons could and pulled it open, nearly racing down the steps in search of his lovely, surprising wife. A broad grin lanced his face as he saw her, just outside of the yew garden, dressed in nothing more concealing than a white nightgown. He looked back at his home, windows lit by the multitude of candles, the moving shapes of servants about their duties, and shook his head.

He laughed aloud and chased her down the rolling grass. He caught her among the trees, her giggles giving her position away.

She smelled of dampness, perfume, and the scent of the spring night. He held his arms around her and laughed into her neck, welcoming the mirth that shook him from his melancholy.

"You will grow chilled, my love," he said, smiling, his hands smoothing a path down her nearly naked back.

"Ah, but m'lord," she said, with answering laughter in her voice, "you are here to warm me."

"I love you, Laura," he said suddenly, and she stilled for the space of a long moment. Then she placed her hands on either side of his mask.

"I know, Alex," she said, her heart filled with tenderness. It was not the first time he had said the words to her, but each time she accepted them like a rare and costly gift. "I knew it from the first."

"Oh, and what else did you know, my eager little wife?"

"That you would be as eager," she said, reaching up and kissing his smiling mouth.

"We have dinner waiting above," he whispered.

"Cook can set it back," was her response.

"We have a nice cozy bed in our room."

"Yes, but we have never made love in the garden."

"We have a multitude of servants, love, who can look out any window, at any time."

"They could not see us well if we were unclothed and hidden in the bushes."

His laughter was infectious, she thought; she could not help but giggle in response.

"I am an earl," he protested with a show of pompous dignity.

"And I am a countess," she reminded him with a loving hug.

"You would not get rug burns this way, Alex," she prodded him.

"But I am apt to be bitten by a thousand willing insects."

"What are a few love bites, more or less?"

He bent and swooped her into his arms, his strength distilled somewhat by the laughter that shook his chest. He proceeded to walk through the Winter Garden with her in his arms. Despite the presence of curious and smiling servants, he entered the front hall of his home with his scantily attired wife in his arms, mounting the great steps leading to the state bedroom with her awestruck eyes fixed upon his mask.

When he lowered her before the doors she smiled.

"That was well done, Alex," she congratulated him.

"I am happy you approve," he said with a bow. "If you think that was good," he said with a flourish, as he once again swept her into his arms, "you should see what happens next."

"I do wish we had taken advantage of the opportunity," she said softly.

"Another time, perhaps, Laura, when the insect population is not waiting for my tender flesh."

"What happens next?"

"Watch and listen, and learn, my love."

She did and did and did.

She rolled over and placed her hand against his back, thinking that she had never felt more deliciously content.

They had, finally, eaten their cold dinner.

In a way, she received her wish, because he had insisted upon them dining in state totally naked among the plants of the conservatory, the star-studded sky their ceiling, their only accompaniment the muted sounds of the night, audible through the open windows.

Her dearest Alex. Her husband.

She had forgotten her ritual, and in the darkness she slid

from the bed and kissed Apollo, and then returned quietly to
the bed. He sat up and welcomed her with a smile, and she
cuddled into his arms as though she had always meant to be
there.

She had. She had always known it.

He brushed back her hair and kissed her.

"What time is it?" he mused, and she glanced at the ormolu clock upon the mantle.

"It is almost morning, love."

He grimaced, thinking of the long journey ahead. Yet he
would not have traded their hours together for something so
mundane as sleep. She had finally told him of her secret, and
he had held her upon his lap and told her she would be the
most wonderful mother in the world.

As he would be the most wonderful father, she had said,
tracing her fingers over his scars as if to heal them.

He sat now in their large bed and absently stroked her
arm, thinking that too soon the dawn would show in the sky
and he would be gone. Too soon.

"Alex," she said haltingly, her voice reedy in the darkness.

"Yes, love."

"Thank you."

He chuckled. "What for?"

"For loving me, and putting up with me, and for so much.
For this wonderful year and our child and listening to my
singing and saying that you love me."

He pulled her closer. "I admit to all of the above, my
darling, except for the singing."

She smiled against his chest.

"You know what I mean," she said, wiggling into a more
comfortable position.

"Yes, love," he said softly, "I do. But gratitude is not what
I would wish from you, Laura."

"Oh? And what would you wish, m'lord?" She felt the fur
of hair upon his chest, and the scars deeply gouged there.

"A little of your inventiveness, perhaps?"

"Are you not tired, m'lord?"

"Hardly," he chuckled, thinking of the instantaneous and stoic rising of his manhood when she had wiggled closer to him.

She slid down into the bed and licked his chest with an eager tongue. What a treasure she was.

He raised her up again and found her face in the darkness, tracing the edge of her jaw with his lips, and then trailing his fingers into the uncoiled mass of her hair.

"Thank you, Laura," he said, his voice soft and low, "for your passion." He bent down and gently smoothed the soft curves of her breasts.

"For your lovely breasts, and these eager tips," he said, pulling gently upon her nipples. She lay quiescent against him, letting him stroke her, her only response a soft moan.

"Thank you for the gift of welcoming me," he whispered, tracing an imaginary line down from the middle of her breasts to her mount, and feeling the wetness already dampening her curls.

"Thank you for the sweetness," he said, dipping his tongue into her mouth, "of your tongue, and of your lips." He bent down and placed her legs across his, smoothing their contours from her toes to the juncture of her thighs. "I love the sounds you make when I am inside you," he said softly in the darkness, and she shivered. "The tiny gasps you make and the nip of your teeth upon my shoulder."

She caressed the side of his face with one trembling hand, and he angled his head to kiss her palm.

"Thank you for not hiding your pleasure, and arching against me when you find release." He stroked her wetness again, and then the turgid nipples that blossomed with his touch. "Thank you for being tight and hot and wet."

"Which of my parts do you prefer, Alex?" she whispered as she traced his lips with a tremulous finger.

"All of them, my love. All tied up in one delectable package."

"It is impolite to refuse a gift, husband," she said, moving her legs and sliding beside him. She pulled his head down and kissed him with soft, wet lips. He shuddered and entered her with one smooth stroke.

She gasped as she felt him as hard as a length of iron. When he bent his head and grasped one nipple between his lips she arched her back and could not prevent the slight moan from escaping her lips.

"Is that what I was doing, wife?" he said teasingly, moving just a little and refusing to slide deeply into her, despite her grip upon his hips. "Refusing a gift?" He pulled out of her tight sheath, and one hand dipped to play in her wetness.

Her hand extended around his back and she pulled his head down once more.

"Do not tease, Alex," she implored, her hips arcing up in little movements to impel him to enter her once more.

"But it is so much fun, Laura," he said, before slipping into her. He felt the sheen of dampness against her skin and licked it away. He bent and retrieved the other nipple, twirling it with his tongue and then the gentle nip of his teeth.

A slight, pleading sound emerged from her lips.

When he slid into her again, as hard as he'd ever been, her back arched and she exploded around him, pulling him into the swirling vortex. It lasted for hours, he thought, hours of almost painful delight, in which she was the only steady force in the universe. She lay weakly beneath him, wondering at it, but accepting with wholehearted enthusiasm the fact that each time it became better, more passionate between them. She sighed.

"You're welcome," she said then, and he held her as laughter overwhelmed them both.

Twenty-four

She held the note tightly in her hand, walked to the paneled door, and locked it with shaking fingers.

Slow, deliberate movements carried her into the conservatory, where she sat upon the upholstered chair behind Alex's desk, the one she had given him for his birthday, the one he had not had a chance to use, the one upon whose gleaming surface rested not one extraneous scrap of paper, nor quill, nor pot of ink.

She read his words again, forcing her eyes to make sense of the words, tracing the elaborate scrolls of his writing with the tip of one shaking finger.

My darling wife,

You have bade me remember Heddon Hall and my rank and added your name to my list of responsibilities as if you were not my greatest joy and my most beloved obligation.

I must leave you now, not because I crave our separation, but because another duty calls to me.

I will miss you with the devotion a saint has for his God, a child for its mother, a man for his beloved.

My love for you wars with my duty, yet I know that should I crave a cessation of this responsibility I would neither be the man you think of me nor the patriot I am.

Each night that separates us will bring dreams of you,

my love. Each sunrise will bring memories of your smiles.

Count the days as those which we must spend in payment for our love, so that when this ends our future will be unsullied by any duty other than that of each to the other and to our children.

Protect yourself, my love, and our child, as I will guard my own life as a gift to you.

I leave you with the words of Shakespeare, whom you love so well—"She loved me for the dangers I had passed, and I loved her that she did pity them."

Your loving husband,
Dixon Alexander Weston
Earl of Cardiff

Alex, her heart screamed, but her eyes remained dry. Alex.

She looked beyond the windows to the Winter Garden, unable to focus on the plants arranged there, simply noting the mass of green and yellow, dusky pink and rose. The yew hedges probably needed trimming, she thought absently, and the roses should be pruned soon. She would have to talk to the head gardener, arrange for some additional mulch to be added to the rose beds. It was, somehow, infinitely important that she not forget those small tasks.

She sat there for a long time, listening intently to the sounds of activity around Heddon Hall, as if the house had suddenly become a living, breathing thing. She heard the gurgle of the water chamber in the dressing room, the scurry of the maid's leather-shod feet in the hall, the quick, promising question called from one of the gardeners to one of the youngest maids and her cheeky response, the soft *tick, tick, tock* of the golden clock centered upon the mantel, the soughing of an early morning breeze that cavorted through the windows of the conservatory.

She smelled the scent of lush earth, black and humid, the

flowers growing in their boxes neatly arranged against the largest windows, the roses from the Winter Garden, the rich tang of lemon polish used to clean the heavy furniture, the hint of beeswax tapers, her own scent, redolent of sleepy satiation and Alex.

Smoothing its parchment folds carefully with fingers too composed, too calm, she bent the note back upon its creases until it lay smooth and unwrinkled upon the polished mahogany. She sat, clutching her wrapper with both clenched hands, and stared at the ivory vellum with its black-etched words as something cracked and broke within her, some undefined innocence that she had long thought shed.

Alex had left her.

How easily he had spoken of duty. How ominous the word sounded, like a death knell in her heart.

She hoped that he had taken his reading glasses, and his warmest coat. She wondered if he had taken the coach and hoped that he had not chosen to ride the distance. His cough had lasted through the winter, even though he had reassured her that it was only the lingering effects of the smoke inhaled at Quiberon Bay.

He would tire himself and work too hard and strain the muscles that had healed completely only during this last year. He would miss meals and the greens the cook prepared especially for him and grow gaunt from lack of proper sustenance.

He would sleep his restless sleep and waken from those occasional nightmares and she would not be there to give him comfort or hold his beloved body close and whisper that she loved him, that it was all right, that it was just a dream.

He would ache for her as she ached for him now, imagining him standing upon the deck of a ship, his mask gleaming in the sun, his gaze fixed upon the ocean's false horizon. He would stand, like the very spirit of the sea itself, broad and unmoving, brave and with honor.

She closed her eyes and saw him, laughing, smiling, teasing her gently. She saw him softly touching her, his grin wide, his chin nuzzling her breasts. She saw his beautiful hand, touched his tongue with the memory of hers.

Oh, Alex.

He had teased her about her love of dancing, had swept her up in his arms and together, listening to the tune he hummed, they had danced upon the boards of the Long Gallery. He had dipped with her and showed her the intricate steps, and when she had frowned and looked at him crossly he had whirled her up against him and held her high and would not release her until she begged sweetly and ceded him a kiss as a boon.

They had explored the grounds of Heddon Hall as they had as children, she racing to escape him and hiding beneath the curved bridge. He, swooping down finally and pulling her, laughing and protesting, into his arms.

She had made fun of his elaborate script and he had promised to overturn the pot of ink upon her head. She had skipped gaily away from him and threatened to throw his quills from the arched window. He had grabbed her and held her and she had ransomed his writing instruments for a kiss.

She had brought him roses from the Winter Garden, and they had argued politics. She had made him try new dishes the cook prepared and he had beaten her soundly at chess. She had debated religion and he had kissed her feet. She had repeated the awful jokes she had heard in the kitchen and beaten him at cards. He had carried her naked from the bath and made glorious love with her upon the floor of their chamber.

She had smiled in the mornings and laughed in the evenings and listened while he played his music in the quiet nights. He had laughed as she sang and tickled her while she slept, and for one day, only one short day, they had planned for their child.

Dear God, Alex.

She loved the rainy days when they had sat alone in the library, a fire lit against the chill. She had sat in the far corner of the room but would catch him staring at her, as often as he would look up and find her studying him. They would both smile softly and look away again, knowing that there would be time, later, to come closer. Sometimes they had not waited, and the old books had witnessed another chapter in their story.

It was, curiously, as if time itself were stopping. As though life were slowing down, second by second, until, soon, it would abruptly halt and become perfectly still, she the only living creature within a solid, immutable bubble of time. Sleeping Beauty's castle was falling under a spell, the spiked thorns beginning to cover every window, the black sun rising to shadow the entire world.

Each of her separate limbs was fading into numbness, the core of her heart beating solidly and rhythmically the only clue that she still lived, still existed. She did not like the hollowness she felt inside her chest. Or the feeling of dread that crept outward from her heart and turned her limbs to ice. She did not want these feelings. She wanted days of sunshine and laughter and the rare and wonderful sound of his laughter. She wanted to massage his hand when the change in weather hurt it, or smooth her fingers against his beloved face.

Alex had left her.

She bowed her head and did not think she could bear the pain, but it was not just within her; it surrounded her. It was there in the room with her and she was a part of it, just as he was part of her.

The armoire would be filled with his scent. The drawers would hold his silk shirts and his cravats; the polished metal buttons from Warwickshire would be in the top drawer. He would have taken his military brush, his shaving gear, but would he have worn that uniform that fitted him so proudly? Would he, even now, be saluted as captain, or would he be the autocratic earl? Where was he? What duty was greater than Heddon Hall, his wife, his child?

Alex.

It became a soft moan.

She stood and turned, looking at the bed she had left only moments before. She had awakened at last, tired from their lovemaking and the demands of her pregnancy. Without opening her eyes she had reached for him, but he had not been there. Only the note had rested upon his pillow, topped by a single lovely, dew-flecked rose.

Alex, please, she whispered soundlessly, and it was a soft entreaty, reaching over miles and past the confines of Heddon Hall, carried on the wind as surely and as certainly as her love sped to be with him.

But she did not cry.

She bent her head and held the parchment close to her breasts, as if he were within its folds. If he had been, she would have kept him tucked against her heart and held him safely, protected from those circumstances and people who would separate them.

Dread curled up within her stomach. They had lived together for one perfect year. One beautiful year of love, memories, and acute happiness. Was one year too much for the gods? Was one year all that she would have to last for a lifetime? The dread uncoiled and entered her heart, and she closed her eyes with a sudden premonition.

She caressed the mound of her stomach, the tiny bulge where their child lay, and prayed that this child would know his father. She had nearly lost him once, but he had returned. Not unscathed, but at least alive.

This time was different.

This time the fear lived and breathed within her heart like a great, dark, winged beast. This time she knew a grief as broad and as deep as the ocean upon which he would soon travel.

This time she knew with a certainty as solemn as it was deadly that he was never coming back.

Twenty-five

"If I did not know you better," she said softly, "I would think you were cheating."

Percival Blake winked at his niece at the same time as he paused in the act of lifting his knight.

"It is very difficult to cheat at chess, my dear," he said with a small smile, "unless one's opponent is not paying attention."

"Is this a lesson in strategy, Uncle Percival," she asked with a matching smile, "or a treatise upon the merits of watching one's opponent?"

"You've taken all the fun out of it," he said with a mock frown and leaned back in the chair facing her. The knight was left on the board, in its original position.

"I appreciate the lesson, Uncle," she said softly, "if not the manner of your executing it."

"My, my, child, you wound an old man."

"Nonsense, Uncle," she said crisply and arranged the pieces to their beginning pattern. "You are neither wounded nor an old man. You affect an entertaining buffoonery, but I have often suspected that you are more learned than Uncle Bevil."

Her younger uncle laughed and looked at his niece appreciatively.

"There can only be one ram, my dear."

"And you have let Uncle Bevil usurp that position?"

"Not usurp, perhaps, but maintain. It takes a great deal of

energy to administer an estate as vast as yours. Perhaps I've never had the energy for it."

"That I cannot accept either, Uncle. I think Uncle Bevil believes himself to be the head of the family, as you allow him to think it."

"My God," he said in mock horror, "you ascribe to me the virtues of a wife!"

Instead of laughing, which would have been her response a few months ago, she looked at him directly, her green eyes laced with something infinitely difficult to see, he thought. It was an emotion she took pains to shield from all of them.

At least, from those who did not have experience to draw upon, who did not recognize that solemn grief for what it was.

She had changed, his niece. In a matter of moments, he suspected, she had put aside her youth and become fully grown. Great loss can bring maturity to those with tender years. Her laughter was hollow, as hollow as her cheeks; her smiles were as dim as her pale lips. She was Laura, but a pale, shadowed imitation of the woman she had been while Alex was here.

He toyed with a chess piece absently, staring at his hands when the look in her eyes became too much to bear.

For the first time in her life she found herself wondering why he had never married.

True, both her uncles had been saddled with a young ward, but that was no serious impediment. She found herself studying Uncle Percival more closely, and conceded that his was a reticent nature, although he could be charming and gregarious when he wished to be. He possessed a sparkling wit, yet his eyes bore a trace of an old sadness. Strange; she had never seen it before.

It was almost like a new word you learned and then, for the next few days, heard spoken constantly. Perhaps, she mused, chewing on the end of one nail, you did not realize the suffering of others until you suffered yourself.

Perhaps she would never have noticed Uncle Percival's old pain, unless she had experienced anguish of her own.

Her question, when it came, did not surprise him. What did surprise him was that it had taken so long for her to ask it.

"Why have you never married, Uncle?" she said softly, and he wished he had the courage to answer her with the first thought that came into his mind.

Why would I want such pain that is mirrored in your eyes? He did not say those words. He answered her with the truth, instead.

"There was a woman once," he said slowly, "a beautiful woman with hair like the mist of a flame and sparkling eyes the color of a forest. She fell in love with my older brother and married him."

She looked shocked, he thought. Shocked and then strangely satisfied, as if an old mystery had finally been solved.

"My mother?" she asked quietly, and did not speak after Uncle Percival nodded once, quickly. That would explain why he had not minded his new duties of caring for his brother's child, why she occasionally saw him watching her with a look of loss on his face, as if remembering something from long ago.

"Have you had no wish to marry again?" she asked quietly.

Would you? he wanted to say but did not. The words, however unspoken, shimmered in the air between them.

"No," he said calmly, and changed the subject, "anymore than I would wish a better chess partner. It is far more thrilling to my ego to have someone I can thoroughly trounce."

"Only if that partner is preoccupied," she said, with a sudden, bright grin that, despite its winsomeness, was not echoed in her eyes. "Try me now, Uncle, and you will find the story has a different ending."

He wished to God her own story would have a different ending, and prayed, once more, that Bevil's errand to London did not bear fruit.

He glanced at his niece, and she looked up from the board. They exchanged a long, wordless look.

It had been almost six months since Alex Weston had departed his ancestral home. Six months in which no word had come. Six months in which Laura had studiously maintained a calm that could not be penetrated.

He had never seen her cry.

Even when her bulk became unwieldy and her visits to Blakemore had to be halted, he had still not seen her lose her composure. It was a daunting thing, this dignity she maintained. It was as if she were frozen inside, waiting, as though nothing had changed since the day Alex had left.

Nothing had changed, he thought, unless it was Laura. She was now heavy with child, the bulk of her swelling girth hidden by the graceful folds of her wrapper. Her difficulty in climbing the stairs necessitated that she limit her trips to once per day, which is why they now sat in the state bedroom, next to the roaring fire. The snow encrusted fields were fallow now, but they would soon be cultivated again, the steward following Laura's instructions to the letter, just as he had all these long months.

When Alex returned he would find that his home had prospered under her care.

If he returned.

Percival blinked and dismissed the thought immediately. He must. The lack of news meant nothing. It was difficult, if not impossible, for anything but military dispatches to be carried during war. Yet the lack of news, even a letter, was not good.

Where was Alex? It did not occur to him that the same question had been asked by his niece every day for months.

Until it was answered a month ago.

"Lady Weston," the secretary said, "I cannot find the expenditures."

"They are in the cupboard, Wesley. Did the earl not show you where?" They sat in the Eagle Tower, ordering supplies for the upkeep of Heddon Hall. It was a formidable task, and would be made more difficult still if they could not find last year's expenses.

She had carried on her duties as Alex would have wished, ensuring the smooth and tranquil operation of their home, the new cultivation being planned, the new strain of cattle recently purchased from market. She knew that he would have wanted her mind occupied with the details even before she learned of his orders to both his secretary and the steward.

It kept her busy by day, but it did not keep her from thinking at night. Thinking and wondering and, most of all, praying. Sometimes, at night, she would light one lone candle and sit in the great bed in their room and stare at the tapestry of the young knight. For the first time the look in his eyes seemed to have dimension. The eyes were filled with determination, or was it a lurking sense of precognition? Was he going to war, or was he returning from it? Did he, too, murmur those daunting words: duty, honor, courage? Did he leave someone behind as he traveled on his quest?

She missed Alex so dreadfully that if it were not for their child, she would have remained in their rooms until he returned, where the scent of his clothes still lingered with hers, where the echoes of their loving seemed to hang, wraithlike, in the early morning hours.

She missed the way she loved Alex, the sharp, piercing beauty of it. To turn and see his black head bent over a book, to see his forceful strides through the gardens or one of the corridors that made a labyrinth of Heddon Hall, to hear his music from the spinet in the Music Room. To see and feel and experience the instantaneous joy she felt in his presence, to know that she could stretch out her hand and he would be there, solid, warm, and loving her.

She missed him. She had Uncle Bevil and Uncle Percival, and Jane, and all of the staff at Heddon, and her unborn child, but none of them were loved in quite the way she loved Alex. None of them, not even her child, could make her heart pound and her senses sing and her face become wreathed with a broad smile just to be in the same room.

She missed him. She sought refuge in her dreams, when the feeling returned with his presence and her mind conjured him up with such detail that she would awaken and turn and it would be long moments before she realized that, again, it was only her mind's pity upon her soul.

She sought fresh air only because she was forced to, ate correctly only for the son who flourished within her. She did all of the things she was supposed to do because he would wish it of her, but all the time she waited for news of him it was with a sick dread.

She had almost lost him once; she did not know what she would do if she truly lost him now. She tried to focus on the future, to listen to her uncles' coaxing words with hope, but nothing seemed to penetrate that horrible dread that grew each day he was apart from her.

The longer he was away, the more she worried, and none of the activities with which she had filled her day seemed to matter.

She finally moved to the cupboard herself, her girth preventing her fluid movements of a few months before.

Did Alex know that he would be gone so long?

The months were etched in her mind and in her heart and in each change that their child had brought to her body. Their child was almost due and still there was no word from him.

Nothing.

She opened the cupboard, forced herself to think only of the supplies Heddon Hall needed, and retrieved the sheaf of papers from the top shelf. She had not gone through them since Alex had left. Perhaps the missing expenditures were here.

"Those are not the ones, m'lady," the secretary said hastily, attempting to gather them before she could carry them back to the table.

"What are you about, Wesley?" she said, smiling, but managing to gather an armful of the falling papers despite his eager assistance, or lack of it.

She placed them on the table and began to unroll the first of them. Wesley stepped back and sighed. She would not be pleased.

She was more than displeased, as she opened the second map, and then the third. The dispatch, wound within the fourth map, caused a frisson of fear to skitter up her spine. She was not a cartographer, but she knew too well what she was seeing. She had no wish to read something Alex evidently had hidden from view for a reason, but the dispatch taunted her until she pulled it from the agitated secretary's hand and carried it to the fire. It was dated a few months after their wedding, that blissful time when all was right in the world and the only thing she and Alex needed was each other. Or so she had thought. She had difficulty deciphering the elaborate scrolled writing, but she had no trouble decoding the scrawled signature: William Pitt.

So, his fine hand was at the root of Alex's disappearance. Alex's mission, whatever it was, was at Pitt's instigation.

"Leave me, Wesley," she said quietly, and the young secretary took the wisest course and left the room quickly.

She had always prided herself on her ability to grasp facts easily—perhaps it was the fact that she wanted to ignore exactly what she'd found that made this process so much more difficult. It took her an hour before she began to realize the significance of the letters. Alex had been working with Pitt.

Pitt had warned of Spain's emergence into the war, and his warning had become fact. Despite Uncle Bevil's reluctance to discuss it, she had learned that Spain had allied itself with France, and the two powers were battling against England for control of the Mediterranean.

She gripped her hands carefully together, and then forced

herself to unclench her fingers. She placed each one of the rolled scrolls into the small fireplace at the end of the room and watched as the fire consumed them. The last, and most damning, letter from Pitt was consigned just as quickly.

Twenty-six

Portugal

He wished to God he was somewhere else.

He wished he could hear something other than the sound of the wind whirling around his head, smashing waves over the forecastle and flooding the decks. The three poop lanterns were lit against the encroaching darkness. The night and the storm were in tandem, and in an hour, maybe two, it would be difficult to tell one shadow from another.

His ship, the *Dominance,* had a keel length of over a hundred and fifty feet, a depth of twenty-two feet, and a tonnage of over two thousand pounds, but she was being tossed on the waves like a child's toy thrown into a shallow pond.

He had ordered a ration of beer and rum an hour earlier, and the men had cheered and jostled each other. An hour before that they had shuffled across the rain-swept deck and jokingly accepted their cold dinner. The Royal Navy still believed that men fought better on a full stomach and with a good tot of rum flowing through their veins.

He had not been able to eat, waving away one of his young lieutenants when he'd offered to stand watch. Years of being on the sea, in foul weather and fair, had left him with a cast-iron constitution, but at this moment it was showing more signs of rust than iron.

He was, he thought irately, getting too damn old for this. Leave the fighting of battles to the younger men, with glory-filled dreams and a belief in their own immortality. He knew, more than any of them, just how damn mortal they all were. If they were blind enough to miss the mask, they sure as hell couldn't miss the glove, which stretched out and pointed to the horizon, where the Spanish ships lay waiting like pregnant geese.

He remained on deck, peering through the gloom for sight of Saunders's ship. The *Dominance* was to follow Saunders into battle, again providing gun support from their cannon.

He wanted, dear God, to be anywhere but here, and if that be cowardice, then let the world call him coward. His honor had been defended by the loss of an eye and a ruined face; he needed no more proof than that.

He was, whether he wanted to be or not, responsible for the fate of more than a hundred men. He felt the weight of this command with every fiber of his body. He had not wanted to be pressed into service. He was only a courier, and a reluctant one at that. He had no choice, however, when influenza decimated Saunders's meager supply of war-seasoned captains. Two days following his arrival, he'd found himself commanding again, a warship aligned at the forefront of the English might assembled against the combined forces of the French and the Spanish.

It was a strange sense of déjà vu he felt, standing on the bridge and watching as they approached the battle. The men had quieted, as one, their voices dropping to a whisper. The wind was more audible at that moment than the men who'd taken up their posts, their stance alert and unmoving. It was an odd quiet, the presage of battle, when each man's thoughts turned to those he left behind, to loved ones and loved things. It was at this moment that all of their longing would be for those in their thoughts and not for the next five minutes. Battle lust had been replaced by something much more powerful: the longing for safe and familiar territory, for the smell of soup bubbling in a kitchen, the touch of a mother's, sister's, lover's hand, shared laughter. Home and hearth. The two took on an added significance now, more than any looming battle. So it had been at Quiberon Bay. So it was now.

This engagement was different from Quiberon Bay in several vital aspects, however. Although an unseasonable storm pounded the decks, it was no gale, and the whistling winds would not blow them off course and onto dangerous shoals. Nor were their orders insane but touched with brilliance. No, their orders were absurdly simple: dismast the Spanish ships; inflict as much damage to the Spanish fleet as possible. Beat them to a pulp, if they could, but effect some destruction.

He was a stranger to this crew, but the existence of his mask and his gloved hand, not to mention the whispers and rumors about his exploits at Quiberon Bay, had given him an aura of invincibility. These men relished battle as his former crew had not, yet with good reason. His former crew had known they were engaged in suicide; this crew felt lucky. He hoped to God it was a justified emotion—he had more reason than ever before to want to stay alive.

His wife and his child.

He had been gone for months already, and by the rumors he'd heard his absence from home would be protracted. He could not possibly hope to return before Laura was brought to bed with his child. God keep her safe, he whispered, and it was not the first time he had uttered that prayer.

His good hand clenched against the railing and he wondered, as they prepared to follow Saunders, if William Pitt had known he was throwing him into combat again. And, if he had known, would it have made any difference to his plan? He'd discovered, in the year he'd spent at the Admiralty, that while it was easy to care about England, it was sometimes difficult to care about the fate of one Englishman. Larger numbers, bigger thoughts, abstract notions, those were what the brilliant minds who controlled the Navy thought of, not one man's wish and fervent desire to hold his wife's hand while she labored to bear his child.

He was grateful that he did not bear the responsibility for

battle strategy; his only command was to perform this day's duty and keep himself safe. To avoid heroics and behave with some sense and protect himself so that he could shortly return to Heddon Hall. To be a good English citizen and a damn good Navy officer, and then hie himself home. It seemed an easy enough task.

The boom of cannon fire cut through his thoughts. Their guns' range was only four hundred feet, and most of the balls and rough chunks of anti-sail iron fell impotently into the sea. He stayed his gunners from firing again until they were closer. He would not waste precious shot on a useless and grandiose show of force.

As their distance narrowed, pieces of iron shot from the Spanish fusillade began to gouge huge holes in their own sails and rain down on the exposed deck. He strolled the upper gun deck, refusing either to seek shelter or return fire. His gunners turned and looked at him, but he would not give the order yet. Their broadsides would be devastating, but only at close range.

He walked briskly between the forecastle and the gun decks, barking out orders that were instantly obeyed. He shouted the order to his lieutenant, and they lumbered against the wind, following the *Royal George*. He lowered his arm, giving the sign to the gunners to begin firing, and they shot double broadsides into a Spanish ship at a range of twenty yards. The cannon belched fire and fury, and at the first explosion he flinched but soon became accustomed to the booming cannonade. He aligned himself with another one of their ships, the *Bretony,* flanking them, and aimed another fusillade against the enemy.

They followed the *Royal George* into the heart of the battle, until they were almost within shouting distance of the Spanish ships. They were blanketed by the thick, greasy smoke from their cannon and the wind that whipped the waves across their decks.

He watched with incredulity as the *Royal George* foundered, hit broadside by the fury of at least a hundred cannon. His own gunners reacted swiftly, pummeling the ship that dared to sink a flagship of His Majesty's Navy.

They fired, relentlessly, but the *Royal George* sank within fifty feet of their port side. Some of his men went over the side, perched on rope ladders to try and save as many men as they could: the rest were occupied with battling the Spanish frigate that loomed closer.

The smoke clouded his sight, filling his nostrils.

He saw nothing for a moment, but then the horrifying sight of another ship, as fully armed as his, as fully manned, running toward them, sails outstretched, their gunners not bothering to prime empty cannon, only holding steady with implacable, unified, and grim determination as their captain made to ram the *Dominance*.

They collided, a jarring screech of splintering wood and shrieking metal combined with the screams of men who had been trapped belowdecks.

He screamed himself, a harsh bellow of rage, a cry of disbelief, a roaring oath to God himself that He would permit this. Not now, he thought, with a frantic and desperate wish to live. Not now, dear God, no!

After that he saw nothing.

Twenty-seven

Bevil Blake did not relish this duty.

He wished, with a somewhat fervent and baseless hope, that he would, miraculously, be spared this task. That God Himself would take this onerous burden from him, or failing that, someone else would volunteer, or insist, or bodily restrain him from performing this most terrible of chores. Percival neither moved nor spoke.

Alex, himself, had thoughtfully and carefully prepared against this day; Bevil had followed his instructions with precision, five futile days in London followed by a few more in transit to Pitt's country estate. Finally, the knowledge he both sought and dreaded was released to him by the power of the former minister's name. Now his feet echoed his reluctance as he slowly pulled himself up the blushed granite steps of Heddon Hall. Had he not dreaded this day ever since his niece's husband left to do Pitt's bidding?

Beside him stood Percival, his face as pale as he knew his own must be. But he did not need a looking glass; the tremulous nature of his own palsied hand was proof enough of his suddenly aged appearance and his palpable dread.

"Dear God, Bevil," his brother said, in a voice that was as low and as halting as his own would have been had he been able to speak. "What will happen to her? She loved him so."

Bevil only nodded. Words did not cross his closed throat easily, and what words he would have been able to utter to answer his brother, had that bodily function been his to command, would have been silly or pointless. How did he tell her? Now that was a question worth answering. His words would be harsh and cruel and without explanation. And what would she say? He forced his mind to veer from the thought of Laura's reaction. It would not make his responsibility of the next few moments any easier. It would not make his duty any less difficult.

"We will help her," Bevil finally said, the long-held responsibility of being the head of their small family pushing the words past his thickened throat. "We are her family. We will be there to help her, any way we can." There was no other choice. But, dear God, must it be him? And who better? he counseled himself sternly. Would you want her to hear the words from a disinterested messenger?

He knew, at heart, that he did not. Since they had been appointed guardians for their brother's child she had bedeviled him and plagued him unmercifully, had indulged in childish tantrums, had disobeyed her nurse and challenged his mind. Yet she had also gifted him with love, and until she had he had never felt the lack of it.

Just as his life had changed from the moment she had put her little hand trustingly into his, he knew that her life from this day forward would never be the same. And, although he wished to be with her and give her what comfort he could, he cringed at the thought that it must be his words to bring her such pain, his voice that must tell the tale.

Simons opened the door and instantly noted the dark suits, the mourning bands, and the sad, resolute eyes of both men. He stepped back, bowed lightly, and then carefully and quickly shuttered his expression against the knowledge of the news they wordlessly conveyed.

There would be no more laughter at Heddon Hall, he thought with sorrow. He realized, at that moment, that he had grown used to the countess, to her smiles. There was not one person in the whole of Heddon Hall who was immune to her charm, not one servant who was not asked about or enveloped in the warmth and love that seemed to surround the smiling countess, even in the dark days since the earl had left his home.

Before that, when the earl was in residence, it had been because of the young countess that the maids no longer scurried belowstairs rather than see the earl. It was common knowledge that the earl's bride did not cower through Heddon Hall—she raced through corridors with laughter lighting her way. She did not fear the masked lord of Cardiff, so surely he was not such a frightful being, after all. Did the halls not ring with their laughter? Did the flushed faces of the more curious maids not bear witness to their loving, even in the light of a sunny day? Did his masked face not bear a smile more readily than a frown?

Heddon Hall had known only joy since she'd first walked through the kitchen garden, not fear. But after this day there would be no more laughter, no shocked looks, no whispering wonder, no bawdy jokes about the earl, his loving bride, and their exploits. No more prayers whispered near attic eaves for the safe passage of the earl back to his ancestral home. No more bobbing curtsy's and flushed faces of maids who insisted upon speaking out of turn in order to banish that look of sorrow on her face. "He'll be back soon, mum." And how many times had he heard that?

"Is your mistress about?" Bevil asked, but the slight inclination of Simons's head focused his attention to the head of the stairs, where his niece stood, frozen, her gaze enveloping the two men.

The uncles wore black mourning bands upon their sleeves. Uncle Bevil stared stonily up at her, and she remembered that expression well. She had been ten years old, but the years had not dimmed her recollection of that look. Of that empathy shining deeply in his black eyes. Of that tightness around his mouth.

"Your parents have died, my child," he had said then, his voice raspy but not without kindness, "but I would have you know that you are not alone in the world. You have me, and your Uncle Percival, now, and we will attempt, in our masculine manner, to make up for your loss."

As he would now. As he would try. Now. The knowledge of the words unspoken, hanging in the air between them, made her clutch the banister tight with one hand. The other went to her belly, and the swift, noticeable kick of her child.

She did not move, nor did she speak, but the look strung between them like the tightest, most painful wire told her all she ever needed or wanted to know. She closed her eyes against the pain of that sudden, lancing knowledge, and swayed. Bevil mounted the steps quickly. He had almost reached her when she seemed to crumple, the movement agonizingly slow and yet so swift that he could do nothing. He had almost brushed her hand when she drooped beyond his reach and fell.

Down the forty-eight steps of Heddon Hall, to land, like a broken bird, at their foot.

She was young and survived the fall with only a broken leg and countless bruises. It was to be deemed a miracle, when the time had come to think of miracles and not of sadness.

Because she was young, she would heal and recover.

Her child would not.

The grinding pain in her abdomen finally roused her. That, and the shouting and the screams from Jane and the little maid, Mary, who saw the blood and the still, fallen figure of her mistress and promptly went into hysterics.

It was not enough, however, for her to remain conscious, as the pain seemed to lance through her like a sword, steel-tipped and wickedly sharp. She gasped as Percival hauled her into his arms and carried her quickly up the steps, past the

238 *Karen Ranney*

doors of the state bedroom, and onto the bed where generations of Westons had been born.

She would have screamed with the agony of it had nature not mercifully blackened the room with a deep and impenetrable fog.

Twenty-eight

"I want to see him," Laura said softly, the words seeming to come from far away. Jane brushed the sweaty tendrils of hair back from her forehead and wished that she had remained unaware of what was happening. They'd no time to fetch the midwife; they had done what they could in those frantic moments.

It had not been enough.

The tiny fifth Earl of Cardiff had not drawn a breath.

Jane blinked back her own tears and wished that Laura would cry.

" 'Tis not a wise idea, love," she crooned, but Laura looked up at her with dry eyes that held an implacable will.

"If you do not bring him to me," she said, her voice faint but fierce, "I will get up and find where they have taken him."

"Do you truly want this?" Percival Blake asked softly from the doorway, interrupting Jane's futile response. It was evident that his niece knew her mind. It was also quite evident that she would not rest until she'd seen her son.

"Please, Uncle, bring him here." She winced only once against the pillow and then levied herself upright, pushing Jane away when her nurse would have laid her gently back against the sheets. The cavernous bed, which had seen generations of Westons approaching both life and death, offered no comfort. The silken sheets that had replaced her birthing bed were already wrinkled and wet where they clung to her drenched skin. The intricately carved headboard pressed a pattern of blooming roses against the softness of her back. She did not feel the discomfort.

Percival looked at her for just a moment before he did as she requested. She had been through too much, his little Laura. He returned in a few moments and lay the tiny bundle in her arms, tightly wrapped in his winding sheet. She looked up at her uncle and her nurse.

"Please," she said, her voice husky, "leave me alone. Just for a little while."

It was Percival Blake who silenced Jane's protestations and pulled her from the room.

She slowly unwrapped the swaddling from her son and bared him in the privacy and silence of the room. He lay on her lap, tiny but perfectly formed.

She smoothed her fingers along his velvety, pale skin, now cold and tinted slightly blue. He appeared almost like a china doll, a porcelain replica of a child who should have lived.

She examined the little half-moons of his tiny fingertips, which lay slack against her palms. This hand should have grasped his father's fingers in a chubby grip, learned how to play with a ball, or to grasp a quill, or hold the reins of his very own pony.

His little feet were perfect, with toes identical to his father's, long and tapering. These tiny feet should have raced through the gardens of Blakemore, feeling the soft brush of grass upon their soles and through the corridors of Heddon Hall and to the magical places she longed to show him.

His long lashes, as raven hued as his father's, drooped softly against a cool white cheek. His eyes should have seen the wonders of the world they could have given him. They should have spied the doves perched in their square little house, and the rolling hills that surrounded Heddon, his birthright, the magic of a summer twilight, the glaring purity of a winter morning.

The tufts of hair upon his tiny, perfectly formed head were

also black, and she stroked its silky softness, combing it into place with trembling fingers. He might have had his father's mannerism of constantly brushing it back with an impatient hand, or he might have peered from tousled locks, uncaring that his view was obscured.

His little bow lips were parted slightly, as if seeking nourishment. He should have cried lustily for mother's milk, learned to speak, to excitedly explain the treasures he had found, to voice his wishes to the three muses.

She felt the stiffness of his flesh as she held him close to her aching breasts. She wanted desperately to heat his cold skin with the warmth of her own. She wanted to feed him life itself from her straining, milk-engorged breasts. Her face contorted into a terrible grimace of pain as she bent and kissed his tiny, cold brow, so smooth and perfectly formed. She arched her head back and stared at the ceiling as if to find God residing above her. She wanted to scream, but instead she merely held this small, precious child close to her heart and wished him alive.

A few moments later she wrapped him again, kissing each soft little spot that she veiled in the shroud before shielding it from the world forever. She left his face free and held him tight against aching breasts that would never be used to suckle this tiny blessed son. Gently, softly, she rocked him within her arms as if to comfort him before his long journey.

She had feared that he would be prone to illness as a baby, had worried about her ability to be a good mother, had anticipated his birth with Alex beside her, comforting her, congratulating her upon her courage, perhaps teasing her in the aftermath.

She had dreamed of his antics as a boy, his excitement about life at Heddon Hall. She had seen him as a child, a boy, a young man.

She had wanted him to be happy and important to himself and to the world.

She had never imagined him dead.

Perhaps, in some distant, far-off place he would meet his father, and Alex would instantly know his son. Perhaps, even now, his little soul was white-winged and escorted to God's side by tiny cherubic angels with the faces of children, who touched his soul as tenderly as she supported his small body.

She hummed to him then, a tuneless melody, a gentle song to speed him to his rest. She hugged him tightly, wishing never to let him go, wishing that he was alive, and his father was alive, or if that could not be, then please, God, please, let her die with them both.

Percival drew him gently from her arms. Her beloved burden was relinquished with reluctance. She looked up at him, her face a ravaged mask of grief.

He was not ashamed of the tears that flowed down his own cheeks, although his niece's eyes remained dry, as if all the sorrow in the world was mirrored by those wide and pain-filled eyes.

"He is so small," she said, her voice barely able to speak the words. "And it is so dark, there."

He did not think he had ever seen such grief before.

He bowed his head for a moment. When he lifted it he softly covered the face of the infant.

She bit her raw lips and again held her arms out for her son. She could not bear the idea of him being enclosed in that great mausoleum with tons of marble surrounding him.

Forever dark.

"It is time, my dear," he said, helpless in the face of her anguish.

Her injuries, and the fact that she had just given birth, would prevent her from attending the small ceremony. Later, when she could rise again from her bed, she would go to the place where they put him. Perhaps, soon, they would bring Alex's beloved body back, and she would lay him beside the son he'd never seen.

She clutched the pillow to her aching breasts and felt her bruised flesh as though it belonged to another. Her physical discomfort only mimicked, in a faint and paltry way, the pain inside her soul.

Her only prayer was a fervent and passionate appeal for death.

But she did not cry.

Twenty-nine

Percival saw her from a distance, knew she had gone to stand before the plaque again. Dawn or dusk, winter or springtime, he had found her there, her fingers tracing the lines of the monument she had erected for Alex, as if that gesture would somehow bring him back. She was no closer to accepting his death now than she had been then.

She heard his footsteps and for a blissful, fleeting moment allowed herself to pretend. She shut her eyes and, until he spoke, it was as if it was true and real. And possible. But he was not Alex.

"I knew I would find you here," he said, his voice not betraying his deep concern. Instead, he forced himself to assume a cheerfulness he did not feel.

"Will it always hurt this badly?" she said, turning and asking the question almost accusingly. She expected a pat reply, sweet and gratuitous and iced with trite phrasing. Instead, she was surprised by his honesty. It seemed that no one else trusted her with the truth lately.

"Yes," he said softly, "it will. Time will blunt the edges of the pain, but you will always feel the loss."

She held out her hand and he gripped it with his own, and then stood beside her, staring at the marker for Alex.

"The years should give you peace," he continued somberly, "but instead they give you finality. A finality that brings its own pain."

"You have never lied to me, have you, Uncle?"

"Should I? These are only truths you will learn yourself. Why should I now mouth platitudes to you?"

"How does one bear it?"

He extended one arm and held her close. How could he tell her that he didn't know? How could he tell her that each person's journey through the valley of the shadow of death was as intimate and personal as each soul's identity? How could he explain that the only way to truly live again was to see death as it was, and endure its essence in life with resigned acceptance?

"By simply living one day at a time," he finally said. "By breathing in and breathing out. By waking and sleeping and eating when necessary. By existing until existence becomes life again. That is all I know."

"I cannot think of living without him," she said softly, and he stood with her, staring over her head at the distant fields of Heddon, at the tall towers that were a landmark for miles around.

"He knew that he might not return," he said, and smiled softly when she turned to him.

"How?"

"How did he know?"

"No. How did he die?"

It was the first time she'd asked. She had accepted the news with a dry-eyed stoicism that he thought strangely disconcerting.

"He was aboard the *Royal George,* my dear. The ship was sunk and all hands presumed killed."

She did not flinch, nor did her shadowed green eyes veer from his.

"Duty," she whispered. "Honor. Courage."

She closed her eyes, and he hoped she would cry.

It was not natural, this inward grief.

He had seen her sob with anguish when Alex had left when she was fourteen. He had seen her tears of joy when he had returned. Yet when he had talked with her in those months since Alex had departed, tears had not come to her eyes.

She had not cried since he left.

"You have had a great love, Laura," he said, his own voice low and emotion-tinged. "Few people can boast of that. One day the perfect year you shared will be golden in your memory. You will be able to thank God that you were blessed with such love. You will know the value of that perfect year, but right now your pain is too great to be anything but angry."

"I am not angry, Uncle," she said, drawing away from him slowly. "I think I would welcome that. I feel nothing at all. Nothing except a great, dark void."

"You will," he said, tipping her face up so that he could see her wide, dry eyes.

"There will come a time when you feel angry at Alex for dying and leaving you. Angry at the world because the world goes on as if he hadn't existed at all. Angry because the world should mourn him, but it doesn't even stop to recognize his passing."

"And when that day comes?"

"Then you will begin to heal. Not to be the same person you were, but a different one. One who accepts."

"I never want to accept his death, Uncle Percival," she said, turning and facing the marker once more.

"It is inevitable," he said, speaking behind her, in the most gentle and resigned of tones. "You may not wish to, but you will."

He was right, Uncle Percival. She wished he had not been, but his words came back to her in full force as the days lumbered by, with nothing to mark their passage but the setting of the sun and the rising of it.

Her life had narrowed to become a hollow, leaden thing, peopled by memories that would not leave her.

Alex, dressed in his uniform, with buttons gleaming, and his hair shining brilliant blue-black in the sun. Alex, with his proud Apollo's face, displaying his rank to the little girl who had worshipped him for so long, not noticing her paleness or her sudden look of fear.

Alex, striding manfully through the gardens as a young man home from school, sent to fetch the young neighbor who would bedevil his life and being pounced upon by a gamine in hoop skirts who would not let him go despite his calling to her nurse, his father, and his brother to rescue him.

Alex, who sat and read to her a new play, who portrayed the villain with leering looks and low, husky voice, while she chuckled and played the virgin caught unaware.

Alex, who grumbled when his hand hurt and did not let her see, until she took it between her own palms and kissed and massaged it to make the pain go away.

Alex, who pretended to be a pirate and made slow, teasing love to her even though she begged for release. Who whispered decadent, wonderful things as she writhed beneath him, or above him, depending upon their mood.

Alex, who carried bouquets of roses to her at midnight, who raided the larder with her and finally taught her how to light a match with patience and skill and many soft kisses.

She could not bear to see the tapestry hanging in their bedroom and had Simons return it to where it had always hung in one of the smaller rooms.

Her own knight, her own Apollo, was never coming back.

She stared at the clean-shaven visage of the young knight once more and saw that, truly, it did not resemble her Alex. Alex's hair was longer, white-winged. There was a sense of elegance to Alex that was missing in the knight, who stood before his destrier and readied himself for war. The smile playing about his lips took on a new meaning. It held only sadness for her now, a slight, self-deprecating smile. Had this knight, too, known that he would not return from the war his king had summoned him to?

For the first time she wondered about the unseen hands that had crafted this likeness with such love. Who had done so, she mused, and thought about the sparkling tears resting on the face of a sweetheart, or a wife, as she slowly eased the threads into place.

The fabric of her own tapestry, as she had childishly and innocently explained to Alex one night, had frayed about the edges, its outlines blurred, its threads abruptly severed. She could not see the picture of it but knew that if she could, it would resemble the most dreary of existences, the most horrible of griefs.

She hated Heddon Hall and its memories, and she hated the kind, concerned looks of those people who loved her. They forced her to be brave and she did not wish to be brave. She wanted to go screaming down the silent corridors and curse God for what he'd done, but she found herself curiously lacking even the impetus for anger at the Creator. She wanted to curse the king and Pitt and all politicians who would make war and sacrifice lives that were not linked to their own. She wanted to curse the apathy of men who sat in closed rooms and sent beloved fathers and sons and husbands and brothers to die so that a few more pieces upon a chessboard would be moved to the right side or the left. Yet even that anger was denied her.

Uncle Bevil and Jane had said that her life should go on, but she wondered why. They said such idiotic things as to what Alex would want. How would they know what Alex would want? He wanted to laugh and be loved and hold her within his arms. He wanted sunshine and bright days, or warm, cheery fires when the weather was damp. He wanted passion and music. He wanted rice pudding and cherry cordial and the mellow taste of brandy. He wanted to hold his child, his future sons and daughters.

Alex had wanted to live.

They watched her with patient eyes and bade her to go about her life again. Why could they not understand that her life had been Alex?

She wanted to be away from those prying eyes that attempted, albeit kindly, to unlock that part of her soul where her grief was kept. They did not truly wish that cavern of darkness opened.

Why should she go about her life again?

She hated herself because she was still alive, and each day brought no imminent presence of death. She hated herself because she breathed, and he did not.

Her heart beat in her chest, and his was still.

Her skin felt cold and wet and warm and his felt nothing.

Her feet touched the ground with reluctant steps and his would never stand upon the soil of Heddon Hall again.

Her eyes could see and his were closed and sightless.

Her fingers touched the keys of the spinet and his would never again play a beautiful melody, or touch her skin, or lift a quill, or a thousand things that fingers might do.

She hated Heddon Hall, because it was his and he was everywhere within it and she could no more escape his presence than she could her own skin.

She suddenly wanted to be far away from this place and the concerned looks and wringing hands of her loved ones. She wanted to be away from the fresh outlines of pristine white marble in the mausoleum. She wanted to be away from the stairs, which she laboriously climbed each day, holding stiffly onto the railing, pausing at the top of them, as if she had seen her child alive upon that step.

She wanted to be away from this place of love and laughter, memories and moments of pure joy.

Into another world. Where she would not be little Laura, loved and loving.

Where she could be as brittle as she felt, and as cold.

Where she could be like the ice that formed upon the walls of the mausoleum that housed her child.

Where she could be as cold as the sea that held her husband's body in a wet and timeless embrace.

* * *

"I do not think she will go to London, Bevil," Percival protested, "not if the king himself commands her."

"Something must be done, though. It has been a year, and she is no closer to shedding her grief than the day it happened."

"Did you really expect her to?" Percival eyed his brother with some surprise.

"No, perhaps not," he admitted, "but I find myself unable to bear her silent grief. If she would but cry, then perhaps some healing could be done."

"She loved him all her life, Bevil. How do you get over a love like that?" If her child had lived, Percival thought, she might have been able to. Now, he did not know if she would ever break through that inflexible shell she had erected around herself.

The difference was in her eyes—eyes that looked dead inside. She moved when she should move and lay down at night when she should sleep and ate when she was forced to and performed like a person, but Percival had the strangest notion that she was not there.

"We must try, Percival. That is a certainty. We must, at least, try. Can you not persuade her to come to London with us? She might do that, for you."

"I do not think she will, Bevil, but I will ask it of her."

She wanted most to die, but if the fates would not allow her that small gift, then she would do the next best thing.

She would go away.

It was a dream that made her agree to Uncle Percival's coaxing. A terrible dream filled with grief and the sound of sobs she could not voice during the day.

"Do you not think he looks like me?" Alex said, smiling. He leaned over and combed back the downy hair from his son's forehead with tender fingers.

"Of course," she said, softly smiling at the two of them.

Her son nursed at her breast, tugging at the nipple with insistence and infant tyranny. His father placed one long finger upon his son's cheek, as if in encouragement of his greed.

"He is a handsome child, is he not?" he asked proudly, allowing his finger to stray across to the fullness of her breast.

"He is," she agreed, finishing and levering the baby to her shoulder. When he burped she lifted his face to hers and kissed him proudly on the forehead.

"Is he not talented?" Alex asked with a broad smile.

She chuckled and held him out for his father. Alex took his son with ease, holding up his solid bulk in the air, proudly surveying him and then lowering him gently.

His son beat his tiny fist against the broad expanse of his father's chest, gripped his chest hairs gleefully between clenched fingers, and gurgled into his face.

Alex laughed, and kissed his soft, warm cheek.

He walked with him perched on his shoulder, treading an invisible path from the conservatory to the bed and back again. Their son showed no inclination for sleep, but seemed to enjoy his father's game. His baby sounds echoed in the silence of their chamber; his parents' smiles reflected their pride in his accomplishments.

As she watched both father and son, a mist rose slowly from the floor, obscuring the multipatterned carpet, dimming the area with its gray, smoky tinge. She reached out one hand for Alex, in sudden fear and awful premonition. He turned and shook his head tenderly at her, his eyes meeting hers. It seemed his gaze mirrored the same awful chasm of grief that was opening up inside her.

Their son rested his head against his father's chest in sweet and innocent trust. Alex smiled, a smile to remember for eternity, a sweet, cherishing smile that carried with it love and memories. Passion and tenderness were there, coupled with a despair and a sadness so real that the tears choked the breath from her chest and blurred her vision.

He stepped back into the cloud that swirled upwards, jealous fingers of mist that veiled his strong legs and grew thicker with each passing, fleeting moment. It swept past his chest, licked at the strong arms that gently held their child, tormented her by enveloping his beloved face from her gaze.

"Alex?" Her arms reached out for her son and her husband and they turned one last time before being encased in the thick white fog.

Alex said nothing as he disappeared, the two of them fading into the mist, shrouded as if they had never been.

Forever gone.

She screamed and flailed upright in the bed.

"Hush," Jane said, stroking back her hair. She would have held her like a child had Laura not scrambled from the bed, shaking.

By sheer force of will she began to relax, even though her heart still beat as furiously as it had in the throes of the dream, and her harsh breathing marred the quiet of the room. She clasped her arms around herself tightly, as if she would splinter into a thousand pieces if she did not, and stared at the darkened conservatory. Only shadows and dark shapes met her eyes, as if he was still standing there, hidden in the darkness, holding their child, watching her.

She knew what it meant. She felt it to the marrow of her bones.

She was going to live for a long, long time.

And they had said good-bye.

Thirty

London

" 'When a man is tired of London, he is tired of life,' "
Laura murmured softly. Her neighbor, a matron with powdered hair and enough jewels to rival those of the crown,
turned slowly and appraised her with interest.

The young woman beside her was attired in a subdued
lavender dress. It shouted of modesty in a sea of billowing,
multicolored fashions worn more with the object of exposing
the female form than adequately covering it. Nor was her hair
powdered, as was the fashion. Instead, her auburn tresses
stood out like a beacon of color amid the starchy locks of
the whirling dancers.

It was, however, the look in her eyes that caught her attention. Deep green eyes that were wide and shadow-filled,
as if their view was not the merriment to be found below the
landing upon which they stood. Instead, their gaze seemed to
be focused upon some distant apparition, some memory that
brought great joy and, at the same time, great pain.

Dorothea, Duchess of Buthe, was very much intrigued.

Laura had drunk just enough wine to blur the evening, just
enough to make it possible to attend the wedding of one of
her former classmates, just enough not to care about what
she said, or to whom.

"And are you simply tired of London, my dear, or life

itself?" The Duchess of Buthe looked carefully at her companion, standing on the broad terrace watching the dancers.

Laura turned, surprised. She had not realized that her comment would be overheard, let alone elicit a response, and one so close to the mark.

The other woman's eyes were kind and so was the gloved hand she laid impulsively on Laura's arm.

"Do not begrudge them their play," she said, her eyes glancing over the expanse of gaudily attired dancers. "Their time will come, as it must to us all. Some sooner than others."

Laura smiled briefly, a quick, polite smile. She would have moved away except for the unyielding hand upon her arm.

"I begrudge them nothing," Laura finally said, the bitter twist to her lips the only clue to her thoughts. She waved the bewigged footman away when he would have proffered more wine.

The woman beside her remained silent, continuing to study her with interest and not a little curiosity. Laura was acutely conscious of the other woman's perusal and damned the whispered words that had come so impulsively to her lips.

She was here only because she had depleted her store of excuses, because the uncles were so worried about her that she had promised to emerge from the town house in order to quell their hovering despair. She was here only because Lucy had been a friend during those interminable years at Mrs. Wolcraft's Academy.

"An, but you do," came the soft-spoken words from the woman at her side. She turned, looked at her neighbor, and, for an instant, met the other's kind and peering blue eyes. Just for an instant, until their intent examination seemed to probe beyond the careful, rigid facade she had erected for this night.

"You begrudge them their laughter and their carefree nature and their sleep at night, restful in their beds. You may even begrudge them the fact that they share love."

"I had not realized my boredom was so apparent," Laura said coolly.

The Duchess of Buthe looked at the lovely young woman beside her and smiled sadly.

"It is not your boredom that shows, my dear, it is your intolerance. The young ones ask you to dance and they do not realize that you long for someone else to hold you in his arms. You listen to the music, but your ears are attuned to the step of one who no longer walks this earth. You see the glitter and yet you long only for the sight of one beloved face."

Laura turned carefully shielded eyes to her neighbor. Erecting a facade around her emotions was a trait she had mastered after so many months. "I have no idea what you mean," she said carefully, as if the words had been rehearsed many times.

"These gatherings are useful for more than perpetuating the marriage mart, my dear. Their sheer numbers offer anonymity. You may speak freely with me and I will not think the less of you for it." Her eyes drifted to the dancers again and she was taken back to another time, another room such as this, many, many years ago. She fumbled in her reticule for a moment and pulled out her card. She smiled softly and pressed it into the young woman's hand. Laura accepted it with reluctance and a studiously polite smile.

"Perhaps it is more tolerable to speak of truth in the company of strangers."

"Perhaps it is wiser not to speak at all," Laura said simply, and wondered at this strange conversation. In the space of only a few moments her aristocratic companion had discerned feelings she had never voiced to another living soul.

"Ah, but with a stranger you can speak of things that otherwise are too filled with anguish to voice," the other woman said, as if divining her thoughts. "Yes," the duchess said consideringly, assessing the young woman beside her, "perhaps a kindly stranger would do you good."

As she signaled a passing footman, who rushed to summon

her carriage, Laura glanced down at the card in her hand. Her lips twisted in an ironic smile. The Duchess of Buthe, a woman sought-after simply because she was a mystery to the ton. Even she had heard the rumors that abounded about the elusive duchess. She was "a personage," as London nobility would say. A woman whose presence at Lucy's wedding was a social coup.

Laura had barely been able to sit through the vows. She had discovered that she was not as dead inside as she had thought, feeling only a sharp, lancing pain at her friend's radiance.

The groom was handsome and wealthy. He had beamed proudly at the sight of his lovely bride.

She could not help but remember a candlelit chapel, with the sound of the wind soughing against the bricks outside and flickering light gleaming on a black mask. She could not help but remember a tremulous hand that reached out and was encased by two others, one warm and soft, the other gloved.

She should never have come to London. She had been here but a few weeks and she was already tired of it. She had had enough. Enough of this life. Enough of London. She should never have listened to her uncles and remained, long past the time they had returned to Blakemore.

Yet she had not wanted to return to her childhood home. Blakemore was too close. Too close to memories. She had said good-bye to Heddon Hall and known that she could never bear to live there again. She had walked through the Winter Garden, had spoken soft words of farewell to each room, had stood within the confines of the Eagle Tower one last time. Finally, when the coach lumbered up to the main doors, she had told Agnes that she would be there soon and ventured into the courtyard one last time.

She stared up at the three muses, thinking it was a childish thing to wish for things that could never come true. Such a thought did not prevent her from one last entreaty. Do not ever let me be hurt so badly again, she leveled at the first. Curse all that comes between me and some form of content- ment, she commanded the second. Judge me with compas- sion, she pleaded to the third, before turning and leaving the courtyard.

She had left Jane behind at Blakemore, the journey being too arduous for her elderly nurse. Yet that was not the only reason she preferred to have only Agnes as her companion. Jane would always be inexorably intertwined with memories of the last year, and the main reason she was going to London was to leave memories behind.

It had taken them forty hours of travel to reach the out- skirts of London. During that time she had forced herself to look beyond the curtained window of the carriage, despite the fact that she had no real interest in her surroundings.

The turnpike roads, supposed to be the most modern of thoroughfares, were in reality only granite cobbles that badly shook the framework of her carriage. Yet even the constant shaking could not penetrate the careful shell she had erected around herself, a shell that grew thicker and more impene- trable the closer they came to London.

She had not wanted to spend another night in a deplorable inn and had hired another driver to spell Wallace. Due to the fact that they rarely visited London, the Blakes had never purchased a home there. She had no choice but to settle re- luctantly into the Weston town house.

It was a decision she had regretted immediately.

Elaine's presence, while not pleasant, had at least prevented the need for an additional chaperone. Yet it was not long before she realized she needed a chaperone from Elaine, to protect her reputation from the other woman's scandalous be- havior. She was, of course, a widow; a wealthy widow who was not subjected to the rules of society as fiercely as she had been when she had been unwed. Yet Elaine's behavior constantly tested the limits of society's tolerance, threatening scandal to the Weston name. Not only would Laura not tolerate that, but she grew to despise each day she was forced to share accommodations with the dowager countess.

Elaine saw nothing untoward about holding bawdy conversations in the drawing room of the town house, amusing her admirers with language that, quite frankly, shocked her, or laughing over practical jokes that seemed boorish to Laura's ears.

Because Beau Nash had bet that he could, a man ran himself to death to make the journey from Bath to London and back within a specified time, whereupon Nash took up a collection for the widow. Elaine seemed to think the whole thing a delightful tale, and regaled her listeners with the story nearly every night. Laura could only turn and walk away.

She had sought peace and all she found was the cacophony that was London.

There was not a moment in the day that was not filled with noise, the constant prattle of her companions, the tinkling laughter of merry voices, the raucous sound of street vendors, the clatter of well-shod hooves or the constant tinny whine of coach wheels upon the cobblestones.

Even the night was not devoid of sound, as the drunken laughter of young men vied with the rumble of carriages and the calls of the watch. Laura wondered about the morals of the ton. There seemed to be an endless parade of drunken nobility in her house, and a few times she had met one of Elaine's night-time visitors on the way out the door in the morning.

The city was explored tentatively, in the company of Agnes, her fierce little maid, and Peter, the tall, stalwart footman. There were no sights in London to excite Laura's enthusiasm. They stood on the newly opened Westminster Bridge and scanned the Thames. Its gleaming surface was so completely covered with small vessels, barges, boats, and ferries that it seemed a forest of masts sat upon the water. It looked as though all of the ships of the world were assembled on the Thames.

All of the ships in the world except the one she most wanted to see.

She journeyed to the Haymarket Theatre, saw the animals at the Tower of London, and listened to the sounds of Handel being performed for the king at the Covent Opera House. Alex would have thrilled at the performances. She simply sat there and scanned the royal box, not bothering to mask her look of contempt as she stared at the homely king, whose machinations had, however unwittingly, meant her husband's death. She strolled in Kensington Gardens, those magnificent acres that Queen Caroline had insisted upon being replanned and expanded. The blooming flowers did not spark her admiration, nor did the elegantly made paths prompt her envy.

Nothing did.

She was not impressed with London, but there were things about the great city and its society that managed to penetrate the fog surrounding her—with shock and disbelief.

She was called upon by sycophants who had learned of her fortune, her widowed state, and her arrival in London through a reliable and swift communication system. She was shocked to discover that she was considered a marital prize. The idea of being solicited and courted for her wealth held almost as much aversion for her as the thought of replacing Alex.

He could never be replaced.

She did not want lies and promises, or flattery and fawning attention. What she truly wanted was to be left alone. She sorted her invitations the easiest way, by having Agnes toss them into the trash without being opened.

She wanted no part of society. Although a countess, she had little use for titled nobility. She would have loved and married Alex if he had remained the earl's second son; his title had held little appeal. Such an emotion was tantamount to heresy in the aristocratic axis of London.

The ton was an enclave of wealthy, bored aristocrats, who existed on two levels: one, sparkling and to be admired; the second, less fastidious and not at all discriminating in important matters. The first impression she had was similar to the great public gardens at Ranelagh or Vauxhall, full of flowers and terraced lawns and promising entertainment. One only had to look beyond the glitter to find that it was neither entertaining nor as beautiful as a first impression might make of it.

In one way, she got her wish; London was nothing like Heddon Hall or Blakemore. London existed with its own rules, its own standards. Everything seemed a little too bizarre, a little too much.

Every woman in London seemed to insist upon greased, powdered, and curled hair, which was dressed high over enormous cushions. Imitation fruit, flowers, and even carefully constructed wooden ships towered in these confections. Enormous mobcaps, which made their heads appear too large for their bodies, had to be worn during the day to protect these artistic endeavors. In order to sleep, the whole contraption must be wrapped in lengths of muslin, and when traveling in sedan chairs the roof had to remain open.

Most of the women in this room wore a face patch, as if dissatisfied with the adornment nature provided. Dresses, although worn over smaller hoops, seemed to expose more than they covered. The low decolletage revealed the brown tint of nipples just below the ruching of bodices. Elaine called her a country widgeon when she refused to lower her own neckline.

The clothes were rich and colorful and expensive. Elaine had paid over sixty-four guineas for a rich dress of crimson velvet embroidered with gold. She could have fed the entire staff at Heddon Hall for a month on such an amount.

Laura had spent enough time in London. The anniversary of her widowhood had been passed at Heddon Hall. She marked each week in London with the same solitary, invisible jot upon a mental calendar.

Where, though, did one go for peace? Where in the world

was there a sanctuary from memories, from dreams? In the end the geography didn't matter. She carried her torment with her.

Laura tucked the card into her reticule, signaled for her carriage, and left the glittering spectacle behind her. When she returned to the town house she wearily climbed the stairs to her room. She opened the drawer of her dresser and extracted her most precious of possessions, placing it gently upon her pillow. She undressed with Agnes's help, divesting herself of the stiff brocade gown with relief. When she had donned her cotton nightdress she bid Agnes good night and extinguished the candles. Only then did she lay down in the bed and open the little music box that had been her wedding present, listening to the sound of each note sparkling in the darkness and the silence of her room.

She hummed a little, following the tune, and it did not matter. There was no one around to criticize her toneless melody.

Thirty-one

"I understand you are an heiress, my dear," the Duchess of Buthe said pointedly.

Laura looked at her, surprised. Money was never discussed in London—the assumption being that if you did not have it, no one wished to know. If you did, then everyone knew it anyway.

It was not the first thing about the duchess that surprised her.

Agnes had roused her at early hour, frantically explaining that the duchess had come to call. Laura had glanced at the ormolu clock and then at the little maid, thinking that morning was a strange time for unsolicited calls. No one ever made calls before noon.

She had spent most of the night in uneasy slumber, her dreams causing her to wake abruptly several times. Yet even this occurrence was not rare; she had learned over the past year that a full night's sleep was as elusive as peace itself.

She knew better than to wish for one night of oblivion. He was there each time she slept, despite her fatigue, despite her weariness, despite the fervent prayers she whispered as she cautiously entered her bed. He had been there every day of her life; he would be there as long as she lived.

She had thought that she had learned to live without Alex, but her mind and his memory laughed at her in the shadows. In those hours just before dawn he came, would always come, showing her not only that would she never be free of him, but reminding her of what she had lost.

As if she could ever forget.

Agnes told her that Elaine had not returned to the town house the night before, and rather than be insufferably rude Laura had no choice but to dress quickly and join her guest in the small drawing room. Jacobs had, thankfully, already supplied tea and morning cakes. She gratefully sank down upon the gold brocade settee, poured her tea, and wondered what the duchess wanted.

It could not be to ascertain the size of her purse. The Buthe fortune was rumored to rival any in the kingdom.

"I have found that it is always good to be well-flushed in such matters," the duchess said cryptically, and sipped her tea from the delicate Spode china. "I myself am fortunate enough to be well-provided-for, but it seems that one needs more and more money as time goes along."

Laura said nothing, simply continued to look at her guest with a puzzled frown between her brows.

"What matters would that be?" she asked, when it was evident that the duchess was not going to speak further.

"Have you any engagements for this morning?" the duchess said instead, placing her cup gently down upon the tray.

Laura wanted nothing more than a little solitude. She had the daunting feeling, however, that the Duchess of Buthe was not going to allow such mundane matters as preference or previous engagements to interrupt her own plans.

"I had arranged for a quiet morning," she said carefully.

Just as she suspected, the older woman did not take the hint.

"Good, then if you will come with me, I have something to show you." She stood, walked to the door, and summoned Jacobs with the royal demeanor of a queen. She gathered Laura's walking cloak, gently propelling her by one arm, and before she knew it Laura was being escorted to the duchess's carriage, a plain black landau with nothing about it to indicate her rank or her wealth. Her initial conclusion was correct—the Duchess of Buthe would not allow any protestations to sway her.

"Of course," the duchess said, "you know that I have gathered who you are. Otherwise I would not have come to call. Your husband was too young to have perished in the service of his country, but death knows no discrimination. He was instrumental in preventing Spain from achieving dominance in Portugal, but I suppose you know that."

The insensitivity of other people was one thing Laura could not seem to tolerate. She saw nothing precious or charming about small blackamoors being made into glorified pets; she did not wish to laugh at others whose infirmities made them the brunt of cruel jokes; she would not take tea with the lunatics at Bedlam and then regale a fascinated audience with stories of drooling and contained madness.

Evidently, the Duchess of Buthe was just as insensitive, probing at a subject that she had vowed would never become fodder for common gossip.

"I do not wish to discuss my husband," Laura said stonily, glancing away from the curious eyes of the older woman. Despite the duchess's regal air of command, there were certain things she would never discuss. Alex was chief among them.

"Of course you don't, my dear. However, it would be unconscionably rude of me not to acknowledge your great loss. I find it strangely disconcerting not to speak of death, as if by ignoring it grief will not exist. You will mourn your husband's passing whether I speak of it or not, Lady Weston. I mention it to satisfy my own sensibilities, if not yours."

She looked at the duchess and then down at her folded hands.

"When my Harry passed away," the duchess continued stubbornly, her voice taking on a less militant and more somber tone, "no one in our acquaintance mentioned his name. It was as if he had never existed at all. He lived and he drew breath and he made a difference to this world. Not speaking of him did not suddenly make him not real."

"Perhaps they did not know what to say," Laura suggested.

"All they need to have done, child, is simply say 'I am sorry; I acknowledge your grief.' They did not even do that. Which is why I acknowledge yours. I will not say something as silly as, 'You are young and you will get over it.' Or, 'Time heals all wounds.' Sometimes you never get over it, and time does nothing but make the ache worse."

The words were so similar to Uncle Percival's that Laura found her interest piqued. She glanced over at the indomitable duchess, who smiled gently at her in response.

She studied her abductor with barely veiled curiosity.

The duchess was dressed in a dark blue silk walking dress that fell in ruffles to her toes, her bodice covered by a white lace fichu. From her elbow, where her tight sleeves ended, flowed white lace cuffs that ended just above her wrists. Upon her head, instead of the customary wig, sat a small hat tilted rakishly over tight black curls that were conspicuously devoid of powder.

Another surprising thing about the Duchess of Buthe's attire was the sight of the shoes peeking from beneath her skirts. They were leather, dyed a brilliant yellow.

Laura's own simple lavender dress seemed even more plain in comparison. Yet fashion, like so many other things in her life, simply did not interest her. She had reluctantly donned her half-mourning colors only because of the uncles, not because the color pleased her, or because her grief was less now than it had been a year before. She had worn black with the same apathy. It was, after all, only a color. Granted, it served a place in society to indicate her status to the world. Yet she wondered if she truly needed outer raiment to convey her condition. It was there in her eyes and in her total disinterest in her environment, other people, or her circumstances in life.

"Is that how it is with you, then?" she asked, wondering

if the older woman's grief had granted her an affinity for others'. If that was true, then the Duchess of Buthe was a rare person, indeed.

The duchess's smile did not dim, but it seemed suddenly filled with poignant memories.

"That is how it is with me," she said gently. "At first, time did nothing more than bring anniversaries and birthdays. Nor did I find that growing older was much of a cure. I was never the same person I had been while loving Harry. I changed, and became someone else. Not of my own choosing, perhaps, but because it simply happened that way. My life is rich in some aspects now, but it will never be the same. I will never be the same."

Laura did not answer her, but stared out at the broad promenade of shops they passed, and the wide streets and avenues. That was how she felt, as though the true person she had been had been consumed in a flame and she was no longer going to be that person any more.

She had always been defined by her love for Alex. Since she was a child her love for him had been a source of amusement for others and deep comfort for herself. For most of her life, since her earliest memories, Alex had been a part of her life. There always, on the fringes, as if waiting for the propitious moment to step in and occupy the place she had set aside for him.

She found, though, that a curious thing had happened since his death. She discovered a void inside herself, a place that had once been occupied by Alex, dreams of Alex, thoughts of Alex, wishes about and for Alex, that was now as dark and as empty as a moonlit moor.

She had built her life upon a foundation of sand and it had shifted beneath her feet. She had given up all her energies and hopes and dreams to that love, and now she had nothing left.

Would she change like the duchess? Would she find, as

Uncle Percival said, something to live for? She prayed for it
to be true, but she did not see how.

As they traveled east, their surroundings grew pro-
gressively more bleak; the houses were built closer together
and the stench from the running sewers was enough to cause
her to hold her lace handkerchief against her nose.

The carriage finally halted before a broad brick building,
its color undecipherable beneath its soot-covered exterior. She
mutely followed the duchess inside the building and stood
for a moment to allow her eyes to adjust to the gloom.

She preferred the darkness.

A woman of indeterminate age, clothed in garments that
would have been better suited to the dust bin, shuffled out
of the crowd within. The duchess calmly stood her ground
and waited until the crone was close enough that the odor
from her unwashed flesh drifted over to Laura. Her hair was
tucked beneath a soiled kerchief, her nose was as broad and
beaked as the most terrible witch in a childhood fairy tale,
and when she grinned, the parody of a smile revealed rotted
stumps of teeth.

She cackled, it seemed to Laura, and her accent was so
thick that she could barely understand her words. She motioned to the women standing behind her, who thrust several
children forward. They were as dirty as the adults, open sores
upon some of their faces, grime obliterating their fair, almost
translucent complexions. She looked at the duchess, who
calmly gathered the children close to her, questioned the old
hag sharply, and then waved to Laura to follow her.

It was not just curiosity that impelled Laura to quickly
follow the duchess. It was an almost hysterical wish to be
gone from this place.

"Do you have anything to do today, child?" the duchess
asked her calmly, as if the footman was not handing the children up beside them. She, herself, was the recipient of a
young girl, no more than four years old, who clung to her
skirts with one hand and thrust her thumb into her mouth

with the other. Her hair was lank and dull, hanging about her shoulders in dirty array. Her face was streaked with dirt, and the tiny tracks of childish tears were the only signs of cleanliness about the child. The other two children were in no better shape. They were all thin, all bore the signs of constant hunger, all wore frightened, dazed looks.

Laura did not know what to think about the duchess's actions. She had seen money exchange hands; the eager, grasping hands of the old woman with her stained and fingerless gloves eagerly reaching for the coins the duchess calmly placed in her palm.

"Have you hired them?" Laura finally asked, when it was evident that the duchess was not going to explain further. It was not beyond reason to think that they were to go into service. Normally, however, the young children treated as pets in large establishments were oddities of some sort, the small of stature, the blackamoors.

"I have just bought them," the duchess said calmly, to Laura's obvious shock.

"That was the parish poorhouse, my dear," the duchess said in a matter of fact way. "These children have no parents, nor kin to call their own. They are English orphans, set upon the streets to make their way. It takes little to convince the overseer to sell them for a few coins."

"Sell them?" Laura repeated, horrified.

"Yes, my dear. You think of it as slavery, do you not? It is, pure and simple. Oh, they would say that the coins gained from the purchase go for the feeding of those remaining, but like as not the money will find no further destination than the pocket of the wardress."

"And the law allows this to happen?"

"It is the law that has supported such a system. Did you know, for example, that vagrants are to be returned to the place of their birth? Or that parishes are allowed to group themselves together for the purposes of providing workhouses and permitted, by law, to farm out children for whatever purpose?"

"Does no one fight for reform?"

"There are many people who do, my dear," the duchess said kindly. "But there still are deplorable customs that continue despite our interference or perhaps," she said wryly, "because of it. Wages are still, in some occupations, doled out at taverns on Saturday night, to encourage drunkenness. Is it any wonder that many working men return home penniless, but happy for one night?"

"It sounds not unlike some of the tales of the nobility I have heard," Laura said, thinking of Elaine's many bawdy stories.

"Poverty and nobility are not that far apart," the duchess said, with no attempt at humor. "Both the poor and the noble attempt, in some fashion, to forget their state."

"I do not understand, though," Laura said, the duchess's earlier question now making sense. "There does not seem to be enough money in the world to alleviate such a situation."

"It is very difficult to change society, Lady Weston," the duchess said with a small smile. "The very least we can do is change one life here and there. That is why I have purchased these children." She smiled brightly and calmly removed the clutching fingers of one of the urchins from her reticule.

At Laura's look, she chuckled. "The children will be given a chance at a better life, my dear. Our orphanages are far better than their current existence. Fresh air, sunshine, a chance to grow healthy and learn a trade, that's what we wish for them."

"And for me? What are your plans for me?"

"To make it possible," the Duchess of Buthe said with a broad smile. "Why, to make it possible, my dear."

The Duchess of Buthe was as much a martinet as Mrs. Wolcraft had been.

Yet if Laura blessed any education during that long day it was not the one she had received at the Academy, or even knowledge gleaned from her uncles', but the strict routine imposed upon her during those days in the kitchens of Heddon Hall.

She asked herself at least ten times why she did not leave, but it seemed there was never the right time to suggest that the duchess's carriage return her home.

There were too many children to wash, too many greasy, lice-infected little heads to soak with vinegar, too many limbs that had never been cleaned of their accumulated filth since the day they had been born. There were too many bowls to fill and too many little mouths upturned like hungry little birds.

She had been tossed an apron, white and starched, and she had pinned it on the bodice of her walking dress. By the afternoon, it was no longer starched and it had lost its pristine whiteness.

It was, instead, spotted with the soup that one of the boys had not been able to stomach.

"Gin," the duchess had replied, when a little boy no more than six had retched upon the floor and continued to heave dryly. She had returned with a mug of gin laced with milk, which she coaxed the child to drink. "We have to wean them from it," she explained, her eyes watching the child carefully, "as much as it was mother's milk. Some were fed it as babies."

One horror seemed heaped upon another as the day passed. The duchess did not stop, even when she slowly closed the eyes of one child and nodded to the footman to remove the shrunken body. "We cannot save them all," she said, escorting Laura to another room. "But we can try," she added, the glint in her eye an odd combination of stubbornness and regret.

Each of the broad, sunny rooms was lined with cots. Upon each cot lay a child in the process of healing, she was told. There seemed to be no end to them as they stretched through the building. It was only a way station of sorts, the more critical to be laid to rest, with more dignity and love than they had known in their short lives. The others, the ones who clung stubbornly to life, were again moved, either to small orphanages set up in the heart of London or, hopefully, to new establishments in the country.

"That is where you come in, my dear," the duchess said, finally resting in the corner of one room where an improvised kitchen had been arranged. "We need funds. I have been as diligent as others whom you have not seen, but we will forever need money. Money to build foundling homes. Money to treat the sickest. Money to alleviate some of the grinding poverty."

"All you need have done was ask," Laura said abruptly, welcoming the irritation. It was a welcome change to the hopelessness she had felt for the last few hours. She did not, however, like being treated as though she had been feeling sorry for herself. This entire day had been an object lesson, she suspected, carefully choreographed by the Duchess of Buthe. "I support many worthwhile charities," she said with a touch of anger.

She did not care that propriety demanded that she be polite. She was tired of being polite. At this moment, with her hair in disarray and her feet being pinched by tight boots not designed for standing for hours and her hands chapped and red, she was angry.

The duchess looked at her, at the glint in her eyes, which was the only expression she had seen there, and smiled softly.

"Do you think I've brought you here as an act of penance?"

"Isn't your aim to make me realize that I should be grateful for all that I have?" Laura bit her lips and turned away.

"Your pain will continue whether you assist these poor unfortunates or not, Laura. It will not matter to you whether you live through your anguish in the confines of your comfortable home, or working here beside those of us who wish to make a difference. It will not matter to you, but it might matter to them," the duchess said.

"Why do you do this?"

The duchess looked around the room. Some of the children were playing together at the end of their cots, some lay as still as if death were looming above them, their eyes staring up at the ceiling, their limbs stretched out upon the cleanest sheets they'd ever known.

"I come from Whitechapel," she said slowly and smiled at Laura's look of surprise. "I was raised by the cook of a great house. Later I became a maid there. Still later, I was married to the owner of that place, a kinder and more wonderful man than I'd ever known. The boundaries of society are still mutable, my dear, but I cannot, in all good conscience, forget my roots."

"There seems so much to be done," Laura said, looking at her own reddened hands and remembering those days at Heddon when she had felt so inept. She felt the same now.

"You may think that your efforts will not make a difference, but a gentle touch to a child who has never felt anything but abuse or scorn does make a difference. A smile to a child who has seen only hatred, a kind word to one who has heard only curses, those things make a small change, true, but a change nonetheless."

Looking into the wise eyes of the Duchess of Buthe, Laura recognized that the older woman was stubborn, inflexible, and quite surely always got what she wanted. She realized something else about the duchess as they stood there in wordless silence, each taking the other's measure; there was pain in her eyes, also, but she had transformed it into an almost infinite capacity for giving.

"What do you want me to do?" she said finally.

The duchess laughed merrily, and several of the children looked at her in surprise. It was quite possible, Laura thought, that they had never heard the sound before.

"I want some of your money, my dear," the duchess said,

with the candor of one who has long sought funds for charitable pursuits, "but I also need your willing heart and strong hands."

Laura did not have any trouble falling asleep that night. She brushed by the shocked servants, wearily climbed the stairs, and slept in her stained and wrinkled dress.

She did not, for once, have dreams of Alex.

Thirty-two

Elaine Weston eased closer to her recumbent lover until their skin was only a scant inch apart, until the hair on his chest seemed to anticipate her, rising up and seeking out her flesh. She chuckled richly, her voice a husky counterpart to the arch of an eyebrow and the teasing look in her eyes. Two sharpened nails stole over that awesome chest, walking like a tiny headless person over corded muscles and skin the color of butternut leather, until she came to the crest of a budded nipple, surrounded by hair bleached golden by both heredity and nature. Without turning her gaze from his intent blue eyes, she grazed the nipple with first the pad of one finger and then the sharpened nail, smiling when her victim hissed a breath and would have prevented her next movement. She did not allow herself to be restrained, but pinched the skin between those two fingers, leaned down, and gently licked the swollen flesh prior to scraping it with her teeth.

"Damn you," he said, but it was more a comment than a curse. She chuckled as she plucked a hair between the two fingers and pulled on it slowly. It was a test of sorts, but the man beneath her neither blinked nor flinched, even as the hair's root was separated from his chest.

"Bitch," he remarked calmly as he reached for her pubis, where he grasped a handful of hair and tugged. She only smiled, and his fingers found a different torture than pulling her hair out by the roots.

"Shall I punish you?" he asked, wondering if she knew

that there were places in London that would love to incorporate her into their membership. Places with dark names and even darker practices.

Elaine Weston was an inventive playmate, her lithe little body tightly packaged into an instrument of sex, but she was amoral as a cat and about as loyal.

She laughed at his comment, arching closer so that his suddenly intrusive fingers would find their target more easily.

He moved his fingers again, until she moaned and moved closer, until there was nothing between his moist flesh and hers. He extended his left arm under her neck, turning her face to his by the simple act of flattening his palm against her ear. She could not move, but it was long seconds before she realized how effectively she was trapped within his embrace.

"Don't ever try to really hurt me, Elaine," he said; the voice was so smooth, so emotionless, that it made her shiver. "If you do," he said, his smile more wicked than she had ever dreamed a smile could be, "I will have to retaliate." He leaned closer, until his breath whispered against her open mouth. His tongue licked her lips slowly, tauntingly. Her mouth opened wider, but he did not take advantage of that wordless invitation.

Instead, he reared back and watched her. It was a calculating look, for all that he was fully aroused. She could feel him against her thigh, the hugeness of him, the engorged flesh of this stallion man who could make her want him with a word, a gesture, a look. She whimpered in her need as his fingers still caressed her, but he would not kiss her, nor would he touch her breasts. He knew how much she liked his rough play, the threat of violence shimmering just beneath the thin veneer of civilized man. He knew she liked his lips on her and then his teeth, and the threat those white, even teeth promised. But still, he would not touch her.

When she would have inched closer he moved even farther away, his delving, exploring fingers the only sign of his interest. He raised his arm effortlessly, forcing her gaze on the odd and shameful tableau being played out between her legs. She could not help but look, even if he had not compelled her to. And if that muscular arm were not supporting her and that smile not lurking around that beautiful mouth of his, she still would not have been able to tear her eyes away.

His golden hand was not subtle; three fingers probed and encouraged and separated slick, wet flesh until a honeyed warmth flowered from her without pretense. Every few seconds those fingers would stop and she would separate her legs wider in wordless supplication, until she could not expand herself any farther for him. His hand glistened from her wetness, his fingers still probed, the little nubbin that was normally hidden now throbbed and wept and thrust up between folds of flesh in anticipation of yet another bold touch.

"Look, my little witch princess," he said softly, as his hand deserted her to caress his own flesh. He handled himself harshly, his eyes open wide, not slitted with need or desire. If he felt desire in that moment, she thought, it was for his own touch, his own flesh. He gripped himself fiercely, rode his own hand, arched his hips up and toward that punishing hand until she could have wept with the loss.

"Do not ever think you're the master here," he said, controlled in this act as he was in everything else. "Do you understand, Elaine?" She would have begged, but she knew better than to do that, or this game would be played again and again until she finally acquiesced. Until she was as docile as he wished her to be.

"Understand?" he demanded again, and when she nodded and whimpered the word he allowed himself to climax, pearled fluid spreading across her belly.

"If you are a good little girl, my dear," he said, still composed despite the force of his ejaculation, "I'll let you do that the next time." He upended her chin with one finger and lightly touched her lips with his tongue. "Would you like that?" When she whimpered again, the Honorable James Watkins levered himself up from the crumpled sheets.

He did not like to remain in bed after having sex, even this kind of sex, without the sheets being changed first. His fastidiousness was just another facet of his personality that the dowager countess did not understand, he thought, as he waited for her outcry at his abandonment. She surprised him, however, and said nothing, even as she lay sprawled in the middle of the bed, legs spread wide open, the flush of her arousal still pinking her cheeks, her eyes lambent and wanting.

"It is a pity you are so poor," she said. It was not quite a pout, not quite an accusation, but he flinched nonetheless.

"It is a pity you're such a whore," he said in return. The smile on her face did not dim.

"Have you no thought of marriage?"

"To you, my dear? I fear I shall have to pass." Hell's gates open wide could hold no more terror than the thought of wedded bliss to the dowager countess. Within an hour of his marriage he would be prime cuckold material.

"To the Countess of Cardiff," she said, not put off by his cruel words. In fact, his total disdain for her was just one of the reasons she desired him so. She was tired of swooning, fawning boys. The Honorable James Watkins was a man.

"Your daughter? How inventive of you, my dear," he said as he thrust his shirt inside the waistband of his trousers. His smile was wolfish as he watched the flush of arousal being replaced by the red of rage.

"I am hardly old enough to be her mother, James," she said, irritated, not realizing that it is very difficult to look the part of outraged nobility while being naked, spread out across wrinkled sheets. He grinned, and she shot him a dark look, but even that was tantamount to a puppy playing with a spider. A poisonous spider.

"Very well," he said, "why the Countess of Cardiff?"

"She is young, reasonably attractive, available, and quite, quite wealthy."

"Your paragon of virtue is also newly widowed."

"It has been almost two years. Enough time to wed again."

"Why me?" he asked, walking slowly toward the bed, wondering if she knew that, instead of a beguiling picture of lust, Elaine looked more like a well-used doxy at the end of a busy evening. He smiled, and she misinterpreted that smile, artfully stretching in front of him, in the mistaken notion that having had a taste he would want the entire sweetmeat. He, on the other hand, had quite enough for one sitting, thank you.

"Why not you?" she purred, opening herself up more for his gaze. His shuttered eyes focused instead on her blue eyes, filled with gleeful malice. "You would have control over all the wonderful Weston money, be close enough to visit from time to time, and have the opportunity to be generous to your relatives."

"I'm assuming you do not speak of my family moldering in Cornwall," he said sardonically. "How could I fail to be generous to such a helpful stepmama, is that your game? Tell me, what will prevail upon the Cool Countess to enter into wedded bliss again? And to such an impecunious soul as I? As an earl's widow, she could do so much better."

"By scandal, dearest," Elaine said, smiling. "Lady Weston has an absolute aversion to casting aspersions upon the Weston name. Compromise the chit, darling, and the plan is foolproof."

It was an indication of how low he'd fallen in the scheme of things that the Honorable James Watkins actually gave credence to the idea.

For about ten seconds.

He was not a marital prize. True, he possessed the symmetry of features and form that had been demanded by sculptors since Roman times; high cheekbones, jutting chin, aquiline nose. His eyes were a clear blue, the artless blue of a newborn babe, the blue of an early opened delphinium, the blue of a frigid brook fed by melting ice. The golden curls adorning his well-proportioned head in artless array provoked envy from debutantes and their mamas alike. He was tall, broad-shouldered, and lean-hipped.

Yet none of his physical attributes could compensate for his lack of that greatest of all requirements for polite society—money. Being without funds, or wealthy, diseased relatives, his only hope of being rescued from his penurious state was fickle luck at the gaming tables or matrimony. Luck had deserted him of late, to the extent that his entrance into one of his favorite clubs was accompanied by a sinking feeling not unlike that a captain might feel embarking on a long and uncertain voyage in a ship of doubtful seaworthiness.

As days and weeks and months of barely surviving in London passed, matrimony began to look less onerous and more necessary. It did not mean, however, that the idea of selling himself to the highest bidder, like a prize bull at auction, was something he accepted with equanimity.

He did not present well.

Most of the matrimonial mothers did not like James Watkins. Oh, at first they were charmed, gravitating effortlessly to his captivating smile, golden good looks, exquisite tailoring, and faultless manners. The transition from besotted to chary normally took less than five minutes, the blooming awareness in the mamas' eyes like a petal fresh opened in the morning's sun.

This metamorphosis was due to another characteristic that James lacked, in abundance. He had no desire whatsoever to be seen as kind. And, should he accidentally evince such an errant emotion, he immediately quelled its existence, to the point that he was seen by the ton as exactly what he most wished to appear—cold, brittle, and just a little dangerous. There was a glint in his magnificent blue eyes that promised heaven and a glimpse of hell, a rakish twist to his lips that hinted at societal restraint but guaranteed recklessness. His laugh challenged the ennui of the ton; his words insulted their values. In fact, everything about him, those very characteristics that threatened these protective mamas, challenged, entranced, and fascinated the Dowager Countess of Cardiff.

She lusted after him, yet it was not only the pleasures of the flesh she sought, but a feeling of acceptance by him. A feeling, despite all its intricacies and convoluted logic, another person might confess as love. Elaine saw it as no such thing. James did not swear undying affection; there was more contempt than fondness in his eyes when viewing her. He was not swayed by threats, coaxing, or sexual blackmail. He was the most supremely autonomous man she'd ever met, and it was because of this potpourri of emotions that she was willing to do anything in the world for him, including placing her lover in Laura Weston's bed. She would even tolerate him being married to that loathsome chit if it meant he would always be available.

In addition, there was all that lovely money to consider. She had grown as tired as he of having to worry about the reduced state of her finances. It was only a matter of time until she had to resort to begging from Laura. Although she'd done many things in her life, she vowed that would never be one of them.

James, however, was having nothing of it.

"No, my dear," he said, donning the rest of his clothes with swift, economical movements. He had, after all, years of practice in both removing his clothes in short order and replacing them just as quickly. "If your countess were a virgin, such an idiotic idea might work. Maybe. But since she's a widow, and a wealthy one at that, the most censure you're likely to produce is a few raised eyebrows. Society is a bit more sophisticated than that."

She raised herself up on one elbow and glared at him. He smiled, thinking that her expression had finally reverted to type. He felt less uncomfortable with Elaine Weston shooting daggers at him than smiling sweetly.

"Then what do you suggest?"

"I suggest you do not interfere in my life, my dear," he

said, his interest captured more by the buttons on his shirt than by her expression.

"She shouldn't have all that lovely money," Elaine said in a soft voice. "It seems a shame that she should have it all."

His laugh was a mixture of amusement and disdain. "And what do you propose to do about that, Elaine? Do you propose to divest her of her fortune?"

"If there was a way," she said simply, meeting his amused look with one totally serious, "that's exactly what I would do."

Thirty-three

The duchess did not take no for an answer, as Laura rightly suspected, and appeared on her doorstep the very next morning. She was needed at the foundling hospital two days a week, she was told, in a tone that brooked absolutely no refusal. Little did the duchess know that Laura gave no thought to protesting. The previous day had not inched by as most of her days had in the past year. The hours had flown, because she was busy and active, imbued with a sense of purpose. A sense of purpose, she realized, which had been lacking in her life for a long time. The day had also bequeathed her an unexpected gift: forgetfulness. She had slept the whole night through without awakening from a dream of Alex.

As the days passed, she scrubbed floors until her knees were red and swollen, hauled buckets of water inside the cavernous building, in return for buckets containing other, less pleasant contents. She cleaned dirty faces swathed in soot and dirty bodies layered with bruises. She combed louse-infected hair and bathed and prodded and pushed and scrubbed. She reheated soup in the huge iron cauldron and fed small stomachs with bowl after bowl of the hearty fare. She sweated over another cauldron, even larger, and assisted with the laundry, until she knew she could not bear to twist one more sheet.

She learned of the two faces of London firsthand. There was squalor and brutality just beyond the gracious squares of stately town homes. There was poverty so prevalent that death was caused by the congested and unsanitary conditions in which London's poor lived. Lice and typhus vied for victims in the houses of those cramped poor. There existed a very real gulf between Southampton House in Bloomsbury and the two-penny lodgings that housed thousands of London's workers.

She stood at the doorway and welcomed the living refuse of London's streets and grew accustomed to the smells of London, the ever-present soot, the sour bite of gin, the stench of unwashed bodies. She would stand and fold her hands, her body still, her eyes closed, her thoughts occasionally straying to another time, another place, another loss, and pray with the others when another child did not survive a vicious beating by a parent or abandonment or starvation or disease, or all of these.

The first time she saw a little boy, nearly two, with coal-black hair and glittering eyes, she nearly turned away. Dixon would have looked the same, but his little body would not have been as gaunt, nor would his flesh be marred by angry-looking bruises. It was the knowledge that this child had never known the love he should have felt, who was never a blessed member of a happy family, that forced her to return, to bury her own pain and bathe him gently and pretend, for just a little while, that the little one was her own child.

Gradually, almost imperceptibly, the children began to penetrate the defenses she had erected around herself. It was not the sights of London, or the glittering society that carefully ignored the squalor just beyond its doorstep.

It was the smiling face of one child that began to make a difference.

One little girl in particular, who would not allow herself to be helped down from the carriage by one of the footmen and who cringed from the touch of Dr. Rutley, sparked something in Laura's heart. The child would only allow Laura to hug her close. After much coaxing she finally told them her name, in a thumb-choked voice, her other hand clutching the towel tight to her emaciated and bruised little body. It was Laura's arms she held tight, like a baby bird whose frail wings had fallen from its body. Laura could believe little Gilly was birdlike—as she hefted the child in her arms, her weight was no more substantial than the hollow bones of a baby sparrow.

Sometimes, she despaired of ever treating such a case with equanimity. When she said as much to Dolly her friend's response shocked and then pleased her.

"Bloody feet of Christ, Laura," the Dowager Duchess of Buthe said, forgetting thirty years of careful diction, a suggestion of her Whitechapel antecedents in her speech, "if I thought you'd ever get used to it, I'd never have invited you to become one of us." Her hand encompassed the figures of those who worked stolidly along with them. Dr. Rutley, who reminded her of Uncle Bevil, with his glowering exterior and warm-as-toast heart. Julie Adamson, the daughter of the Earl of Cheswhire, who worked as diligently as Dolly, but who tired quicker than the rest. Probably due, Laura thought, to the fact that she still bore the small scars upon her face from measles and, although lucky to have survived, was slow to regain her strength. Madelaine Hobert was one of their staunchest workers, although her pedigree stemmed from survival, not the ton, in direct opposition to Matthew Pettigrew, a viscount. He was an earnest worker, as diligent and softly spoken as Julie, and on those occasions when great hordes of children were not pouring into the hospital, there was an interested look in his eye when he viewed the shy girl.

There was not time, however, for looks of any sort other than that quick discerning eye that scanned a child's flushed face. There was too much likelihood, in even their cramped and crowded conditions, of disease spreading to allow themselves to relax for even a moment.

There never seemed to be a free minute, and at the close of day, when Laura looked up, the darkness outside prompted Dolly to exclaim about the lateness of the hour. As if, Laura thought smiling, she would have left before the littlest ones had eaten their soup and been tucked into bed. As if darkness were a more reliable clock than the soft, whispered good nights from the children.

Her anger grew in proportion to the abuses she saw. Her eyes sparkled with rage when forced to deal with the wardress of the poor house; her sense of outrage grew with each refusal for change at the highest seat of government. She could not understand how a country that amassed the world's greatest military might could not spend a little of its wealth on the welfare of its tiniest citizens.

She found herself humming to the youngest of the children, who looked up at her clean and smiling face as if she were one of God's angels. She was moved by the slightest gesture. A picture laboriously scrawled upon a bedsheet with a small bit of coal did not cause her to wince and think of laundry. A little girl's smile when she was pronounced free of lice seemed to be the epitome of beauty and filled with infinite promise. She listened to the sound of the healthier children practicing their letters under the strict guidance of a young Lord Hawley and washed dishes with the Duchess of Buthe. She did not notice that her time at the foundling hospital increased from two days a week to four and, finally, from four to six.

She did not notice her own smile, fleeting at first and then evident during most of the day, except on those saddest of occasions when a child did not survive. She did not notice her eagerness to rise in the mornings and be about her duties. She did not notice the looks of others when she dressed in serviceable dresses of cotton and put aside her velvets and brocades. She did not notice that her hair was sometimes unbound and damp tendrils clung to her cheeks, and that the children reached out with grimy hands to see if the flame of her hair was warm, in truth. She did not notice that instead of flinching she warmly accepted hugs and shy kisses bestowed by tiny pursed lips.

She grew adept at returning stolen articles to their rightful owners and noticing which one of the children seemed to have slippery fingers. She gave orders for clothing and could quickly discern which little girl would be pleased with a rose smock and which by a yellow.

When her laughter punctuated the clamor in the crowded room she did not notice that the rare and joyous sound of it caused the others to glance at each other and nod. She did not notice when the Duchess of Buthe began to rely on her more, trust her judgment and solicit her advice.

The young woman who had braved society's displeasure and possible scandal by donning a mobcap and going in search of the only man she'd ever loved was not a prudish miss. The woman who had survived the last two years of grief and despair was tempered by fire, and more than confident of her ability. She also fiercely detested the false mores and social rules of the decadent, inbred society in which she lived.

She was just the sort of person who could convince those in power that England should care for her children.

If she had to visit every single member of the Houses of Lords and Commons in order to do it, she would make someone wake up and notice. She would make someone care.

"Lord Carnahan," she said with some asperity, a few weeks later, "there is a wealth of good works to be done by England. Not the least of which is modifying the poor laws."

"I cannot think, Lady Weston," the portly Lord Carnahan replied, his jowls hanging at the level of his chin and waggling whenever he breathed or spoke, "what would replace them, if they were repealed. There have always been the poor, haven't there?" He looked up at her with confusion in his red-rimmed eyes, their circles so deep and pronounced that for a moment she believed she was listening to a bloodhound given the power of speech. She shook her head as if to clear it and addressed the issue at hand. Namely, funding for a series of orphanages to help house and feed the children abandoned on London's streets.

Lord Carnahan, however, was acting just like the rest of the men to whom she'd paid an impromptu visit. As if a woman's mouth were to be used for kisses only, and not to frame words that needed to be said. And as if her head was an ornamental appendage suitable only for the adornment of a hat. She yearned to tell a few of the unenlightened men that just because she possessed breasts did not mean she also lacked brains, but decided that restraint was more fitting than wit in this instance. She needed their assistance, not their rancor, and a wiser move was to nod and smile, and then do as she pleased.

She was empowered by the poor children she saw every day. Should she never return to the orphanage or the foundling hospital again, she would still see those little faces, all upturned like fragile porcelain made flesh, God's handiwork to be protected and cherished, not farmed out to work for a pence and treated worse than London's scavenging dogs.

Unfortunately, word of her visits meant that only a few of the prestigious members of Parliament were available in their chambers when she came to call; their wives were suspiciously "out" when she left her card at their homes.

She sighed, settled her hat firmly upon her head, and strode from Lord Carnahan's office in a combination of despair and acute irritation. Once outside she breathed deeply, clearing her lungs of the overpowering stench of whiskey that had permeated the good lordship's suite.

There weren't enough nights in a month to give a ball or a rout, or sponsor some sort of entertainment to solicit funds, and although both she and Dolly were wealthy, the need encompassed more than the sum total of both fortunes. No, there was only one course of action, and that was to convince the government to assist in sponsoring orphanages. If that could not be done, at least she might be able to convince them to censor those absurd poor laws, which propagated the dumping of children on London's streets and made it too easy to simply forget the poor or take advantage of them. Most of the victims were under the age of twelve and suffered terribly from the neglect.

If she had to, she would call Pitt out of retirement, and that pithy old gentleman could sponsor her legislation. In fact, that irascible, gout-ridden Machiavellian schemer owed her more than a little legislative derring-do. William Pitt owed her.

The more she thought about it, the more apropos the thought seemed. Let Pitt convince, cajole, use his sleight of hand. She'd never once heard from him following Alex's disappearance and death. Not one sympathy card, not one letter of commiseration. Nothing. William Pitt owed her more than he possibly knew.

And, by God, the debt was going to be paid.

Hester Pitt opened the missive that arrived in that day's post with a curious eye to the feminine hand that had addressed it. There was no question whatsoever that it was feminine; all those sweeping sworls and flowing letters did not suit well her husband's masculine cronies. She waved it back and forth in front of her nose but was unable to detect a scent, nor did the wax seal seem inclined to indicate something indelicate. It was only a crest of some sort. The fact that her husband had correspondence was not a singular thing, but it was indeed odd to receive something not sealed in a diplomatic pouch, or hand delivered from Parliament itself. Therefore, with much trepidation, in case he felt that she had ventured too far in her care of him, Hester Pitt grasped the letter in one hand and her frothy skirts in another, and proceeded to mount the steep stairs that led to her husband's study. When she laid the curious letter upon his desk, near his elbow, he only bent his glance to it once before dismissing it from his concerns. She sighed, knowing that it could sit there for months and he would never be curious enough to open it, and she would never know who the female was who wrote to her husband.

London had eschewed him; England had forgotten him. In a long and happy marriage, only in the last year had Hester Pitt had her husband all to herself. There were no battles to fight, no Parliaments to sway, no insane or germanic king to swear at while wearing a mask of cordial obeisance.

He heard her sigh and smiled, his eyes red-rimmed but filled with fondness as he spied his wife and her barely restrained curiosity. "Do you wish to read it, my dear?" he asked, having seen in a scant second what had taken her a few moments to discern. It was not that she was less adroit at thinking, only that she had less experience at the deciphering of codes and therefore styles, which had led him to his instantaneous conclusion. That yes, this letter was probably written by a female hand, and no, he didn't care if he ever read it.

She smiled at his knowledge of her and reached forward to take the letter, slitting it open with one slim finger, leaning forward to read it beside the glass globe of the candle's chimney. At first she scanned it quickly, then smiled as she read the sender's name. As she read further, she pressed the fingertips of one hand across her mouth, as if by the holding of her lips she could refrain from expressing . . . what, damn it? What did his wife try to hide?

"Well?" he asked, curiously impatient now that he'd seen how absorbed she was in the mysterious letter. "Have I a female admirer, wife, and you refuse to inform me of that fact? Life is speeding by, dear wife; I could use the compliment of another's wistful gaze."

She nearly laughed then and that, if nothing else, empowered him to reach across the desk and gently retake the letter from her, claiming his possession once again.

He slanted her a look only the king and a few indolent subordinates had seen and began to read:

Dear Sir,

Although I'm sure you do not remember our associa-
tion, I will remind you of my husband's name in the
hope that it will again awaken you to his place in your
memory.

Dixon Alexander Weston, the fourth Earl of Cardiff,
was your loyal man, true to a fault, if the fault be leav-
ing his wife and estates behind for England and En-
gland's cause.

I am sure that none has called you to task for his
death, just as I am sure that you sleep with the ease of
a babe. Yet, lest you sleep too soundly, I would beg a
favor on my husband's name and in my husband's mem-
ory, for a cause my husband would find not only just,
but right and proper.

He could not believe that he was being harangued verbally
by someone he had met only once, and that was attired in a
mobcap. No, that was not correct; she had nearly sat on his
feet and made him privy to their most intimate association.
He cleared his throat and continued reading. When he'd
reached the bottom of the letter his eyes widened and his
reaction caused his wife to giggle, placing both hands across
her mouth as if to stifle the noise.

"Good God," William Pitt said as he scanned the words
once more, in the mistaken belief that he had misread them.
"She wants my help, dear Hester," he informed his wife, who
was very familiar with the last sentence.

If I cannot obtain the assistance of someone with your
great abilities, the unbelievable Lady Weston wrote, *I feel it*
only fair to warn you that I have in my possession certain
documents, which, should they be sent to those currently in
power, might constitute interesting reading.

Damn that woman, he thought, recalling his last letter to
the Earl of Cardiff. Dated after he'd resigned, his instructions
to Alex could be construed, by less charitable associates, as
treasonous. If he were ever to come back into power, that

letter must be destroyed. Even the threat of that letter ever seeing the light of day must be eliminated. "Damn woman," he said, shaking with restrained fury. "Damn, damn, damn."

Thirty-four

Heddon Hall

It was time.

The months in London had brought her some measure of peace, and with it, knowledge. She knew she would never again live at Heddon Hall, but Laura wanted to see the grand old house once more. Perhaps it was a trial, but she performed it with the resolute strength she had shown in the two years since word had come of Alex's death. Two years since her own small son had died before being given life. Two years in which all who knew her, with the exception of Uncle Percival, had counseled her to forget her past and go on with living.

As if there was a timetable for grief. One year and the pain is muted. Two and it becomes acceptable. Three, then four, five, was it magically forgotten?

Was loss transmuted to a faint, easily accepted memory after time? If that was so, then she had not followed the timetable at all.

Her loss was as fresh today as it had been on that day two years before.

The only thing that had changed was her. She was young, but she felt as old as the ancients. She was wealthy, but she felt like the poorest beggar. She looked the same, but she felt altered, as though the changes in her life had eaten their way through her soul and must soon appear on her face.

She had read a fairy tale once, in a collection of German stories, about a magic princess who comes upon two children. "I will grant you a choice," she told them, "but you must choose wisely. The first choice is to have a happy childhood, but you must pay for your happiness in your old age. The second is to have a miserable childhood and yet the remainder of your life will be radiant."

The two chose.

The first little girl chose to be happy now, for after all, she was only a child, and to children the future is far away. She was a gloriously happy child until she grew up, lost her home, and was forced to lead a life of poverty, begging for scraps of food.

The second child decided to delay her happiness and chose, instead, a radiant future. She was orphaned and lived in poverty until she became an adult, when she caught the eye of a neighboring prince, fell in love, and lived happily ever after.

The magic princess saw her again, as an old woman upon her death bed, her beautiful and loving family gathered around her, a broad smile upon her lined face. "Why did you choose the second path?" the princess asked the old woman, once a poor child. Most of the children to whom she had given the choice had taken the easiest path of fulfillment now.

"Because," the old woman explained, "I was taught that I must have the worst first, so that I could enjoy the best. 'Tis why I always had to eat my vegetables before I could have my dessert."

Laura realized that she had taken the easiest path, with a childhood filled with mostly sunshine and laughter, brightness and promise. True, she had been orphaned, but because of the uncles she had never really felt the lack.

Now, and for the rest of her life, she would pay for those years of happiness, and for that one shining year in which she had lived so blissfully and so carefree.

She rode the pony cart to the bridge spanning the Wye, just as she had so long before, and dismounted with reluctance. She stood beside the dovecote and listened to the cooing of its inhabitants. There, just over the gentle swell of bridge, was Heddon Hall. Could she actually go back there again? It had been a year since she had left. Only a year. Barely a year. An achingly long year.

She climbed up the bridge and stood for a moment, looking down into the rushing, gurgling water and then, gathering her skirts in her hands and her courage in her heart, she walked up the incline to the Winter Garden.

She was no longer the child who had visited here. She was not quite the bride whose memories overlay each foot of springy turf. She was the widow who knew herself in both those guises and into whose mind poured such a hodgepodge of memories that she was assaulted by them.

"Alex! Alex! No fair! You can't claim a forfeit that way! You cheated!"

"No, Alex, I'm sorry; it's a wonderful fish, but it's too wonderful to eat. Darling, please throw it back."

"Alex, I miss you. Be safe, my love, be safe."

She did not realize that her nails were gouging into her palms until she felt the pain. She bowed her head, took a deep breath, and forced herself to take the path toward the mausoleum. Stopping in the garden, she tore off a solitary pink rose from the bush, and it was this rose that she lay upon the marble shelf that surrounded her baby son. She fingered the chiseled marks still so sharp and clean and new.

She did not stop beside the plaque she had erected for Alex. The pain of that loss hurt too much, and she wanted only numbness now. She wanted to say good-bye to Heddon Hall, but she did not think that she could ever say good-bye to Alex.

Even on those mornings when she was not expected either at the hospital or the orphanage, or when Dolly did not have another errand for her to perform, she filled her hours with activity, so that thoughts of him would not intrude.

Even now, it was too painful.

Since she had been a small child her days had been filled with him, her hours marked by either his presence or his absence. Yet her love was dead. Her husband was dead. He was never coming back. Uncle Percival and Dolly were right. The intervening years had not made the pain easier, it had only reinforced the reality of it. She still turned in the night for comfort, but he wasn't there. He would never, never, never be there again. It was a litany she repeated to herself every day, and yet the words did not make the reality easier to bear.

She entered the great hall and allowed Simons to take her cloak.

"Are you well today, m'lady?" he asked somberly, as if she had just been out for an airing and not been gone a year.

"I am fine, Simons, and you?" she responded, smiling.

"As well as can be expected, m'lady," he said, answering her smile with his own.

"And the staff?"

"Still worthless, m'lady," he said, his lips turned down at the thought of the constant chore of keeping servants at Heddon Hall. None liked the solitude and the recent rumors. Ignorant bumpkins, he thought with a scowl, as if the Earl of Cardiff would haunt his ancestral home.

She looked up the expanse of steep steps that led to the state bedroom and slowly mounted them, keeping her eyes upon those double doors. She did not allow any thought to creep into her mind, no memories, nor voices of ghosts to cloud her vision. She held resolutely to the banister and lifted herself up until she came to the landing.

She slowly opened the doors with the key Simons had slipped into her hand and closed them just as silently, just as carefully. She did not see Simons's worried glance.

She saw nothing but the past whirling up to face her, as if time had gone backward and then was rushing forward in a futile effort to keep up with the present.

"Thank you, Laura, for your passion. For your lovely breasts and these eager tips. Thank you for the gift of wel-

coming me. Thank you for the sweetness of your tongue, and of your lips."

She turned, and the great green bed was still in place, carefully dusted every week, she had no doubt. In the center of the room was the circular table upon which a bowl of roses had once stood as a centerpiece until she and Alex had toppled it in their games.

"Do you want me, Lady Weston?"

"Yes," she said, turning her eyes to meet his mask. *"Always,"* she added with a soft smile.

The door next to the desk led to the dressing room, where the armoire probably still contained a few of Alex's possessions. She did not have the courage to see.

Nor did she open the door, because she would have seen the fold-down tub and the pipe that led to the reservoir upon the roof, and the bath would only bring back memories of their splashing each other like children.

"Stop! Have pity on my ears!"

"You have no pity, or you would not constantly abuse my sensibilities, sir!"

"It is not your sensibilities I wish to abuse, sweet Laura, 'tis your lovely body."

"One song for one tryst?"

"You bargain like a fishwife."

"No, only like a wife."

She walked into the conservatory instead, seeing how lush the plants had grown, how much of the glass they now encompassed. She sat on the chair next to Alex's desk, only for a moment, and then stood abruptly and left the room.

Ghosts lived here. Happy ghosts. Loving ghosts.

She would intrude no longer.

She made a major change, however, that afternoon.

Although she vowed never to return to Heddon even after the uncles moved here, she could not forestall the urge to take the handsome knight from his niche upon the wall and remove him to the Eagle Tower.

Simons helped her hang him upon the wall facing the arched window, and she thanked him and stood surveying their handiwork.

Here is where he should be, where his gaze could stretch out over the vistas that belonged to Heddon Hall. She turned and looked out the window herself, down into the kitchen gardens, remembering when she had come in search of Alex, plotting and planning. How foolish she had been, but oh, how glad she was now that her innocence had fostered such courage.

She allowed her gaze to roam to the hills, half shrouded in morning mist, to the green, sloping terrace that led down to the Wye.

This was Alex's land. It should have been his son's. It should have belonged to generations of Westons, all stretching out until the end of time.

This is what Alex had fought for. The land, and the peace that surrounded it. His duty and sense of responsibility had led him farther than he wished, as her feeling of responsibility toward London's children led her deep into dark alleys and stinking pest holes. His courage was stalwart despite the odds, as the children she nursed each day fought against all of their obstacles and managed to survive. His honor was such that he could not turn his back upon his country when it needed him, any more than she could turn her back on the children who asked for little and expected less.

Duty, courage, honor. She would hear those words and always remember Alex.

Her love, her friend.

There, in that silent morning as she stood in the Eagle Tower, watching as the brave sun's rays dispelled the mist, she finally began to accept the truth, as total and as unchangeable as the sun itself.

It was accepted not with tears or anger or passion.

It was accepted from the heart of one who knows, instinctively, what a great gift has been bestowed. Even if that gift was taken away too quickly, its presence would always linger in her heart, touching her soul with magic and majesty.

"Good-bye, my love," she whispered, and the morning sun tenderly lit the knight's face, touching his far-seeing eyes with a solitary beam, bathing his half-smiling lips with radiance.

It was a final farewell.

Thirty-five

Prussia

It was bad enough that he had a ship shot out from under him, he thought with sheer disgust. To compound that disaster by being captured by the French and allowed to molder in a dank prison ship was a horror that his mind veered from remembering.

To be turned over to one of England's allies, following the Treaty of Paris, was a light of hope, but to be held as hostage was beyond reason!

Dixon Alexander Weston, fourth Earl of Cardiff, prisoner of the French and now an unwilling guest of Frederick of Prussia, was an angry man.

He was damn furious and made his point well known to George III's emissary, a thin and fragile-looking man whose courier duties were due more to his relation by marriage to the secretary of state than because of his abilities as a statesman.

Even now he sat, clutching his leather valise close to his chest, his knees drawn up, feet barely touching the floor, his frame dwarfed in the elaborately scrolled and tufted chair.

Alex looked at him in sheer disgust.

"I don't care what the hell you have to do, man," he said finally, after listening to the man's fawning explanations for nearly fifteen minutes. "Get me out of here!"

He had suffered bodily from his incarceration by the French, and although he was treated with great civility by the

Prussians, he wanted nothing more than to return home. His limp was worse and he had accumulated a few more scars, but they were negligible next to the torment of his soul and the supreme boredom of his mind.

Frederick's own physician had tended to him, making recommendations for rest and recuperation that he had no choice but to follow. That had been over five months ago! Five agonizing months in which he desperately, fervently prayed for freedom each day.

He was well enough to travel—had been as fit as he ever would be—for three months. In fact, he would gladly walk home to England and carry this birdlike emissary on his back if need be.

Damme, he wanted his wife!

Laura. With luck, Laura had not lost faith. With luck, she had not given up hope.

He wanted his wife and his child and he wanted Heddon Hall. Freedom was only a few politicians' speeches away.

He paced in the ornate bedroom that had been graciously offered to him, but the gold-leafed and frescoed interior did not make the room less of a prison. Nor did it diminish the knowledge that two armed guards stood stiffly outside the door and blocked his passage and his freedom.

He stared at the little man sent from England to placate Frederick and wondered how the hell he could possibly accomplish that goal. Frederick had felt betrayed—hell, he had *been* betrayed—by the terms of the Treaty of Paris, and retaliated by confining three of His Majesty's subjects in a childish act. He was not likely to be swayed by the timorous words of a man who looked more like a mouse than a subject of King George.

The little man, who sat hunched over his leather valise and squirmed uncomfortably beneath the intense gaze of the earl, was more than surprised to be told of the presence of English subjects. He was shocked. He frankly had no orders concerning this contingency.

Alex slammed his fist down on the table and did not care when one of the fragile figurines crashed to the floor and shattered into a thousand fragments.

"Can you reach Pitt?" he finally said, his rage fueled by the little man's silence. He handed a letter he had penned with great care and not a little grief, since his spectacles had been lost during the battle. If anyone could get him released from this lavish prison, William Pitt could, whether or not Pitt still was active in politics. England had lost a great statesman when he'd been forced to resign; it had lost a better negotiator. If this birdlike man would allow his letter to be conveyed to Pitt, Alex's chances of being released were suddenly almost favorable. "I've enclosed a letter for my wife, which I would appreciate being left untouched," he said as he turned over the packet to the emissary. He hoped that his carefully blocked letters would at least convey his feelings to Laura.

Dear God, what she must be suffering!

The little man nodded like a wise bird, took the packet and placed it in his diplomatic pouch.

"I will see that he receives it," he said slowly, his voice high-pitched and wheezing. "I will also do what I can, Lord Weston, to see you freed."

"You damn well better do more than that, my friend," Alex said between gritted teeth. "Get me out of here." Why the hell had George sent such an incompetent to placate Frederick? If he were the leader of Prussia, he would be angrier than before, which did not bode well for either his release or the other two Englishmen rumored to be held under Frederick's genteel imprisonment.

The birdlike gnome drew himself up to his tallest height, which barely reached Alex's chest, and fixed a beady stare upon the intransigent earl.

"King George will be apprised, my lord," he said imperiously. "But the King of England does not negotiate under threat, sir."

"Damn it, man, I don't care how the hell he negotiates! Get me home!" Alex finally shouted, and the little man with his leather valise and his coached words scurried from the room with all of the delicacy of a crab.

He turned back to the window. Home; dear God, he wanted home. He wanted the misty, rolling hills of England, the stately, towering edifice of Heddon Hall, the placidity of a life that was not measured by man's cruelty to his fellow man.

Most of all, he wanted his wife. And his child.

He wanted laughter that surrounded his senses and plummeted into his soul and washed it clean. Green eyes that hinted of dense summer forests, or the spring dew upon newly bladed grass. Freckles that were the kisses of fairies, or spots of sun-kissed skin. Lips that curved sweetly into a smile that lifted his heart or were compressed into a daunting expression of displeasure.

He did not notice that his own lips were formed into a tender smile. He wanted a voice like the song of sirens, low and lilting, so that words were enhanced by her speaking them. A mind that craved no limitations and was filled with pockets of trivialities nestled alongside great thoughts. He wanted her quoting at him and beating him at cards. He wanted her singing in a tinny voice, and teasing him with laughter. He wanted peace, forgetfulness, and his wife.

Laura.

He leaned his forehead against the cool window and wished himself home. Home.

William Pitt clutched the wrinkled and torn letter with trembling hands, the messenger's dust-coated figure fading away, the room itself diminishing to obscurity as he read the words written in an almost childish scrawl. He lifted incredulous eyes to the messenger once more and noticed, finally, the livery the poor man was wearing. So, the king had surfaced from his playacting long enough to show some sense.

He had argued vehemently against the Treaty of Paris for three and a half hours, until his throat had grown hoarse and his words faded into echoes, but England, Bute, and King George still deserted Frederick of Prussia. It was, of course, the final straw.

No, *this* was the final straw. He waved the letter in front of the young man unfortunate enough to have been chosen for this particular mission. "Have you lost the letter to his wife, you fool?" he asked, his voice not the brilliant orator's of a few years before, but the tremulous tones of a man growing increasingly more frail and elderly.

"No, sir," the messenger said, having taken the precaution of backing up a step before responding to the irascible minister. "His Majesty decreed that it should be sent directly to the countess. Sir." That last was a hastily appended gesture of respect.

Pitt's wife, a more compassionate soul than he, sent the messenger to the kitchen, where tea and bread was procured before the young man began his long journey back to the palace. His quarrel was with the king, not with his minions. Pitt snorted, hobbling from one end of the room to the other in an awkward gait, for once the pain of his gout-poisoned legs superseded by the anguish of his mind. Damn!

"Is it bad news?" Hester's anxious voice interrupted his pacing.

"Let us say, my dear, that it is only one more sign of how our illustrious monarch had slipped the moorings of a rational mind."

"Is he really mad?"

"I do not know, dear," Pitt said, "if he is simply as stupid as his grandfather or truly mad. I suspect it's the inbreeding. Too damn many generations of it. Cousins marrying cousins, niece wed to uncle. Makes a good English soul shiver to think of it, the perversions these damn Hanoverians can list on their family tree."

His wife's shocked giggle caused him to smile and took his mind momentarily from the pain in his legs. He had rarely, over the years, talked politics with her, but he had been so bored of late that her gentle acceptance of his conversation was something he not only appreciated but had come to crave. She occasionally asked the most probing questions and never acted the part of sycophant.

He wanted to be listened to by men of reason. Or, if that was too much, by God, he wanted some sanity to prevail. But it was too evident, in the fact that he had still not been granted an audience, in the rumors that swirled around him like a tattered cloak, that reason and sanity were *not* going to prevail, that reasonable men with logical minds had departed the corridors of the palace like rats starved of a food source.

England deserved better. His country, the birthplace of legends, of gallant warriors, the home of burly farmers, parchment-skinned grandmothers, apple-cheeked babes deserved better. They were rulers of an empire strung across the world and they warranted a better ruler than an increasingly erratic monarch whose favorite occupation was playing at politics or conversing with his boyhood tutor.

What had he once said? "I have two beliefs: England, and the fact that I am what she needs." He still believed in England, but he also knew a darker, less palatable truth. England was in danger, and there was nothing he could do about it. Not as long as King George marched on into madness.

"I think," he said, reading the letter once more, "that this guilt, however, is shared equally. My honesty prevents me from laying the blame upon King George. No," he said, quietly but firmly, his eyes looking not at this missive but recalling another letter, accusing and angry, "this is something I must address."

Thirty-six

Shelby, Duke of Carrington, blew across her full, white breasts and thought himself a rake.

Laura tapped him on the shoulder with her fan, harder than was deemed polite, but otherwise paid no attention to his overtures. The fact that she ignored him did not deter his exploits. He dipped two fingers into his port and sprinkled the droplets across the melons of her upthrust breasts, but she only glanced at him, irritated beyond measure, and wiped herself dry.

She could never understand why some mild-mannered men turned into licentious satyrs after a few glasses of wine. She sighed, carefully edged away from the duke, and wished fervently for this evening to be over.

During the past few months she had found herself in the rather distasteful position of being a lure to the fashionable set—a hostess whose invitations were prized because they were so infrequent. The commonplace prompted only ennui among the ton. The fact that the milling guests were invited only to contribute to a growing Orphanage Fund seemed to have no effect on the enthusiasm of those who attended.

Tonight, however, had been a disaster.

Tonight her noble guests had been served up more than costly spirits and a meal crafted by a superb chef. Tonight she had provided fodder for their whispered conversations for weeks, if not months.

Finally, after what felt like hours of endless tuning that

scraped along her nerves, the opening strains of violins lilted through the air, luring her guests to the parqueted ballroom floor. Those who did not dance made no pretense of not studying her avidly, their sharp-eyed speculation barely concealed behind a polite mask of civility.

She smiled and moved from guest to guest, chatting an inane social banter that was the meat of London conversation. The fact that her smile was forced, a rictus of muscles she had carefully crafted into a polite and serene gesture, was unnoticed and undetected by its recipients. She had declined four invitations to dance by the time she had crossed the room. Her excuse, spoken in a low, emotionless voice, was that her duties as hostess dictated her presence somewhere else. None of her fervent male admirers noticed that the Countess of Cardiff never danced.

She did not comport herself as a widow as much as she did a woman whose husband was absent. The great Cardiff heirloom was never absent from her finger, and although she no longer wore mourning, her very demeanor was that of a woman who expected her husband to walk in the doorway any moment, after a long absence.

Even now, two years since his death, she found it hard to believe that Alex would not appear and question her absence from Heddon Hall. Not a day went by that she did not stop and think to herself, I must tell Alex this. Or, what would Alex say? Until reality surfaced, and she realized that never again would she be able to talk with Alex. Never again would he be able to comment upon an amusing anecdote, or challenge her ideas, to laugh with her at the foibles of the ton, to tease her from the melancholy that seemed to descend upon her even in the midst of a crowd.

The more matronly women gravitated to her side, as if she were not as young as some of the debutantes among them. The younger women sought her out for guidance, as if she were poised between two worlds—too young to be old, but too experienced to ever be young again. She spoke less, and guarded her responses more. There was a reticence about her, a circumspection that was present even in her dealings with Uncle Bevil, her solicitor, or the staff. Only with Uncle Percival did some of her guard descend. Only with Dolly did she allow some of her emotions to show.

She had truly lived up to that idiotic appellation with which society had labeled her—the Cool Countess.

Until tonight.

What she truly wanted now was a bath and bed and an end to the sharp-eyed speculation of her guests. Instead, she moved back into the dining room, intent on final instructions to Hendrickson. A midnight supper was to be offered to her guests, none of whom showed the slightest interest in leaving before dawn.

Why should they leave? The entertainment she had provided was destined to keep the gossip mills busy for months. She winced once again at the memory.

"Come, dear, it is not that bad," Dolly said kindly, following her into the deserted room and noting the look of distress on Laura's face. She surmised, quite accurately, that she was remembering the scene in the dining room a scant hour before.

"Yes, Dolly, it *is* that bad," Laura said with a weary smile, "and if you weren't such a good friend, you would admit it."

"That horrid woman." Elaine Weston, the Duchess of Buthe thought, had not begun to suffer the justice her words demanded. What Laura had done, while extraordinary, especially for her, paled in comparison with some of the ton's more rapacious members. She had not danced naked upon a table with a rose between her teeth and then denied it to a hundred witnesses the next day. Nor had she foisted a bastard off upon a titled husband or taken a lover and supported him in the same house in which her husband and children resided. She neither stole nor gambled, and she paid her bills within tradesmen's terms, which was odd for the nobility and made

Karen Ranney

her a saint in the shopkeepers' eyes. In truth, she could be construed as proper, ladylike, and boring. Well, almost boring.

"I should never have tolerated her for that long," Laura admitted, "but I had other things on my mind."

Dolly looked at her friend, the young woman who'd worked so hard and so diligently in a cause she'd made her own. This past year had brought many changes, but despite the fact that Laura Weston had rejoined the world of the living, there would always be, she suspected, that look of sadness in her eyes.

"What is done is done," Dolly said simply, "do not don a hair shirt, I beg you. Elaine bears the responsibility for tonight."

Laura looked around at the long dining table, now bared of its silver settings and its famous Weston candelabra. She was as responsible as Elaine, if not more.

It had all started innocently enough.

She had been surprised to find Elaine in attendance, escorted by a fatuous Lord Hawley. Surprised and a little displeased, but Lord Hawley was, in Dolly's estimation, an excellent example of money going to rot. He had been invited tonight in order to tap him for a portion of those substantial funds. Laura could not very well show him to the door when she'd seen whom he had chosen to escort.

She realized soon after she'd returned to London that she would have to make other living arrangements. She did not want to hear Elaine's ribald stories or gibes about her own reputation. She did not want pointed remarks concerning her own married state or lack of it. Above all, she wanted to escape that secretive smile that played around Elaine's perfect bow lips and the glint of malice in her eyes.

The closest Laura could come to describing it was cruelty, but even that was opined and not proven. Unless, of course, you looked closely at the arms of Elaine's young maid and saw the small and vicious black bruises there, as if someone had pinched her with relish, twisting the flesh until the pain must have been intense. The girl would not discuss it with Laura, and she was left with the helpless and uncomfortable feeling that there was more to Elaine than she knew.

As a child, Laura had instinctively recoiled from Elaine. As a young woman, she had been appalled by the other woman's jeering comments toward Alex. As a grief-stricken widow, she had yearned for there to be some common ground between them. There was something else about the woman that bothered her, and it was a week before Laura could put a name to the emotion. There was only hatred in Elaine Weston's eyes. On those rare occasions when they were both at the town house, Laura would turn suddenly and glimpse Elaine staring at her, before that gaze was carefully averted. At first she had doubted her impression, but recently there was no mistaking the meaning of that cold stare.

Those blue eyes were filled with malevolent intent.

If once Elaine had indicated that she felt any sadness at all for Alex's loss, Laura would have extended the hand of friendship to her. Elaine, however, remained the same person she'd always been, intensely focused on only herself, as if the world outside her skin was of little use to her.

If there was never an open confrontation between them, it was more likely due to the fact that Elaine knew she was dependent upon Laura's charity than the fact that she wished her well.

As Elaine divested herself of the black silk cloak lined in scarlet silk, Laura had forced herself to be pleasant to the woman, although she had not seen Elaine since she'd moved out of the Weston town house. She and Elaine moved in very different circles.

"You look well, Laura," Elaine said, adjusting her elbow-length gloves and then pressing a finger to her immaculate coiffure, a towering powdered headpiece adorned with red silk flowers and a tiny bird perched precariously at an angle. The flowers were duplicated at her waist and the bodice of the gown, which plummeted to an obscene depth. The dress was shocking, in decidedly bad taste, and undoubtedly exorbitantly expensive.

It was, however, pure Elaine.

"Thank you, Elaine," she responded calmly, and nodded to Lord Hawley, who was looking at the Dowager Countess of Cardiff as if she were a prize beyond price. Laura pitied him. The squat little man with his balding head and his overflowing paunch evidently did not realize that his only allure for Elaine stemmed from the size of his purse and his power, not from his adoration.

"Widowhood agrees with you," Elaine said sotto voce, gliding past her, a cat's smile on her heart-shaped face.

Elaine hated the sniveling bitch.

The little chit was performing good works now and, once again, was the subject of gossip. The monster's bride was the subject of many a drawing room whisper, as if she were a sacred icon for the jaded appetites of the ton. The Cool Countess would gain yet another nickname, something sweet no doubt, an appellation that echoed society's sneaking admiration for her.

Laura gritted her teeth, formed her lips into a strained smile, and forced herself to greet the remainder of her guests.

Due to the sheer number of guests attending the party, she and Elaine managed to avoid each other's presence until dinner. Elaine was seated at her right, in the middle of the table, in deference to her sex, if not her rank. On Elaine's right was the Honorable John Melbourne, to her left, Marcus Hathaway, the brilliant doctor.

It was a diverse group, distinguished by their wealth and their differences and by the fact that Laura disliked the posturing of society, the cruel jokes at the expense of others so much that she went out of her way to invite those who were considered social outcasts to her home.

It took Elaine only seconds to realize that her dinner companions were among that group. She spared only moments on the conversation of John Melbourne, whose speech impediment was so pronounced that it brought jeers from a less polite group of people. At Laura's table he was allowed to form sentences laboriously and without censure. Nor was anyone so gauche as to comment upon Marcus's lameness, or his twisted and short arm.

Both men had been frequent guests in her home, and both men were considered friends.

Laura hoped they still spoke to her after tonight.

Elaine quickly dismissed John Melbourne as unworthy of her attention. She turned impatiently and stared at Marcus with slitted eyes, not masking her derision as she pointedly stared at his withered arm, visible through the carefully tailored coat. She edged away from him in a gesture of affront and then glared at Laura as if she had altered the seating arrangements to deliberately offend her sensibilities.

Laura suspected that the only people truly offended after this dinner would be her friends.

"La, dear," Elaine said, her voice mockingly sweet and carrying over the low murmur of conversation, "London was wrong to call you the Cool Countess."

Laura turned from her companion on the right. Jonas Hanway had played a prominent part in helping Captain Coram to establish his celebrated Foundling Hospital, in addition to forming the Marine Society, which helped clothe common seamen during the war and established more than twelve thousand boys in professions in the Navy. She glanced at Elaine, not bothering to mask her displeasure at the sound of that nickname.

She had disliked it ever since she had first been informed by Dolly that her appeal stemmed from her aloofness. She was a widow, and a chaste one at that, which only imbued her with a certain unapproachable status that challenged even the least rapacious man in their group. The man who broached the Cool Countess's icy fortress was to be congratulated. The fact that none of them had so far succeeded only added to her mystique.

She knew she was an enigma to them. She was a virtuous woman in an age when virtue was prized by the stuffy Georgian court but dismissed quickly behind closed doors. She was a fantastically wealthy woman who squandered her fortune on London's neglected children. She was the widow of a peer but was equally at home conversing with butlers and gin-ridden hags. She did not gossip about others, nor was her name linked with any lover or friend.

"Oh, and why is that?" she responded calmly, as she motioned for Hendrickson to begin the second course.

"Why, I do believe you would be better served by calling you Beauty and the Beasts," Elaine said, seemingly oblivious to the sudden audible gasp from her dinner companions and the immediate cessation of conversation. As one, the group at the long dining table stared at Elaine, then at Laura. Laura could feel the flush begin in the region of her chest and spread upward to her hairline.

"But I recall," Elaine continued, interspersing her comments with tiny forkfuls of lake trout, as if the occupants of the room had not suddenly stilled and were hanging on to her every word, wineglasses suspended in midair, forks resting on white Limoges china, "that you always craved the bizarre. I wonder, dear, if it was the way you were raised, to seek the abnormal over the normal?"

Laura carefully placed her wineglass on a crystal coaster, folded her hands in her lap, her gaze not veering from her unwanted guest.

"You seem to surround yourself with the strangest people." She glanced at the men seated beside her with contempt. "First that freak of a husband, and now these odd specimens."

Laura noted that neither of her friends lifted their gazes from their plates, which they seemed to be studying with compelling interest.

They did not deserve this.

She did not deserve this.

Alex did not deserve this.

In that moment she recalled all of the other times she had been the brunt of Elaine's barbed tongue—as a child, visiting Heddon Hall, guilty of nothing more than being naive and female. As a young woman in love, when Elaine's words had been the cause of so much pain and remorse. As a bride on her wedding night, when she had been so uncertain and unsure and confrontation was the last thing she had wished for. When she had first come to London and a word of kindness would have been so welcome, but all she had received from the dowager countess were taunting insults. She stared at the woman who was related to her late husband by marriage only, but who had the right to wear, and shame, the Weston name.

Dolly, who was seated to her left, placed a restraining hand on her arm, but Laura shook it off gently, smiling reassuringly at her friend. She stood, her movements smooth and composed. The eyes of her guests veered from the petite woman attired in shocking red to the vision of their hostess, serene and lovely in ivory lace. Only her hands, clenched at her sides, indicated her outrage.

Elaine had made a grave error, and that was expecting Laura to remain as still and silent as she had many times before. She would no longer be the brunt of Elaine's tasteless jokes, nor would she allow the woman to taunt her, and others, any longer.

She had gone too far this time by publicly mocking Alex's memory.

She wondered why she did not remember more of her next actions or the steps that led up to it. All she could recall was that she was surfeited by a desperate need to silence the dowager countess. She wanted Elaine to leave her house, leave the dining room, but most of all, leave her presence.

She reached her side midpoint at the table at the same time Elaine stood, her short stature dwarfed by Laura's willowy height. Later Laura wondered how the wineglass had come so conveniently to her hand, not remembering that the

Honorable John Melbourne had gallantly offered up his own in a gesture of complete accord.

Wine and flour do not mix, nor did wine live in complete harmony with Elaine's makeup, although skillfully and artfully applied. Her scream of outrage, as Laura calmly threw the contents of the glass in her face, mingled with the chuckles of her less sympathetic dinner companions and the shocked gasps of others, creating a cacophony of sound that propelled Hendrickson into the room. He nearly skidded to a halt in midstep, the sight of his gentle and benevolent mistress in the act of shocking the ton almost enough to banish the usual impassive stare from his face.

It was enough to make the footman smile.

"Our guest will be leaving, Hendrickson," Laura said coolly, still holding the empty goblet. "Now."

Elaine's exit from the room was followed by the departure of Lord Hawley, his florid face punctuated by a scowl of outrage.

"You should have emptied the soup tureen over her head, my dear," Dolly said, interrupting her reverie.

"What a horrid waste of good food," she said, and they both smiled.

"We shall have to think of a new nickname for you, my dear," Dolly said with a smile. "Somehow, after tonight, I do not think the Cool Countess will be very apt."

"I can imagine what names I'll be called now," Laura said, rolling her eyes to the ceiling. The affinity of the ton to apply labels to people never ceased to amaze her.

"Perhaps the 'Avenging Archangel'?"

"Somehow I don't think I'm the angel type, Dolly."

"Hmm, perhaps not. I have it," she said, with a triumphant smile, "the Champagne Countess!"

"It wasn't champagne, Dolly; it was wine."

"You let a little thing such as the facts get in the way, dear," Dolly said fondly, eyeing her friend with gentle interest, noting gratefully that her stricken look was gone, replaced by a smile now, a genuine smile.

Laura's humor was not restored for long, however, as she wondered at the form Elaine Weston's retribution would take. Elaine, she suspected, could be a formidable enemy.

Thirty-seven

Blakemore House

"She wants Blakemore," Bevil Blake said in shock as he waved the letter at his brother, who was calmly pruning a rare form of hibiscus.

Percival looked up without concern, even though it was a rare day indeed when Bevil ventured into the greenhouse. Bevil was the financier of the two, comfortable in a book-strewn room, ecstatic to be given the task of tallying long columns of figures all day long. It would have driven him insane. Which was just as well, since his penchant was for the outdoors and good, green, growing things.

"Well, it's hers, isn't it?" he said, dipping the cutting he had taken into a special batch of root stimulator, a rancid combination of beet parings, rainwater, manure from the stables, and a dollop of honey.

"Of course," Bevil said, nodding, "but she says that she doesn't want to dispossess us, and she'll give us Heddon Hall in return." The legalities of that move were completely foreign to him, but even now, his brain yearned to attack the problem.

"Can she do that?" Percival asked with interest. The gardens at Heddon Hall were much bigger than Blakemore; some of the plants there were priceless grafts. The roses alone were rumored to be over two hundred years old.

"I suppose she can," Bevil said absently, returning to the letter and scanning it once again. For a moment he allowed himself the luxury of pretending to occupy Heddon Hall. What a joy it would be to be able to haunt its immense libraries, to sit in a colored stream of light emitted from the famous stained-glass windows. What hedonistic indulgence to have a major domo the caliber of Simons in charge. Imagine not having to worry about staffing problems any more. To think that he would get his tea on time and his housekeeper would not forever be indulging in those little sulks. He almost rubbed his hands together in anticipation.

"Does she say why she wants Blakemore?" Percival put down the pruning shears and advanced on his brother.

"No, she just states that she needs a place where children can run and play."

"Haven't we enough children now?" Percival said, glancing out the window and smiling. Gone was the quiet of Blakemore. Gone was the stultifying peace that wore upon any sane man's nerves. He noted the signs of activity with a grin. A month ago the children had started arriving, and Blakemore was now overrun with the sounds of childhood. The unnatural quiet of the London children, confronted with the broad fields and clean air of Blakemore, had lasted but one day, and now the air seemed filled with shouts of "Jane, he's got my ball!," "I don't want to bathe," and other, blunter sentiments offered up in Cockney slang. All in all, it was a momentous and welcome change from the silence that normally surrounded them.

Percival strode to where Bevil stood and pulled Laura's letter free from his brother's grasp, scanning it as quickly as Bevil had.

He smiled as he read the letter. So, his niece had more grandiose, adventuresome plans. He smiled, thinking of the young girl who had not wanted to conquer the world as much as she wanted to snare Alex Weston's heart. Well, now Laura was out to master the world. All the welcome signs were there. She was, despite herself, or perhaps because of it, beginning to live again.

"What's she up to?" Bevil asked, knowing quite well that his niece and his brother sometimes spoke to each other of things closest to their hearts. It was not as if he didn't have feelings, but he wasn't apt to verbalize them the way Percival did. He didn't slight his brother one whit for his ability, nor for his closeness to their niece. They were just different people, and over the years had learned to accept and appreciate the differences and the similarities in their natures.

"Damned if I know," Percival said, grinning, "but knowing you, my tenacious brother, I'm sure you're going to find out."

Bevil only scowled at him. Of course; was he not the practical one?

The soiled letter, incongruously wrapped by a wide blue ribbon affixed with an imposing red seal, sat atop the silver salver. She slowly withdrew her gloves, one finger at a time, staring at the missive with astonished eyes. She picked it up and slipped it into the pocket of her cape.

As the bedroom door clicked shut, she retrieved the letter, quickly peeling away the seal of the secretary of state and its accompanying note. She sat, heavily, in a chair beside her dressing table, her incredulous eyes reading words from beyond the grave.

My dearest love,

Distance separates us, but that is the only impediment. Neither time nor the machinations of government or politics can truly divide us.

I sit at a table, bare but for a candle, which marks the passage of time in slow droplets upon the face of the bottle that holds it.

The same breeze that threatens the flame brings with it the scent of your hair, your lilting laugh, and with that memory I am transported beyond the portals of time itself. As a child, you fascinated me. As a woman, you enthralled me. As my wife, you empower me.

My dearest, dearest, darling, I am but a mortal man, for all that I would wish otherwise. I am chained to my circumstances and to Frederick's gentle enslavement even though my mind flows free and wild like the spring wind. I ache to touch you, to prove that you are real and that I am real and that whatever has been between us exists no longer to separate us.

I will be with you soon, my darling and our life will be once more what we wished it to be.
Your loving husband,
Dixon Alexander Weston

Her heart beat too heavily, too loudly. Her breath was too tight, as if someone had tied cotton string at the base of her lungs.

She touched the parchment to the flame of the candle. His swooping signature was the first to blaze, and the letter acted like a torch, illuminating the ivory complexion, her soft, full lips. The rest of the paper flashed, burning swiftly.

Elaine Weston, Dowager Countess of Cardiff, her delicate face almost twisted beyond recognition by rage, dropped the ashes into the chamberpot and left the maids to wonder why.

London

"I do not know why you will not move to Heddon," she said calmly, ignoring her uncle's scowl. It was the same scowl he had worn the day she summarily announced she would never return to Mrs. Wolcraft's school. A week later she'd arrived for her second semester.

"I will not move anywhere until I find out what you are planning," he said stubbornly.

Her uncle did not look at all shocked, she thought with a

smile, as she outlined her plans for Blakemore. He looked vastly pleased with himself, as if he himself had thought of the plan.

"But," he protested, when she had finished, "you cannot simply deed us Heddon Hall."

"Why not?" she asked calmly. "It is mine." Alex's solicitor had made that fact too clear. In fact, their combined wealth was more than she could spend in her lifetime. It would have been more, she thought, with a small sad smile, than her children and their children could spend.

"Yes, but it has been the Weston home for generations," he explained patiently. Legally, she could burn the place down if she wanted to, of course, but there was the moral issue at stake. It simply wasn't right. Bevil Blakemore wasn't certain why, but it just did not feel like the correct thing to do. An attitude that, had he been foolish enough to have mentioned it, would have shocked both his brother and his niece, who knew him as the most pragmatic man alive.

She looked at him calmly, her gaze direct and unflinching. "There is no true Weston left, dear uncle," she said quietly.

He looked down at the floor. What she said was true. Alex's second cousin had a different surname. There would be no more Westons to trace a distinguished dynasty down through the years. Which was a damn shame, wasn't it? He shook himself mentally. Not what his niece needed to hear.

"All right," he said finally. "Blakemore is yours, and Percy and I will reside at Heddon Hall, but on one condition."

She smiled. "Name it."

"You must not deed it to anyone, not even to us." He held up his hand when she would have spoken. "Heddon Hall is yours and should remain yours."

"Uncle," she said softly, not meeting his kind and knowing eyes, "I have said good-bye to that part of my life. I will never go back there."

"Never is a long time, Laura. Each and every time I have issued such a dictate I have found myself recanting it soon enough. Be careful that you do not speak the word too soon. No, you must promise me not to deed the Hall to anyone but retain full ownership."

"Very well," she said, smiling fondly at her uncle. "I promise. I will also attempt to refrain from utilizing the word never."

"Wise girl," he said, smiling broadly at her. Part of his glee resulted from the prospect of having the redoubtable Simons looking after him in the near future, part of it from anticipating the excellent luncheon his talented niece would no doubt serve in a few moments. "I am cautioned to learn of the latest court gossip, or Percival will not let me back in the door. Is it true that Pitt may come back to power?"

Laura grimaced, wondering if her uncle would be shocked to learn of her blackmail. She might have personal antipathy for the man, but even she had to admit that England had no steadier course than when Pitt was at the helm. She had not heard from him, but she did not doubt that, should he return to power, he would address the repeal of the poor laws. Pitt was a crafty politician, and no politician could afford to ignore her thinly veiled threat.

"The king's tutor still holds the reins, Uncle, but for how long no one knows. I cannot help but wonder what would have happened had Prince Fred not died. As it is, Bute is not held in much favor by the general population, for being too close to the king's mother and for being a Scot. I think that, however, is an insult to the Scots."

"Is it true that his coach was attacked?"

Laura smiled wryly. "Not only his coach but the windows in his house were broken, and people gathered outside of it and sang bawdy songs. Surely the king will notice all of the antipathy toward Bute. He has not truly been popular since the Treaty of Paris."

"It was a bad deal, that. Too damn generous to Spain and France, and we insulted Frederick of Prussia with the terms. Wouldn't be at all surprised if the man declared war on us.

Would that the king had more insight into the workings of his own government."

"Yes, but he is only twenty-five," she said.

"And half mad, I hear, or is it only gossip that speaks of his odd rashes and incomprehensible behavior?"

"I move in circles greatly separated from the court," she said tactfully, "but I have heard the rumors, too."

"I can understand why you spurn that lot," he said, smiling. "You always had too much intelligence."

"I don't know if it's intelligence or simply impatience. The court operates on mistrust and deceit and is not as glittering as people would make it. It is, frankly, boring. What I find abhorrent is that there is one standard for nobility and another for the common man. And the kindest thing I can say about George III is that he likes to sit and make toast with his wife."

Bevil laughed. "Well, it could be worse, perhaps," he admitted.

Laura looked at her uncle and wondered how.

Was not a mad king and an incompetent minister bad enough? She was infinitely grateful that the only thing she needed to be concerned about was the welfare of children.

"There," Laura said wearily, finally standing, "that should do it." She looked at the neatly packed trunk with a welcome sense of accomplishment. It had taken them two days to create order out of chaos. She had not imagined that she could accumulate so much in just one year in London.

"M'lady," Agnes said, with the same fervor and mothering tones of Laura's old nurse, "you go sit somewhere. You work too hard on chores that the maids could do." She frowned at her mistress in mock censure and left the room to fetch tea.

Laura wondered if Agnes had forgotten that she had once worked as a kitchen apprentice at Heddon Hall. She smiled, and looked over her bedroom, now cleared of the clutter that had marred it for several days.

She had made the decision only a few weeks before and it had taken almost that long to implement it. Although London was home to Dolly, the city had never held much fascination for her. She was a country girl at heart, despite her wealth and her rank. She loved sunsets without the stench of soot, the sweet smell of gardens abloom with fresh spring flowers. She wanted lonely dirt roads to walk upon and the scent of clean air untainted by London's chimney pots. She missed the silence of summer nights and the cold, crisp white snow that remained crisp and white, not trod underfoot by rumbling carriages and turned a dirty gray color.

Most of all she wanted a sense of newness, a sparkle to her life that had been missing for so long. She wanted a feeling of beginning again, a fresh start someplace where there were no memories of either her past or her struggle to overcome that past.

She thought she had found it.

Blakemore was beyond her capabilities. She loved her childhood home almost as much as she loved Heddon Hall, but the thought of moving to either place was to sacrifice all of the gains of the past year and become mired in that awful grief that had consumed her at the beginning.

Now she thought she had found it. A small house, really, that needed to be enlarged to accommodate the children who would soon reside there. Five miles from Blakemore, it was close enough that the uncles could visit. Close enough that if she wanted to see Heddon Hall, it would not be an arduous journey.

She smiled at that paradoxical thought. She could not live there, but she still did not want to banish that grand old place from her memory. It was too much a part of her, too much a part of who she had been and still was.

Yet Heddon Hall and Blakemore belonged to the past, and although she might wish to visit there from time to time, she could never live there anymore than Lady Weston could become little Laura Blake again.

The visit to Heddon Hall had proven that.

Agnes bustled in with the tray, nearly tripping over one of the trunks they had laboriously packed. She threw the rounded trunk a glance of censure and then set the tray on the table beside her mistress.

"You just sit and rest, m'lady," she coaxed, "and I'll finish the rest of it."

Laura smiled at her industrious maid, watching as she fastened the straps. In two days Uncle Bevil would arrive to assist them in their move, and she suspected that Agnes was as glad for their departure from London as she.

"Wait," she said, just before Agnes closed the last of the trunks. She walked to her bureau, now empty of all clothing except that which she would need for the next few days. She opened the top drawer and pulled out the music box. Her fingers traced the Cardiff emblem, etched in gold. She did not open its lid or hear its tune, however. She knew it by heart, each tinkling note.

"Here," she said, handing her most precious belonging to Agnes. "Pack this in the one for storage," she said resolutely.

"But, m'lady," Agnes stammered.

"Do you not know your Bible, Agnes?" she asked, looking not at the music box still held tenderly in her maid's outstretched hand, but at something far more distant.

Laura Ashcott Blake Weston, who had somehow lost her penchant for quoting elusive platitudes, found that she could remember this one as if it was carved on the wall before her.

"To every thing there is a season and a time to every purpose under the heaven. A time to be born and a time to die; a time to plant and a time to pluck up that which is planted; a time to kill and a time to heal; a time to break down and a time to build up; a time to weep and a time to laugh. A time to mourn and a time to dance." The rest eluded her, and she was grateful, because for some inexplicable reason her throat felt as though a band were being tied around it, constricting all further speech.

"Please," she whispered, and Agnes, in a swift movement that hid her own sudden blinding tears, whirled and packed the music box into the trunk bound for storage.

Thirty-eight

"Where is my wife, madam?"

Elaine Weston stared at him, her ashen face and wide blue eyes the only sign of her shock.

Jacobs had carried the news of their visitor himself, his impassive face wreathed in a smile, as if the sight of her too-oft resurrected stepson would be a pleasing one. She'd wasted no time in dressing, had only thrown on a wrapper and descended the staircase to test the truth of his words. She halted, now, on a middle step, her left hand gripping the banister with such strength that her knuckles showed white and bony.

The monster had returned. She shut her eyes at the full import of that news, and then opened them again. He was still here. He was no ghost, no amorphous shape. That he had survived his incarceration by the French she knew well from the letter she had burned. Somewhere, however, a tiny flicker of hope had made her believe and wish and dream of his eventual demise at Frederick's hand.

Was he more than human? Would he always manage to bedevil her life, this monster? No, he was all too real.

He watched her compose herself with barely veiled irritation. Would no one speak in this too silent house? First Jacobs stammering and groveling, too excited to answer his questions about his wife. Then his stepmother's unwelcome appearance.

Granted it was morning and the hour was early, but where was Laura?

If he must, he would search every room until he found her. His slight movement toward the stairs roused Elaine finally, and she held up one hand as if to restrain him from mounting the steps.

"She is not here," Elaine said with deceptive calm, still reeling from the sight of him, large and looming in the foyer.

He looked fit, she thought. Older, true, with lines around his mouth that had not been there before, and swooping wings of silver etched into his midnight-hued hair. The black mask was in place as usual, his attire as rich as if he'd just returned from court, a black upon black that the earl chose over more resplendent clothing.

"What the hell do you mean, she's not here?"

He was still mutilated, however, and a look of derision crossed her face as her eyes swept along his mask, then lowered and took in the sight of his glove.

He did not miss his stepmother's contemptuous perusal. It was not the welcome he had expected. He calmly removed his cloak while studying her, biding his time while trying to dismiss an uncomfortable and growing sense of unease. All was not as it should be.

His frantic journey from the admiralty, where he had been informed of his demise, now seemed out of proportion to his welcome. There, he had been fawned over enough to make his blood churn. They had wanted him to see the minister, but he had curtly refused. He had given up too much for king and country; he would not give up more time.

It was a stroke of luck that Laura was in London. That, he had learned from one of the clerks at the admiralty. He would be spared the long journey to Heddon Hall before their reunion. A reunion that had been delayed too damn long by solicitous remarks, concern over his health, his fatigue, the effects of his incarceration, his hunger.

All he wanted now was his wife and his child.

The servants bustled in from the kitchen, led by the little maid who used to bring his breakfast tray. She almost fainted at the sight of the Earl of Cardiff standing nonchalantly in the foyer of his London home.

"Oh, sir," she said breathlessly, "it *is* you!"

It seemed to be a sentiment echoed by them all, as they filed into the hall, excitedly talking, their beaming smiles interspersed by reverent bobbing.

It seemed as though his resurrection resulted in varying degrees of shock, he thought, not without a trace of ironic humor. At least the servants seemed glad to see him.

"So it is," he agreed amicably. Mary blushed and withdrew, bobbing a curtsy to him.

He turned to Elaine again when they were alone.

"I will ask you just once more, madam," he said, his soft tones belying his mounting anger. "Where is my wife?"

He had pictured her welcome, her beautiful face wreathed in a smile so broad and so blinding that it would breach the passage of time itself. His arms craved the feel of her held tightly to his chest; he had wanted the soft touch of her flesh enfolding him, the sound of her voice as she said, "I love you, I love you," the sigh of her breath as her lips touched his scars and healed other wounds not so readily apparent, but just as deep.

Time, the most grievous injury of them all. They had stolen time from him, and the last shreds of his credulity. His faith in his country had been shaken, the rightness of his cause had been questioned, his loyalty to his king had been examined.

In the end, duty, courage, and honor embodied only three things in his life. They had been distilled, these high ideals, into the only things that mattered—Laura, their child, and Heddon Hall.

It was not to be.

"I'm sure I can't say, Alex," Elaine said serenely, her composure regained. She remained standing on the second step, so that the earl would not tower over her.

"She does not inform me of her whereabouts," she told him, a small tinkling laugh punctuating her words. "You know London, Alex; it is so full of sights and sounds and experiences. Who knows what, or who, Laura is currently enjoying?" She smiled brightly at him, noting that the gloved hand clenched.

"Has she taken a page from your book, then, Elaine?"

"Life is for the living, Alex," she responded sweetly, her smile growing in direct proportion to the rigidity of his stance. "You have been gone long. Would you expect any woman, especially one as sought-after as Laura, to remain faithful?"

"Words such as faithful sound strange coming from your lips, madam," Alex said acridly.

His little Laura. How sweetly she had appeared in his dreams. How gentle her touch on those nights when he could not sleep, but lay awake listening to the moans of countless prisoners housed belowdecks. He had seen her then, as if she had appeared before him in the flesh. Her smile enticing, her hair swirling around her like a cloud, her lips promising and delivering oblivion and sweet release.

Laura, with her bright laughter and her wit. Had she tired, after all, of being loyal to a shadow?

He flinched from the greater fear, one he'd thought buried deep but that came unbidden to his mind: Had she tired of being wed to a monster?

"And my child?" he asked softly. His stepmother's smile did not dim. Of course, he could not have known.

"I am sorry, Alex," she said in mock sympathy. "He never breathed, although Laura took it better than most. Perhaps it is just as well; a child would have tied her down, whereas London offers so many delectable diversions."

So much for dreams, he thought bitterly.

"I had a son, then," he said shortly.

Again she smiled softly, and he was too attuned to his own inner anguish to see the look of malice in her eyes.

"Where is she?"

"La, Alex," Elaine said, glancing up at the graceful fanlight above the door. "It is well into morning and she has not come home. How should I know?"

His homecoming turned to ashes in his mouth, a bitter, vile taste. His wife had, evidently, not mourned him; his child was dead. The bright enthusiasm and urgency that had sped him toward England now dimmed like a tarnished piece of fool's gold.

It would have been better had he died a thousand times rather than face this.

"Shall I tell her that you inquired about her whereabouts when she returns?" Elaine asked sweetly, as he whirled and strode through the foyer of his London town house, intent on any movement that would carry him as far away from this place as possible.

"Tell her anything you damn well please," he spat out, and brushed by the butler too quickly for the man to do anything but hurry to get out of his way.

He slammed the door shut behind him and did not see the calculating look on his stepmother's face.

The monster would waste no time establishing dominion over his fortune again. But what the misshapen earl did not know was that she had no intention of remaining in leading strings. If the last two hellish years had taught her nothing, they had reinforced her belief that money was the root of power and freedom. She had no intention of begging, or groveling for a pittance. No, no more.

Unless she ensured that the Earl of Cardiff was mortal, that is exactly what her life would become. She would once more be doled out a miserly allowance. Her tradesmen's bills would be due and payable; her relationship to the widowed countess enough to have mollified all but the most demanding shopkeeper these past few months. Her life in the city would be a thing of the past, and she would be forced to molder in the country, the glittering extravaganza that was London beyond her means.

Not unless she did something. Now.

It would be another double tragedy to inflict the Weston family, another catastrophe to mar the Cardiff line, another set of appalling circumstances for the ton to speculate about and to ponder. The dear oft-resurrected Earl of Cardiff and his lovely wife. What a pity they had to die together. What a pity.

Thirty-nine

"You bloody silly cow," James said softly.

She was bemused by the husky timbre of his voice, knowing that James at his quietest, his softest, was also James at his most predatory, most dangerous.

"Don't you have the wits God gave a snake, you silly woman?" he said, advancing on her, his smile mean and intent.

It was the type of smile, Elaine thought, that the king's executioner might wear. She shivered and would have backed away, but there was nowhere to go. These rooms were small and cramped and smelled of fish and cabbage. They were not large and airy like gentlemen's lodgings should be.

"You're insane if you think there's any way I will go along with this idiotic scheme, you stupid, stupid, woman," he said, his smile replaced by rage, his dulcet tone harsh and rasping now, as if he had walked through something invisible to her eyes, something hanging in the air that stripped him of all his charm, leaving only the anger. "Don't," he said imperiously, wiggling a finger in her face, "get me confused with someone who gives a bloody whit about your future, Elaine. Don't get me confused with someone who cares."

"Have you got a better idea?" She'd trusted him, trusted him enough to bring her plan to him, and now he was throwing it back in her face.

"Why are you laboring under the delusion that your problems are my problems?" he asked softly. "Do you think just because I spent a few hours in your bed that now our fates are inexorably linked, somehow?"

"I have to do something."

"And your idea of a solution is to murder a bloody earl and his countess?" His snort of laughter ate at her pride. "No, my little pearl of beauty, killing them seems a little overdone, don't you think?"

"Don't be so enamored of titles, James," she said, stung. "I hold the rank of countess."

To her discomfiture, James laughed, a great bark of a laugh. "No, my love, you're nothing more than a slattern, who managed to convince someone once upon a time that she was quality. A pretty little piece of goods you are, though, I must admit. But it's plain to see you married into your title. No noble family would brag about producing you as progeny."

Her glare was enough to take the finish from the bureau. "Don't presume to preach to me about nobility," she said, her chin jutting into the air, facing his insouciant charm with a rigorous expression of haughty disdain. It was a look she had practiced in the mirror for hours. It left James Watkins coldly unmoved but wondering the exact age of the dowager countess.

"I will admit to stupidity, rash judgment, even desperation, dear Countess. But my depravity does not extend to murder."

"Have you fallen into riches, then, dear James?" she asked sweetly, desperate to recoup something from this odd and dissatisfying conversation. It was not going as she had planned. His blue eyes were penetrating and contemptuous, as if they peered into her soul and found it somehow wanting. The sneer on his face could not be construed as a fond smile.

"Why the volte-face? Why, I'm about to be married, dear chit. To a lovely, high-browed girl who, incidentally, is a virgin. What do you say to that, Countess? A virgin for old James. Think you I will like the feel of that?"

"What would your new family think of your past, dear

James?" she asked, and it was her turn to wear a look of rage, fueled as it was by a sense of abandonment. "What do you think your pretty little bride will think when she hears of your exploits, my charming love?" She'd known he had to marry, known it from the first, just as she'd known that it might be a course she herself could not escape again. Why else would she allow that pompous boor, Lord Hawley, to escort her to one boring event after another? Yet somehow this was different, with him wetting his lips at the thought of money and virtue tied up in one package.

Lucifer, her golden lover. She hated him at that moment, more than she hated Laura or even the misshapen earl. They never changed; their antipathy was so constant you could tell time by it, like the sundial in the Winter Garden at Heddon Hall.

He'd used her. She'd supported him, and he had used her. She had only a few coins left. Only a few, and now James was leaving her.

"Go threaten someone else, Elaine," he said with a wisp of a smile. "My little bride thinks herself a healer of sorts, a believer in second chances. I'm sure your vile tales will only encourage her to try to save me even more than she's already wont to do.

"Remember this, though, dearest Elaine," he said, his smile widening, "two can play your little game. What would the earl think if he knew murder was your aim? What would he think after learning of all your plotting and scheming? Who has the most to lose, Elaine? You or me? Do me the favor of leaving my rooms quickly, before I forget my patience and the fact that, unlike you, I have noble antecedents."

He turned away from her.

That gesture of contempt was too much for Elaine.

At first he did not see the gun she pulled from her reticule. He only saw that her hand trembled and tears sparkled in those lovely blue eyes, eyes that he'd seen convincingly portray almost every human emotion. He laughed, genuinely amused by her last gesture of histrionics. By God, he would miss the bitch. She served up spice to his life, but then again, pepper could not be sprinkled upon every dish.

"Do not be so foolish, love," he said, his mocking tone replaced by genuine amusement. " 'Twill avail you nothing, this scene, except to shame you further."

"What have I got left?" she asked him, and it disturbed him that her voice was calm, despite the tears that rolled unchecked down her rouged cheeks. Her voice was too dispassionate, and for just a moment he began to feel very worried indeed.

"I am getting older, James," she said softly. She smiled at herself, at such honesty "Oh, 'tis true, I assure you. I have no money, nor hope of being more than a drain on my dear, dear stepson. I have no home that is mine; now the man I love has betrayed me. What have I got to lose?"

His amusement was out of context, he supposed, facing down the muzzle of a gun as he was. But the thought of Elaine Weston believing herself in love was tantamount to believing that pigs really could fly. Not bloody likely.

"Elaine," he said rashly, in view of the gun and the stoic, unbending look on her face, "what we had cannot be called something as noble as love. Granted, I will admit to a certain fascination with your body and your responses, but I can assure you, it does not stem from so ornate a sentiment as fondness. If ever I were to feel that troubling emotion, my pet, I should reserve it for babies and puppies. No, Elaine, what you are feeling is a good and grand case of lust. Which, my dear, is quite over."

"So," she said, "you will not help me?"

"In murder? You must be out of your bloody mind. Murdering a member of the nobility may be an easy task—after all they're human too; but I'd not go to Newgate for the likes of you."

"Then good-bye, James," she said softly, and for just a

moment he thought he witnessed indecision on her face and wondered if she would shoot him, after all.

He reached out and grabbed the barrel of the gun and gently pulled it from her grip. He was careful not to let his amusement show, however, until the unstable Lady Weston departed his pathetic set of rooms.

It was with absurd and acute relief that he watched her walk through the door, her pride in tatters, her dreams in ruins, but her murderous intent intact.

Forty

"Sir," a voice spoke hesitantly from the fog. Bevil Blake halted, one hand reaching for his cane with its cunningly concealed stiletto, conscious of the everpresent threat of footpads and other ruffians who earned their living by robbing visitors to London.

"Sir," the voice breathed again from the high, thick hedges surrounding the entrance to his niece's town house. He peered into the darkness, but it was so complete that all he saw was an amorphous shape, clad in a shapeless, ankle-length cloak.

"Reveal yourself," he said, more harshly than he'd intended. The shadow reluctantly disengaged itself from the wall, moving less with malevolent intent than with a caution of its own. He drew closer to the streetlamp, a halo of light muted by the fog.

He stiffened as the shadow approached him, his eyes straining in the darkness. He expelled a sigh of relief as he saw who summoned him.

She was young; barely twenty, he supposed. The cloak concealed her shape but did nothing to mask the dark stain upon one side of her face, its tentacles extending down to her throat. Her anxiety added a sharpness to her already pinched features.

"What is it?" She moved reluctantly closer, conscious of the Weston town house lying just across the square.

"Sir, be you the uncle?" she whispered, and he frowned.

"Who are you seeking, girl?"

"A friend, sir. A friend to Lady Laura Weston."

"Why?" he demanded peremptorily.

"Sir," the voice trembled a little. What she was doing was dangerous. If the dowager countess ever discovered that she had slipped away from the kitchen, where she had been sent to fetch her a light supper, then . . .

She resolutely pushed that thought away. The time had come for courage, for speaking out. The fact that she was merely a servant, and her accusation leveled against a member of nobility, was not what frightened Maggie Bowes. No, what made her tremble was what she'd heard while pressing her ear against the door of James Watkins's lodgings, and the look in the dowager countess's eyes this afternoon when she'd emerged from those rooms. The fierce, enraged look that made her eyes appear mere slits and that mouth pinched as if she'd smelled something too strong. The fact that she wore that look out in public, upon the streets of London, was the most telling sign. All who knew the dowager knew only the sweet and facile face, not the ugly one tempered by anger.

It was not enough that the dowager countess hated the lovely Lady Weston, a sweeter and kinder lady than any Maggie had ever known. Had not Lady Laura always remembered her name and inquired about her family? Had she not noticed those bruises upon her arms and wanted to know who had so ill used her? Did she not now devote her money and her time to all the little ones who had no one to look out after them?

Maggie squeezed her eyes shut and prayed for courage. *The time has come, Maggie girl,* she told herself, *to do the right thing.* Too many things had happened for her to remain silent any longer.

Not the least of which was Samuel.

Dearest Samuel, who professed not to notice her ugliness, who had declared his love for her and their dreams of the future. To escape servitude and emigrate, perhaps, to another place where they might be able to buy land with their carefully hoarded wages. To farm again and depend upon themselves, not the vagaries and whims of their employers.

It was Samuel's secret that had tipped the scales. Samuel's knowledge of the groom's actions on that fateful day when both the old earl and his heir had perished on the icy roads. Dear Samuel, who could live with his secret as little as she could live with her own accumulated knowledge. Especially after this afternoon. Dear God, but the evil woman must be stopped.

"Speak your mind, girl," Bevil Blake said more kindly as he noticed the trembling of the figure in front of him. She twisted her hands nervously, then peered up at him with a courage that was hard won.

" 'Tis the dowager countess, sir," she said tremulously. "She's an evil one. 'Twas her who hates Lady Laura, who told lies to the earl. Now she has plans, sir. Evil plans, sir, as God Himself is my witness."

"Girl, you ramble," he said impatiently, unable to interpret her short, frantic speech. "Explain yourself."

" 'Tis the Earl of Cardiff, sir. He's come back."

"Alexander Weston?" Bevil was stunned. "He's alive?"

"Yes, sir. Came to fetch his wife back." Maggie's eyes glittered with unshed tears. And wasn't this a story just like a fairy tale?

"When did this happen?" He did not wish to frighten the girl, but he wanted news, and he chafed at the time it took for her to frame her thoughts.

"This morning, sir."

"Where is the earl now?"

"I don't know, sir," she said, made more anxious by the barely constrained impatience of the man before her.

Bevil whirled and called for his coachman, when one roughened hand was laid across his sleeve.

"Sir," Maggie Bowes said, with the same determination that had seen her through two years of the dowager countess's physical and emotional abuse, "there is more, and Samuel and I decided that someone should know."

He thought, later, that the fog was a perfect and sinister backdrop to the words the young maid spoke that night. His mind reeled with the knowledge of Elaine Weston's plans for Laura and Alex, of her actions involving the late earl's death. He decided that he must act quickly upon his newfound information. Only then could he do what he most wanted to do.

Find Alexander Weston.

Forty-one

The carriage was closed, the curtains drawn against the chill of the night; no coat of arms marred its pristine black surface. It sat alone on the side of the cobbled road, enveloped by the encroaching fog.

The thick, cloudlike mist seemed to both muffle sounds and accentuate them. The world was cocooned in cotton sound, all melted together to give an eerie feeling to the night. Yet the snort of a restless horse, the tinkle of a bridle, the whisk of harness, the bawdy laughter from a nearby tavern, all seemed more audible, magnified.

As was the dowager countess's low, throaty chuckle.

With one hand she drew her hood against her face; with the other she clutched a drawstring bag. Only a few coins remained, but it would have to be enough. It was the supreme irony that it was the earl's own gold she would use to purchase his and his wife's death. She would have gladly paid a greater price, had she the money. Yet it was unlikely that the men she would hire this evening would demand more. There was no sense paying more than what was needed.

She had long since decided that if a miracle did occur, and the grotesque earl reappeared, then he would soon be persuaded to follow in his father's footsteps. There were creatures in London who would do the deed for a paltry sum, less than she might spend on a new gown. As it was, it would cost her less than that.

It was money well spent.

What was one more footpad on the streets of London? It would require only one swift movement, a shadowy shape, a deadly thrust of a hidden knife, and she would be unfettered finally, free to enjoy the money that should have been hers all along.

The earl's demise would be accomplished swiftly, his own coins buying satisfaction and temporary loyalty. He had cheated the fates twice; he would not cheat them any longer. As to the countess, she did not care if Lady Weston was sorely used first and then put out of her misery. Let them have a little fun with the bitch and then kill her.

After all, was London not a dangerous place for the unwary? She smiled.

James was wrong; the deed was absurdly simple to execute. At the thought of her former lover, her fingers clenched around the almost empty bag. Later; she would handle him later.

Maggie huddled up against the corner of the carriage, grateful for the darkness that hid the countess from her view and her own fearful look from the other's peering eyes. She did not doubt that the evil woman could see in the dark, though, not unlike a slithering, wicked cat. Her heart beat so loudly that she could hear it, and even her hands clasped nervously and tightly in her lap did nothing to still the trembling that shook her body.

It was not just the disreputable part of town they were in, or the fact that their carriage stood alone and without guards, the coachman having gone in search of the men the countess had bid him seek out. No, that was not the only reason she was deathly afraid.

The coach lurched as a tall man clad in an enormous greatcoat filled the doorway and then was righted as he lifted himself into the sanctuary of the draped carriage.

He settled himself onto the seat opposite the dowager countess, too close to Maggie. She slowly pulled her skirts away from his muddy boots.

Elaine smiled and extended the bag of coins toward the stranger. She kept her head carefully averted. There was no need for her own identity to be discovered; she merely wanted the deed done.

"Who?" he demanded harshly, his voice too loud in the silence of the carriage.

She told him then, as he grasped the coins greedily. A small laugh escaped her. Too easy; again it had been too easy.

Her congratulatory thoughts lasted only a moment.

Her hired companion pulled off the hat that had shielded most of his features and pushed open the carriage door with a swift movement. In the light spilling from a nearby tavern he looked even more ethereal than before, her avenging Lucifer.

"I told you it was a bloody stupid idea, Elaine," James Watkins said, smiling. It was not a gentle smile, but perhaps in the depths of his blue eyes there was pity. He turned and handed the bag of coins to Bevil Blake, who stood just outside the carriage.

"You'll find no traffic in death this night, Elaine," Bevil Blake said, "unless it is your own." He stepped back to allow the magistrate's men to enter the carriage, ignoring both her screams and her shouts of retribution.

She cursed James then, her vivacious face transformed into one crazed and totally devoid of beauty. She shocked Bevil Blake and the others who were with him as she lunged for him, attempting to rake her nails across her former lover's face. It took three strong men to restrain her in her rage.

James merely stepped back, out of range, well aware of her capacity for duplicity and her gutter tactics. Nothing she could do would surprise him, which was only one of the reasons he'd decided to cooperate with Bevil Blake when he'd knocked on the door of his lodgings this evening. The fact was, he really didn't traffic in murder; wanted no part of it, in fact. He had not sunk that low, even though his standards had reached the waterline, even for him.

"I will kill you for this," Elaine hissed, straining for his face. Maggie blanched and retreated, in case the dowager wanted to vent her rage on any available target. Wise course, thought Bevil Blake.

He circled the carriage and opened the opposite door, neatly pulling the little maid from the countess's reach, stunned at the look of demonic rage that transformed her features. He thought that if her many admirers could see her now, there would be none to call her beautiful.

"Madam," he told the Dowager Countess of Cardiff, a woman who by all rights should never have worn that title, "the only one to die for their crimes will be yourself. Of that, I can assure you."

Elaine Weston would be tried for the murder of her husband and her stepson. There was no need for her to maintain a pretense of innocence. The authorities had already spoken to Samuel. He had told them all of the groom's confession before he had left Heddon Hall. The groom was beyond their reach, having emigrated, no doubt, to the colonies. Not so the Dowager Countess of Cardiff. Scandal be damned, he thought; she deserved everything she would receive. Granted, nobility was exempt from many of society's strictures, but murder was murder, and even her rank would not protect her now.

Let her stew in Newgate for a while, he thought. The dank atmosphere would soften her anger, though he doubted it would bring remorse. Even now she was not so filled with contrition for her deeds as she was rage that she was discovered. At least in Newgate she would not be able to harm those who had been harmed enough by fate itself.

Forty-two

The London night seen through her bedroom window looked no different than it ever had, Laura thought.

The fog rolled in, a moist cloud of vapor blanketing the street with an eerie mantle, like egg white beaten to a froth. If not for the fog, she could see to the corner, where the Weston town house stood. The exterior of the house was simple, almost plain, with a series of well-proportioned windows level with the sills. A railing of black wrought iron separated the property from the street and supported two lantern holders, empty now. The two Doric columns flanking the front door were surmounted by a graceful fanlight, which remained dark and inhospitable. There, just there, only a few feet from her own door, he had stood, had paused perhaps in taking his leave. There his feet had stepped. There his eyes had traveled. There he might have seen her own carriage, might have glanced, unconcerned, apathetically, toward her own window. There he had heard the sounds of carriages, of barrow girls calling out their wares. There the wind might have whipped his cloak from off his shoulder or teased that raven hair.

He was alive and she had not known.

Should something not have alerted her? Should she not have realized, somehow? Should she not have felt him, the beating of his blood, the pounding of his heart, the slow breaths?

She had not known.

She had not known.

All these many months, these years, she had not known.

She shivered, crossed her arms over her chest, and watched the street intently, as if the swirling fog was infinitely more important than the news her uncle had brought.

When, after long moments, she did not turn, nor speak to him, he finally grew restless and not a little worried at her composure.

Or was it composure? he wondered. Was she simply so shocked that she could not understand the import of the news?

He had been prepared for hysterics. Perhaps even for her fainting. He had certainly been prepared for tears, and had tucked an extra handkerchief into his pocket for just such an eventuality. He had not been prepared for her stoic silence, or her coldness.

What was wrong with his niece?

"Do you not comprehend, Laura?" he said finally, his worry giving way to irritation.

"Yes, Uncle Bevil," she said calmly, too calmly, still not turning from the view through the glass. "I do understand."

"Alex is alive, child. Alive!" he nearly shouted.

"Yes," she agreed. She clutched her arms tighter to her chest as another shudder racked her body. She had the absurd feeling that she must hold herself very tightly. If she did not, she would splinter into a thousand tiny shards, and then she would be unable to piece herself back together again.

"Have you nothing more to say?"

"What would you have me say, Uncle?" she asked, the words expelled from her chest in one long sigh.

"Well, something a damn sight more exciting than what I've heard," he muttered. She was acting as if all of his frantic activity this night had been for naught, he thought.

First, the trap for the dowager countess, an action that still left a sour taste in his mouth. Then the interview at the Admiralty, where he had to pull in every favor he'd been owed over the years in order to find out the truth concerning Alex's

appearance in London, two years after a memorial service
had been held for him and a damn plaque lovingly erected
in his memory.

His last gesture of this frantic night had been the courier
dispatched to Percival, with a letter detailing the events of
the last few hours.

He had finally returned to Laura's town house near midnight, anxious to impart the news to her.

Now his niece was acting in such a way that he doubted
his own sanity. Instead of rushing to Heddon Hall, certain
that Alex would have returned to his ancestral home, she was
not making any plans at all. She was too calm, too rational,
and too damn cold for his tastes. She continued to stare out
the window, as if seeking her future there.

"I seem," she said haltingly, as if the words would not
slide past some invisible barrier, "to be speechless, Uncle.
Isn't that strange?"

He looked at his niece, the woman who was no longer the
girl he had known so well, and recalled what she had had to
bear in these past years. No, perhaps it was not so hard to
understand at all. She had run the gamut of emotions from
deep love to despairing grief, buried her husband and her
child, mourned for them both in an intensely private way that
defied his past experience and his knowledge of the female
sex.

No, perhaps it was not so hard to understand at all.

"Child," he said gently, skirting the trunks that dotted the
room and laying one hand upon her rigid shoulder. "Time is
all you need. Time to come to grips with this wonderful news.
Time to absorb it all."

"Perhaps," she said, gently but firmly pulling away from
his tender touch.

"Perhaps Alex is at Heddon Hall, my dear, waiting for
you."

For just an instant of time, she wanted to laugh.

Alex at Heddon Hall. Just like before. As if nothing had

ever happened. The past was to be rolled back like a wave suddenly commanded to halt its advance from the ocean and not reach the shore.

What her uncle expected of her was just as impossible.

Yet where was the joy?

Memories came unbidden to her mind and threatened to destroy her tenuous composure. She shook her head as if to clear it. She did not want to see Alex in her mind, his tall, broad frame filling a doorway, his slanted smile. She did not want to hear his warm laughter or his teasing words. She did not want to smell the scent of him, something so rare and Alexlike that she could never quite describe it. She did not want to recall his swift and compelling grace that belied his injured leg, or see the beauty of him despite the mask and his scars.

Uncle Bevil was right; she could not absorb it all yet. But where was the delirious joy? Where was the laughter, the thankfulness, the excitement?

"You will want to go home," he said, in the tones of a born strategist.

"No," she answered him swiftly, without thinking.

"No?" He eyed her incredulously. "Alex will expect you there."

"Will he?" she asked, and finally moved away from the window. She turned and glanced impassionately at her uncle. He was not prepared for that steady and direct gaze.

"Then, if you will not return, what will you do?"

"Uncle Bevil," she said calmly, "at this moment I do not know." She glanced at the trunks, arranged throughout the room. Perhaps she would still leave. Perhaps. She had not lied to him. At this moment she was incapable of making a decision.

She heard the sound of her uncle's angry departure from the room and shut her eyes tightly.

He was dead, and now he was alive.

Why, dear God, did she feel nothing?

From the moment she had known of his death she had prayed for this moment. She had bargained with a harsh God for his return. She had sought his life by being willing to trade her own. When it was evident that miracles would not happen, that no message would be brought of his magical and mystical resurrection, she had gradually, slowly, begun to accept his death.

At first she had had to step through the pain, because there was no way to avoid it. A hole in her soul had been created by Alex's death. She carried it with her, as a tortoise would carry its home, complete and self-sufficient. Then, as she became used to its presence in her life, a curious thing had begun to happen. She had found herself changing to encompass it, to surround it and make a place for it in her life. She felt as though she was no longer herself, as if she had been lost on a long, dark road, desolate in its blackness, empty of even the tiniest flicker of light. Totally and completely alone, with no sound of another traveler or the smallest noise of a foot tread to mar the absorbing silence. This person who inhabited her body was someone else borrowed for a time, until she could find her way back from the darkness.

The grief she had felt each day had never left her; it had simply become a part of her.

And now her uncle expected her, as they would all expect her, to shed that pain and anguish as if it were a cloak, and be about the business of living again.

How could she pretend to be that same person?

The old Laura had ceased to exist. The old Laura was a pampered, sheltered darling who assumed that life would always offer the same predictable existence. Who knew that she could get her way with a smile. Who could lie and rationalize her own selfishness because she had always been applauded and approved of. Who knew that she would be granted love because she loved in return. Who was certain that bad things would not happen to her because she was a good person.

That child had known nothing of duty, even less of courage. That girl had been reckless and impulsive, had challenged fate itself and expected to emerge the victor. The old Laura had wept at anything that remotely stirred her, had been moved by the sight of pink roses, and expected everyone within her range of influence to realize how charming and loving she was.

That Laura had died.

She had realized, during the last two years, that not only must she learn to live without Alex, but she must learn to live with her new self.

She was older and wiser, with a wisdom forged in pain. She was conscious, despite her relative youth, of how mortal she was, how fleeting life itself was. Her time with the children had only reinforced that belief, that knowledge of the frailty of human existence. When each tiny victim was laid to rest she was once more impressed with the fragility of human nature. She did not spend her time in frivolous pursuits. She did not care for fashion, for aimless chatter, for the ennui that seemed to grip the nobility like an invisible vice.

She did not defer to anyone, not even the uncles, when making a decision. She administered her own wealth and spent it where she deemed it would do the most good. She lived where she wanted to live, sought the company of those she wished to be near. Now she weighed the pros and cons of each decision with deliberateness and foresight, whereas before she would have rushed into circumstances headlong, without a thought to the consequences. She fought the delays of bureaucracy with dogged determination and the jaded attitudes of society with the same resolve. She challenged men who made laws and she'd threatened William Pitt!

No, she was no longer that same child.

This Laura would not have resorted to idiotic games or

trickery in seeking an audience with Alex. She would not have been the selfish child who resented the time they spent apart. She would not have tolerated Pitt's machinations in her marriage, but would have challenged the man to know her husband's whereabouts the minute Alex had disappeared. This Laura would have been furiously angry at Alex's departure instead of grief-stricken. She would have followed him rather than remain meekly behind, even if it had meant giving birth amid the carnage of war.

She would have demanded his love instead of accepting his rare declarations with gratitude. She would have been his partner, his helpmate, his equal, instead of an adoring child who could not quite believe her good fortune.

Alex had given her love and passion, but his death had bequeathed her an unexpected gift.

It had forced her to grow up.

It was ironic to her that she had longed to tell Alex what she had learned, yet it was because of Alex's death that she had learned it at all.

She was no longer the same adoring child.

She had been like a candle, burning quickly and with a bright, brilliant flame. She had burned herself up for Alex and when there was no more of her left she had scraped together the mass of hardened, puddled wax and begun again. This time with a slower, more steady flame that was not as bright, but not that easily extinguished.

Alex was her past, representing what she had known herself to be, summoning memories by his presence. Alex had been her childhood idol, her god, her one friend. She felt cut off from that past now, as if the child she had been—the girl who had loved him so desperately—was another person.

She could see that person in her mind's eye, but she was a stranger. That life was another's life. Those experiences belonged to someone else, as if two souls lived within her body. One belonged to a child, a young girl with such hope and such innocence and such courage. The other, to a much wiser woman.

It was not bitterness that caused that division. Death, itself, was the only catalyst that could have accomplished it. She, too, had died, and her rebirth had been accomplished slowly, in torturous steps. Each day she had had to begin that long discovery of reshaping herself from what she had been.

Everything that had been normal was normal no longer.

Everything that had been usual was now unusual.

He had left, and she had been forced to learn to live with his departure, his death, and, finally, her new identity.

Now he had returned, like a phoenix from the ashes.

She did not wish to return to the past. She did not want to roll back time, as if these great changes had not occurred. To be the careless, hopeful, childish Laura, with such strong convictions and such certain knowledge. Who could give up her pride without a thought, who could invest so much of herself into that great love she had felt and shared.

She knew, now, that her knowledge was as nothing, her strong convictions only the stuff of childish dreams. Her pride was once again in place, her capacity for love dulled by the stern voice of caution.

Now he was at Heddon Hall and she should return to him, as if nothing had happened, take up the remnants of her life, and return to what and who she had been.

She could not do it.

She was both stronger and yet more delicate. She did not know, frankly, if she had the strength for Alex's love.

Uncle Bevil could not understand. Could Alex?

She no longer willingly accepted pain as the reverse of that great and magical love he offered. She did not want anguish as a price she must pay. She preferred the dulled existence of the past two years to the agony she had suffered when she lost him the first time.

How could you love just a little?

Alex deserved no less than the full measure of her devotion, not bits and pieces of herself doled out when she felt safe. He deserved a wife who loved him in the way he should be loved, fully and completely, with no thought to the consequences.

Would she always withhold something, in order not to be hurt so terribly again? Would she always be careful and cautious?

Once, Uncle Percival had said that she would feel anger, and only then would she begin to heal.

She had never felt anger before, never felt free enough or strong enough for fury. She had wanted to be angry, God knew, but she could never summon the energy for it. The damning, infuriating power of anger had escaped her.

She was not prepared for the rage that suffused her now.

She whirled and faced the window again, and suddenly wanted to strike both fists against the pane and shatter it.

She wanted to curse at the world. She wanted to pull down the barrier of composure that had sheltered and protected her emotions for so long.

"It is not fair," she whispered in the silence of the room.

"I can't do it," she shouted a moment later, as anger whirled within her, summoning all the dormant rage that had lain still and untapped within her.

She who had never felt anger before was now surfeited by it. She was desperately, fiercely angry at him for leaving her. He had left her when she had needed him most. He had left for England and William Pitt, and she did not think she could ever forgive him for it. He had left because duty called him; not Heddon Hall, not his wife, not plans for the future. Damn duty. He had left her a note, rather than face her and accept the burden of her grief and her pain. He had left, and their son had died, and he had not been there, and she had been unprepared and too damn young to accept the burden of that, but forced to do so. All during that long year, when her life was comprised of only the bitter taste of ashes, when she had felt such despairing grief, he had been alive, and yet no word had come.

She didn't think she could ever forgive him for that.

He had plotted with Pitt and spent his nights in secret conjecture, investigating and counseling the great minister on naval strategy.

She knew she could not forgive him for that.

"Damn you, Alex!" she shouted.

It did not strike her as ironic that all the anger she should have vented in those long months since his death was now heaped upon Alex's head.

She placed both hands against the cool glass and bowed her head between her outstretched arms. In the quiet of the room she could hear the sound of her heart beating frantically in her chest.

She had been presented with the most wonderful and terrible offering of all—the return of the loved one whose death had altered her life.

It terrified her.

Forty-three

Heddon Hall

He had dreamed of his return.

Like a fool, he had imagined her welcome, envisioned her tears of joy, relished the thought of the sweet warmth of her flesh. He had seen his son in his mind, a toddler hiding behind his mother's skirts, eyeing him with a timid glance that rapidly changed to a fearless, protective stance. He would have knelt on one knee, and that little warrior would have come closer, recognizing his father at last.

He passed through the arched iron gate that led to the mausoleum and stood at the entrance before he forced himself to brave its marble coldness. Inside was a small niche carved for his son. The words chiseled into the stone were without comment. They simply listed his birth and his death on the same day. His palm remained braced against the marble slab, absorbing the cold into his skin.

His face was a stoic mask that only mimicked the black leather that partially covered it.

This was to be his homecoming, then: an absent wife and a dead child.

He should have stayed in Prussia.

Something broke in him then, as he touched the marble slab. Something that had remained strong and vigorous despite his punishment by the French and Frederick's intransigent stubbornness in not releasing him sooner. Something that had been brave and daunting and fearless and had kept him going even though men died around him every day.

He bowed his head and did not think he could bear it.

"She thought you dead," Percival spoke softly from behind him.

"I thought her constant," Alex said coldly, not turning.

"There are two things you must see," Percival said calmly, gently placing his hand on the younger man's shoulder, leading him outside of the crypt, where a small monument was placed.

Alex stared at it, slowly tracing his fingers over the marble.

> *For Alex*
> *My Husband*
> *My Love*
> *My Friend*

He finally turned away.

He did not speak.

"She came here almost every day," Percival said, noting the stiffness of the other man's stance. "Sometimes, during the first year, we could find her here at any hour. She found it hard to leave at night, as if your son would be fearful of the encroaching darkness."

Still Alex did not speak, but Percival was having none of it.

"There are things you must know, Alex," Percival said stubbornly, refusing to budge, refusing to be sent away by the other man's stubborn silence.

"There is nothing you can say that will ease my homecoming," Alex said with a mocking laugh. "Nothing other than to tell me that this is a bad dream, that Laura awaits me inside Heddon Hall. Tell me that my son lives. If you will but do that, I will listen to whatever words you have to tell me. If not, then bid me farewell, because I cannot stomach more."

"And if I would tell you things that would change your mind?" Percival asked cautiously. "I cannot summon the dead, Alex, but I can tell you of Laura."

"I do not wish to hear of my perfidious wife," Alex said.

"You would believe what others say of her, Alex? Instead of judging her actions?" Bevil's message had been less taciturn than usual; he had been careful to explain all that had occurred in London. "Why do you put so much credence in Elaine's words? Is she such a worthy judge of character, then, Alex?"

"My stepmother is a bitch, Percy, but a consistent one. If she lied, then where is Laura? Has she flown to my side? What actions of hers do I judge, Percival?"

Neither mentioned that another man might have sought Laura out, to learn the truth of her feelings in person. Percival was too aware of the rigid pride of the other man, and Alex too mindful of his shortcomings. He'd had one perfect year with Laura before she realized, evidently, all she had given up in the name of love. One perfect year that had to last a lifetime.

"It seems Elaine spoke only truth, after all," Alex said, his voice raspy and harsh, belying his churning emotions.

"There are other things you should see before you form an opinion, Alex. I do not lie," Percival said somberly. It was only the unflinching look in the older man's eyes that finally propelled Alex down the steep grass incline to the stables.

"Tell me, then," he said, after several long, silent moments had passed. The man at his side merely motioned him onward.

"I beg of you an indulgence, Alex," Percival began, knowing that the man was suffering, yet knowing that mere words would not make him understand. "Bear with me until we reach Blakemore. Then I will tell you and show you."

Alex turned and looked at his companion. Percival wore a slight smile, and his eyes were crinkled at the corners. Damn, this was no game.

"It seems I have nothing but time left, Percival," he said ironically. "No wife, no child, no welcome."

Percival shut his eyes when Alex laughed, a great booming laugh that carried with it no humor but vast mockery.

Percival was relieved that he seemed to accept his terms and did not question him until they passed through the Winter Garden. He felt Alex stiffen beside him. Only then did he voice the question that burned on his tongue.

"Where is she?"

"In London," Percival said calmly. "In her own home. She could not stomach Elaine's company for long, I'm afraid. Had you questioned but one of the servants you would have discovered that."

Alex said nothing to that remark, only shot a sharp glance at his wife's uncle.

The trip to Blakemore was made in silence.

As they entered the green, sloping courtyard that fronted his wife's childhood home, he began to notice the signs of activity.

Children seemed to be everywhere.

He counted ten of them, engaged in occupations as diverse as sitting on the grass and listening to a story being told by Jane or playing in the gardens. One was attempting, however unsuccessfully, to assist the gardener; still another was bouncing a ball upon the cobblestone walk.

"Do you not see something strange about these children?" Percival asked him.

Alex looked around and then shook his head, bemused.

"Look again," Percival coaxed, but Alex could see nothing extraordinary. There was one small child seated on the steps of Blakemore, only a few feet from their mounts. Percival smiled at him, coaxing the lad to come closer. He bent down stiffly and pulled the boy up to sit in front of him on the saddle. The child smiled, a radiant, peaceful smile, and Alex felt something in his heart turn.

"This one's name is Dix," Percival said, combing the little

boy's hair out of his eyes. "He's only two. The same age your son would have been, had he lived." He waved to the other children, then turned and smiled at Alex.

"They all have black hair and, with few exceptions, black eyes. The little girls, for the most part, have hair as brightly orange as Laura's as a child." He smiled softly, an infinitely gentle smile. "I don't think she realizes what she's done. I don't think even Bevil has noticed. There are three other country houses she has made into orphanages, but the children at Blakemore are special."

Alex did not speak. He looked out among the children once more, turning his gaze from the little boy who sat trustingly upon Percival's horse. It was true, they all looked the same, little boys with hair of black, so black that it shimmered blue in the sun. Their cheeks were rosy, their frames small, too thin, but already showing the signs of love and care.

"She cannot have more children," Percival said gently, beginning to speak now, just when Alex wished to God he would shut up. He blinked and turned his mount but heard the words nonetheless. "She thinks herself responsible for your son's death, and for a long time did not want to live." He told him, then, how it had happened.

"She is as scarred inside her soul as you are on your flesh, Alex, and I do not know how you will reach her. I have never seen anyone mourn as she mourned, or anyone lose the spark of spirit inside as Laura did when she thought you dead. It was as if the fire were extinguished behind those bright eyes."

Alex did not speak but glanced around him at the children playing unconcerned on the grass.

"She wears a mask of her own, I think," Percival said. His words would have surprised his brother, but they would not have shocked his niece, who had realized long ago that, of the two, Percival was more able to understand the anguish she had suffered.

"She acts as though she is still the same, but she is not. She lives, as we all do, but she only suffers an existence.

Only in the past year, when she has been so busy with these children, have I seen a spark of the old Laura return."

"Then why, for God's sake, is she not at Heddon? Or are you telling me now that she still does not know that, like Lazarus, I have returned from the dead?" Alex almost shouted, but Percival detected the emotion behind the rage.

He smiled, a small sad smile.

"When Laura was little I used to tell her that she should not be so enamored of you. Do you know what she told me?"

He could see the back of Alex's head, the slight gesture.

"She told me that I was the one who was wrong. I can hear her little voice now, piping with that high-pitched tone that little girls have, 'Uncle Percival,' she said, 'he's mine. He may not know it now, but he is. Dixon Alexander Weston will always be mine, until the day I die.' "

"That does not explain her actions," Alex said curtly, the lump in his throat making his voice sound thick.

"I also remember what she was like when you were gone. I found her often beside the mausoleum, as if she summoned your spirit there. One day is particularly vivid to me. She was standing with her hands pressed against the plaque she had erected for you, as if she could connect with you somehow. When I urged her to go inside because of the light rain that had begun to fall she shook her head and said that she wanted to stay. Then she said the strangest thing. 'I would kill myself, Uncle, if I did not think that God would hold me apart from Alex's spirit in punishment. But perhaps I'm dead already.' Do you know, she has never cried? Not once. She holds her grief inside of her as though the shedding of one tear would unloose a flood that could never be stopped."

"That still does not answer why," Alex said, cursing the fact that his voice betrayed him by its tremulous nature.

"You asked for the truth. It is in her own words, Alex. She said that she would love you until the day she died and, in a sense, she died along with you."

Alex turned then, and Percival was not unduly surprised

by the sight of his lips pressed together in a thin line, as if
to suppress his emotions.

"Are you saying that it is over? That there is nothing left
between us?"

"I am not saying that, Alex. What I am saying is that it
will take patience, compassion, and more empathy than you
can imagine. If you asked me to speculate, my answer would
be that she is afraid, Alex, desperately afraid. She has given
so much and lost it all. What did you expect her to do? Exist
in a timeless state until you came back? She is a human
being, sometimes wrong, sometimes right. You have both been
dealt a blow, Alex. You have suffered, but know this, if you
doubt all else. While you were fighting the French and the
Spanish, Laura was fighting her own battle. While you were
imprisoned, so was she. While you lived through a hell on
earth, Laura's hell was as encompassing."

"Then what in God's name do I do?"

"Love her. Believe in that love," Percival said simply. "If
you do, it will sustain you. If you do not, you will live a
lonely existence with only the presence of plants and insects
to keep you company." He smiled then, a small self-depreca-
tory smile that held years of bitter memories.

Alex turned his mount, returning home to Heddon Hall
with a great deal to think about.

Percival Blake watched him, gently set little Dix back upon
the steps, and followed slowly.

Alex strode past the Winter Garden, through the inner
courtyard and beyond, to the bridge that spanned the Wye.
He stood there for the longest time, gazing down at the river,
its clean and sparkling depths a mirror to his own soul.

Laura. He had thought of her as though she were an icon.
He had prayed to Laura more than he had prayed to God
himself. He had held her fast in his heart; little Laura.

Laura, holding her doll under one arm and staring at him
with worshipful eyes. Laura, reading in the garden, her green-
eyed gaze following him everywhere. Laura, learning chess

at his side and plaguing him with questions until he manfully decided to test her mind, for all that she was a mere female. He had learned that day, to his discredit, that she was a worthy opponent.

Laura, with her stubbornness, and her kitchen duties; Laura, with her nightly kisses to Apollo, the ill-named knight; Laura, with her flashing smile, attired in nothing but her silken flesh, mounting him as if he were a horse, swiftly impaling herself upon his shaft and shouting her release.

He had thought of her safe at Heddon, in comfort and luxury, surrounded by people who loved her, tending their son with the same devotion she had extended to him.

He had never thought of her as different, changed.

He had frozen her in time, just as Percival had accused, his lovely little bride, his to awaken.

While he had thought of her as a token of all that he had held dear, she had known him as lost, dead.

He had his thoughts of her, and his hope for the future. A hope that, somehow, had never died. She had not even had that. She had been left with only memories to draw upon, no hope for the future, only a despairing grief.

Once, he had thought that although she was gentle, compassionate, warm, and loving, she was untested by life. He had thought that she would never understand his own melancholy after the cannon misfired, would never understand how he had wanted, once, to give into deep, black despair, to dream of death rather than to keep living.

Once, perhaps, but not now.

Now, he realized, Laura would not only understand, but had been as tested as he.

Percival was right: They had each fought their own wars. Each had been involved in his own struggle for survival.

He had the sudden, shocking notion that her battle had been the more difficult.

Forty-four

Blakemore

"Good lord, but that's an ugly man your uncle hired," Dolly, Duchess of Buthe said, entering the drawing room. A dusty apron was pinned to her bodice and the hem of her dress bore the unmistakable signs of wood shavings. Dolly could never avoid the lure of supervision. As it was, the carpenters involved in enlarging Blakemore's kitchen watched her departure with a collective sigh of relief.

"I hope he's a genius with horses, because he's certain to scare the children to death."

Laura looked up from her desk. "What new man?" She had barely begun to tally the figures for the construction. They were a little overbudget, but that did not concern her. What bothered her the most was that they were behind schedule, badly behind schedule, which meant that someone had to supervise all the work in order for it to be done on time. There were too many children waiting for a safe haven, a place far from London.

She had not wanted to return to Blakemore, but Dolly had almost bullied her into coming back.

"You have few choices, my dear," Dolly had said. "Your trunks are packed, your house let for the season. You can spend a few days there before you make other plans."

Dearest Dolly. But for her, she would have no friends.

She had agreed to return to Blakemore only if Dolly accompanied her and, surprisingly, Dolly had simply responded that if she had not been invited, she would have followed anyway.

Dolly and Uncle Bevil had become friends immediately, both of them being practical people. It was with Uncle Percival, though, that Dolly's demeanor changed. Laura had watched in fascination as Dolly became almost flirtatious around her more reticent uncle. She watched with outright wonder as Uncle Percival shed his mask of shyness and became almost courtly in his pursuit of her friend.

She could not help but smile at both of them.

"The groom your uncle hired," Dolly repeated for the second time. Laura caught herself and nodded, returning to her work. She did not see the small smile playing around Dolly's lips, or the softening of her eyes.

"Good heavens, Laura, must you pore over those figures all day long? You look pale as a sheet."

She suspected she was pale from the shock she had received, and the fact that she had not slept well since hearing the news.

She had not yet come to grips with Alex's resurrection, although it had been over a week.

Night after night she had stood at the window, wondering where he was, what he was doing. Most of all, wondering about his thoughts, his feelings.

Would he ever understand?

Did he hate her for their son's death?

Or—and this was the most terrible question of all—would he love the woman she had become or prefer the girl she had been?

Seven days, in which she had hidden from the world, returning the carefully inscribed letter to Simons, who had made the trip between the two great houses with dignity and formal demeanor. Who, when she had simply and wordlessly returned the unopened envelope to him, had only sighed and placed it carefully in his pocket.

"Are you sure, m'lady?" he had asked then, in that grave, Simonslike voice. She had only smiled and barely restrained herself from patting the man's cheek in a comforting gesture. He looked so sad, then, that she could not help but grieve for him. She wished that something she could say would make some sense, and that those few magical words would make him murmur, "Ah, I see now why." But, of course, there were no such words, or if they existed, they were lacking from her vocabulary.

She did not want to read Alex's words. She did not wish to see his sloping signature, filled with such power, such arrogance. She did not want to feel.

She was not ready.

She did not know if she would ever be ready. Was there enough time in the world to prepare herself for this confrontation?

It had only been a week. One week, in which all the dormant emotions she had thought long dead now sprang to the forefront of her mind.

Memories of him. Dear God, the memories of him.

The soft, rasping whisper of his voice, his deep, resonant laughter, the grin that turned up those mobile lips. The smooth hardness of his body as it was pressed against hers, the magic of his mind as they dueled with words and sought to challenge each other at chess. His compassion and understanding, his reverence for all those things that she, too, held dear.

A week. Only one week.

She was more frightened than she had ever been.

Each night, when she finally, fitfully dozed, she did not sleep well, as though her mind conspired against her heart. Her dreams roused her in the middle of the night, when she would sit up in her bed and look toward Heddon Hall. She could sense him there, awake and wondering about her, too. She could almost feel him searching her out, beckoning to her, imploring her.

Last night, in the darkness, she had dreamed the most disturbing dream of all.

They stood together in the state bedroom, she clothed in a serviceable nightgown similar to the ones she had worn for more than two years, he naked, bathed by the moonlight streaming in from the conservatory window.

He scooped her up into his arms effortlessly, carrying her through to the conservatory, where he lay her gently upon a sheet covering the marble floor. It was cool to the touch, icy upon her back. She raised up on one elbow and watched him as he knelt beside her.

He was not scarred, this Alex, but bore the beloved face she remembered so well from her childhood. He knelt, bunched up her nightgown in his strong, tanned hands, and eased it over her head.

Then he did the strangest thing.

He anointed her body with his tears. Where one fell he lapped and bathed the spot with a tender tongue and then a deep kiss.

"What are you doing?" she asked him in a tear-clogged voice. He placed one gentle hand behind her head and raised her to a sitting position, enfolding her in his arms.

"I am blessing you, my love," he said tenderly, and kissed her parted lips. His lips tasted of salt and sweetness and hot moisture. All Alex, firm and hard and soft. She sighed against his mouth and his words pooled on her tongue.

"Love me, my darling," he whispered, and the words seemed to be embedded in her soul. She entwined her arms around his neck and pulled him down to her, feeling the hard strength of him next to her supple softness. His hands smoothed the places his kiss had tasted, dipped lower, and felt the wetness between her thighs, stroked her with silky movements that made her dig her heels into the sheet and arch against him.

He soothed her with a whisper and then lowered his mouth

to her breasts, feeling the tightness, the pebbly stones of her nipples reaching for his eager, lapping mouth.

She arched again, and her moan was muted by her own compressed lips, lips that opened quickly when his mouth descended once again to touch hers. His tongue licked her lips open, and then once again departed for a tender, eager nipple. This time, when he sucked and pulled and rasped it with a hot tongue, she moaned aloud, never noticing when the sound seemed to echo in the silence of the room. He cupped her full and heavy breasts and suckled upon her as if she could feed him forgetfulness. He plundered her breasts as he plundered her mouth, until she was writhing open-mouthed and wanting beneath him.

She pulled that beloved head close to hers and whispered to him, words of wanting and needing and the fire that ached to be quenched by him and only him.

He bathed her body with cooling kisses that turned molten hot when he dipped between her legs, blessing her by the power of his love. He licked and lapped, and she begged for release and begged him to love her, but he would not cease.

When she awoke it was with a sense of loss as heavy and deep as when he had died and left her.

In the silence of the night-filled room, with only the molten air shimmering around her sweat-drenched body, she stared out the window toward Heddon Hall.

Dear God, it had been so long, and yet not long enough. Never long enough to forget him.

She could feel him there, waiting, wondering, patient.

Never long enough to forget the pain.

Anguish lingered in the shadows of her bedroom and her mind. It was more than a hint of pain; it was a tangible threat.

To go to him now would be to risk everything, to dare to step across a threshold, a chasm of danger. She would be suspended above an abyss of nothingness because she knew, in some deep and dark place in her heart, that if she ever lost him again, she would die of it.

As she had nearly died of it before.

To go to him now would be her greatest act of bravery, and she did not know if there was that much courage in the world.

"Come," Dolly said imperiously, "you have worked over those ledgers long enough. It is time you took some fresh air. We'll escape this menagerie for a while. Go and dress in your new habit, and I'll summon the horses."

She extracted the book from Laura's grasp and pointed toward the stairs. Laura sighed helplessly, recognizing the implacable look on Dolly's face for what it was. What she really wanted was a good night's sleep, she thought with irritation. Yet she wondered if she would ever be able to sleep again.

She shook her head to dismiss her thoughts and agreed to change. When she returned to the foyer she was surprised to see that Dolly was not attired in her own habit.

"No, child, I think you will profit from the solitude," she announced, and nearly shoved her out the door.

She smiled at her friend's strange notions of solitude as she was surrounded by chattering children. They stood on the steps and watched as her horse was brought around.

The groom was attired in dun-colored trousers and a frayed cotton shirt, its color once white but now dotted with offal and other colors whose origins she preferred to ignore. He bent toward her until his back was parallel to the ground and tugged on the forelock of his shaggy black hair.

Hair that was etched with silver.

He cupped his palms together, which was difficult since one hand was badly deformed and gloveless.

She felt her heart still in her chest.

"M'lady," he said in a low, servile voice. He bent down and would have retrieved one reluctant boot, placing it in his hand, had she not stepped away.

She did not move except for that one hesitant step.

She could not.

"Alex?" she said, her voice seeming to come from far away.

Fear was dying swiftly in her heart as she stared at the man she had always loved. How easy it was to be afraid until she glimpsed that beloved face.

Oh, God, Alex.

Something began to crack within her heart, an icy shell that she had erected around her thoughts and her feelings and whose barrier had been surmounted easily by her dreams of him. A shell that had been too long in place and whose presence had no part between the two of them. As she stared at him, it shimmered and began to splinter.

He lifted his bared face to look at her directly. He had never exposed himself to the daylight before, but now he did. In view of the children and Dolly and the other London servants, who must have derided him and made him the object of many a callous joke.

The man who craved his privacy with fanatical fervor now exposed himself in the full view of any who would see. Who had roamed through his own home at midnight, rather than let the servants see his hesitation, now bent and bowed before her as if he were the lowliest servant.

He stared at her, thinking that she had never looked so lovely. He ached to put his arms around her, but he did nothing but stand and watch her.

Her face had filled out, her lips had grown more full, her hair seemed to glisten with gold highlights. How well he remembered it wrapped around him. Her eyes were wide and green, sparkling like the most valuable emeralds. He smiled into them, but they were frozen and staring, as if viewing a ghost.

"Alex?" she said again, and he tugged his forelock with one grimy hand.

He was still Alex. Older, with a few more scars upon his face and a look in his eyes it pained her to see.

She did not notice the one small tear that escaped the corner of her eye and rolled down her cheek.

He did, and remembered Percival's words.

Do you know, she has never cried? Not once. She holds her grief inside of her as though the shedding of one tear would unloose a flood that could never be stopped.

"Why?" she whispered, and he looked into those wide green eyes he had dreamed about for so long and knew himself home at last.

"You came to me once in the guise of a servant," he said simply, "to reach me and convince me of your love. Could I do less?" He reached out one hand and touched that one tear with a tender finger.

Laura. Dear God, Laura. He thought his heart would swell and explode.

She saw him from far away, the distance measured not only in years but in her capacity for pain.

He smiled softly, and she closed her eyes.

"Laura," he said gently. How low his voice was and how resonant. Her name upon his lips was enough to bring back all the memories she had kept carefully concealed and sheltered in her mind. It was enough to summon the anguish, the despair. But it was also enough to breech the defenses she had erected around herself and kept carefully intact all these years.

She was no longer Lady Weston; she was Laura Ashcott Blake, a small and fearless child with a love so strong and powerful that it swept aside barriers of propriety, her own humiliation, and an ingrained sense of pride.

Time became compressed and mutable as she was thrust into the past. She moaned, but the sound of it was low, almost inaudible.

He smiled gently at her, then turned and walked away.

It was the hardest thing he'd ever done.

There would be time enough for her to come to him.

He had not lied to Percival: All he had in the world now

was time. Time to recover the one person he could not live without.

She stared at his retreating back and felt the chasm shift back into place, until the world was firm and solid again.

She knew, in that moment in time, when he walked away from her, that she would cherish him as long as she would live and perhaps beyond death itself. She would seek to be beside him, not because he was the other half of herself, not because she could not live without him. She had survived, she had lived, she had carved out a life without him. No, she sought to be beside him because she wanted to be with him. This was the man her heart had chosen when she was only a child. This man. She had matured and grown and lived a little more, but the girl was wiser than the woman.

The girl had recognized her love and had not been fearful of it.

The girl had not been afraid of the power of that love and the pain it might hold.

She knew, in that moment, that there would be times in which they would be separated again. That one day death would truly come to one of them, leaving the other to live as long as life decreed before they met again.

She recognized that great love carries a price of great torment if it ends, but it also bestows a greater and more valuable gift.

She had never truly felt alive except with him, this stalwart man who had braved his deepest fear to come to her.

She had never felt such excitement, such awareness of life around her, as if the very air was charged with his presence.

Yes, she might be hurt again and feel the anguish and the pain that made her want to die with him, but until that day came he would gift her with love. Love that defied trite words or even description, that carried with it tenderness and passion and laughter and friendship. Love that made her eyes sparkle and her breath stop when she saw him and imbued life with more meaning and more purpose.

Alex was love. That child who still resided within her, who had been so much wiser and braver than the woman had been, shouted at her.

In that moment the barrier that had begun to crack disintegrated and crumbled into icy shards to lie at the base of Laura's soul. As she stared at his retreating back, they transformed themselves into healing tears—tears that she had never felt strong enough or brave enough to shed.

At first he did not hear her choked reply.

"Alex!" she finally screamed, running after him, throwing herself into his strong arms much as she had as a child. Instead of being assaulted by a flurry of hoops, calico, torn lace, and Laura Blake's flushed and tearful face, he was enveloped by the lovely warm figure of Laura Weston, his wife, his love, his friend.

He swung her up into his arms, neither of them noticing when Dolly wiped her eyes with a hastily procured handkerchief, continuing to watch them unashamedly from the front steps of Blakemore. Laura did not notice when all of the children who had begun to look upon her as their surrogate mother began to cheer and raised such a noise that Jane tossed her book upon the ground and attempted to restore order to her charges.

"Alex," she repeated over and over like a hallowed prayer, interspersing that one word with tiny kisses that brushed against his beloved face burned by the sun and by the wind touching its exposed and tortured skin. "Alex," she whispered, as the tears began to flow in soft droplets that bathed his face.

"Alex," she sobbed, as he effortlessly carried her past a broadly smiling Dolly and shocked servants arrayed in the hallway. She did not stop sobbing his name until he came to her room and sat with her on the bed with her gently imprisoned in his arms.

The torrent began.

Tears flooded her heart and cascaded down her face, wetting his shirt as she clutched fistfuls of it. Tears that she wept because he had left and died, returned and lived. Tears because their son had died and she had felt so alone and so responsible. Tears because she could never give him another child. Tears that started as soft dripping drops and turned into great gasping sobs that racked her body and rid her of the poison of pain.

She did not know that she spoke as she cried, telling him of her anguish. She was not aware that she pounded his chest with her clenched fist and railed at him for leaving her, and then gripped him fiercely with greedy fingers that could not stop stroking him. Nor did she realize that his own tears mixed with hers, as he held her tenderly within the broad shelter of his arms.

They clutched each other in love and support and total security and knew themselves home at last.

Epilogue

Heddon Hall

She was there when the crested carriage rolled to a stop before the front steps of Heddon Hall. No child clutched her skirts, no baby marred her pristine bodice; she was alone for once, which in itself was an oddity. She waited until Simons had opened the door to the carriage, a duty he had nearly begged to accomplish. She allowed him the act of demeaning himself, if that was what he truly wished. By the perspiration dotting his brow and his rapturous smile, it evidently was.

A feminine foot descended first, followed by frothy lace and velvet, and Laura extended her hand to Lady Hester. When the other figure appeared she pressed her mouth into a semblance of a smile and performed a perfunctory gesture of greeting. A curtsy it was not.

William Pitt, newly made Earl of Chatham, surveyed his hostess with an eye to strategy and negotiation. After all, if he wanted those letters back, and the continued services of the Earl of Cardiff, he was prepared to pay. It was not coin this countess craved. It was assistance, pure and simple, and although his keen mind skimmed past the thought of being forced to repay favors, he supposed it was long overdue, even by his standards. But he didn't have to like it.

"I understand congratulations are in order, sir," Laura Ashcott Blake Weston, Countess of Cardiff, said to the new earl, by her tone allowing him to ponder the slight, amused smile on her face. Was she reminding him, by any chance, that her husband's title was two hundred years old and that even her own noble antecedents preceded his by many decades? Dammit, he didn't care if she was, the cheeky little minx. He was damned if he was going to be needled all week. He turned to his wife and, by a quick glance at the servile butler, requested that Lady Hester be taken someplace to rest and recuperate from the journey.

Only then did he turn to his hostess, who cruelly left him standing on those poisoned stumps of his.

"Well, Lady Weston," he said, well-versed in the art of intimidation and deciding to try it, "what is it, exactly, that you want?"

"Sir?" she said in her sweetest voice. "I crave nothing but that which excites your brain to speech."

"Is that Shakespeare?"

"No," she said, smiling, "Weston."

He harrumphed a little longer, his florid face increasing in hue as her stance was unmoving. As still as some damn statue, he thought.

"Very well, Lady Weston," he said, capitulating. "I will do my best to assist you in your task of raising money for your orphanages. And I will lend what weight I can to legislation for reform. More than that I cannot promise."

"Pitt's promise is good enough," Laura said, her green eyes large and innocent.

"Very well, Lady Weston. Does your husband know I've been blackmailed?" Damn woman didn't have to grin like some sort of resident of Bedlam.

"Blackmail, sir?"

"Are you going to let me have those letters?" He fell into step beside her as they slowly mounted the steep steps of Heddon Hall.

"They were burned long ago, sir," she said calmly, smiling slightly.

"You're a conniving woman, Lady Weston," he grumbled, "a devious personality."

"If you believe so, sir," she said, smiling and reaching out to help steady him with a hand to his elbow. The old dear was getting on in age, for all that shining, avaricious intelligence peered out from beneath those bushy eyebrows. "Allow me to show you to your rooms, sir," Laura said, extending an arm and assisting her gout-ridden guest up the stairs of Heddon Hall.

Her smile was bright enough to light a fire, William Pitt thought, and it didn't fool him one bit. He suspected the letters still existed. He'd watch this countess very carefully. Very carefully, indeed.

Dixon Alexander Weston held his infant son upon his lap, while two children sat at his feet, clamoring for yet another story of naval warfare.

He surmised that since Laura was nowhere around, it would not hurt their bloodthirsty little appetites to be regaled with one more tale. It was, after all, the only way to speed them to bed.

He had plans for tonight, plans that did not include his brood's interference.

Little Alex snuggled close to his chest, his tiny head nodding in sleep, and his father looked down at him with more than doting fondness. It was proud, paternal devotion.

He might not have sired this child, or any of them, but he was as much a father to his family of ten as if he and Laura had conceived them all.

It was not for lack of trying, he thought, with a grin.

He was halfway through his story, his daughter's enraptured expression mirroring her brother's, when his wife discovered them.

All three wore the same guilty expressions, and she stifled

a smile as she took the baby from her husband. The infant was the only one not to be chastised.

"Really, Alex," she said, the sparkling look in her eyes softening her words, "must you? Just before bedtime? Now they'll have nightmares."

He looked more than guilty, he looked horrified, she thought. As if the children's dreams might interfere with his plans. This time she could not stop the grin that wreathed her mouth, or the look that passed between them.

Simons had already alerted her to the meal set aside in the state bedroom, and the fact that Alex had instructed the nursery staff to ready the children for bed an hour early. Not only that, but Uncle Bevil was wearing a distinctly pleased expression that indicated he knew full well what was on Alex's mind. He had worn that expression for over a year now, as though he and he alone was responsible for Alex's resurrection.

He was a doting uncle to their brood, as much as he had been to her. Heddon Hall rang with the sound of childish laughter and the groans of the older children, who were marched upstairs to the schoolroom for their daily lessons.

Nor was Blakemore immune to new life. Over a hundred children resided there, playing in the gardens that had once been inhabited by one lone child. The lush and blooming landscape was still overseen by Uncle Percival. That is, since he had returned from his wedding journey with his new wife, Dolly.

The two older children obeyed her slight gesture reluctantly. It was not often they had their father all to themselves. The trust established for the orphanages took a great deal of their mother's time, but William Pitt still demanded a share of his.

Laura looked at her husband, the man who had the power to sway Parliament, the gifted speaker before the House of Lords, the adviser to the Minister of England. He was still scarred, but he would always be handsome to her. He was Alex.

The name itself had the power to motivate the entire staff at Heddon Hall. It is for Alex, she would say, and the servants would sigh inwardly, knowing that she would not be moved. It was an explanation that everyone around her knew was as unshakable as the deepest faith.

She prayed that life would never become less sweet than it was right now. Just this afternoon they had stood before the muses, surrounded by their brood, as Alex told them the history of the statues. She'd noticed several of her children staring intently at the three gargoyles, and wondered what wishes were being said to the stone figures.

She still visited the mausoleum and placed roses on the tiny marble slab that encased her infant son. Once, Alex had found her there and had held her tenderly as they both wept again for their loss. Yet each time she rescued another child from the slums of London, it was as if little Dixon's spirit still lived.

Life was full, exciting, and busy. It was not easy planning a romantic dinner, either with their schedules or with a brood as large as their's.

However, she was more than willing to acquiesce to any of Alex's plans.

She did wish sometimes that they could escape to the gardens, or have one night of uninterrupted pleasure.

Not that they didn't try, and often.

He smiled at the flush suffusing her face and did not wonder at her thoughts. He knew them well.

He grinned back at her and watched her hips sway seductively as she carried the baby to the nursery, the children trailing in her wake.

Had anyone told him, a year ago, that his life would be as full and as rich as it was now, he would have blessed their precognition, but would have doubted it with all his heart.

Now he could only revel in it.

Only one small episode had marred their new life, and that was the death of his stepmother. Her body had been found in the cell at Newgate, her legs splayed wide, her throat neatly cut. Who had been the instrument of her death? They did not know, nor were any explanations forthcoming, despite numerous bribes to greedy guards.

He could summon no sorrow for her passing.

Maggie and Samuel were on their way to the Colonies, their dreams of their own farm possible because of Bevil Blake's gift. There was not enough money to pay for Maggie's courage, he thought, and had added his own funds in a gesture of thanks.

He retreated to their room, bathed and emerged from the dressing room clad only in his brocade robe. In a few moments, with Laura's return, he would wear nothing at all.

He had long ceased wearing his mask, and his ravaged face did not seem to scare the children at all.

Occasionally, when they ventured out of doors, he would wear an eyepatch, but even that was dispensed with in the comfort of his home. His children accepted him with as much love as their mother. He smiled as he walked to the center of the room, surveying the dinner laid upon the circular table, and the mass of candles arrayed as a perfect backdrop to Laura's beauty.

This room held such memories for him, he thought, and smiled again, wondering what was taking her so long. The young scamps were probably begging for another, tamer story, and she would give it to them. Yet her mind would be on other things, he knew. He had not missed that look in her eyes; eyes that were as passionate and filled with love as he had always remembered.

She entered the room softly, touching his back and burrowing her nose against the softness of his robe.

"I must bathe," she said softly, and he wondered if he could convince her to let him play the maid. He turned, enveloping her in his arms.

She shivered with anticipation and then smiled, a blinding smile of such pure love that he could only sigh and nuzzle her neck with his lips, feeling the pulse beat rapidly there. His hands cradled her breasts through the fabric of her dress. Her nipples lay heavy, like stones, against his palms.

"Oh God," she said suddenly, her stance stiff and frozen as she remembered their guests. "The Earl and Lady Hester have arrived." She had totally forgotten their invited presence. She leaned her forehead against her husband's chest and moaned.

He only chuckled.

"He can wait," Dixon Alexander Weston, fourth Earl of Cardiff said, decades of autocracy imbuing his voice with purposeful and arrogant intent. "They can both damn well wait."

"They can?" she asked, raising her head. Her gaze was laced with mischief and longing.

"I've given up too damn much for Pitt," he said, growling against her skin. "No more," he murmured, "and certainly not this." He wasted no further time on speech, so intent was he on converting his wife's laughter to blissful moans.

And when the time had come for Laura Ashcott Blake Weston, beloved wife of the fourth Earl of Cardiff, matriarch of the Weston dynasty, to look back upon her life, what she saw did not surprise her, but only brought a full and serene smile to her lips.

The tapestry of her life was dotted with threadbare spots, where grief or pain or loss had eaten through like hungry moths. But those faint traces, instead of detracting from the resplendent tones and rich hues of the intertwined threads, only intensified their splendor.

It was a work of art created not with a needle but with duty, courage, and honor, sprinkled liberally with laughter and hope.

Author's Note

William Pitt was a fascinating personality; in some ways a more impressive minister than Winston Churchill. Pitt was considered a brilliant leader in wartime, but lacked patience for peacetime statesmanship. A minister empowered by the common man, he probably made a tactical error when he became the Earl of Chatham, an honor bestowed by King George III. The common man never quite forgave him for elevating himself above them.

The Seven Years War, lasting between 1756 and 1763, was the struggle for dominion on several continents of Prussia and Britain against France, in alliance with Austria and Russia. The Battle of Quiberon Bay actually occurred, and Admiral Hawke was awarded a huge stipend, by 1759 standards, for his brilliant plan.

In 1760 England was beginning to enter a new era, in which fastidiousness and a concern for health was to dominate how both the poor and the ill were treated. Sweeping changes in the poor laws were not implemented until the nineteenth century, but in the 1700s there existed people who fought for social reform.

Whenever we are tempted to think that the 20th century is traumatic and tumultuous, we should remember the latter half of the 1700s. In 1756 the Seven Years War began; in 1775 the Battle of Lexington heralded the American Revolution. In 1789 the Bastille was stormed—the French Revolution had begun.

I hope you enjoyed Laura and Alex's story. Heddon Hall is modeled after an estate in England that, unfortunately, has been allowed to fall into ruin. Perhaps if you stood within the walls of this magnificent old home, you might hear the faint sound of laughter. Or is it just the brush of leaves against the crumbling brick?

Taylor—made Romance From Zebra Books

WHISPERED KISSES (3830, $4.99/5.99)
Beautiful Texas heiress Laura Leigh Webster never imagined that her biggest worry on her African safari would be the handsome Jace Elliot, her tour guide. Laura's guardian, Lord Chadwick Hamilton, warns her of Jace's dangerous past; she simply cannot resist the lure of his strong arms and the passion of his *Whispered Kisses*.

KISS OF THE NIGHT WIND (3831, $4.99/$5.99)
Carrie Sue Strover thought she was leaving trouble behind her when she deserted her brother's outlaw gang to live her life as schoolmarm Carolyn Starns. On her journey, her stagecoach was attacked and she was rescued by handsome T.J. Rogue. T.J. plots to have Carrie lead him to her brother's cohorts who murdered his family. T.J., however, soon succumbs to the beautiful runaway's charms and loving caresses.

FORTUNE'S FLAMES (3825, $4.99/$5.99)
Impatient to begin her journey back home to New Orleans, beautiful Maren James was furious when Captain Hawk delayed the voyage by searching for stowaways. Impatience gave way to uncontrollable desire once the handsome captain searched *her* cabin. He was looking for illegal passengers; what he found was wild passion with a woman he knew was unlike all those he had known before!

PASSIONS WILD AND FREE (3828, $4.99/$5.99)
After seeing her family and home destroyed by the cruel and hateful Epson gang, Randee Hollis swore revenge. She knew she found the perfect man to help her—gunslinger Marsh Logan. Not only strong and brave, Marsh had the ebony hair and light blue eyes to make Randee forget her hate and seek the love and passion that only he could give her.

Available wherever paperbacks are sold, or order direct from the Publisher. Send cover price plus 50¢ per copy for mailing and handling to Penguin USA, P.O. Box 999, c/o Dept. 17109, Bergenfield, NJ 07621. Residents of New York and Tennessee must include sales tax. DO NOT SEND CASH.